About the Author

Amanda McCabe wrote her first romance at sixteen – a vast historical epic starring all her friends as the characters, written secretly during algebra class! She's never since used algebra, but her books have been nominated for many awards, including the RITA® Award, Booksellers Best, National Readers Choice Award and the Holt Medallion. In her spare time, she loves taking dance classes and collecting travel souvenirs. Amanda lives in Oklahoma. Email her at: amanda@ammandamccabe.com

Regency Scandals

Regency Scandal:

Dissolute Ways

AMANDA MCCABE

MILLS & BOON

First Published in Great Britain 2020
By Mills & Boon, an imprint of HarperCollins*Publishers*
1 London Bridge Street, London, SE1 9GF

REGENCY SCANDAL: DISSOLUTE WAYS © 2020
Harlequin Books S.A.

The Runaway Countess © 2013 Ammanda McCabe
Running from Scandal © 2013 Ammanda McCabe

ISBN: 978-0-263-29831-4

MIX
Paper from
responsible sources
FSC™ C007454

www.fsc.org

This book is produced from independently certified FSC™ paper to ensure responsible forest management.

For more information visit: www.harpercollins.co.uk/green

Printed and bound in Spain
by CPI, Barcelona

THE RUNAWAY
COUNTESS

Prologue

London—1810
The most spectacular marriage in London...

Jane Fitzwalter, the Countess of Ramsay, almost laughed aloud as she read those words. They looked so solid in their black, smudged newsprint, right there in the gossipy pages of the *Gazette* for everyone to see. If it was written there, so many people thought, it had to be true.

Once she had even believed in it herself, for a brief moment. But not now. Now the words were hollow and false, mocking her and all her silly dreams.

The beautiful Ramsays, so young, so wealthy, so fashionable. They had a grand London house where they held grand balls, great crushes with invitations fervently sought by every member of the *ton*. A grand country house where they held grand shooting parties, and the laughter and merriment went on until dawn. Lady Ramsay's hats and gowns, stored in their own grand wardrobe room, were emulated by all the ladies who aspired to fashion in London.

And everyone knew the tale of their marriage. How the young Lord Ramsay glimpsed the even younger Miss Jane Bancroft across the crowded salon full of tall, waving plumes at her Court presentation and strode past the whole gawking gathering to demand an introduction. How they danced together at two private balls and once at Almack's and went driving once in Hyde Park, and Lord Ramsay insisted she marry him. Her guardian wasn't sure, having doubts about the couple's youth and short acquaintance, but they threatened to elope and the next thing society knew they were attending a grand, glittering wedding at St George's.

Grand, grand, grand. The life of the beautiful Ramsays was the envy of everyone.

But Lady Ramsay, now slightly less young and much less naïve, would gladly sell all that grandness for a farthing. She would give it all away to go back to that sunny day in Hyde Park, her shoulder pressed close to Hayden's as they sat together in his curricle and laughed. As they held hands secretly under the cover of her parasol. On that day the world seemed to stretch before her in glorious, golden promise. That day seemed to promise everything she had dreamed of—love, security, a place to belong, someone who needed her.

If only they could start again there and move forwards in a whole different way. But sadly that was impossible. Life would simply go on again as it had done already, because they were the Ramsays and that was the way of their world.

But she was heartily sick of this world of theirs. She had expected that Hayden's title would give them security in the world, a security she never had with her own family, but she had been foolish. She hadn't realised how a title took over everything else, became everything. That a title gathered empty friends, empty marriages.

Jane let the paper fall to the floor beside her bed and slid back down amid the heaps of pillows. It was surely very late at night by now. Her maid had tried to close the satin curtains at the windows, but Jane wouldn't let her. She liked seeing the darkness outside, it felt safe and comforting, like a thick blanket wrapped around her. The moon, a silvery sliver sliding towards the horizon, blinked at her.

Out there beyond her quiet chamber there were balls still twirling on with music and dancing and wine, laughter and conversation. Once she would have been in the very midst of one of those balls, laughing and dancing with the rest or gaily losing in the card room. Now the thought of it made her feel faintly ill.

She rolled on to her side to face the crackling blaze in the marble fireplace and her gaze fell on the bottle of laudanum the doctor had left for her. It would take away all the memories, draw her off to a dream-land, but she didn't want that, either. She had to think now, to face the truth no matter how painful it was.

She pressed her hand to her stomach, perfectly flat again beneath her linen nightdress. The tiny bump that had been growing there, filling her with such joy, was gone. It had been gone for days now, vanished as if it had never been. Lost in a flurry of agonising spasms—and Hayden was not with her. Again. When she lost their child, the third child she had lost so early, he was off gambling somewhere. And drinking, of course. Always drinking. Now there was only that hollow ache to remind her. She had failed in her duty. Again.

She couldn't go on like this any longer. She was cracking under the pressure of their grand lie. She had thought she was getting a new family with Hayden, yet she felt lonelier than she ever had before.

Suddenly she heard a sound from downstairs, a crash and a muffled voice. It was explosively loud in the silent house, for she had sent the servants to bed hours ago. Hayden wasn't expected back until dawn.

But it seemed he had come home early. Jane carefully climbed out of her bed and reached for a shawl to wrap around her shoulders. She slowly made her way out to the staircase landing and peered down to the hall below.

Hayden sat sprawled on the lower steps, the light of the lamp the butler had left on the pier table flickering over him. He had knocked over the umbrella stand, and parasols and walking sticks lay scattered over the black-and-white tiles of the floor.

Hayden studied them with a strangely sad look on his handsome face. The pattern of shadows and light carved his starkly elegant features into something mysterious, and for a moment he almost looked like the man she had married with such hope. Could it be possible he was as weary of this frantic life as she was? That they could somehow start again? Despite her cold disillusionment, she still dared to hope. Still dared to be irrational.

Jane took a step down the stairs and at the creak of the wooden tread Hayden looked up at her. For an instant she saw the stark look on his face, but then he grinned and the brief moment of reflection and hope was gone.

He pushed back a lock of his tousled black hair and held out his hand to her. The signet ring on his finger gleamed and she saw the brandy stain on his sleeve. 'Jane! My beautiful wife waits to greet me— how amazing.'

As Jane moved slowly down the stairs, she could smell the sweet-acrid scent of the brandy hovering around him like a cloud. 'I couldn't sleep,' she said. She hadn't been able to sleep for days and days.

'You should have come with me to the Westin rout, then,' he said. 'It was quite the crush.'

Jane gently smoothed back his hair and cupped her palm over his cheek. The faint roughness of his evening whiskers tickled her skin and the sky-blue of his eyes glowed in the shadows.

How very handsome he was, her husband. How her heart ached just to look at him. Once he had been everything she had ever wanted.

'So I see,' she said.

'Everyone asked about you there,' he answered. He turned his head to press a quick, careless kiss into her palm. 'You're missed by our friends.'

'Friends?' she murmured doubtfully. She barely knew the Westins, or anyone who had been there tonight. And they did not know her, not really. She always felt shy and uncomfortable at balls, another way she failed at being a countess. 'I don't feel like parties yet.'

'Well, I hope you will very soon. The Season is still young and we have a brace of invitations to respond to.' He kissed her hand again, but Jane had the distinct sense he didn't even feel her, see her. 'I hate it when you're ill, darling.'

Feeling a tiny spark of hope, Jane caught his hands in hers and said, 'Maybe we need a little holiday, a few weeks in the country with just us. I'm sure I would feel better in the fresh air. We could take my sister, Emma, from school to come see us. It's been so long since I was with Emma.'

As she thought about it she grew more excited. Yes, she was sure a holiday would be a wonderful thing. A time in the country at Barton Park, just the three of them, no parties, no brandy. She and

Hayden could talk again, as they used to, and be together—maybe make a new baby. Try one more time, despite her fears. They could leave the grand Ramsays behind and just be Hayden and Jane. That was what she had once hoped for so much.

But Hayden laughed at her words, as if she had just made some great joke. He let go of her hands and sprawled back on to the steps. 'Go off to the country now? Jane darling, it's the very midst of the Season. We can't possibly leave now.'

'But it could be—'

Hayden shook his head. 'Staying in London would do you more good than burying yourself in the country. You should go to parties with me again, enjoy yourself. Everyone expects it of you, of us.'

'Go to parties as you do?' Jane said bitterly as her faint, desperate hope faded away. Nothing had changed. Nothing *would* change.

'Yes, as I do. As my parents always did,' he said. 'It's better than wallowing in misery alone at home.'

Jane wrapped her arms around herself, feeling suddenly hollow and empty. Cold. 'I am tired. Perhaps I will go away by myself to visit my sister. Poor Emma writes that she doesn't like her school and I miss her. I just need some time away from London. I want to go home to Barton Park for a while.'

Hayden closed his eyes as if he was weary of her and this conversation. Weary of her emotions. 'If you like, of course. You will have to return before our end-of-Season ball, though. Everyone expects that.'

Jane nodded, but she already knew she would not be back for any ball. She couldn't return to this life at all. She needed to find her own soul again, even if she couldn't make Hayden see that he needed to save his.

He gave a faint snore and Jane looked down to find that he had drifted to sleep right there on the stairs, in the middle of their conversation. His face looked so beautiful and peaceful, a faint smile on his lips as if he had already floated out of her life and into the one he had chosen for himself long before he met her. She leaned down and softly kissed his cheek and smoothed back his hair one last time.

'I'm sorry, Hayden,' she whispered. 'Forgive me.'

She rose to her feet and stepped over him, going back to her chamber and closing the door quietly behind her. It didn't even make a sound in the vast house that had never really been hers.

Hayden stared up at the ceiling far above his head, not seeing the elaborate, cake-icing whorls of white plaster. He barely felt the hard press of the stairs at his back, either, or the familiar feeling of a headache growing behind his eyes. All he could see, all he could think about, was Jane.

He closed his eyes and listened carefully, but she was long gone. There was only silence since she had tiptoed away and softly closed her chamber door behind her. Even his butler, Makepeace, had given up on him and left him lying there on the stairs. Cold air swept around him from the marble floor of the hall.

He had truly become what he never wanted to be—his parents.

Not that he was really like his father, oh, no. The elder earl had been all about responsibility and proper family appearances. It was Hayden's mother who had liked the parties, liked the forgetfulness of being in a noisy crowd. But they had both liked brandy and port too much and it killed his father in the end.

His mother, rest her giddy soul, was done in by childbirth, trying one last time to give his father another son.

A spasm of raw, burning pain flashed through Hayden as he remembered Jane's face, as white as the sheets she lay on after the first baby was gone, thin and drawn with pain.

'We can try again, Hayden,' she had said, reaching for his hand. 'The doctor says I am truly healthy, there's no reason it won't work next time. Please, Hayden, please stay with me.'

And he'd taken her trembling hand, murmured all the right, reassuring things, but inside he was shouting—*not again.* Never again. He couldn't hurt her again, couldn't see her go through what his mother had.

When he first saw Jane, saw the young, hopeful light in her pretty hazel eyes and the sweet pink blush in her cheeks, he felt something he had thought long dead stir inside of him. A curiosity, maybe, an excitement about life and what might happen next. It was more intoxicating than any wine, that feeling Jane gave him. And when he touched her hand, when she smiled up at him…

He only wanted that feeling she gave him to last for ever. He had to have her and he never stopped to think of the consequences. Until he was forced to.

He'd done Jane a great wrong in marrying her so quickly after they met, before she could see the real him. No matter what he did now it seemed he could not make her happy. He couldn't even see what she wanted, needed. She always looked at him so expectantly, so sadly, with those eyes of hers, as if she was waiting for something from him. Something he couldn't even begin to fathom.

So he ran back to what he *did* know, his friends and their never-ending parties. And Jane grew sadder, especially when the babies were lost. Three of them now.

Hayden pushed himself slowly to his feet and made his careful way up the stairs. There was no sound beyond Jane's door, just that perfect, echoing silence. He pushed the door open and peered inside.

Jane lay on her side in the middle of the satin-draped bed countesses had slept in for decades. Her palm was tucked under her cheek, her thick, dark braid snaking over her shoulder. The moonlight fell over her face and he saw she was frowning even in her sleep. She looked so small, so vulnerable and alone.

Hayden knew he had let her down very badly. But he vowed he would never do it again, no matter what he had to do. Even if it meant letting her go.

'I promise you, Jane,' he whispered as she stirred in her sleep. 'I will never hurt you again.'

Chapter One

Three Years Later

Was it an earthquake in London?

That was surely the only explanation for the blasted pounding noise, because Hayden knew that no one in his household would dare to disturb him with such a sound in the middle of the night.

He rolled over on to his back in the tangled bed-clothes and opened his eyes to stare up at the dark green canopy above his head. Pinpricks of light were trickling around the edges of the tightly closed window curtains, but surely it *was* still the middle of the night. He remembered coming home from the club with Harry and Edwards, stumbling through the streets singing, and somehow he had made it up the stairs and into bed. Alone.

Now he felt the familiar ache behind his eyes, made worse by that incessant banging noise.

The room itself wasn't shaking. He could see that

now that he forced himself to be still. So it wasn't an earthquake. Someone was knocking at the bedroom door.

'Damn it all!' he shouted as he pushed himself off the bed. 'It is the middle of the night.'

'If you will beg pardon, my lord, you will find it is actually very near noon,' Makepeace said, calmly but firmly, from the other side of the door.

'The hell it is,' Hayden muttered. He found his breeches tangled up amid the twisted bedclothes and impatiently jerked them on. His shirt was nowhere to be found.

He glanced at the clock on the fireplace mantel, and saw that Makepeace was quite right. It was going on noon. He raked his hands through his tangled hair and jerked open the door.

'Someone had better be dead,' he said.

Makepeace merely blinked, his round, jowly face solemn as usual. He had been with Hayden's family for many years, having been promoted to butler even before Hayden's parents died when he was twelve. Makepeace had seen too much in the Fitzwalter household to ever be surprised.

'To my knowledge, my lord, no one has shuffled off this mortal coil yet,' Makepeace said. 'This letter just arrived.'

He held out his silver tray, which held one small, neatly folded missive. Hayden stared at it in disbelief.

'A letter?' he said. 'You woke me for *that*? Leave

it with the rest of the post on the breakfast table and I'll read it later.'

He started to slam the door to go back to bed, but Makepeace adroitly slid his foot in. He proffered the tray again. 'You will want to read this right away, my lord. It's from Barton Park.'

Hayden wasn't sure he had heard Makepeace right. Perhaps he was still in bed, having a bizarre brandy-induced dream where letters arrived from Barton Park. 'What did you say?'

'If you will look at the return address, my lord, you will see it's from Barton Park,' Makepeace said. 'I thought you might want to see it right away.'

Hayden couldn't say anything. He merely nodded and took the letter carefully from the tray. He closed the door and stared down at the small, neatly folded missive. It glowed a snowy white in the dim, gloomy room, like some exotic and deadly snake about to strike.

It did indeed read 'JF, Barton Park' in a neat, looping handwriting he remembered all too well. The last time he received a letter from that address had been three years ago, when Jane wrote a brief note to tell him she had arrived at Barton Park and would be staying there until further notice. Since then he had sent her monthly bank drafts that were never cashed and he hadn't heard from her at all. He would only know she was alive because his agents reported it to him on a periodic basis.

Why would his estranged wife be writing to

him today? And why did he feel a blasted, terrible spark of hope as he looked at the paper? Hope wasn't something he deserved. Not when it came to Jane.

The haze of last night's drink cleared in an instant as he stared down at the letter in his hand. All his senses seemed to sharpen, three years vanished and all he could see was Jane. The way the light glowed on her dark hair as she laughed with him in their sunlit bed. The rose-pink blush that washed over her cheeks when he teased her. The way she stared up at him, her eyes shining with emotion, as he made love to her.

The way all that heat and light had completely vanished, turned to cold, clear, hard ice, when she turned away from him. When she threw away their marriage and left him.

Now she was writing to him again.

Hayden slowly walked to the fireplace and propped the unopened letter on the mantel, next to the clock. Leaving it there, like a white, reproachful beacon, he went to the window to pull back the curtains and let the light in. When Jane left, it had been a chilly, rainy spring, the busiest part of the Season. Now summers and winters had passed, and it was almost summer again. A time of warmth and light, and long, lazy days.

What had Jane been doing all that time? He had tried not to think about that over those long three years, about Jane and what her life was like now. Every time she came through his mind he shoved her away, buried her in cards and drink, in late nights where if he didn't sleep he couldn't dream. They were better off apart. They had been so young and foolish when they married and she was safer away from him. He had convinced himself she was just a pale phantom.

Almost.

Hayden unlatched the window and pushed it open. Fresh air rushed into the stale room for the first time in days, a warm breeze that was another reminder that summer was coming. That his life really couldn't keep going on as it had, in a blurred succession of parties and drinking. That was the way it had always been, the way his parents' life had been. It was all he knew, all he had been taught. But what could take their place? Once he had known, or thought he had known, something different. But it was an illusion in the end.

Hayden turned away from the bright day outside and caught a glimpse of himself in the mirror across the room. For a second he didn't recognise himself. His black hair needed cutting and was tangled over his brow. He had lost weight and his breeches hung from his lean hips. His eyes were shadowed.

'Jane would never know you now, you disreputable bastard,' he told himself with a bitter laugh. He pulled open his wardrobe and reached for the first shirt hanging there. He pulled it over his head and splashed some cold water over his face. He wanted a brandy to fortify himself for reading Jane's letter, but there was none nearby.

He had to read it now.

Hayden took the letter from the mantel and broke the seal.

'Hayden,' it began. No 'dear' or 'beloved'. Right to the point.

It has been some time since I wrote and I am sorry for being rather quiet. Matters have been so very busy here. As you may remember, Barton Park has been neglected for some time and it has taken up so much of my attention. I believe I have made it quite comfortable again and Emma has left school to come stay with me permanently. We go along very well together and I hope that you are well too.

The reason I am writing is this. It has been a long while since we lived together as husband and wife. It occurred to me that we cannot go on this way for much longer. You are an earl and must have an heir, I know that very well. I am also well aware of how difficult and expensive a divorce would be. But you are a man of influence in London with many friends. If you wish to begin proceedings, I will not stop you in any way. My life here is a quiet one and scandal cannot touch it.

I will not stand in the way of your future. I

trust that, in honour of what we once had, you will not stand in the way of mine.
Sincerely,
Jane.

Hayden was stunned. A divorce? Jane wrote him after all this time to say he should seek a divorce? He crumpled the letter in his fist and tossed it into the empty grate. A raw, burning fury swept through him, an anger he didn't understand. What had he expected would happen with Jane? Had he just thought they would go along in their strange twilight world for ever, married but not married?

The truth was he had avoided thinking about it at all. Now he saw he must. Jane was quite right. Even though he avoided considering his responsibilities as much as possible, he needed an heir. When Jane lost the babies, that hope was gone as well as their marriage. It was like his poor mother all over again, only Jane had luckily been spared the fate of dying trying to give her husband a spare to go with his heir. Jane was saved—because she wisely left. Yes, she was right about it all.

But something else was there, something she did not say in that polite, carefully worded little letter. He wasn't sure what it was, what was really going on with her, but he was sure there was more to this sudden plea for a divorce.

My life here is a quiet one and scandal cannot affect it.

How quiet *was* her life at Barton Park? He had heard nothing of how she really lived in the years since they had parted. No one ever saw her and, after the initial ripple of gossip over their separation, no one spoke of her. They treated him as if he was a single man again, as if Jane had never been. Now he wondered what she did. Why she wanted to be away from him in such a permanent way.

Suddenly he knew he had to see her again. He had to know what was really going on. She had left him, left their life together without a backward glance. He wouldn't let things be easy for her any longer.

No matter what Jane thought, she *was* still his wife. It was time she remembered that. Time they both remembered that.

Hayden strode to the door and pulled it open. 'Makepeace!' he shouted.

'My lord?' came the faint reply up the stairs. Makepeace always disapproved of Hayden's strange habit of shouting out of doors.

'Call for my horse to be saddled. I am leaving for the country today.'

Chapter Two

~~~~~~~~~~~~~~~

'*Who is that?*'

Hayden's best friend, Lord John Eastwood, looked around at Hayden's sudden question. It had been a long, dull day, hanging about at the royal Drawing Room, watching all that Season's crop of fresh young misses make their curtsies to the queen. John's sister, Susan, was one those misses and he had been recruited to help her. Hayden in return was recruited to help John survive the deadly dullness of it all.

Only for John would Hayden brave such a place and only after a stiff gulp of port. They had been friends ever since they were awkward schoolboys, drawn together by a shared humour and love of parties. John's family took Hayden in on holidays when his own family was too busy for him.

But even for the Eastwoods he was regretting venturing in there, to the over-gilded overheated room stuffed with girls in awkwardly hooped satin-

and-lace gowns and towering plumes—and their sharp-eyed, avidly husband-hunting mamas.

A new young earl like Hayden was just a sitting duck, or a fox flushed out of hiding. He wanted to run.

Until he saw her.

She stood amid the gaggle of white-clad girls, overdressed just like them, with the tall headdress of white feathers in her dark hair threatening to overwhelm her slender figure. She was silent, carefully watching everything around her, but she drew his attention like the sudden flicker of a candle in the darkness.

She wasn't beautiful, not like so many of the pretty blonde shepherdess types clustered around her. She was too slim, too pale, with brown hair and a pointed chin, like a forest fairy. Yet she wore her ridiculous gown with an air of quiet, stylish dignity and her pink lips were curved in a little smile as if she had a secret joke no one else in the crowd could know.

And Hayden really, really wanted her to tell him what it was. What made her smile like that. No one had caught his attention so suddenly, so completely, in—well, ever. He had to find out who she was.

'Who is that?' Hayden asked again, and it seemed something in the urgency of his tone caught John's attention. John stopped grinning at his current flirtation, a certain Lady Eleanor Saunders, and turned to Hayden.

'Who is who?' John asked.

'That girl over there, in the white with the silver lace,' Hayden said impatiently.

'There are approximately fifty girls in white over there.'

'It's *that* one, of course.' Hayden turned to gesture to her, only to find that now she watched him. Her smile was gone and she looked a bit startled.

Her eyes were the strangest colour of golden-green, and they seemed to draw him in to her, closer and closer.

'The little brunette who is looking this way,' he said quietly, as if he feared to scare her away if he spoke too loudly. She had such a quiet, watchful delicacy to her.

'Oh, her. She is Miss Jane Bancroft, the niece of Lady Kenton.'

'You know her?' How could John know her and he could not?

'She had tea with Susan last week. It seems they met in the park and rather liked each other.' John gave Hayden a sharp glance of sudden interest. 'Why? Would you like to meet her?'

'Yes,' Hayden said simply. He couldn't stop looking at her, couldn't stop trying to decipher what was so immediately and deeply alluring about her.

'She's not your usual sort, is she?' John said.

'My usual sort?'

'You know. Dashing, colourful. Like Lady Marlbury. You've never looked twice at a deb before.'

Hayden couldn't even remember who Lady Marlbury was at the moment, even though she had been his sometimes-mistress for a few weeks. Not when Miss Bancroft smiled at him, then looked shyly away, her cheeks turning pink.

'Just introduce me,' he said.

'If you like,' John said. 'Just be careful, my friend. Girls like her can be lethal to men like you and you know it.'

Hayden couldn't answer that. When was he ever careful? He wasn't about to start now, not when feelings were roiling through him he had never felt before. He set off across the crowded room, leaving John to scramble after him.

And Miss Bancroft watched him approach. She still looked so very still, but he saw her gloved fingers tighten on the sticks of her fan, saw her sudden intake of breath against the satin of her bodice. She wasn't indifferent to him. Whatever this strange, sudden spell was, he wasn't in it alone.

'Miss Bancroft,' John said, giving the girl a bow. 'Very nice to see you again.'

'And you, Lord John,' she answered, her voice low and soft, musical, with a flash of gentle humour in its depths. 'It is a most dutiful brother who would brave a Drawing Room for his sister.'

John laughed and half-turned. 'May I present my very good friend, Hayden Fitzwalter, the Earl of Ramsay? He especially asked to make your acquaintance. Hayden, this is Miss Jane Bancroft.'

'How do you do?' she murmured. She made a little curtsy and slowly held out her hand to him.

Her fingers trembled a bit as he folded them in his own, and her cheeks turned a deeper pink. Jane, Jane.

And in that moment he was utterly lost...

Curiosus Semper.

Careful Always. Jane had to laugh as she tore a trailing veil of ivy away from the stone garden bench and saw the motto carved there. The letters were faded with time, encrusted with the moss and dirt of neglect, but they were still visible. She would wager her ancestors never could have foreseen how sadly ironic those words would be for their family.

She stood up and dusted some of the soil and leaves from her gloved hands. Her shoulders ached from kneeling there, clearing away some of the tenaciously clinging vines, but it was a good ache. Work meant she didn't have to think. And there was plenty of work to be done at Barton Park.

As she stretched, she studied the house that loomed across the garden. Barton Park had belonged to the Bancrofts for centuries, a gift to one of their ancestors from Charles II. Legend had it that the house was part of the payment in exchange for that long-ago Bancroft marrying one of the king's many cast-off mistresses. But the marriage, against all odds, was a happy one, and the couple went on to make Barton Park a centre of raucous parties and all sorts of debauchery.

Just the sort of place Hayden would have liked, Jane often thought. Perhaps if she had been more like that first mistress of Barton Park things between them could have worked out. But the Bancrofts that followed were quieter, more scholarly, and not as adept at accumulating royal gifts. Their fortune dwindled until by the time of Jane's father there was little left but the house itself, which was already crumbling with neglect.

Little but the legend of the treasure. The old tale about how one of the first Barton Park Bancrofts' many licentious guests had dabbled in highway robbery and had hidden his ill-gotten treasure somewhere in the garden. Jane's father, as he grew sicker and sicker, had become obsessed with the idea of this treasure. He told Jane the story of it over and over, even sending her out to try digging in various spots around the grounds.

Then he died and her mother had told her different tales. Harder, more bitter stories about the truth of a woman's insecure place in the world, of how finding the right husband—a *rich* husband—was all that mattered. Jane was frightened to think she might be right. Money and position could bring security, of course, and she craved that so much after the uncertainties of her childhood. But surely there must be more? Must be some chance of a happy family? Of being a good wife and mother, despite the poor example she had always seen before her.

Then her mother also died and Jane went to have a London Season with her aunt while Emma was sent to school.

Both those destinations had ended badly for the Bancroft sisters. Jane had found she had more of her fanciful father in her than she ever would have thought. She had imagined she had found a fairy tale, a happy-ever-after with Hayden, until she discovered she was in love with an illusion, a man who never really existed except in her dreams. She didn't know how to fit into his world and he couldn't help her. They had been so young, so foolish to think that they could even try, that their passion in the bedroom could be enough to make a life together.

So her father had been wrong in relying on fairy stories. But so had her mother. A rich husband was not all a woman needed.

Jane tossed her trowel and garden gloves into a bucket and examined the house. Barton Park was not a large dwelling, but once it had been very pretty, a red brick faded to a soft pink, centred around a white-stone portico and surrounded by gardens, a mysterious hedge maze and a pretty Chinoiserie summerhouse. Now the stone was chipped, some of the windows cracked and the lovely gardens sadly overgrown. She hadn't gone in the hedge maze at all since she moved back.

Jane did her best. She and Emma lived on a small

bequest from their mother's family, which Hayden could probably claim if he wanted, but it was surely too insignificant to interest him. It paid for their food, a cook, a maid, fuel for the fires, but not a carriage or a team of gardeners. No grand parties, but she had had her fill of those in London. She had found she wasn't at all good at them, either attending or hosting them. There could be money from Hayden, but she couldn't bring herself to touch it.

Jane sighed as she pushed the loose tendrils of her brown hair back into her scarf. Emma was sixteen now. In a couple of years she should have a London Season, though Jane had no idea how to pay for it or how to weather London gossip in order to launch her.

Not that Emma seemed in the least bit interested in a Season. She was a strange girl, always buried in books about botany or running off to the woods to collect 'specimens' or bring home new pets like rabbits or hedgehogs. She liked the quiet life in the country as much as Jane did. They both needed its peace. But Jane knew it couldn't go on for ever.

That was why she had forced herself to write to Hayden after all these years. It had taken days of agonising before she could take up that pen to write the letter and even more before she could send it. Then there was…

Nothing. The days had gone by in silence with no answer at all from her husband.

Her husband. Jane pressed her hand to her stomach with the spasm of pain that always came when she thought those words. She remembered Hayden as she had last seen him, sprawled asleep on the stairs of their London house. Her husband, as beautiful as a fallen angel. How horribly they had disappointed each other. Failed each other.

She tried so hard not to think about him. Not to think about how things were when they first married, when she had been so naïve and full of hope. So dazzled by Hayden and what he gave to her. By who he was and the delights they found together in the bedchamber. She tried not to think about the babies, and about how losing those tiny, fragile lives showed her how hollow and empty everything was. She couldn't even fulfil her main duty as a countess.

During the day it was easy not to think about it all. There was so much work to be done, the gardens to be cleared, the meagre accounts to go over, a few neighbourhood friends to call on or join for tea or cards. But at night—at night it was so different.

In the silence and the darkness there was nothing but the memories. She remembered everything about their days together, the good and the bad. How they had laughed together; how he had made her feel when he kissed her, touched her. How in those moments she had felt not so alone any longer, even though it was all an illusion in the end. She wondered how he was now, what he was doing. And then she wanted to sob for what was lost, for what had never really been except in her dreams.

Yes. Except for those nights, life would be very

tolerable indeed. But it wasn't just Emma's future she needed to think about, it was her own. And Hayden's, too, even though the future had never seemed to be something he considered. He was an earl and also an orphan with no siblings. He would need an heir. And for that he would have to be free, as complicated and costly as that would be. She had to offer him that.

And she needed to be free, too.

Jane pushed away thoughts of Hayden and the unanswered letter. She couldn't worry about it now. She scooped up the bucket and made her way along the overgrown pathway to the house. They were expecting guests for tea.

As she stowed the bucket next to the kitchen, the door suddenly flew open and Emma dashed out. She held a wriggling puppy under one arm and the dirty burlap bag she used for collecting plants over the other. Her golden-blonde hair was gathered in an untidy braid and she wore an old apron over her faded blue-muslin dress.

Even so dishevelled, anyone could see that Emma was becoming a rare beauty, all ivory and gold with their mother's jewel-green eyes, eyes that had become a muddy hazel on Jane. Emma's beauty was yet another reason to worry about the future. Emma might be happy at Barton Park, but Jane knew she couldn't be buried in the country for ever.

'Where are you going in such a hurry?' Jane asked.

'I saw a patch of what looked like the plant I've been seeking by the road yesterday, but I didn't have time to examine it properly,' Emma answered briskly. 'I want to collect a few pieces before they get trampled.'

'It looks like rain,' Jane said. 'And we have guests coming to tea soon.'

'Do we? Who? The vicar again?' Emma said without much interest. She put down Murray the puppy and clipped on his lead.

'No, Sir David Marton and his sister Miss Louisa. Surely you remember them from the assembly last month?' Their last real social outing, dancing and tepid punch at the village assembly rooms. Emma would surely remember it as she had protested being put into one of Jane's made-over London gowns and had then been ogled and flirted with by every man between fifteen and fifty. Sir David had danced with her once, too, then he had spent the evening talking to Jane.

'That old stick-in-the-mud?' Emma said with a scoffing laugh. 'What is he going to do, read us sermons?'

'Emma!' Jane protested. 'Sir David is hardly old—I doubt he is even thirty. And he is not in the least bit sermon-like. He and his sister are very nice.'

'Nice enough, I suppose, but still very stick-in-the-muddy. When he danced with me at the assembly he kept going on about some German philosopher with terribly gloomy ideas. He didn't know anything about botany. And his sister only seemed to care about hats.'

'Nevertheless, they *are* nice, and they are to be our nearest neighbours since they took over Easton Abbey,' Jane said, trying not to laugh at her sister's idea of proper social discourse. 'You need to be here when they call. And properly dressed, not drenched from getting caught in the rain.'

'I won't be gone long at all, Jane, I promise,' Emma said. 'I will be all prim and proper in the sitting room when they get here, ready to talk about German philosophy over cakes and tea.'

Jane laughed as Emma kissed her cheek and hurried away, Murray barking madly at her feet. 'Half an hour, Emma, no more.'

'Half an hour! I promise!'

Once Emma was gone out the garden gate, Jane hurried through the kitchens, where their cook was making a rare fine tea of sandwiches and lemon cakes, and went up the back stairs to her chamber. Emma wasn't the only one who needed to mend her appearance, she thought as she caught a glimpse of herself in the dressing-table mirror. She could pass as the scullery maid herself.

And somehow it seemed so important that Sir David and his sister not think ill of her appearance.

As she tugged the scarf from her hair and untied her apron, she thought about Sir David and their recent meetings. He was a handsome young man, in a quiet way that matched his polite demeanour. With his sandy-brown hair and spectacles, he seemed to exude an unobtrusive intelligence that Jane found calming after all that had happened before in her life.

She enjoyed talking to him and he seemed to enjoy talking to her. When she had declined to dance at the assembly, saying only that her dancing days were behind her, he did not press her. But he was kind enough to dance with Emma and listen to her talk about plants, even though Emma seemed to find him 'stick-in-the-muddy'.

So when Jane had encountered him and his sister in the village, it seemed natural to invite them to tea. Only to be a friendly neighbour, of course. There could be nothing more. She was a married woman, even though she had not seen her husband in years.

She was a married woman for now, anyway. And she could not quite deny that when David Marton smiled at her, sought her out for conversation, she felt something she hadn't in a long time. She felt— admired.

Even before she left London she had begun to feel invisible. The one person whose admiration mattered—her husband—didn't see her any more and all the chatter in the fashion papers about her gowns and her coiffures didn't matter at all. Nothing mattered beyond Hayden's indifference. She started to feel invisible even to herself, especially after she had failed in her main duty to give her husband an heir.

Back home at Barton Park she had started to feel

better, slowly, day by day. She had started to feel the sun on her skin again and hear the birds singing. The weed-choked gardens didn't care what she looked like and Emma certainly didn't. Things seemed quite content. So it had come as quite a surprise how much she enjoyed Sir David's quiet attentions.

She leaned towards the mirror to peer more closely at her reflection.

'No one in London would recognise you now,' she said with laugh. And, indeed, no one *would* recognise the well-dressed Lady Ramsay in this woman, with her wind-tossed hair and the pale gold freckles the sun had dotted over her nose. She reached for her hairbrush and set to work.

She suddenly felt giddily schoolgirlish in how much she looked forward to this tea party.

Chapter Three

'Ramsay? By Jove, it *is* you! Blast it, man, what are you doing in this godforsaken place?'

Hayden slowly turned from his place at the bar. He had just been asking himself that very thing, What was he doing in a country inn, sipping at tepid, weak ale, running after a woman who clearly didn't want him, when he could be in London, getting ready for a night out at balls and gambling clubs?

He had just come to the startling realisation that a night out gaming and drinking wasn't something he would miss very much when he heard those shouted words. They were a welcome distraction from his own brooding thoughts.

He turned away from the bar and saw Lord Ethan Carstairs making his way across the crowded room towards him. Lord Ethan was not what Hayden would call a friend, but they were often in the same circles and saw each other at their club and across the gambling tables. Lord Ethan was rather loud and didn't hold his liquor very well, but he was tolerable enough most of the time. Especially at moments like this, when Hayden needed distraction.

'Lord Ethan,' he said. 'Fancy seeing you here. Can I buy you an ale?'

'I won't say no to that,' Ethan said affably as he leaned against the bar next to Hayden. To judge by his reddened cheeks and rumpled hair, and the dishevelled state of his expensive clothes, he had been imbibing the ale for quite a while already. 'My damnable uncle is making me rusticate for a while. Says he won't increase my allowance until I learn some control and I am completely out of funds.'

'Indeed?' Hayden asked without much interest as he gestured to the innkeeper for more ale. Everyone knew that Ethan's Puritanical uncle, who also held the Carstairs family purse-strings, disapproved of his nephew's wild ways. Hayden sympathised. His own father had so often been disapproving.

And now here he was, drowning his doubts in drink. Just like his father. That was certainly something he did *not* want to think about.

'Most unfair,' Ethan grumbled. He took a long gulp from his glass, the reached into his pocket and took out a small, gold object he twirled through his fingers. Hayden recognised it as an old Spanish coin the man often used as a lucky charm at the card tables. 'I'm on my way to some country pile to wait him out. But what are *you* doing so far from town?'

Hayden shrugged. He might as well tell the truth.

All of society would know soon enough, when he either came back to London with Jane by his side or instigated scandalous divorce proceedings. 'I am on my way to Barton Park to see Lady Ramsay.'

'By Jove!' Ethan sputtered. 'I had forgotten you were married.'

'My wife is delicate and prefers the country for her health,' Hayden said, as he always did when someone asked about Jane. They seldom even bothered any longer.

'I see. I remember they said she was a pretty little thing.' Ethan's gaze narrowed, and for an instant it was as if the ale-haze cleared in his bloodshot-blue eyes. 'Barton Park, you say?'

'It's her family home.'

'I think I have heard of it. Isn't there some tale of treasure or some such there?' Ethan laughed, and that instant of clarity vanished. 'We can both rot here in the country for a while, then. Damnable families.'

Damnable families. Hayden almost laughed bitterly as he sipped at the terrible ale. He wasn't even sure what it felt like to have a family, not now. He had been alone for so long it seemed like the only way he could be. The only way he could avoid hurting anyone else.

Once, for a moment, he had seen what it could be to have a real family. He had a flashing memory of a sunlit day, of Jane with her dark hair loose over her bare shoulders, smiling up at him. She took his hand and held it against the warm skin of her stomach, where he could feel the swell of their child. The first child that was lost.

He knew now that that was the most perfect moment of his life, but it had only been an illusion. Jane was done with him now. But he wasn't done with her. Soon enough she would see that.

'I have to be on my way,' Hayden said. He pushed his half-full glass away. 'Good luck with your rusticating, Carstairs.'

Lord Ethan blinked at him. 'Same to you, Ramsay. Maybe we'll meet again soon.'

Hayden nodded, though really he was quite sure they wouldn't. He left the stale-smelling room behind for the innyard. As he waited for a fresh horse to be brought around, one of the servants said, 'It looks like rain is coming, my lord. Might be best to wait to ride out.'

Hayden peered up at the sky. It had been a pale blue when he arrived at the inn, hazy with country sunlight, but now he saw the servant was right. Grey clouds were gathering swiftly and the wind was colder.

But the thought of going back inside to drink some more with Ethan Carstairs was most unappealing. He had already waited too long to go after Jane—he needed to get on with the business of confronting his wife.

'I haven't far to ride,' he said as he swung up into the saddle. But he hadn't been gone long from the inn when the lowering skies burst open on a clap of thunder and rain poured down.

Hayden was glad of the cold, it seemed to drive him onwards and cleared his head. He galloped faster down the narrow, rutted lane, revelling in the speed and the wildness of the nature around him. All too often in London he felt closed in, trapped by the buildings and the noise, by all the people watching him.

Here there was nothing but the trees and the wind, the dark clouds sweeping in faster and faster over his head on the rumble of thunder. Maybe that was why Jane had run here, he thought as his horse leaped over a fallen log in the road and galloped onwards even faster. Just to be able to breathe again.

He urged the horse on, trying to outrun the raw anger that had burned in him ever since he had read Jane's letter. Even if she was tired of her London life, she had duties, damn it! Duties as his wife and countess. She had left them, left him, behind. And now she wanted to abandon them permanently.

She had to see how impossible her suggestion of divorce was. He had to *make* her see.

A bolt of sizzling blue-white lightning suddenly split the sky, cleaving a tree beside the road only a few feet away. With a deafening crack, a thick branch split away and crashed into the road. Hayden's horse reared up and the wet reins slid from his hands at the sudden movement.

He felt himself falling, the sky and the rain and

the mud all tumbling around him. He crashed to the ground and pain shot through his leg as it twisted under him.

Hayden cursed as loudly as he could, but he was drowned out by the shout of the thunder. The horse scrambled to regain his footing and ran away down the lane. Hayden tried to push himself up, to balance on his good leg, but he fell back to the mud.

He shoved back his sodden hair and stared up into the leaden sky. He laughed at the storm. It seemed even nature wanted to keep him away from Jane.

'Are you all right?' he heard a woman call. He twisted around to see her running towards him through the misty sheets of rain, like a ghost.

She looked vaguely familiar, not very tall and too slender in a faded, rain-spotted dress. A loose braid of wet golden hair lay over her shoulder and a barking puppy ran in circles around her. But despite that nagging sense that he should know her, he didn't really recognise her as she ran down the lane towards him.

Until she knelt beside him, completely careless of the rain. She stared up at him with bright green eyes, pale and clear. He remembered those eyes. He had seen them at his wedding when Jane proudly introduced her sister. She had been younger then, scrawny and awkward. Now time had moved on and she had grown up.

And he remembered that Jane had written that

her sister lived with her now. He had to be close to Barton Park.

'Emma?' he said.

She sat back on her heels, her eyes narrowing with suspicion. 'Yes, I am Emma Bancroft. How do you...?' Suddenly she gasped. 'Ramsay? What in the hell are you doing here?'

'Does your sister let you curse like that? Most unladylike,' he said, suddenly aware of the utter absurdity of his situation. He was sitting in the rain, in the middle of a muddy country lane, arguing about propriety with the sister-in-law he hardly knew.

He laughed and she frowned at him as if he was an escaped bedlamite. He certainly felt like one.

'Of course she doesn't let me,' Emma said. 'But she is not here and this situation clearly warrants a curse or two. What are *you* doing here? Aren't you supposed to be in London?'

'I was, but now I'm on my way to Barton Park. Or I was, until that infernal horse threw me.'

Emma glanced over her shoulder at where the horse had come to a halt further down the lane. 'Are you hurt?'

'I think I twisted my leg. I can't stand up.'

Her frown of suspicion vanished, replaced by an expression of concern. Perhaps like her sister she was too soft-hearted. 'Oh, no! Here, let me help you.'

'I'm far too heavy for you.'

'Nonsense. I'm much stronger than I look.' She wrapped her arm around him and let him lean on her as he staggered to his feet. She *was* rather strong, and between them they managed to hobble over to the fallen branch.

'Stay here, Ramsay, and I'll get your horse back,' she said. 'You need to get out of the rain and have that leg looked at.'

She dashed away, leaving her now-silent dog to watch him suspiciously in her place. She returned very quickly with the recalcitrant horse.

'We aren't far from Barton Park,' she said. 'I can lead you there, if you can manage to ride that far.'

'Of course I can ride that far, it's just a sprain,' he said, even though his leg felt like it was on fire and he could see blood spotting his rain-soaked breeches.

'Good. You'll need to save your strength for when Jane sees you. She doesn't know you're coming, does she?' Emma asked matter of factly, as if she ran into estranged relatives every day.

Hayden gritted his teeth as he pulled himself up into the saddle. The pain washed over him in cold waves and he pushed it away. 'Not yet.'

To his surprise, Emma laughed. 'Oh, this day just gets more interesting all the time.'

Emma tried not to stare at her brother-in-law like a lackwit, tried to just calmly give him directions to Barton Park as he pulled her up on to the horse behind him and set them into motion, Murray running alongside them. But she just couldn't help it. She couldn't believe Lord Ramsay was actually there, that she had actually stumbled on him right in the middle of the road as she tried to hurry home for tea.

Whatever was he doing there? It couldn't possibly be good. As far as Emma knew, Jane hadn't even talked to him in all the time since they came to live at Barton. Jane never even talked *about* him, so Emma had no idea what had happened in London.

But she did have imagination and it had filled in all sorts of lurid scenarios that could drive her kind-hearted, responsible sister away from her husband. Ramsay had become something of an ogre in Emma's mind, so her first instinct when she saw him there in the road had been to run from him as fast as she could. Especially after what had happened to her at school, with that odious Mr Milne, the music master. He had been enough to scare her off men for ever.

And yet—yet she remembered that one other time she had met Ramsay, on the day he married her sister in that elegant town ceremony. He had looked at Jane then as if all the stars and the moon revolved only around her and he had held her hand so tenderly. And Jane had been radiant that day, as if she was lit from within. Emma had never seen her sister, who tended to worry over everyone else so much, so very happy. Emma had even known she could endure her hated school because she knew Jane was happy in her new life with her husband.

What had gone so wrong? Why was Ramsay here

now, after so long? Emma was bursting to know, but she just said calmly, 'Turn right up there at the gate.'

'Thank you, Miss Bancroft,' he said through gritted teeth. When she glanced up at his profile, she saw he looked rather pale. He was probably in more pain than he wanted to show, just like a man.

'I hardly think we need to be so formal,' she said teasingly. 'I'm your sister. My name is Emma.'

A flash of a smile touched his lips. 'I do remember your name, Emma.'

'That's good. If you turn left here, you'll see the house just ahead.'

'Thank you,' he said again. 'So, Emma, what are you doing running about in the rain?'

'It wasn't raining when I left,' she said. 'And if you must know, I was collecting some specimens.'

'Specimens?'

'Plants. For my studies.' And she really had taken a few cuttings of the plants. He didn't need to know her other errands. No one had to know, not yet, that she was hunting for the lost Barton Park treasure.

Emma tucked her sack closer to her side and felt the reassuring weight of the small journal in its pocket. She had found it in a forgotten corner of the Barton library last month. She had been hoping to find old plans of the gardens, but this book was even better. It was a journal belonging to the young cousin of the first mistress of Barton Park.

It seemed this girl had been a poor relation, sent to stay at Barton to gain some Court polish. Emma didn't know her name, but she had quickly been drawn into her sharply observed tales of the people and parties of the house back then. Barton was so quiet now, silently crumbling away with only her and Jane living there, but once upon a time it had been full of life and scandal.

Then the journal's writer had fallen in love with one of the naughty guests—the very man who had stolen the treasure and hid it somewhere in the gardens. Emma had been combing its yellowed pages for clues ever since.

Surely if she could find it, their worries would be over. Jane could cease working so very hard, could lose that pinched, concerned look on her face. Jane had always been the best of sisters. Emma only wanted to help her, too.

But she didn't want Jane to know what she was doing. Emma didn't want to be compared to their father, so caught up in useless dreams he couldn't help his family. So she did her detective work in secret, whenever she could. And she had found nothing yet.

She had also never told her sister about what had really happened at school with Mr Milne. That was only for her nightmares now, thankfully. She was done with men altogether.

'There's the house,' she said. It loomed before them in the misty rain and she was glad he couldn't yet see the dwelling clearly. Couldn't see how shabby it was. If only she had had time to warn Jane! Then again, maybe the surprise was better.

But if she had vague hopes that Ramsay's leg would slow him down enough to give her a head start into the house, they were quickly dashed. He held on to his saddle and carefully slid to the ground, his jaw set in his handsome, hard-edged face.

Emma leaped down and ran up the front steps to throw the door open. Murray dashed in, barking, his muddy paw prints trailing over the old, scarred parquet floor.

'Jane, Jane!' she shouted, completely abandoning propriety. She had only seconds to warn her sister. Then she could watch the drama unfold.

Jane emerged from the drawing-room door, her eyes wide with astonishment. She had changed from her garden clothes to her best day dress, a pale green muslin with a high-frilled collar. Her brown hair was carefully pinned up and bound with a green-ribbon bandeau. For a second, Emma couldn't decipher why her sister was so dressed up on a rainy afternoon.

Then the Martons, Sir David and his silly sister, appeared in the doorway behind her and Emma remembered in a flash. They had guests. *Respectable* guests, who for some unfathomable reason Jane wanted to impress.

'Emma, whatever is the matter?' Jane demanded, while Sir David looked rather disapproving and his sister giggled behind her handkerchief.

'He is here!' Emma cried. She couldn't worry about the Martons right now, not with Ramsay so close behind her.

'Who is here?' Jane said. 'Emma, dear, are you ill?'

Across the empty hall, the door opened again, letting in a blast of rain and wind. Ramsay stood there, silhouetted in his greatcoat against the grey sky outside. For one instant there was a flash of something raw and burning, something real, in his eyes. Then it was as if a blank, pale mask dropped down and there was nothing at all.

'Hello, Jane,' he said calmly. 'It's been much too long. You are looking lovely as always.'

Emma swung back around to look at Jane. Her sister's face had turned utterly white and Emma feared she might faint right in front of everyone. But when Emma moved to take her hand, Jane waved her back.

'Oh, blast it all,' Jane whispered. 'Not now...'

'You can't feel it move yet,' Jane said, her voice full of laughter. 'It's much too soon.'

Hayden laid down beside her on the sun-splashed bed anyway and rested his cheek on the gentle swell of her belly under her light dressing gown. It was early; the doctor had only just confirmed that Jane was truly pregnant. But his wife already seemed blooming. She wasn't quite as thin and her cheeks were pink. Four months married and now a child on the way. Their first child.

She laughed again as he carefully touched the small bump. Her skin was so warm, so sweet, so alive. 'You won't break me, Hayden. The doctor says I am quite healthy.'

Hayden fervently prayed so. He didn't know what he had ever done in his misbegotten life to deserve a wife like Jane, but he knew he couldn't lose her now. His heart ached just to think of her laughter, her quite, calm presence, being gone in a flash.

Just like his mother.

Jane seemed to sense his sudden fear. She gently smoothed a soft caress over his hair. 'All will be well, Hayden. I am sure of it. And in a few months, we will have a little lord or lady. The beginning of a new family for us. Just like we talked about on our honeymoon.'

Their honeymoon—those perfect, sweet days and nights, just the two of them all alone in the country. They had almost become buried under the noise and rush of London life since they returned. Jane had seemed a bit lost as a new countess, with so many eyes upon her, but now she looked perfectly content. A new family was on the way, their *family. It could be very different from what he knew with his parents. He could make it different.*

But still the tiny, buried spark of that old fear lingered...

Chapter Four

'Won't you introduce me to your guests?'

Hayden. Hayden was here, standing in her house. Jane was sure she must have fallen and hit her head, that she was lying on the drawing-room floor having dream visions. One minute she was serving tea, trying to make polite conversation as she worried about Emma wandering around out in the rain. And the next she was facing her husband.

Her husband. It truly was Hayden, after all these years. She stared at him, frozen, stricken. Her dreams of him had been nothing to the real thing. Hayden was even more handsome than she remembered, his elegantly sharp-planed face drawn even leaner, harsher with his black hair slicked back with the rain.

His eyes, that pure, pale blue she had once so loved, stared back at her unwavering. For an instant she went tumbling back to that moment when she first saw him. She was that romantic girl again, hopeful, heartstruck, so sure that she saw her own passionate need reflected in those eyes. So sure he was what she had been longing for all her life. Hayden, Hayden—he was here again!

She almost took a step towards him, almost reached for him, when he suddenly smiled at her. But it was not a smile of joyful welcome. It was sardonic, almost bitter, the smile of a sophisticated stranger. It made Jane remember what had become of her romantic dreams of marriage and the man she had thought was her husband. He had been living his fast life in London while she was healing here in the country. Hayden was truly only a stranger now.

Jane's half-lifted hand fell back to her side and the haze of dreams cleared around her. For a moment she had seen only Hayden, but suddenly she was aware of everything else. The rain pounding at the windows. Emma beside her, her golden hair dripping on to the floor, watching her with a frown of concern. The Martons just behind, witnessing this whole bizarre tableau of unexpected reunion.

The way that Hayden leaned heavily on the wobbly old pier table. There was a tear in his finely tailored breeches and spots of blood on the pale fabric muted by the rainwater.

Jane's throat tightened at the realisation that he was hurt. 'What has happened?' she asked hoarsely.

It was Emma who answered. 'I found him on the road,' she said. 'His horse had thrown him and his leg was so hurt he couldn't stand.'

'Thrown him?' Jane said. Surely that was impossible. Hayden was one of the finest riders she knew. Despite her fears and doubts, she couldn't help but be concerned he was truly hurt.

'A lightning strike startled the horse,' he said, remarkably calm for a man who was standing drenched and wounded in his estranged wife's house. 'I fear I'm interrupting a social occasion.'

'I— No, not at all,' Jane managed to choke out. 'Merely tea with our neighbours. This is Sir David Marton and his sister, Miss Louisa Marton. May I present Lord Ramsay, my—my husband.'

'Your husband?' Miss Louisa cried. 'Why, how very exciting. We were not expecting to meet you here, my lord.'

'No, I imagine not,' Hayden murmured. 'How do you do?'

Miss Louisa giggled while Sir David said nothing. Jane sensed him watching her, but she couldn't deal with him now. She had to take care of Hayden. She forced herself to move, to go across the hall and reach for Hayden's arm.

For an instant he was stiff under her tentative touch and she thought he would jerk away from her. But he let her thread her fingers around his elbow and swayed towards her.

Up close, she could see how carefully rigid he held his body, the bruised-looking shadows under his eyes. He felt thinner, harder than he had the last time she had touched him. But his smell was the same, that clean, crisp scent of sun and lemony cologne and man that had once made her long to curl up beside him and inhale him into her very heart. There was the faint undertone of ale, but the brandy was gone.

'We need to get you upstairs and send for the doctor,' Jane said quietly. He was obviously in more pain than he would ever reveal.

'I can go,' Emma said.

'No, permit me to go for the doctor, Lady Ramsay,' Sir David said. 'Louisa and I have the carriage and Miss Bancroft should be by the fire.'

Jane glanced over at Sir David, surprised by the offer. He didn't smile, just looked back at her solemnly and gave her a polite nod. The tea had been going rather well, she suddenly remembered, until this most unexpected interruption. Unlike Emma, Jane rather enjoyed hearing about philosophy, books and ideas, and Sir David was an intelligent, pleasant conversationalist. He had seemed to enjoy talking to her as well, and if nothing else his company gave her hope that life would not always be so lonely. That life could be—nice, rather than chaotic or painful.

Then Hayden appeared.

'Thank you, Sir David,' she said. 'That is so kind of you.' He nodded and took his sister's arm to lead her away. She waved at them merrily over her shoulder.

Emma tactfully withdrew, leaving Jane alone with Hayden for the first time in three years. Jane took a deep, steadying breath. She had to help him just as she would anyone else who showed up on her doorstep in a storm. He was merely a stranger to her now.

But he didn't *feel* like a stranger as she took his arm again. His eyes weren't those of a stranger as he looked down at her. Once he had known her so well, better than anyone else ever had. He had known her body as well as the secrets of her heart. She had trusted him so much, allowed him to see so much.

She had bitterly regretted that ever since. She could never let herself be so vulnerable again.

She turned away from the blue light of his eyes. 'Let me help you up the stairs,' she said softly.

'Do you have no butler or footmen?' Hayden asked. 'Those stairs look rather precarious.'

Jane almost laughed. 'We have an elderly cook and a shy little maid who is no doubt cowering in the pantry right now. I'm the only help available, I fear.'

Hayden nodded grimly and let her hold on to his arm as she led him slowly up the stairs. She sensed he was trying to lean on her as little as possible, even as his jaw was set with the pain. She never really noticed the staircase any longer, it was always just *there*. But now she saw it through his eyes, the missing carved posts, the chips in the once-gilded balustrade, the loose boards in the risers.

'I usually use the back stairs,' she said. 'But they are rather a long walk from here.'

Hayden nodded again and together they concentrated on getting to the landing. At the top, they faced the long corridor lined with closed doors and Jane realised there was no choice. She had to take him to her room. Besides Emma's, none of the other chambers were habitable.

She pushed open the door and led him over to the old *chaise* next to the window. He lowered himself down to its faded cushions, still looking up at her with those eyes that seemed to see so much. Seemed to remember her, know her.

Jane remembered that when he was drinking, when he was caught up in his London life, he didn't seem to see her at all. Why was he here, now, finally looking at her when she had at last gained a small measure of contentment?

'What do you want, Jane? What in God's name will make you happy? You have everything here.'

Those long-ago words of Hayden's suddenly rang in her memory. The frustration in them, the anger. And she remembered her own tears.

'All I want is for you to spend time with me,' she answered, so confused that he couldn't understand without her saying anything. That he didn't know.

'I was with you all last night, Jane.'

'At a ball.' A ball where they had danced once and then he had disappeared into the card room. He had not even made love to her when they got home near dawn. And the times when they had made love, when it was only the two of them alone in the

darkness, were the only times she felt sure he was really with her.

'Let's go back to Ramsay House, like on our honeymoon,' she had begged, trying not to cry again. She was so tired of crying. 'We had such fun there.'

'We have duties here, Jane. Don't be ridiculous.'

'Duties!' And that was when anger overtook the hurt confusion inside of her. 'Duties to do what? Go to the races with your friends? Play cards? You are surely needed at your estate.' Needed by her. *But she dared not say that again.*

'You don't understand,' he had answered coldly. 'You are new to being a countess. But you will learn.'

Only she never had learned how to be the sort of countess he wanted. A woman at ease in the racy environs of society. A woman who could give him an heir. A woman his friends would admire. She gave up even trying, especially after she lost the babies.

'You should change out of your wet clothes,' she said. 'I'll see if I can find something in my father's old wardrobe.'

She turned away, but Hayden suddenly reached out and caught her hand in his. His fingers were cool and strong as they twined with hers, holding her with him. It felt strange, new and wonderfully familiar all at the same time. She stared down at him, startled.

A smile touched his sensual lips, an echo of that bright, rakish grin that once drew her in so completely.

'Will you not help me out of my wet clothes, Jane?' he said. 'You used to be so good at that...'

Jane snatched her hand away. 'I'm glad the fall didn't damage *everything,* Hayden. You can take them off all by yourself, I'm sure.'

More flustered than she would ever admit, Jane whirled around and hurried towards the door.

'Jane,' he called.

She stopped with her hand on the latch. 'Yes? What now?'

'Who was your visitor?'

His tone had flashed from teasing and suggestive to hard, demanding. As if he had any right to demand anything of her any longer!

She glanced back at him over her shoulder. The stark grey light from the window surrounded him, blinding her. 'I told you, the Martons are our neighbours. We were having tea.'

'Is that all?' he said. He sounded ridiculously suspicious.

'Of course,' Jane snapped, suddenly angry. He knew nothing of her life at Barton Park, just as she knew nothing now of his London life. She didn't *want* to know; she could imagine it all too well. And she was sure he did nothing so innocent as take tea and talk about books with his neighbours.

'What are you even doing here, Hayden?' she said. 'Why now?'

Hayden shook his head and, as Jane blinked away that unwelcome prickle of tears, she saw how weary he looked. He slumped back on to the *chaise* and she knew this was not the moment for any long-delayed quarrels and confrontations. Those could wait.

'I will fetch some dry clothes and some water for you to wash,' she said and slipped out the door.

Once alone in the dark corridor, she leaned against the wall and impatiently rubbed at her aching eyes. She had already cried enough tears over Hayden; she wouldn't shed any more. She would find out what he wanted then send him on his way so she could resume her life without him.

That was her only choice now.

The door closed behind the doctor and Hayden let his head fall back on to the worn cushions of the *chaise* and closed his eyes. His whole body felt as if he had gone three rounds at Gentleman Jackson's Saloon and then got foxed and fallen off his horse on top of that. He felt battered, bruised and exhausted, and his leg burned fiercely, especially after all the doctor's poking and prodding.

But the pain of his leg was nothing to the pain of seeing Jane again. He wasn't expecting the bolt of pure, hot longing that would hit him just from seeing her face. Touching her, feeling her nearness. He had thought he had forgotten about her in the busy noise of his life, that their separation was nothing. That he didn't miss her. That she was just a distant acquaintance.

But then she stepped out of the doorway and the

sight of her face hit him like another lightning strike, sudden and paralysing. Almost like the first time he saw her and couldn't turn away from the light of her shy smile. Couldn't turn away from the hope she kindled inside him.

In that moment before she saw him, she had looked concerned about her sister, her hazel-green eyes soft with worry. Until she glimpsed him and they froze over like a spring tree branch in a sudden frost. Her slender shoulders had stiffened and he had the feeling that she would have fled if all her weighty good manners and pride hadn't held her there.

Jane always had exquisite manners, was always concerned about the people around her. Including those blasted visitors today? What was their name— Marton? Yes, that Marton was too good looking, too polished and perfect and serious. Damn him. Somehow Hayden had imagined Jane saw no one at all here in the country.

He shifted on the *chaise* and his leg sent out a stab of fresh pain in protest. There was the soft sound of voices outside the door, one of them the doctor's, stern and gravelly.

The other was Jane's, a gentle murmur, and its very softness hurt him even more. It made him think of the first time he came home drunk, after they returned to town from their long honeymoon at Ramsay House and he left Jane one night to go to the club with his friends. Those days alone with Jane had been so golden, so perfect and peaceful, unlike any he had ever known before in his life.

Then his friends had laughed about his new 'settled and domestic' ways, about how he would soon become one of those men who followed their wives about London like puppy dogs.

Hayden couldn't be that way, couldn't depend on anyone. Need anyone. He had seen how that had killed his parents. After his flighty, beautiful mother died in childbirth, his father couldn't bear it and followed her soon after. He had always vowed never to be like them. Yet he could see then how much he was coming to rely on Jane. That very night, his first night back at the club as a married man, he only wanted to leave his friends and go home to her. He couldn't have that. So he drank more than his fill of brandy to prove it.

Just as his father had always done.

And Jane had spoken to him softly that night as well. Had watched him with those concerned eyes as Makepeace helped him up the stairs.

'Not to worry, my lady,' Makepeace told her. 'This is merely what young men do in society.'

'But surely Ramsay does not...' she had said. Then she learned that Ramsay did and he saw that bright hope die in her eyes. He had killed it.

Hayden opened his eyes and found himself not a callow newlywed at his town house, but alone in a strange room with Jane's familiar voice outside.

He studied the chamber for the first time since she brought him in there.

It wasn't a large room, but it was cosy and warm with thick blue curtains at the windows muffling the patter of the rain. There was the old *chaise*, a small inlaid desk piled with papers and ledgers, and a dressing table cluttered with pots and bottles and ribbons. The bed was an old one, dark, heavy carved wood spread with an embroidered coverlet. A dressing gown was tossed across its foot and a pair of slippers had been hastily kicked off on the faded rug beside it. A screen across the corner was also hung with clothes.

This had to be Jane's own room, Hayden realised with surprise. He recognised the silver hairbrush on the dressing table; he had run it through the silken strands of her hair several times, winding the long, soft length of it around his wrist. The smell of her lilac perfume still hung in the air.

He had forgotten what it was like to live with a lady, to be surrounded by cosy, feminine clutter. Why would she put him in here of all places?

The door opened and Jane herself appeared there. Emma peeked in behind her, her eyes wide with curiosity until Jane gently but firmly closed the door between them.

'The doctor said your leg is not broken, but the wound is a rather deep one. You'll have to stay still for a few days and let it heal,' she said. Her face was as still and smooth as a marble statue's, giving away nothing of her real thoughts.

Nothing about how she felt to have him in her home.

'Is this your own room, Jane?' he asked. His voice came out too rough, almost angry, and he felt immediately guilty when she flinched. He had never known quite how to behave around her—except in the bedchamber, when they knew how to be together only too well.

'Yes,' she said. She plucked up the silky dressing gown from the bed and stashed it behind the screen. 'I'm afraid we have few guests here at Barton, so only my room and Emma's are ready to be occupied. I can stay with her tonight and we'll tidy another chamber in the morning.'

'I can sleep in your drawing room,' he said, forcing himself to be gentler, quieter. Jane's face was turned from him so he could see only her profile, that pure, serene, classical line of her nose and mouth he had always loved.

He suddenly longed to push back from the *chaise*, to grab her into his arms and pull her against him. To kiss her soft lips until she melted against him again and that ice that seemed to surround her melted. Until she was *his* Jane again.

But he knew he couldn't do that. The walls between them had been built too strong, too thick, brick by brick. He had done that himself. He had wanted it that way.

But he still wanted to kiss her.

'You're ill,' she said. 'I'm not helping you all the way downstairs again just so you can injure yourself once more.' She took a small bottle out of the pocket of the white apron she wore over her pretty green dress and put it down on the desk. 'The doctor left that to help you sleep. I'll bring you some water and something to eat. You must be hungry after your journey.'

'Jane,' Hayden called as she turned towards the door.

She glanced back at him over her shoulder, her hand poised on the latch. There was a flash of something, some emotion, deep in her hazel eyes, but it was gone before he could decipher it.

And he had forgotten what he wanted to say to her. No words could bridge this gap. 'Who is that man Marton?' he blurted.

Jane's lips twitched, but she didn't quite smile. 'Oh, Hayden. We can talk in the morning. The inn sent on your valise, I'll bring it up so you don't have to wear my father's shirt any longer.'

'Jane…' he shouted again, but she was gone as quickly and quietly as she had arrived. And he was alone with his thoughts, which was the very last place he ever wanted to be.

Chapter Five

Hayden was asleep.

Jane tiptoed carefully into the room and set her
tray down as gently as possible on the dressing table.
She didn't want to wake him. She had no idea what
she would say to him. There were so many things
she wanted to know. Why was he here? What did he
want? Was he going to agree to a divorce?

And yet there was a part of her, a deep, fearful,
secret part, that didn't want to know at all.

She eased back the edge of the window curtain to
let in some morning light. Not that there was much
of it. It still rained outside, a steady grey *drip-drip*
against the windows and the roof that she prayed
wouldn't spring a leak. Not now, with Hayden here.
It was bad enough he had seen Barton Park in all
its shabbiness.

She turned to study him as he slept on the *chaise*.
He hadn't moved to the bed, but was stretched out
under an old quilt on the *chaise* where she had left

him. The bottle of laudanum was untouched, yet he seemed to sleep peacefully enough.

She tiptoed closer and studied him in the watery grey light. It had been so long since she saw him like this, so quiet and unaware, so lost in dreams. She remembered when they were first married, those bright honeymoon days at Ramsay House, when she would lie there beside him every morning and watch him as he slept. She would marvel that he was *hers*, that they were together.

And then he would wake and smile at her. He would reach for her, both of them laughing as they rolled through the rumpled sheets. It seemed like everything was just beginning for them then. What would she have done if she knew that was all there would be?

Yesterday she had thought Hayden looked different, like a hard, lean stranger dropped into her house. Yet right now he looked like *that* Hayden again, like the husband she had loved waking up with every morning. In sleep, the harsh lines of his face were smoothed and a small smile touched the corners of his lips as if he was having a good dream.

There were no arguments, no tears, no misunderstandings. Just Hayden.

Jane couldn't help herself. She knelt down by the *chaise* and reached out to carefully smooth a rumpled wave of black hair back from his brow. His skin was warm under her touch, but not feverish. She cupped her palm over his cheek and a wave of terrible tenderness washed over her. She hadn't realised until that moment just how much she had really missed Hayden.

Not the Hayden of London, the Hayden who had no time for his wife, but the man she had wanted so much to marry. How had that all fallen so very apart?

Suddenly his eyes opened, those glowing summer-blue eyes, and he stared up at her. His smile widened and she couldn't draw away from him—it was so very beautiful. His hand reached up to cover hers and hold her against him.

'Jane,' he said, his voice rough with sleep. 'I had the strangest dream…'

Then his gaze flickered past her to the room beyond and that smile vanished. That one magical instant, where the past was the present, was gone like a wisp of fog.

Jane pulled her hand away and pushed herself to her feet. She brushed her fingers over her apron, but she could still feel him on her skin. He rolled on to his back and groaned.

'How are you feeling this morning?' she said. She turned away and poured out a cup of tea on the tray.

'Like I was dragged backward by the heels through miles of hedgerow,' Hayden answered. He scowled at the cup she held out. 'Do you have anything stronger, perchance?'

She was definitely not giving him brandy. Not

now, while she had the control. 'No, just tea. You didn't take the laudanum the doctor left?'

He shook his head and sipped cautiously at the tea when she held it out to him again. 'I had the feeling I would need a clear head today.'

'You should eat something, too, then I can change your bandage.' Jane gave him the plate of toast and sat down on the dressing-table bench. 'What are you doing here, Hayden?'

He chewed thoughtfully at a bite of the buttered bread before he set the plate aside. 'Because you wrote to me, of course.'

'But I never intended for you to come here!' Jane cried. 'You could have just written back to me.'

Hayden gave a humourless laugh. 'My wife demands a divorce and she thinks I should just write back a polite little letter? Saying what? "Oh, yes, Jane dear, whatever you want." It's not that simple.'

Jane closed her eyes tightly against the sight of Hayden sitting there in her bedchamber, so close, but so, so far. 'I know it's not simple at all. But surely we can't just go on as we have been for ever. You need a real wife, an heir. And this sham of a marriage—'

Hayden suddenly slammed his plate down on the floor. 'Our marriage is not a sham! We stood up in that church and made our vows before all of society. You are the Countess of Ramsay. My *wife*.'

Jane couldn't bear it any longer. He was right; when she walked down that aisle there had been nothing of the sham about it. She had wanted only to be his wife, to live her life with him. But nothing had turned out as she expected, nothing at all. And when the babies, their last hope, were gone...

'I have never really been your wife, have I?' she said, her voice thick with the tears she had held back for such a long time. 'We never wanted the same things, I was just too foolish to see that back then. We were so young and I didn't know what would happen.'

'What is it that you want, Jane? What have I not given you?' He sounded confused, hurt.

Yourself, she wanted to shout. But she could never say that. She had built her pride up again, inch by painful inch, here at Barton. She couldn't let it crumble away again.

'I couldn't give you an heir,' she said quietly. 'I couldn't be the kind of grand countess you needed. So I gave you the chance to move forwards in your own way.'

'Or perhaps you want the chance to marry that man Marton.'

Jane gave a choked laugh. Maybe she *had* harboured vague hopes of moving forwards with David Marton, or someone like him. Someone kind and peaceful, who wouldn't break her heart all over again. But that had only been a dream, so far from reality. She had to be done with dreams. They had never brought anything good.

'Sir David has been kind to me, yes,' she said as

she turned away from Hayden and fussed with the clean bandages and the basin. 'So has his sister.'

'You've made many friends here, have you? To replace the ones you left in London?'

Jane didn't like his tone, dark and suspicious, almost disgruntled even. He had no right to be suspicious of *her*, not after all that had happened in London. Not after Lady Marlbury. She twisted the bandage in her fist.

'What friends did I ever have in London?' she said. 'Everyone we ever saw was *your* friend. I had to fit into your life, even if I was a very square peg in a very round hole. So, yes, I have made some friends here. The neighbours and the villagers are kind to Emma and me, they don't gossip about us. They don't laugh at us behind our backs. I'm not lonely here.'

'You were lonely in London?' he said and sounded incredulous. 'What did you not have there? What did I not give you? I tried to make you happy, Jane. I gave you what any woman could want.'

'Oh, yes,' Jane cried. She could feel her emotions, so tightly tied down for so long, springing free and spiralling beyond her control. The pain and anger she'd thought gone were still there. But so was the tenderness. 'You gave me houses, carriages, gowns and jewels. What else could a woman possibly want?'

Except love. A family. What she had wanted most when they married. There they had failed each other.

'What did you want from me, Jane?' he said, a near-shout.

'You left me alone.' She spun around to face him. Her handsome husband. The man she'd loved so much. *He* was all she had wanted. And he couldn't give her that. 'When the babies were—gone. When I tried to tell you what I needed. I was so alone, Hayden.'

He shook his head. There was such confusion in his eyes, even though she'd told him this before. Tried so hard to make him see. 'You just laid there in your room, Jane. You wouldn't go anywhere, wouldn't talk to anyone.'

'There was no one to talk to,' she whispered. Oh, she was so tired of this, of the pain that wouldn't end. It *had* to end. She had to end it.

She went and knelt down next to him with the bandages and quietly set about changing the dressings on his leg. It was hard to be so near him, to feel his heat, smell the familiar scent of him and know what couldn't be again. What had never really been, except in her imagination.

'Are you happy here, Jane?' Hayden asked softly.

She nodded, not looking up from her task. 'Barton is my home. I've found a—a sort of peace here.'

'And friends?'

'Yes. And friends. Emma and I belong here.'

He was silent for a long moment and sat very still under her nursing attentions. 'We cannot divorce. Surely you must know that.'

She nodded. She *had* always known that, even with that wild hope that made her write to him in the first place. Men like Hayden, with titles and ancient family names, couldn't divorce. Even when their wives proved unsatisfactory.

'But perhaps we can reach some arrangement that would work for both of us,' he said. 'I don't want to go on making you unhappy, Jane. I never wanted that.'

Surprised by the heaviness in his words that matched her own emotions, Jane glanced up at him. For just an instant there was a sad shadow in his eyes. Then he smiled and it was gone.

'My money should be good for something when it comes to you, Jane,' he said, lightly.

Jane grimly went back to her task. 'I never wanted your money.'

'I know,' he answered. 'But right now that's all I have to give you, it seems.'

Hayden frowned as he studied the array of silver items laid out before him on the cloth-covered dining-room table. Patches of each piece sparkled, but other patches were still dull and pock-marked, streaked in strange patterns.

'Blast it all,' he cursed as he threw down the polishing rag. He had to be very careful what he asked for here, it seems.

When he hobbled downstairs at what he thought was a reasonably early hour for the country, Hannah the maid sniffily informed him that Lady Ramsay and Miss Emma were already working in the garden and, if he wanted breakfast, tea and toast would have to suffice. And when he had asked—nay, near begged for a task, she gave him this. Polishing the Bancroft silver that, from the looks of it, had been packed away for approximately a hundred years with no polish coming near it.

How hard could it be to polish a bit of silver while his leg healed up? Wipe things up a bit, maybe get Jane to smile at him again as she once did.

Not so easy as all that, it turned out. He polished and polished, only to partially clean up a smallish tray, a chocolate pot and a few spoons. The newly shining bits only seemed to make the rest of it look shoddier and there were still several pieces he hadn't touched at all.

Hayden had to laugh at himself as he tossed down the rag. It seemed 'butler' wouldn't be his new job. He would have to find some other way to surprise Jane.

Jane. Hayden ran his hands through his hair, remembering how she looked at him as she nursed his leg. For just the merest second there, he had dared to imagine that she even looked happy to see him again. For just a moment, it felt like it had when they were first together, and the laughter and smiles were easy.

And for just that second the hopes he had pressed down and locked away so tightly now struggled to be free again. He had to shove them away and forget them all over again. He had to just remember what came after those hopes died and he realised he could never make Jane happy. That they were only an illusion to each other after all.

But there, in the quiet intimacy of the candlelight and the rain, with Jane's scent and warmth wrapped around him again, it didn't *feel* like an illusion. It felt more real, more vital than anything else in his life.

Then those shadows drifted across her eyes again and she turned away from him. He still didn't know how to make her happy.

He pushed away the silver in front of him and used his borrowed walking stick to push himself to his feet. Labouring away here all alone in this gloomy room wouldn't make Jane smile at him again. And gloomy it certainly was. It was a long, narrow, high-ceilinged room, probably once very grand. Now the furniture was shrouded in canvas, and paler patches on the faded blue wallpaper showed where paintings had once hung. The rug was rolled up and shoved against the wall. Several crystals were missing from the chandelier.

And yet Jane seemed happier here than amid the fashionable grandeur of their London house.

Hayden heard a burst of laughter from beyond the closed dining-room doors. He limped over and eased it open to peer into the hall just beyond.

Jane and Emma had just come dashing in, apparently after getting caught in a sudden morning rain.

Their hair tumbled down in damp ropes and Emma was shaking out a wet shawl.

Jane dropped the bucket she was carrying and shook out her wet skirts. The thin muslin clung to her body, which was as slender and delicate as ever, and just as alluring to him. But what caught his avid attention was the look on her face. She looked so alive, so happy and free as she laughed. Her eyes sparkled.

He remembered how it had felt that first time he took her hand, as if her warmth and innocence could be his. As if the life he had always led, the only life he knew, wasn't the only way he had to be. That he could find another path—with her.

Maybe it was this place, this strange, ramshackle, warm-hearted place, that had given his wife that air of laughing, welcoming life. Because here she bloomed. With him she had faded and he had faded with her. Yet here she was, his Jane again.

His hope. And he had never, ever wanted to hope again.

'Well, Lady Ramsay. What do you think of your new home?'

Jane laughed as Hayden lifted her high in his arms and carried her over the threshold of Ramsay House. He twirled her around so fast she could see only blurry glimpses of an ancient carved ceiling and dark-panelled walls hung with bright flags and standards. It didn't look like an especially aus-

picious honeymoon spot, but Jane was so happy with Hayden she didn't care where she was.

From the outside, as they drove up in their carriage pulled by cheering estate workers, Ramsay House was a forbidding grey-stone castle, austere and sharp-lined. She half-expected knights to appear on the crenellated ramparts to throw boiling oil at her, but instead the steps were lined with smiling servants who tossed petals as she emerged from the carriage and called out, 'Best wishes to Lord and Lady Ramsay!'

Lady Ramsay. *The name still sounded so strange. It couldn't possibly belong to her,* be *her. The same hazy strangeness that had enveloped her ever since she had walked up the aisle to take Hayden's hand only vanished when she was in his arms. There she felt as if she belonged. There she never wanted to be anyplace else.*

'I'm sure it's lovely,' she said, laughing as he spun her around faster and faster. 'But I can hardly see it, Hayden!'

He finally twirled to a stop and slowly lowered her to her feet. They held on tightly to each other as the room lurched to a stop around them.

'You can make any changes you want to it, of course,' Hayden said. 'You are the mistress of Ramsay House now.'

Jane tilted back her head to examine the room closer. Just like the turrets and arrow slits outside, the inside looked like nothing so much as a me-

dieval great hall. There were even a few suits of slightly tarnished armour, and ancient battleaxes and swords hung between the battle flags. There were no softening rugs or chintz cushions, no flower arrangements or haphazard piles of books, as she was used to at Barton Park.

'I don't think this place has had any changes made since about 1350,' she said uncertainly. And surely she wasn't going to be the one bold enough to tear it down and start again.

Hayden laughed. 'I don't think it has. About time for it to be brought into the nineteenth century, don't you think?'

Jane caught a glimpse of a painting hung at the far end of the room and hurried over to look at it more closely. Unlike the rest of the furnishings, it had a modern look about it. It was a family group, three people seated in a semi-circle in this very medieval space. An older man with his grey hair tied back in an old-fashioned queue, scowling above his tightly tied cravat, and a younger woman next to him, dressed in an elegant blue-silk gown and lace shawl. Her glossy black hair, piled high atop her head, matched that of the little boy playing with a toy sword at her feet.

It should have been a cosy family scene, but the artist had captured some rather disquieting details. None of the three looked at each other. The woman had a distant, dreamy look in her eyes, where the man seemed unhappy at everything around him. The boy was also engrossed only in his toys. It almost seemed to be three separate paintings.

Jane felt Hayden come to stand behind her, his body warm against hers. 'This is you and your parents?' she said.

'Yes. I remember sitting for this—it was terribly dull and I was far too fidgety for my father's liking,' Hayden said, his tone deliberately light. 'This is the first thing you should get rid of. Banish it to the attics.'

Jane suddenly realised how very little she knew about Hayden's family. Only that he was an only child whose parents were long dead, much like her own. But nothing about what they were like when they were alive. 'What should we put in its place?'

'A portrait of you, of course. Or maybe not.'

'No?' Because she wasn't the real Lady Ramsay?

'Maybe I would want to keep your image all to myself in my own chamber,' he said teasingly.

Jane spun around and threw her arms around Hayden, unable to bear looking at the strangely melancholy painting any longer. She closed her eyes and breathed in deeply of his delicious, comforting scent.

'Perhaps you should show me your chamber now,' she said. 'So I can see what sort of painting might be needed.'

Hayden laughed and scooped her up in his arms again. 'That is one command I can happily obey.'

He carried her up the stone staircase and along what seemed to be endless twisting corridors, until he opened a door at the very end of the last hallway. Jane barely had a glimpse of a very large carved bed, a massive fireplace and green-velvet curtains at the windows before Hayden spun her around in his arms.

'Blast it all, Jane, but I've been wanting to kiss you for hours and hours,' he said hoarsely. 'All the way from London.'

'What are you waiting for, then?' Jane whispered. 'I've been wanting the very same thing...'

Their mouths touched softly at first, tasting, learning. Remembering last night after their wedding.

He kissed her so gently, once, twice, before the tip of his tongue traced her lower lip and made her gasp with the sudden rush of longing. She grabbed on to his shoulders tightly to keep from falling and whispered his name.

'My beautiful wife,' Hayden moaned, and pulled her even closer as their kiss caught fire. Their lips met in a burning clash of need and want, and the rest of the world completely vanished. There was only the two of them, bound together by a passion that refused to be denied.

And Jane knew that truly this was where she was meant to be. With Hayden. In his arms, there was no doubt, no fear. No worry that they were too young, that they had married too quickly. She had been right to say yes to Hayden.

They belonged together and that was all that mattered.

Chapter Six

Jane tossed the handful of weeds into a bucket and stood up to stretch her aching back. It was much like every other day here at Barton, taking advantage of the lull in the rain to work in the garden. Emma was darting around with a book in one hand and a trowel in the other, no doubt collecting more botanical specimens, while Murray chased sticks and barked, and their maid, Hannah, hung out the laundry.

And yet it wasn't like any other day, not really. Because Hayden sat on the terrace, watching them all.

Jane tried to ignore him. The clouds were gathering again and she had work to do in the garden before they were forced to go inside. In fact, she had been trying to ignore him completely for the two days he had been at Barton.

It hadn't been too hard to avoid him. He stayed in the guest chamber they had hastily cleared out.

Hannah carried his meals to him, scurrying in and out as fast as she could. Emma took him books to read and Jane checked on the bandages after dinner. After their quarrel that first night, they were scrupulously polite, exchanging few words.

It made Jane want to scream. Careful, quiet, distant politeness had never been Hayden. That was what had drawn her to him in the first place, that vivid, bright life that burned in him like a torch. He shook up her careful life, turned it all topsy-turvy until she wanted to run and dance and shout along with him. Be alive with him.

She hadn't realised at the beginning the other side of that beckoning flame. She hadn't realised how very hard married life would be. She had been so young, so romantic, with so little experience of men like Hayden and their world. When she had left London, she had wanted only the quiet she found at Barton, and that was her healing refuge. Her chance to get to know herself.

But quiet sat uneasily on Hayden. The silent tension between them, under the same roof, but not in the same world, only reminded her how long they had been apart.

She held up her hand to shade her eyes from the grey light and studied him as he sat on the terrace. His black hair shimmered, brushed back from the lean angles of his face, and his finely tailored green coat and elegantly tied cravat made him stand out from the shabbiness around him. His polished boot rested against the old chipped planter and he leaned on the walking stick Emma had unearthed from somewhere as he solemnly studied the garden.

He looked like a god suddenly dropped down from the sky. He didn't belong there any more than she belonged in London. They didn't belong *together.*

Yet he had dismissed any talk of divorce.

Jane sighed as she tugged off her dirty garden gloves. Soon enough he would be on his way, as soon as the doctor said he could travel. Then they could go back to their silent, distant truce, their limbo.

But she was afraid she would have to work at forgetting him all over again.

She made her way to the terrace and sat down on the old stone bench next to him. They were silent together for a moment, watching as Emma and her dog disappeared into the tangled entrance of the old maze.

'How are you feeling today?' Jane asked.

'Much better,' he answered. He gestured towards the maze with his stick. 'Should she be going in there?'

Jane laughed. 'Probably not. The maze hasn't been maintained in years, it's surely completely overgrown with who knows what. But it's hard to tell Emma what not to do. She is sure to do it, anyway.'

Hayden smiled down at her, the corners of his eyes crinkling in the light. 'Unlike her sister, I dare say,' he said teasingly.

'Very true. I always tried to do what I should.' Jane sighed to think of how hard she had worked to be what everyone wanted, to take care of everyone. And look how that ended up. 'I think Emma has the right idea.'

'I should have taken better care of you, Jane,' he said quietly.

Jane was shocked by those words. She turned to look at him, only to find that he still watched the garden. 'In what way? You said it yourself—you gave me everything I could want.'

'I gave you what I thought you must want. A fine house, a title, jewels, gowns.' He softly tapped the end of the stick on the old stones of the terrace, the only sign of movement about him. 'Yet it occurs to me that I never asked if *you* wanted them.'

'I— Yes, of course I did,' Jane said, confused. 'Emma and I never had a home after our parents died. It was all I wanted.' And, yes, she had wanted the title, too. It seemed to stand for continuity, security. Yet it turned into something very different indeed.

'But you didn't want *my* house. Not in the end.' Hayden suddenly turned to look at her, his bright blue eyes piercing. 'Are you happy here, Jane?'

'Very happy,' she said. 'Barton isn't a large place, as you've seen, and it needs a great deal of work. But it's my home. It reminds me of my parents, and when we were a family. It gives me a place to—to…'

'A place to belong,' Hayden said quietly.

Jane looked at him in surprise. She wasn't quite used to this Hayden, the man who listened to her, thought about what she really wanted and not what he thought she *should* want. 'Yes. I belong here. And I want Emma to feel that way, too.'

Once she'd wanted to give Hayden that as well. Wanted their home to be with each other. But that couldn't be in the end and there was no use crying any longer.

'Yes,' she said. 'A place to belong. Barton gives us that now. Leaky roof and everything.'

'Jane!' she heard Emma call, and she looked up to find her sister waving at her from the rickety old gate that guarded the entrance to the garden maze. Emma's hair was tangled, with leaves caught in the blonde curls, and her dress was streaked with dirt. 'Jane, I reached the maze's centre at last. Come see what I found.'

Jane laughed and hurried down the terrace steps towards her sister. She hadn't known what to say to Hayden. It was so long since he talked to her like that, since he looked at her as if he was trying to read her thoughts. It reminded her too much of the old Hayden, the one she knew all too briefly before he vanished.

She couldn't bear it if that Hayden reappeared now, when she had finally begun to get over him.

'Emma, whatever are you doing in there?' Jane said, laughing as Emma grabbed her hand. 'You look like a scarecrow.'

'Oh, never mind that,' Emma cried. 'You have to come see, Jane! It's the loveliest thing.' She glanced over Jane's shoulder and her delighted smile widened. 'You come, too, Ramsay. I must say, you are looking much more hale and hearty this morning.'

Jane turned to see that Hayden had left his seat on the terrace and was walking towards them on the overgrown pathway. The pale light gleamed on his hair and his smile seemed strangely unsure. Not his usual confident, carefree grin. It made her heart start to thaw just the tiniest bit more, made her want to run to him and take his hand.

He already seemed different here than she remembered when they parted. Quieter, more watchful, more careful. It utterly confused her.

But she knew one thing for certain. She could *not* be drawn back to Hayden Fitzwalter. She couldn't be caught up in the bright, chaotic whirlwind of him again. Her heart couldn't stand it.

'I'm sure Hayden should be resting, Emma,' Jane said. 'We can't drag him all over the garden.'

'Not at all,' Hayden said. 'I don't think I could stand to rest for another second without going crazy.'

Emma happily clapped her hands before grabbing Jane's arm and leading her through the entrance to the maze. Hayden followed them. Jane couldn't see him, but she could hear the tap of his stick on the gravel and feel the warmth of him just behind her.

The tangled hedge walls loomed around them, blocking out the day, and it seemed as if the three of them were closed into their own little world. Emma's dog barked somewhere ahead of them and the sound was muffled and echoing.

'How long has this maze been here?' Hayden asked.

'Oh, ages and ages,' Emma said. 'Since the Restoration at least. They were very fond of places where they could hide and be naughty, weren't they? But it hasn't been used in a long time.'

'When we were children, we were forbidden to come in here,' Jane said. 'My mother was sure we would be lost for ever and our nanny told us wild fairies lived in the hedges, just waiting to snatch up wayward children.'

'I never saw any fairies, though,' Emma said, sounding rather disappointed.

'But you come in here now?' said Hayden.

'Emma has begun exploring a bit,' Jane answered. 'I have enough work to do just tending the main flowerbeds.'

'It's too bad, because this could be so lovely,' Emma said. She tossed a quick grin back at them. 'Rather romantic, don't you think? Just imagine it— moonlight overhead, a warm breeze, an orchestra playing a waltz…'

'No more novel reading for you, Emma,' Jane said with a laugh. 'You are becoming too fanciful.'

Emma turned another corner, leading them further and further inwards. Jane saw now that her sister must have spent even more time exploring the maze than she had thought, for Emma seemed to know just where she was going.

'Not at all,' Emma said. 'But just picture it, Jane! Wouldn't this be a marvellous place for a costume ball? Especially *here*.'

They turned one more tangled corner and were in the very centre of the maze. Jane almost gasped at the sight that greeted them, it was so unexpected and, yes, so romantic.

Amid the octagonal walls was a small, open-sided summerhouse topped with a lacy cupola. It had once been painted white, but was now peeling to reveal the wooden planks beneath, and some of the boards had fallen away to land on the ground, but it was still a whimsical and inviting spot. An empty, cracked reflecting pool surrounded it, lined with statues of classical goddesses and cupids staring down at its lost glories.

Emma was right—this would be a perfect spot for a costume ball. With torches, music, dancing, the light on the pool…

And Hayden taking her in his arms to waltz her across the grass. She remembered he was such a good dancer, so strong and graceful that she had seemed to float at his touch. Had seemed to forget everything else but that they were together, holding each other, laughing with the exhilaration of the dance and being young and in love.

No! Jane shook her head, refusing to remember how it was to dance with Hayden. She hurried up the steps of the summerhouse, but if she was trying to escape that way she saw at once it wouldn't work. The round space was surrounded by wide benches that once held lush cushions and at its centre hung a swing.

Just like the one in the garden at Ramsay House.

Jane whirled around to leave, only to find that Hayden stood behind her on the steps. The over-hanging roof cast him in a lacy pattern of shadows, half-hiding his face. He glanced around the small space, and she saw that he remembered, too.

'Push me higher, Hayden!'

He laughed in her memory, the sound as strong and clear and perfect as if that day had returned to the present. She felt again the heat of the sun on her skin, the way her loose hair tickled the back of her neck. His hands at her waist, holding her safe in the very same moment he sent her soaring.

'You can't go any higher, Jane,' he insisted. And yet she knew she could, only with him. She seemed to soar into the sky, so very free. Until she landed back on earth and Hayden kissed her, his lips so warm on hers, the passion between them flaming higher than the sun.

So very perfect.

But perfection never, ever lasted more than a mo-ment.

Jane stared up at Hayden now, caught halfway between that golden day and the present hour. 'I—I don't think this swing would be safe to use.'

'Not like the one at the lake at Ramsay House,' he said quietly, roughly.

'Not at all like that one.' Jane brushed past him and hurried back down the steps. Emma was chasing Murray around the clearing, laughing, and Jane watched them as she tried to breathe deeply and remind herself that the Hayden she knew that day of the swing wasn't the real Hayden.

Just as that girl hadn't been the real Jane. That was all just a silly dream. Then she had lost the babies and she woke up.

She had to stay awake now, and guard her heart very, very carefully.

Had Jane always been so beautiful?

Hayden watched his wife as she ran along the garden pathway towards the terrace, laughing with her sister. Of course Jane had always been beautiful. She had drawn him in from the first moment he saw her, with the way all her emotions flashed through her large hazel eyes, with the shining loops of her dark hair he wanted to get lost in. Yes—Jane had always been so very beautiful.

But she had also been pale and somehow fragile, moving through the world so carefully. Everyone in London had wanted to emulate her, her elegant clothes and hats, everyone had wanted invitations to her small soirées. Yet still that air of uncertainty clung about her. He had been so sure he could banish it, that he could make her happy while still not making himself vulnerable. When he couldn't, the frustration and anger consumed him.

Here at Barton, Jane wasn't uncertain at all. Her pale skin had turned an unfashionable, but attractive, burnished gold. She was still slender, but she didn't look as if she would break. As she twirled around in a circle with her sister, laughing with glorious abandon, she looked carefree.

Happy.

That was what he wanted so much to give her, where he had failed. When they were together, he had watched that fragile hope in her eyes fade to silent sadness, but he couldn't seem to stop it, no matter how hard he tried. He couldn't really know what she wanted and he didn't have it in him to discover it. He didn't know how to even begin.

How could he? He had learned nothing of emotions and connections from his own parents, nothing but how to be what they and society expected him to be—a rake and a scoundrel. A failure. He didn't know how to be anything else, even for Jane.

For an instant, Jane and Emma's laughter faded and the overgrown gardens melted, and he stood before his father's massive library desk.

'Never was a man cursed with such a worthless heir!' the earl had roared, while Hayden's mother lounged on the sofa, drinking her ever-present claret and smirking at her son's latest peccadillo. It was all she ever did. *'If only your older brother had lived. You have disgraced us for the last time, Hayden. Ob-*

viously there is something in you, some curse from your mother's family, that won't allow you to be a true Fitzwalter. You are a wastrel and a fool, and I wash my hands of you! You are no son of mine.'

It was during a diatribe very like that one that his father had an apoplexy and keeled over dead on the library carpet, not long after his mother died trying to give her husband one more son. So his 'wastrel' son killed him in the end. And Hayden never saw any reason to rise above the low expectations set for him so long ago.

Until Jane. By then it was too late. And he hadn't protected her from the very things that brought down his own parents. He couldn't fail her like that again.

'Hayden, come dance with us!' Emma called, twirling in a circle.

Hayden was jerked out of the sticky tentacles of the past and dropped back into the present moment in the garden at Barton. Emma ran over to grab his hand, and Jane watched him with a bemused half-smile on her face.

At least she wasn't frowning at him for the moment. He wished she would *really* smile at him again, as she had that day on the swing at Ramsay House. She had laughed then, too, letting her wariness drop away and letting herself be free with him. The memory of that smile was like a secret jewel he had cherished over all these years.

But he knew he hadn't yet earned another. Maybe he never would.

'I don't think Hayden is up to dancing yet, Emma,' Jane said. 'Besides, it looks like the rain is coming back. We should return to the house, don't you think?'

Emma pouted a bit, but nodded and dashed off after her dog towards the terrace. Jane picked up her bucket and looped it over her arm before she fell into step with Hayden as they made their slower way back.

'I hope we didn't keep you up too long today,' she said quietly. 'How does your leg feel?'

'Much better,' he answered. 'The exercise does me good. I could become far too indolent, lolling by your fire and eating your cook's cream cakes.'

Jane laughed. 'Somehow I can't picture you being indolent, Hayden. You were always dashing off to a race or a boxing match. Always seeking—something.'

'I don't feel like dashing around so much here,' Hayden said, and he was surprised to realise those words were true. In the few days he had been at Barton he found his whirling thoughts had slowed. He hadn't felt that old, familiar itch to be always going, doing. And not just because of his leg. Because of being around Jane again, around her serene smile.

He glanced down at Jane where she walked beside him. He knew now what it was he saw in her here, what he could never give her—contentment.

He looked back at the house. In the daylight it was easy to see how shabby Barton was, how many things needed to be done. New windows, the roof patched, the garden cleared. He remembered how Jane would speak of it after they were married, as if it was a tiny spot of paradise. A place of happy memories, so unlike his own family home. She'd wanted to visit it with him, but there was never time. Now he saw her 'paradise' was merely a small, ramshackle manor house. But she did seem happy there.

'You work too hard here, Jane,' he said.

She shrugged. 'I don't mind the work. I want to help Barton and working helps me forget—things.'

Things like the fact that she was married to him? Hayden stabbed his walking stick hard against the ground to try to ease the pang that thought gave him. 'You are just one person. These gardens are too much for you.'

'I can't do all I would like, of course,' Jane said calmly, as if she was completely unaware of his inner turmoil. 'But real gardeners are expensive, so I do what I can.'

She was a countess, *his* countess. She shouldn't be working at all, Hayden thought fiercely. She should be lounging on a satin *chaise*, approving the designs of the best gardeners there were to be had and then watching her dreams take shape.

'I can tell you love it here,' Hayden said.

Jane really did smile then, a *real* smile that brought out the hidden dimple in her cheek he had once loved discovering. It almost felt as if the sun burst forth after a long, long night.

'I do love it,' she said. 'It's as if I can still sense my parents here and Emma is so happy. I know we can't go on like this for ever, but—yes, I love it here. I wish…' Her voice faded and she looked away from him.

'You wish what, Jane?' Hayden reached out to gently touch her hand and, to his surprise, she didn't pull away from him.

'I wish that we could have come here when we first met,' she whispered. 'That you could have seen it then.'

'Do you think things would have been different?'

Jane shrugged again. 'I don't know. Perhaps not. We are really such different people inside. I was just too foolish to see it then. Or maybe I just didn't want to see it. But at least we could have been together here for a while.'

They reached the terrace and Jane turned away to put down her bucket. 'Do you feel like dining with us tonight?' she said. 'It won't be London cuisine, but one of the neighbours did send over some venison today and cook makes a fine stew.'

One of the neighbours—like that David Marton? Hayden remembered how she had smiled at the man, how he seemed to belong here in a way Hayden himself never really could.

'I'd be happy to dine with you tonight,' Hayden said tightly. 'I'm feeling much better, Jane, really. I should be out of your way very soon.'

Jane glanced at him, an unreadable gleam in her

eyes. 'There's no hurry, Hayden. Not when you are just beginning to recover here.'

She slipped through the doors into the house, leaving Hayden alone on the terrace. He studied the overgrown gardens, the tangled flowerbeds and the ragged pathways. He *had* failed Jane. He had not been able to make her happy. But he saw now there was one thing he could give her that would surely make her smile.

If he could just find a way to make her accept it.

'Did you have a dog when you were young, Hayden?' Emma asked. 'Do you remember it?'

Hayden grinned at her. He couldn't *help* but smile at her as she gambolled with her puppy in front of the fire after a most congenial dinner. There had been much laughter and chatter about inconsequential, funny things. Even Jane had laughed and exchanged a warm glance or two with him across the small table.

Or at least he fancied she did. Hoped she did.

Jane definitely smiled now as she looked up from the account book she studied. 'Hayden is not exactly old and decrepit now, Emma. I'm sure he can remember whether or not he had a dog.'

'Despite my stick? And my grey hairs?' Hayden said, waving the stick in the air. He nearly had no use for it any longer, yet he found himself strangely loath to let it go. It would mean he was well enough to leave Barton Park and he wasn't ready to do that.

Emma made a face, and tossed a ball across the room for Murray to run after. 'Of course you aren't old, Hayden. Just—oldish.'

'Thank you very much for the distinction,' Hayden choked out, trying not to fall over laughing.

'So,' Emma went on, 'did you have a dog?'

'Not a good dog like Murray,' he said. 'My father was quite the country sportsman and kept a pack of hounds, but I wasn't supposed to go near them. And my mother had a rather vicious little lapdog who loathed everyone but her. But she quite adored it for some strange reason.'

Emma's pretty face crumpled. 'Oh, poor Hayden! Everyone should have a dog to love. You must play with Murray whenever you like.'

As if Murray agreed, he bounded up to Hayden and dropped his slimy toy ball at Hayden's feet, marring his polished shoes.

'Er—thank you very much,' Hayden muttered doubtfully.

'I'm not sure Hayden would really thank you for the favour,' Jane said. 'Emma, dear, could you fetch me the green ledger book from my desk in the library? I need to check something here.'

Emma nodded, still looking most saddened by Hayden's lack of boyhood pets, and hurried out at a run with Murray at her heels. Hayden glanced over at Jane and found her regarding him with something in her eyes he hadn't seen in a very long time— sympathy.

It made him want to snatch her up in his arms and hold her so very close, twirl her around in sudden bursts of joy as he once did when he would come home to Ramsay House and find her waiting for him so eagerly. Yet hard-learned caution kept him in his seat, across the room from her. He didn't want to frighten her, not with everything hanging between them so delicate and tentative.

'Emma is most enthusiastic in her interests,' he said.

Jane laughed. 'Indeed she is. And you are very kind to her. I suppose it's a good thing I never wanted a lapdog in London, they sound like fearsome little beasties.'

'Oh, they most certainly are. Fifi was fierce in guarding my mother and biting everyone else who ventured near, a veritable tiny Cerberus. But if you *had* wanted one, if it would have made you smile, I would have fetched one in a trice and laid it at your feet.'

Her smile flickered and she looked down at the book open in front of her. 'A dog might have added a little—warmth to the house, I suppose. But not one that would insist on biting the ankles of every caller. I wouldn't want to drive away all my friends.'

Hayden couldn't stop himself asking—he had to know. 'It wasn't all so very bad, was it, Jane? We had some good times.'

She glanced up at him, and her hazel eyes were bright. A tentative smile touched her lips. 'No, it certainly wasn't all bad. I remember some lovely moments indeed.'

'Like when the estate workers at Ramsay House unhitched our carriage horses and pulled us to the house themselves for the honeymoon?'

Her smile widened, giving him a quick glimpse of the sweet, wondrous girl he'd first met. A quick moment to dare to hope. 'And when I found you had ordered my chamber filled with flowers! I could barely move in there.'

'And when we swam in the lake?'

'You were a terrible swimmer,' she said, really laughing now. 'I thought you had drowned for one terrible moment.'

'I only did that so you would feel sorry for me and kiss me.'

'Which I did—and more, much more there in the summerhouse.' Her cheeks suddenly turned pink, and she turned away. 'No, it wasn't all bad. I was just so young then, so foolish. I thought everything would always be just that way.'

'We aren't so young now, Jane. We've been married five years and spent barely two of those years together,' Hayden said, suddenly feeling very urgent. Somehow they had to connect again. 'Surely we can talk. Perhaps I could even make you see me as you once did. The real me.'

For she was the only one who had ever *truly* seen him, just him, Hayden the man and not the earl. The man he was and the man he really wanted to be. And like an idiot he had thrown that rare treasure away.

Emma came running back in just at that moment, not giving Jane time to answer. But she *did* smile at him and, for the moment, that would have to be enough. Until he put his plan in order.

'Keep your eyes closed,' Hayden said sternly as he helped his wife down from the carriage.

Jane laughed and shook her head, but she didn't move away from his guiding hands on her shoulders or try to remove the blindfold tied over her eyes. 'This is ridiculous, Hayden! I have seen your town house before.'

'It wasn't my town house,' he said. 'It was my parents'. More accurately, my mother's since my father did not care for it. But now it is our *town house. I've had it completely refurbished, attics to kitchens, to make it ours.'*

He helped her up the marble steps just as Makepeace, the butler who had presided over this place ever since Hayden was in leading strings, opened the front door and gave a deep bow. 'Welcome home, my lord, my lady. I trust you had a pleasant time in the country.'

'Most refreshing, thank you, Makepeace,' Hayden said.

Jane stumbled a bit on the top step, but Hayden held her fast with his strong arms. Refreshing said the very least of it. It had been—amazing. Beauti-

ful. Transcendent. She had never imagined being so close to another person could be so wonderful.

He led her through the grand rooms, the beautiful drawing room decorated in the very latest à la greque fashion, the music room with its gilded pianoforte and harp, the dining room with its vast expanse of polished table and many, many perfectly aligned, brocade-cushioned chairs waiting for elegant parties.

Parties she would have to host.

A full-length portrait of Hayden's beautiful black-haired mother, in full countess splendour in velvet robes and coronet, peered down at her haughtily from her carved frame. A little white dog peeked out from her fur-trimmed hem, but it didn't make her look at all cosy. She looked rather fearsome. And now her job was Jane's. Her world was Jane's and it was one Jane knew hardly anything about.

Suddenly some of her silvery glow of happiness tarnished at the edges.

But Hayden still held her hand, and she clung to it. He led her up the stairs and into a large suite of rooms, all done in blue-and-silver satin, with a massive carved bed curtained and draped in blue velvet and piled with embroidered cushions. A dressing gown, all frothed with swathes of tulle, was spread with a dazzling array of silver and crystal pots and bottles and brushes.

'And this is yours,' Hayden announced proudly. 'I had it completely redecorated for you in a way

you would love. My room is right there through that door, so we can be together every night.'

Together every night. *Jane wished the night would start right away as she stared around the overwhelmingly elegant room. A room fit for a countess. A room fit for a woman she was not. How could she make this room, this life, her own?*

She suddenly felt very, very cold. Ramsay House had been a dream and she was waking up.

She slowly untied the ribbons of her bonnet and looked about for somewhere to put it down. A maid-servant she hadn't even seen bustled over to take it with a curtsy.

'Do you like it?' Hayden said confidently. He was already sure she had to. It was the best of everything after all.

But it was not the room she would choose. A comfortable, shabby, pretty pink room for reading and talking—and kissing. 'It is beautiful.'

'I'm very glad to hear it.' Hayden kissed her cheek quickly and strode towards the closed connecting door. 'Settle in, enjoy yourself. Ring for the servants if you need anything at all. I'm going to change my clothes and go to the club just for a while. It's been some time since I've seen my friends.'

'The club!' Jane whispered. He was leaving her, right now, all alone in this new house.

'Just for a short time. You must be tired from the journey, you won't want me hanging about while

you rest. Mary will bring you supper here on a tray, won't you, Mary?'

'Of course, my lord,' the maid said quickly. 'I am here to help her ladyship with anything at all.'

'There you go, my dear,' Hayden said with a smile. He was obviously happy to be back in town. With or without her. 'Look around the house, let me know if you want to change anything.'

And then he was gone, the door swinging closed between them. Jane slowly sat down on a chaise by the marble fireplace and shivered, wishing a fire was laid. But it wasn't the chilly house making her cold. It was the sudden realisation, as quick and unwelcome as a dunking in a snowbank, that this was her life now, her life as a countess. And she had no idea how to begin it.

Chapter Seven

'Lord Ramsay sent this to you, my lady,' Hannah announced, in a grand voice Jane had never heard from the maid before. 'Grand' was never required at Barton.

She looked up in surprise from the trunk she was sorting through with Emma. Hannah stood in the bedchamber doorway, holding out a neatly folded note on a silver tray she had unearthed from somewhere.

'Isn't Lord Ramsay downstairs, Hannah?' Jane asked, dusting off her hands on her apron.

'Yes, my lady. In the old library.'

'Then why would he...?' Jane stared at the note. Yesterday in the maze, and then later at dinner with Emma, had been—different. Laughing with Hayden, talking with him rather than quarrelling, she was sure she caught a glimpse of the man she once thought she had married. He seemed serious, interested in life at Barton. There was even a strange, swift flash of sadness she couldn't quite work out, lost quickly in the laughter of a game of Pope Joan with Emma.

But then today the rain started again and Hayden retreated to her father's dusty old library. Now he was sending her notes instead of coming to talk to her. She was completely baffled by him.

'Aren't you going to read it?' Emma asked.

Jane suddenly realised Emma and Hannah were staring at her, their eyes wide with curiosity. 'Yes, of course,' she said briskly and reached for the letter.

It wasn't sealed, and when she unfolded it she saw Hayden's familiar bold, untidy scrawl. She remembered the last time she saw that handwriting, on the notes he would secretly send her behind her aunt's back when they were courting. She still had them, carefully tied up in ribbon at the bottom of her jewel case, unread since those heady days.

Would you do me the honour of having supper with me in the dining room at seven this evening? Sincerely, Hayden.

Jane almost laughed aloud at the absurdly formal words.

'What is it, Jane?' Emma asked.

'He invites me to dine,' Jane answered, folding the note and tucking it in her apron pocket. 'In my own house?'

'Indeed?' Emma said. Her voice sounded far too innocent. Jane turned to study her sister's face, which was written with a comical expression of false surprise.

'What do you know about this?' Jane demanded.

'Why, nothing at all! It sounds as if he would just like to spend time with you,' Emma said. 'Maybe he's just not sure *you* want to spend time with *him*.'

Spend time with Hayden? Once that had been all Jane wanted in the world, but it had never come to pass. He was always rushing away somewhere.

But now he was here in her house, trapped by the weather and his injury, and he wanted to dine with her. What would they even have to say to each other, after all this time?

Yet she had to admit—she was curious. And just the tiniest bit excited.

'Will you go?' Emma asked.

'Of course. I have to eat some time,' Jane said. She turned back to Hannah. 'You may tell his lordship I will meet him in the dining room at seven.'

Emma clapped her hands as Hannah left with the message. She whirled back to the trunk they had been sorting through and tossed out a pile of gowns. They spread over the faded carpet like a vivid rainbow of shimmering silks and delicate muslins.

'What will you wear?' Emma said. She caught up a pale blue silk trimmed with dark blue velvet ribbons and pearl beading. 'This one? It's very pretty and the colour would look splendid with your eyes.'

Jane knelt down to study the tangle of dresses. Much like Hayden, they seemed like visitors from another world, this rich array from the finest London modistes. She had brought out the trunk only a few weeks ago when Emma needed a dress for the assembly. Once upon a time, shopping for these gowns had been a consolation to her, a refuge of sorts. She hadn't wanted to see them, remember the places she once wore them. The grand parties where she hadn't been able to measure up to society beauties.

The blue gown had gone to a reception at Carlton House, where she had dined amid the most luxurious of furnishings and watched tiny fish swim down a channel along the middle of the dining table. Where there was music and champagne and buffet tables piled with delicacies, all for the most illustrious people in the land. But what she remembered from that night was watching Hayden laughing and whispering with the statuesque, red-headed Lady Marlbury.

A woman who was rumoured to have been Hayden's mistress before he married. And that night it looked very much as if they were renewing the connection.

Jane carefully laid aside the blue gown and took up a pink muslin trimmed with cherry satin and froths of cream-coloured lace. It had gone to a garden party, which she had attended alone with some so-called friends. Hayden wasn't even there.

'This one, I think,' Jane said.

'It's very pretty. You should let me dress your

hair,' Emma said. 'We could use some of the red rosebuds from the garden to make a wreath.'

Her sister sounded far too enthusiastic about hair and gowns. 'Emma, did you have a hand in this strange dinner invitation?'

Emma started to shake her head, but then she nodded sheepishly. 'Not very much, though. When I showed Hayden the library this morning, he asked me to help him inspect the dining room, too. That's all. Really, Jane, I think he just wants to talk to you alone, in a civilised setting.'

'But why go to the trouble? He only needs to come up here and ask to talk to me.' Though Jane was sure they had said everything they needed to say to each other. Talking now would only rip open old wounds. Make her want things she knew were lost, just as she had when Hayden laughed with her last night.

Emma shrugged. 'I don't know. But I do think he wants to try to fit in here. Just be nice to him, Jane, please.'

'I'm always nice!' Jane protested. And she had tried with Hayden. Tried until she couldn't bear to try again.

She slipped her hand into her apron pocket and felt the crackle of the note there. Maybe, just maybe, she could dig deep and find it in herself to try one more time? Just for dinner?

'Help me find the pink slippers that go with the gown, Emma,' she said. 'They should be in here somewhere...'

* * *

Emma hummed a little tune as she skipped down the stairs, Murray's claws skittering on the wooden floor behind her. From behind the closed dining-room door she could hear the sound of furniture being moved, the clink of fine porcelain and silver being unpacked, and upstairs Jane was dressing in some of her pretty London clothes.

It was more activity than Barton had seen in a very long time and it felt as if the house was waking up around them. As if a whole new day was dawning.

Emma turned towards the library and gave a little spinning turn on the newly polished floor. Everything was going so very well. Jane looked happier, smiling more, even laughing, and no one deserved to be happy more than her sweet sister did. And Hayden wasn't the ogre Emma had come to imagine when she had seen how distant Jane was in their first weeks back at Barton last year.

Emma didn't know the whole tale of her sister's marriage. Jane had never been one to confide her troubles in anyone else, just as Emma never told Jane about Mr Milne. But Emma's imagination had filled in tales based on novels she read about city lives and gossip from the girls at her old school. Hayden became almost a monster of unkindness and rakedom in her mind.

But when she found him injured on the road and brought him home, she'd seen he wasn't what she imagined. He seemed almost like Jane. Sad—seeking.

Of course, that didn't mean Emma wouldn't kill him if he dared hurt Jane again.

She closed the library door behind her and hurried to the shelf where she spent so much time, the section that held volumes and documents on the history of Barton and the neighbourhood. That was where she had found the original journal and where she had come to think the maze held the secrets to the treasure. She had to keep on with the hunt; she was so close now.

Jane slowly made her way down the stairs, hugging her wool shawl closer around her shoulders. Somehow the house, *her* house, felt strange, as if she walked through halls and rooms she had never seen before. Lamps were lit along the way, the flickering amber light blending with the waning daylight streaming through the windows. It made everything look magical.

Jane pressed her hand against her stomach to still the nervous flutters. It was ridiculous to be anxious. She was merely going to have a meal in her own house, with Hayden.

Alone with Hayden. That was the uncertain point. For such a long time, when they were alone they either fought or fell into each other's arms. Neither had ever done them much good. She'd spent all those months at Barton trying to forget and find a way to move forwards.

She'd even thought she *had* moved forwards, until he suddenly appeared on her doorstep. Until yesterday, when she saw that swing and remembered all the good things that once were. Until he laughed with her and Emma, as if the past was truly past.

She hurried through the drawing room, towards the closed double doors that led into the dining room. They seldom used those rooms any longer and the furniture was shrouded with canvas covers. It made everything feel even stranger, more unreal, as did the echoing quiet of the house. Usually Emma and her dog were running around, the cook was banging pots and pans as loudly as she could in the kitchen and Hannah was singing as she dusted.

For such a small household, they made a lot of noise. Far more than the fully-staffed, impeccably run London house. But tonight even Emma was being quiet.

Jane paused as she reached for the door handle. She couldn't hear anything in the dining room. What if Hayden wasn't really there? What if he had changed his mind and run off back to London, despite the muddy roads?

Half-sure she would find the room empty, she pushed open the door.

The long table, which had been covered and empty for so long, was polished to a high gleam, set off by dozens of candles lit along its length and set on the sideboard. Two places were set at the far end with her mother's china and silver that had been packed away for safekeeping, and wonderful, enticing scents of cinnamon and stewed fruit emanated from the covered dishes on the sideboard. Her mother's portrait had even been taken from the attic and hung back in its old place on the faded wallpaper.

Jane took it all in, amazed at the transformation, until her gaze landed on Hayden. He stood behind the chair at the head of the table, dressed in a fine velvet-trimmed blue coat and faultlessly tied cravat, his glossy black hair smoothed back from his face.

'Have I suddenly been transported to a different house?' she said with a laugh. 'This can't possibly be Barton Park.'

A smile cracked his cautious façade and he hurried over to take her hand. He raised it to his lips for a soft, lingering kiss, and Jane shivered at the sensation of his mouth on her skin. It had been so very long since she had felt that. She'd forgotten the immediate, visceral reaction she always had to his touch.

'It's amazing what a bit of polish can do,' Hayden said as he led her to the chairs. 'Emma found the china and most of the candle holders in the attic, along with the portrait.'

'I knew she was up to something!' Jane cried. 'She is becoming much too good at subterfuge.' She sat down in the chair Hayden held out and arranged her skirts as she watched him sit down next to her.

The candlelight shimmered over him, turning his skin to purest pale gold.

'She seemed very excited to help me set up a small surprise for you,' Hayden said. He reached for a ewer of wine and filled their glasses. 'She agrees with me—you work far too hard here.'

Jane sipped at the sweet, rich red liquid and wondered where he'd unearthed it. 'I told you, I like the work. It keeps me occupied.'

'And there was nothing to keep you occupied in London?'

Jane set the glass down with a thump. 'Did you bring me here to quarrel again, Hayden?'

He shook his head. 'The very last thing I want to do is quarrel with you, Jane. I'm so weary of that and you deserve better.'

'Do I?' She swallowed hard past a sudden lump in her throat. She did deserve better; they both deserved better than the half-life they had lived together. She'd always wanted him to see that, to tell him that things could be different, but she had never found the right words. Until she didn't believe it herself.

Hannah hurried in with a tureen of soup and Jane couldn't say anything at all. As they sampled the first courses of what looked like the most elaborate meal Barton had seen in a long time, she asked him about his friends in London, how Ramsay House was faring, anything but the two of them. Anything but what happened between them before.

Anything but the lost babies.

And slowly, as the candles sputtered lower and the darkness gathered outside, as Hannah served the elaborate meal and more wine was poured, something very strange happened. Jane started to enjoy herself.

'Oh, that didn't really happen!' she said, laughing helplessly. 'I can't even believe it.'

'Of course it really happened.' Hayden grinned at her, looking rather like a naughty schoolboy telling a joke he knew he shouldn't. 'You remember Lady Worthington's pet monkey. She always insisted on taking the blasted thing to every party and it always escaped.'

'Yes, but her footmen also captured the poor creature before it could wreak too much havoc.'

'Not this time. The wretched thing proved too wily for everyone and stole Prinny's hairpiece before carrying it up to the chandeliers. When he dropped it into the soup, Mrs Carlyle swore it was an immense African spider and, in all her shrieking and flailing, tore the cloth right off the table. Along with all the dishes. Luckily the bottle of port right in front of me was spared.'

Jane pressed her napkin to her mouth, giggling at the wild images Hayden's dry, matter-of-fact rendition of the tale conjured up in her mind. She had forgotten that about Hayden—that he could be so very much *fun*. That he could see the ridiculous in any event and make her see it, too.

'I do wish I had seen that,' she said. 'But I'm glad Emma didn't. She would have demanded a pet monkey.'

Hayden refilled her wine glass and she suddenly realised that his was still half-full. He had been drinking remarkably little that night.

'To keep the dog company?' he said. 'That creature barks more than any canine I've ever seen. Perhaps he needs a friend.'

'She does adore Murray,' Jane said, sipping at the wine. It felt good to sit and just talk with Hayden, to be comfortable with him. Even though she knew such a moment couldn't last long, not with them. 'He was the runt of a litter one of the local farmers had and she rescued him. He's better than the last pet. It was a hedgehog and a rather ill-tempered one.'

'She said she collects plant specimens as well.'

'Oh, yes. She'll show you her laboratory if you give her the slightest encouragement.'

Hayden sat back in his chair and watched her, a half-smile on his lips. 'You *are* happy here, aren't you, Jane?'

'Of course,' she answered in surprise. She'd thought Hayden was far beyond noticing or caring whether she was happy or unhappy. Surely he could never think someone could be happy in the country. 'It's always been my home. You would think it much too quiet, though. The most excitement we ever have is when the vicar comes to call, or there's an assembly in the village.'

'They say the hunting is good around here,' he said. He toyed with the stem of his glass between his long, elegant fingers, and Jane found herself mesmerised by the movement. By a flashing memory of what those beautiful hands could do.

She tore her stare away from him and took a quick bite of the lemon-trifle dessert on her plate. She nearly choked on it. 'It is. My grandparents even helped start the local hunt club—they were avid riders. I'm sure Emma would enjoy the sport, too, but we can't afford to keep horses.'

Hayden nodded and Jane noticed that a shadow seemed to flicker over his face. But he never stopped the slow, lazy turning of the glass. 'You could let me help you, Jane.'

'No,' she said, suddenly feeling cold. 'No, I can't do that.'

'As much as you seem to want to fight the fact, I *am* your husband,' he said, so calm, so rational. It almost made her want the old, heated quarrels they had when he drank. They were easier for her to dismiss than this new, quiet, solemn Hayden. The man who was a stranger and yet also someone she knew so intimately.

'As if I could ever forget that,' she said.

'Then let me help you. It's the least I can do after how I treated you.'

'How you treated me?' Jane choked out. Like when they fought? Like when she only wanted his attention, the one thing that wasn't hers? Like when he refused to understand her? Or when she refused to understand him. Refused to try to fit into his world, because it was not hers at all.

'I wasn't all I should have been,' he said. 'I didn't really know how to be a husband. We were so young when we married. But I would like to learn how to be your friend, if you will let me. The past is gone. We must live in the present.'

Before Jane could even think out what to say to those extraordinary words, Hannah hurried in to gather the plates from the table. Jane slumped back in her chair, glad of the interruption, the moment to gather her scattered thoughts. Hayden was right— going over old quarrels, things that were past and done, would do them no good. They had to find a way to move forwards. But how? How could she stop the pain, once and for all?

Especially when he sat right beside her, with his beautiful eyes, the warmth and smell of him, re- minding her of all she had once hoped for. All she still might long for, deep down inside, if she couldn't keep those wild emotions tightly bound down.

'Walk with me on the terrace?' Hayden said as Hannah left the room, china clattering. 'I think the rain has stopped and it's a fine night outside.'

Jane nodded. She could use the fresh air, the chance to clear her head and speak to him ratio- nally again. When he drew back her chair and of- fered her his arm, she hesitated for a moment before she took it. He felt so warm and strong under her touch, so familiar and yet so foreign all at the same time. Her head whirled with how quickly they could veer now between distant politeness and falling back to the old intimacy.

Hayden led her through the old glass doors on to the terrace, limping just the merest amount on his bad leg. He had left the walking stick behind tonight. The night was dark and cloudy, lit only by the diluted, chalky rays of moonlight and the candles in the windows. In the distance she saw the maze, dark and mysterious, almost frightening, but the only thing she was really, vividly aware of was Hayden at her side.

'Do you remember the night of the Milbanke ball?' Hayden asked quietly.

Jane laughed. 'Of course. How could I forget? That was when you first asked me to marry you. I was shocked out of my wits. You probably were, too.' They'd walked on a terrace much like this one, hiding in the shadows together while the noise and colour of the party whirled on beyond the open doors.

'I *was* shocked,' Hayden said. 'I never meant to blurt out those words to you like that, with no skill or charm. But once I said it—I knew it was right.'

Jane leaned on his arm and closed her eyes as she thought back to that night. It seemed so long ago now, those shimmering moments when it seemed as if every impossible dream was coming true. It also seemed so close now, on this other warm, soft night.

Yet they weren't the same people they were then.

She had been so disappointed so many times until that hope simply withered away. Surely Hayden felt the same. It became so clear to her that he thought he was getting something, someone, else when he married her. That they didn't really know each other at all. They had met and married in such quick, dizzying succession.

But that night at the Milbanke ball had been pure magic. So perfect that even now she felt the memory of it wrap around her and enfold her completely in its beautiful illusion.

'I thought it was right, too,' she whispered. 'When you kissed me, it felt like perfection, and I was sure we could never be parted again. But life can't always be like that.'

Hayden suddenly stopped, and Jane opened her eyes to blink up at him. His face was concealed in the night and he turned to clasp both her hands in his. 'I wanted to make everything perfect for you, Jane,' he said roughly. 'I wanted to make you smile every day, to erase that worry in your eyes once and for all. Instead I only made your life more difficult.'

Jane was astonished at his words, so stark and simple, so laden with hurt. After they married, he had kept every vestige of true emotion, true thoughts, hidden from her behind the wild whirl of parties and the fashionable life. She never would have imagined he felt that way at all.

'I was the one who was wrong,' she said. 'I was so silly, so sheltered behind my eccentric family. I didn't know what being your wife, being a countess, really meant. I could only see *you*. I only wanted to be with you. But marriage is never just two people, is it? It's so much more.'

He was quiet for a long, tense moment, until Jane feared she'd said something wrong. She tried to slip her hands out of his, but he wouldn't let her go.

'When I was growing up, my parents didn't talk to me often. When they did it was always about duty,' Hayden said. 'The duty of a Fitzwalter, of an earl.'

He laughed, but Jane could hear the bitter tinge to it. Hayden never spoke of his parents to her when they were together, or of his life before he met her. She knew nothing about them, except that they died years before, his father of an apoplexy and his mother in childbirth.

'Hayden…' she began, desperate to tell him that his attractions as a husband to her had been everything about him *but* his title. His humour, his sense of fun, his good looks, the way he held her hand, the way she felt when he kissed her—she had wanted all those things so much. The title scared her to tears. The life he led in London scared her in its strangeness.

And she had been right to fear it in the end.

'No, Jane, let me say this,' he said. 'I wanted to give you everything I could, everything I thought you wanted. But I could give you nothing, could I? Not even a child.'

Jane's stomach seized with a sharp pain at the mention of the babies. That one thing she'd longed for above all others—Hayden's child, a new family, a new start. The thing that would never be. She would be too afraid of the pain even to try now.

'Hayden, please, no' was all she could say. She closed her eyes against the tears she couldn't afford to cry any more and tugged at her hands. Still he held on to her.

'I'm sorry, Jane,' he said simply, starkly. 'I'm sorry.'

'Oh, Hayden,' she choked out. 'Once those words were all I wanted from you. But now…'

'Now it's too late,' he said, a terrible ring of finality in those four simple words.

They stood there together in silence, holding hands, so close she could hear his breath, yet far apart. As far as the moon behind the haze of clouds.

'Dance with me,' Hayden suddenly said.

'D-dance? What about your leg?' Jane stammered. As usual, Hayden was too quicksilver for her.

'Like we did at the Milbanke ball. And my leg is fine. Perfectly up to a simple waltz.'

'There's no music.'

'Just imagine it. Remember it.'

His arm slid around her waist and the fingers of his other hand twined with hers. He drew her much closer than he had that night, under the watch of her aunt. Their bodies were pressed so close together she could feel his heartbeat echo through her.

He hummed the tune of that remembered waltz under his breath, ragged and out of tune and far too endearing. He was still the marvellous dancer she'd once known, despite his leg, and soon they were spinning and twirling over the terrace, his arm guiding her steps until they once again moved as one. Faster and faster, until Jane laughed helplessly and clung to him.

They whirled to a stop, out of breath, hearts pounding. Jane stared up at him, marvelling that she could fall into him again so quickly.

'It's been so long since I danced,' she said.

'Jane,' he said hoarsely and she saw a light shift in his eyes. Suddenly his arm tightened around her and his mouth came down to touch hers.

She went up on tiptoe as he kissed her, twining her arms around his neck to hold him against her. She felt his touch at her waist, dragging her even closer.

They still fit together so perfectly, their mouths, their bodies, their touch, as if they were made to be just so. Her body still wanted his so very much, still remembered every night they'd had together. She parted her lips and felt the tip of his tongue touch hers and the kiss slid down into frantic need. She wanted this so much, wanted to forget the past and have only *now*. To fall into him and be lost all over again.

Her head fell back as his lips trailed away from hers and he pressed a hot kiss to the sensitive curve of her neck. She shivered as his mouth trailed over her shoulder, the soft upper swell of her breast above her bodice. He remembered every spot that made her most wild with want for him.

She buried her fingers in the silk of his hair and sighed at the intense feelings that poured through her. At the connection that still coursed between them like lightning.

She felt him draw back, felt his kiss slide away from her, but he still held her against him. His arms were around her waist, pulling her up so his chin could rest atop her head. The rough, uneven rhythm of their breath mingled. Their heartbeats pounded out a frantic drum tattoo of need and want and fear.

Jane caressed his shoulder, her hand shaking.

'Oh, Jane,' he muttered. 'You see what you still do to me?'

She laughed. 'This was always the easy part between us, Hayden. Kissing, lovemaking—it was always so perfect. So wonderful. It always made us forget everything else.'

But 'everything else' always waited there, lurking in the shadows around them. It always came back to remind her that Hayden didn't, couldn't, love her as she longed for.

'Jane…' he began, but she backed away from him, shaking her head. She didn't *want* all those other things, not now, not on a night that had been so special.

And she definitely did not want to cry in front of

Hayden. 'I must go look in on Emma,' she managed to whisper. 'Thank you for dinner, Hayden, and for our dance. It was—delightful.'

And she spun around and ran away before he could see her tears.

Hayden watched Jane go, her skirts swirling around her as she hurried up the stairs. He wanted to follow her more than he had ever wanted anything in his life, but something even more powerful held him back. Something that told him if he pushed her now, if he grabbed her in his arms and refused to let her go, she would drift even further away from him.

He raked his fingers through his hair, listening as her rushing footsteps faded away and the door to her room closed. He sat down on the step and braced his fists on the old, warped wood as he tried to make sense of all that happened tonight.

Hayden did not like to think. Drinking, carousing, horse racing, dancing—they erased the need for thought, for doing anything but being in that one moment. It had been like that his whole life, just as it had been for his father before him. Nothing else mattered then, not being the earl, not what he had failed to do. Only the speed and movement, the slow slide into forgetfulness.

But Jane had made him stop and think from the first time he saw her. Her quiet seriousness made him see things in a different way, made him *want* to be better. That he failed at that wasn't her fault. He'd chased her away and run back into his old ways. Almost forgotten how he felt when he was with her.

Only a few days back in her company, and it all came rushing out again. Without the barrier of drinking between them, he saw how Jane was here in the country. The pale, brittle, fragile Jane he remembered from the last days in London was gone. She was beautiful and strong here. And deeply, deeply wary of him. Rightfully so. He had failed her as a husband. He hadn't even really tried.

Hayden pounded his fists hard against the stairs as he envisioned the raw pain in Jane's eyes when he mentioned the babies. He hadn't been there for her then; she didn't want him here now.

He had to find a way to change again.

'How did the dinner go?' he heard Emma ask, breaking into his brooding thoughts.

He looked up to see her leaning over the banister from the landing, staring down at him. Her blonde hair tangled over her shoulders and she held a squirming Murray under her arm. For once even the puppy was quiet.

He shook his head and Emma groaned. 'That bad, was it?' she said as she hurried down the stairs to sit down beside him.

'It wasn't bad at all at first,' Hayden answered. Emma had been such an enthusiastic help in setting up the surprise for Jane, he hated to disappoint her, too. 'We talked and laughed, just like when we were on our honeymoon. We danced…'

'You got Jane to dance?' Emma exclaimed.

'Yes. We used to love dancing together.'

Emma shook her head. 'She won't dance at all now. Even at the assembly, when that stick-in-the-mud David Marton asked her.'

Marton again. It seemed the man could do, be, whatever Hayden couldn't for Jane. 'Marton asked her to dance?'

'Yes, but she made me do it instead. It was quite dull.' Emma thoughtfully stroked Murray's black-and-white fur where he lay on her lap. 'So what went wrong?'

'I fear I have hurt your sister too much for one dance to make much difference,' he admitted.

'Then you must keep on trying! And on and on, until she sees how much she misses you.'

Against his will, he felt a touch of something strangely like hope. 'She missed me?'

'I'm sure she does. She seldom talks about you or your life in London and she always tries so hard to be cheerful for me. But I see how sad she looks sometimes, when she thinks no one is around. Whatever happened, I'm sure it can't be so bad that it can't be fixed. You must keep trying.'

Hayden had to laugh at Emma's stubborn certainty. Perhaps there *was* hope, if Jane truly missed him. If he could change, and show her that he had changed, maybe they could make a new sort of life.

For the first time he saw the faint, faraway light of something he never thought to have—hope.

'You know, Emma,' he said, 'I always wanted a sister.'

Emma laughed. 'And I always wanted a brother. You could possibly do well. But don't make me sorry I decided to help you.'

Chapter Eight

'Are you quite sure you feel like doing this?' Jane asked Hayden anxiously as they walked out of Barton's gates on to the lane. The drying ruts of mud sucked at her sturdy boots, but couldn't hold her down. 'Your leg…'

'It's much better,' he insisted with a laugh. 'You don't need to fuss any more, Jane. I know I'm capable of walking into the village without collapsing.'

Jane had to laugh, too. She *was* fussing, even though it was quite clear Hayden could take care of himself. For the last two days, since their dinner alone and the kiss that sent her life spinning, he had worked in the garden, cleaning flowerbeds with her between the rains. He dug through the piles of old books in the library with Emma. He played cards with her in the evenings, much to her giggling delight. He took Murray for walks.

And he drank only small amounts of wine and walked her to her chamber door every night, leaving her with a kiss on the cheek. She wasn't sure if she was relieved or disappointed by that sweet salute. Kissing, and all the delicious things that went along with it, were always the things the two of them got exactly right.

But she did know she was utterly mystified by this new Hayden. He was so attentive, so interested in what went on at Barton. He fit into their quiet life, as if he had merely been the last piece of the puzzle that needed to be slid into place.

Back in London, where every minute had been so full of wild, dizzying activity, she would never have pictured Hayden in his shirtsleeves digging about in the garden with her—and laughing about it. She always felt slightly on edge, waiting for his game to be over and the Hayden she'd come to see as a wild stranger emerge again. She waited for the moment he grew tired of them and left, never to be seen again.

Yet he was still there. And he showed no signs of leaving Barton.

Jane was afraid she was becoming all too accustomed to having him there, to working alongside him as they talked quietly of inconsequential things, and of watching him laugh with Emma. She'd only just begun to pick up the shards of her scattered life. She'd have to cry all over again when he did leave.

But today didn't look like it would be that day. The sky was overcast, but the rains hadn't started again. Emma wanted to walk into the village to see if there was anything new at the bookshop and Hayden immediately agreed to walk with them. It would be the first time in days that they had left their cosy nest at Barton and went out among other people. The village was not London, of course, but Jane still didn't know what would happen.

Emma dashed ahead of them with Murray, her bonnet dangling by its ribbons down her back. Hayden walked next to Jane, close but not touching, and they went in silence for several long minutes.

'Do you often walk into the village?' he asked.

'Not very often,' Jane answered, glad of something neutral, easy to speak of. 'We're so busy at Barton. But this is an easy walk on a fine day and Emma likes to visit the bookshop. We've been once or twice to the assembly rooms, too. There are a surprising number of fine musicians who live nearby and play for the dancing. It's not a grand London ball, but most enjoyable.'

'And does Emma enjoy the dancing as much as she does the bookshop?'

'Not nearly as much, I fear,' Jane said with a laugh. 'But I try to find her what society I can.'

'Perhaps there are no worthy dance partners for her.'

'Perhaps not. But then I am not sure what she would consider "worthy". She spurns whatever young man offers her attention.'

'And do you also dance at the assemblies, Jane?'

There was a strangely intent note in Hayden's

voice, as if suddenly they weren't merely chatting. Her steps slowed as they came to the small clearing where the road split off in two branches. One led into the village, the other to an old farmhouse that was half-burned and falling in on itself. A river ran along the roadside there, out of sight down a sloping bank.

Usually the waters were placid, a fine spot for a picnic on a nice day, but now it was swollen from the rains and she could hear the rush and tumble of it over the rocks. Emma had vanished down by its waves and Jane could hear her calling after Murray.

'Of course I don't dance,' she said. 'I am an old married lady. My job is to chaperon Emma.'

'Yet surely you have friends you talk to at parties? You said you did.'

What was he really asking? Jane turned to study him, but his face was shadowed under his hat. 'A few. But not as many as you have in London.'

He gave a harsh laugh. 'I don't have friends in London, Jane, as you rightfully pointed out. I have people I know.'

'What of Lord John Eastwood? Is he not your friend?' John Eastwood had been the best man at their wedding, a friend of Hayden's from schooldays, and he was the only crony of Hayden's she'd really liked. He actually talked to her. And he seemed so sad after the sudden death of Lady Eastwood. Jane had hoped John could help Hayden after their own marriage crumbled.

'John has been in the country lately,' Hayden said shortly.

'Then what of—?' Jane clamped her mouth tightly shut on the words. She'd almost blurted out 'What of Lady Marlbury?' But she didn't really want to know if he saw Lady Marlbury.

'What about what?' he asked.

'Nothing,' she said quickly. She called for Emma and hurried on towards the village, away from the river and the burned-out farmhouse. Away from the past and her own emotions of what had happened there.

The village was a small one, just a few cobbled lanes and a green centred around a stone thirteenth-century church and the long, low building housing the assembly rooms. Even though Jane didn't make the walk in very often, everyone there knew her. And they all seemed to be out that afternoon, hurrying in and out of the shops, strolling on the shady green, shaking rugs out of windows.

Everyone called out greetings to Jane, looking curiously at Hayden until she stopped to introduce him. Then their surprise turned to smiles. Jane knew they'd all wondered about her as the months went on and she stayed alone at Barton, Lord Ramsay nowhere in evidence. No one had ever been rude enough to ask outright where he was, though Louisa Marton had hinted once or twice. But now they were all so clearly happy to see them together.

Jane was half-afraid Hayden would be bored in the village. The tension of their short conversation by the river still lingered between them, taut as a rope binding them, but holding them apart.

But he went with her into the shops, carrying her purchases and conversing affably with everyone who stopped them. He was friendly, joking, chatting about farming matters and local gossip quite as if he was deeply interested in them. Jane was astonished; this was not the Hayden she'd come to know in London. This was the Hayden who had been with her all too briefly at Ramsay House on their honeymoon, the one who had slipped away from her.

'I didn't know you had read about sheep cultivation in the country,' she said as they stepped out of the draper's and turned towards the bookshop to fetch Emma.

Hayden laughed. 'I have all sorts of hidden interests, Jane. But you mustn't tell anyone. Wouldn't want to ruin my reputation as a care-for-nothing, would we?'

She had so many questions flying around in her mind. Why would Hayden hide his true intelligence, especially from her? She opened her mouth to ask him more, but suddenly a woman called, 'Lady Ramsay! Lady Ramsay, how lovely to see you again.'

Jane turned to see Louisa Marton rushing towards them across the street, the plumes on her bonnet waving. David Marton walked behind her, more cautious.

'How do you do, Miss Marton? Sir David?' Jane said. She remembered Hayden's irrational jealousy when he had arrived at Barton and found the Martons there. How he had asked her so closely about Sir David and her 'friendships' in the village. She glanced up at him from under the brim of her straw hat, but his face was blandly polite. Only the slight narrowing of his eyes as he looked at Sir David showed he was thinking anything at all. 'You remember Lord Ramsay?'

'Oh, of course we do,' Louisa said with a giggle. 'Don't we, David? It's no wonder we haven't seen you in a few days. You two must be very busy.'

'There is certainly much to be done at Barton, Miss Marton,' Hayden said. 'I'm very grateful my wife has had such good friends to help her while I've been away on business. I wouldn't want her to be lonely.'

'Anyone would be honoured to stand in as a friend to Lady Ramsay,' David said quietly. 'Especially when she is most in need of one.'

The two men stared at each other in a long, tense moment as Louisa giggled and Jane tried to think of something—anything—to say. Finally the strange atmosphere was broken when Emma came hurrying out of the bookshop and they turned towards home after making their farewells to the Martons.

'We shall see you soon, I hope, Lady Ramsay!'

Louisa called after them. 'I will have a small musical evening soon, which I do hope you will attend...'

'What did the Martons want?' Emma asked as they walked back past the burned-out farmhouse. 'Sir David looked positively animated there for an instant, which is more than I can usually say for him.'

'Don't be rude, Emma,' Jane chided. 'The Martons have been very kind to us.'

Emma shrugged and went on to chatter about the new books she had found all the way to the gates of Barton Park, so that Jane and Hayden could say nothing to each other. Jane thought that was just as well, since she wasn't sure what she would want to say, anyway. Once they were on the pathway to the house again, Emma ran up the drive ahead of them and they were alone for a moment.

'So the Martons are proud to be your good friends?' Hayden asked quietly.

'I told you,' Jane said, exasperated by his strange attitude. 'They are near neighbours and Sir David is widely read and has many interesting opinions, even if Emma does think him dull. So, yes, they are friends. Did you think I would just sit here alone while you ran about London? That I would make no life for myself and my sister?'

'You never had to be alone, Jane. We could have shared the life in London. You could have had friends there.'

She shook her head, suddenly so tired. This was

something they had quarrelled about before and there was no solution. No moving back or forwards.

Suddenly Emma gave a shout, and Jane saw her dashing back up the drive towards them. 'Jane, come quickly! It's the most amazing thing.'

Bewildered, Jane hurried after her sister until they turned the corner in sight of the house.

It really was the most amazing thing. There was *work* being done on Barton. There were several men climbing about on the roof, busily fixing the patches that had been worn away in all the rain. Others were examining the cracked windows and hauling barrows of debris from the garden.

'What is this?' she cried. She spun around to face Hayden as he limped closer to her. 'Did you do this?'

He gave a sheepish smile. 'Surprise, Jane. I thought you might be tired of moving those buckets around every time it rains.'

'Hayden,' she said slowly. She could hardly credit what she was seeing right before her—and that Hayden had thought of this all on his own. 'I— shouldn't let you do this. It's too much.'

'Of course you should. You've let me into your house; you won't take money from me. I want to do something for you and for Barton Park. Patching the roof is the least I can do now.'

He wanted to do something for Barton? Jane was amazed and touched. Against her will, she felt herself softening towards him just the tiniest bit. She'd seen a side to him today she hadn't in a very long time, and it made her feel reluctantly—hopeful. Maybe Barton did have the power to change people.

'Well,' she said, 'if you insist on patching the leaky roof, who am I to deny you?'

Hayden laughed and took her arm to walk with her towards the house. 'Now you are coming around to my point of view, Jane. I knew you would eventually…'

Chapter Nine

❧❧❧

'Are you quite sure you don't mind helping me find books, Hayden?' Emma asked, her voice muffled from where she knelt under a haphazard pile of volumes.

Hayden smiled down at the top of her head, the straw crown of her bonnet just visible. 'Of course I don't mind. Why should I?'

Emma handed up two books for him to hold. 'It just doesn't seem like a little village bookshop would be your natural habitat.'

Hayden studied the store, the jumbled shelves jammed with volumes, the streaked windows, the old, white-haired proprietor, Mr Lorne, who obviously knew Emma very well as he had kept back a stack of books for her. It was quiet and overly warm, smelling of lavender and book dust, its own little world. 'It's true I'm not much of a reader. But I fear I would have been in your sister's way while she made the grocery order and I don't think I should try to get in her black books any more than I already am.'

'Hmm—not much of a reader. Nor much of a country dweller, I would say,' Emma said. She handed him another book and rose to her feet, brushing the dust from her skirts. 'Have you always lived in town?'

'When I was a child I lived at Ramsay House with my parents, but I don't go there often now,' Hayden answered. 'I suppose I do prefer city life.'

'Really? Why?'

Hayden shrugged, still not quite used to his sister-in-law's forthright, curious nature. It was so unlike anything he had ever known in his own family. He also wasn't used to looking too closely inside himself, the dark corners and cobwebbed passages. 'I like to keep busy, I suppose.'

'And there isn't enough to keep you busy at Ramsay House? Jane said it was quite vast.'

'So it is. And I have an excellent estate manager to keep it going for me.'

'It's not quite the same as taking care of it yourself, is it? Not if it's home, as Barton Park is. I missed it so much when we were gone from it.'

'I'm not sure Ramsay House is much of a home,' Hayden admitted, surprised to find himself saying words he had barely even thought before. But there was something about Jane's innocent sister, about the whole intimate world of Barton and its environs, that forced him to be honest. 'I never felt I really belonged there until Jane was there with me.'

Emma's eyes widened. 'But then why—?'

She was interrupted when the shop door opened with a tinkle of bells and someone called her name. As she hurried to greet her friend, Hayden moved to a quiet corner behind a bank of shelves. He pretended to examine the books, but in his mind he was suddenly back at Ramsay House. With Jane.

He had a flashing memory of carrying Jane over the threshold, the two of them laughing. Jane's laughter as she wrapped her arms around him and sent them both tumbling to the bed. The taste of her skin under his lips, the sound of her sighs. There, in bed, when they were alone, he could make her happy.

It was only when they left their sensual cocoon that he couldn't decipher what she really wanted.

Hayden stared at the rows of volumes before him and wished there was a book that could tell him, finally, what to do for Jane. How to make things right.

He heard an echo of merry laughter and, for an instant, thought it was another memory of one of their too-brief moments of happiness. But then he saw that Jane stood outside the shop window, chatting with someone, laughing at some joke. She looked as she had in those days when they dashed together through the gardens at Ramsay House, her face alight with joy, young and free.

But this time he wasn't the one to put that happiness there. Hayden had the sudden, terrible realisation that he had always let Jane down. He had swept her off her feet because he wanted her so much, then he hadn't known how to keep her. He hadn't even tried and he had no one to blame but himself. His parents had taught him badly and he hadn't even thought to escape them.

It was he alone who hadn't been the right husband for Jane. And that thought struck him like a shotgun blast.

Jane glanced through the window and saw him watching her. Her laughter faded and a frown flickered over her face. He had to prove himself to her, that was all. But how could he do that, how could he make it up to his brave wife, when he didn't know where to start?

'Hayden, you are dreadful! You must be cheating,' Emma cried as she tossed her cards down on the table. 'That is the third hand you've won tonight.'

Jane had to laugh at the disgruntled look on Emma's face. Her sister loved to play cards, but Emma was also easily distracted and often lost track of the game. She could only keep up with an experienced gamester like Hayden for a short while.

But Hayden never let Emma feel like he was 'letting' her win, or like she was slow-witted for losing. The two of them seemed as if they could play for ever, something Jane would never have expected.

But then Hayden wasn't behaving at all as she would have once expected.

Hayden grinned as he gathered up the scattered cards. 'A gentleman never cheats, Emma. Luck is with me tonight.'

'Luck is always with you,' Emma grumbled. She turned to Jane and added, 'It's most unfair, isn't it, Jane?'

Jane plied her needle carefully through the linen she was mending. 'Life is always most unfair, Emma dear.'

'Indeed it is. I wish the rain would stop,' Emma said. They could hear the drops pattering at the sitting-room window. It had started when they sat down to dinner, a slow, steady drip that would make the already muddy roads even more impassable.

So Hayden would have to stay even longer.

Jane studied him as he shuffled the cards and dealt them between him and Emma again. They hadn't spoken much since their quarrel in the village that afternoon, but he seemed to be in a good humour again. He'd laughed and joked over dinner, making Emma giggle with tales of London gossip. Everything was so comfortable between them all tonight, cosy almost.

Once, this had been all she longed for with Hayden. A happy family life for the two of them. It was the one thing he couldn't give her in the end— the one thing they couldn't give each other. To see it before her now made her heart ache at how bittersweet life could be. Emma was right—things were most unfair.

Jane had been angry at his too-quick assumptions about David Marton, that was true. Hayden had no right to say such things to her when he was no doubt engaged in all kinds of debaucheries in town! But now, wrapped up in this warm evening, she couldn't hold on to her anger any longer.

Especially when they hadn't needed to get out the buckets to catch the drips from the old roof, thanks to his efficient workmen.

'One more game, Emma, then off to bed,' Jane said, twisting the needle through the cloth.

She expected an argument. Emma was a night-owl who could happily stay up until dawn. But Emma just nodded and gave a strangely sly smile as she studied her new hand of cards.

'Of course,' Emma said. 'I have some notes to make on my new plant specimens, anyway. You can take my place at cards, Jane.'

Jane shook her head. 'I don't play cards any longer.'

Hayden shot her a quizzical glance, but he didn't say anything until the game ended and Emma bid them goodnight. Once she had left, Murray trotting at her heels, the room seemed deeply quiet. She could only hear the soft slide of the cards between his fingers, the fall of the rain, the rustle of the linen under her needle. But she was intensely, burningly aware that he sat just across the room from her. That he watched her.

'You don't play cards?' he said suddenly, the words tossed out into the heavy silence. 'I remember you were a wicked opponent at whist.'

Jane shook her head. 'I even had to give up such old-fashioned games. I hated losing far too much and Emma has become too good a player.'

'Emma is certainly an enthusiastic opponent,' he said. 'But are you sure you didn't stop because of me?'

Startled by his stark question, Jane dropped her mending to her lap and stared at him. He looked back at her, unwavering, unblinking, his blue eyes dark and solemn. 'I— Well, yes. I didn't like what you became when you played deep in the card rooms. So intense, so—feverish. It was as if I didn't know you there. But then again…'

Her words stuck and she shook her head again. She was so accustomed to stuffing her true thoughts and emotions down deeper and deeper, so deep that Hayden couldn't see them and thus hurt her even more. She didn't know what to do with this new Hayden, this still, watchful, serious Hayden.

'Then again—what, Jane?' he asked.

'Then again, I often felt like I didn't know you at all,' she admitted. 'When I saw you at balls, in the card rooms, with your friends, I was sure I had only imagined the man I thought I married. He vanished so utterly and you never seemed to know me at all.'

He nodded and stared down at the pack of cards in his hand. A straight, frowning line creased between his eyes.

'I should have come here when you asked me to,' he said.

'What?' Jane said in surprise.

'That last night, before you left London, you asked me to come here with you and Emma for a holiday. I should have done it.'

Jane couldn't believe he even remembered that. He'd been so foxed that night on the stairs, she'd been so sure he remembered nothing about it. And when she left the town house the next day without a word from him, she was sure she was right. That he didn't care at all.

'Barton is a special place, isn't it?' he said. 'I've never felt like a house could be this way.'

Jane knew that very well. Barton was her home. But she would never have thought he could see it. 'What way?'

'Like a real home,' he said simply.

Jane's heart pounded at those stark words. *That* was what she had tried to tell him so long ago; why she tried to get him to come here with her. Why did he see now, when it was too late?

She tried to laugh, but the sound came out all choked. 'Perhaps it will be, now that you have fixed the roof.'

'That was the least I could do. I owe you so much, Jane, and yet you won't accept anything from me.'

'You don't owe me anything, Hayden,' she said. She didn't want debt between them, not any longer. She'd only wanted to leave him, leave the mistake of *them,* behind so she could find some way to move forwards. But all that effort was shattered when he showed up here.

'Your family must have been so happy here,' he said. 'You never talked about them, except for Emma.'

'You never spoke of your family, either.'

His lips twisted in a strange, bitter little smile. 'My family isn't really worth talking about. My parents were most typical of the aristocratic sort. Nothing worth analysing.'

Jane had to laugh. 'My parents weren't typical at all.'

'Then what were they like?'

She closed her eyes and pictured them as they had once sat in this very room. Her father huddled over his books, her mother's lips pinched tightly together as she watched him. Baby Emma playing with her blocks by the fire. Barton Park fading and crumbling around them even back then. But there was also that sense of security and belonging, that sense she wanted to bring to her own family.

'They were—eccentric,' she said.

'That sounds intriguing. Eccentric in what way?'

'Well, did I ever tell you the tale of the Barton treasure?'

Hayden laughed and, despite everything, she still

revelled in that sound. 'Treasure? Not at all. I can't believe you kept such a thing from me. It sounds positively piratical.'

'And if anyone likes all things piratical, it's surely you,' Jane said with a laugh. She told him what she knew of the Barton Park treasure and how it was lost in the mists of time.

'But even though that was a mere legend,' she ended, 'it captured my father's imagination when he was a boy. And by the time Emma and I were older, it completely took over his life. He spent days and days poring over old family papers looking for clues and maps. My mother hated his obsession, hated how it took over everything else. My father just said she would be glad once he found the treasure and we were all rich.'

She glanced up to find Hayden watching her closely, his chin propped on his palm.

'I take it he never found it,' Hayden said.

'Obviously not.' Jane waved around at the shabby room, the faded wallpaper peeling at the edges and the mended curtains. 'He died before he could even find a real clue, while I was still a girl. My mother followed soon after, probably in a fit of rage that he had escaped her without leaving the promised treasure. That was how I came to be in London, with an aunt I hardly knew and who wasn't best happy to be suddenly saddled with two nieces.'

'And then you met me.'

'Yes,' Jane said, remembering the bright, perfect

dream of that time she had found Hayden. 'And that is the strange, sad tale of my family at Barton Park.'

'Sad?' he said. 'It's an odd one, no doubt. Eccentric, as you said. But was it sad? Were you unhappy here?'

'Not at all.' Jane was surprised at the truth of those words, at realising why it was she had longed to come back to Barton. 'Anyone with a conventional life would have thought we must be most unhappy, but Emma and I never felt so. We had a freedom most girls never know and we were always sure we belonged here. That we belonged to each other.'

'I was always quite sure I did not belong at Ramsay House,' Hayden said. Despite the simple sadness of those words, his tone was calm and matter of fact, as if everyone's life was like that.

She knew so little about Hayden's family. His parents were long dead when she met him and he never spoke about them. At Ramsay House she'd seen their portraits, but all she could glean from them was that his mother had been a beauty with her son's blue eyes and his father was very stern and unsmiling.

When she asked Hayden about his childhood, all he would say was, 'It was most typical.'

She knew *typical* for a young man of his station meant tutors and school. Not the slightly chaotic and shabby life she and Emma knew here at Barton. But what was it like when he was with his parents?

'What was life like at Ramsay House?' she asked.

Hayden shrugged. 'Quiet most of the time. My mother was seldom there; she preferred town life.'

Like her son? Maybe that was why he was the way he was. 'And your father?'

'A countryman through and through. He was most happy with his horses and dogs, or when he was walking the fields or visiting tenants. Ramsay House was everything to him. Duty and the family name, all that. I was a disappointment to him all round.'

'How could you possibly be a disappointment to them?' Jane cried. 'A handsome, popular young heir. What more could they want?'

'My brother, I suppose.'

'Your brother?' She was shocked. She'd never heard of any sibling before.

'Did you not know I had an older brother? He died as a child, before I was born, But my father was quite convinced he would have been the perfect heir. Serious and dutiful, dedicated to all things Ramsay. Not an irresponsible gadabout like the son they were stuck with. I finally ceased to go to Ramsay House on my school holidays, just so I wouldn't hear the same conversation all over again. John Eastwood's parents kindly took me in instead. Then I only had to hear about my shortcomings in letters. It all worked out very well.'

He sounded joking, as if he were merely recalling amusing peccadilloes from the past, but Jane knew him too well to be fooled. She had come to sense that there was something he hid deep inside, some hurt he covered up in drink and parties, something he would never reveal to her. Until now.

Jane's heart ached as she turned his words over in her mind. It ached for the boy he had once been, who surely only wanted to be accepted in the role he had to play. But when nothing would satisfy his father, when nothing could compare to a boy who was dead…

What else could he do but close off his heart? Live up to their low expectations until they became the truth. Until neither he nor anyone else could tell where the ruse ended and the real Hayden began.

'I'm so sorry, Hayden,' she said. 'They were wrong to believe those things. If only they could have seen the earl you've become.'

Hayden gave a bitter-sounding laugh. 'They would be just as disappointed as ever. My father would be happy to proclaim he was right, though I certainly get my taste for brandy from him. And my mother died in childbirth, trying to give my father another son long after she should have ceased bearing children. Poor Mother. But did I not disappoint you, too, Jane? In the end.'

She shook her head, her eyes aching with tears. Just in those few words she had learned so much, saw so much. Her sweet Hayden. How she missed him, missed the man she'd fallen in love with and first been married to. How deeply she wished he would come back.

Yes, she had been disappointed once. She had been confused and angry. But now she perhaps had the first inkling of why. She didn't know how to tell him that. She had to show him.

Jane feared she would start crying at his words. Hayden tried to make them sound light, inconsequential. But she'd never heard him say much about his family before; she'd only known they had died before she met him. And now she could hear the old, but still raw, pain in his voice. The pain that told him he could never build a real family. She slowly rose to her feet, went to kneel beside him and took his hand in hers.

His eyes widened in surprise. Before he could say anything, before she could remember everything that lay like a gulf of hurt between them and change her mind, she rose up to kiss him. She pressed one swift, soft kiss to his lips, then another and another, teasing him until he half-laughed, half-groaned and pulled her even closer against him. So close nothing could come between them at all.

He moaned against her lips and deepened the kiss, his tongue lightly seeking hers, and Jane was lost in him all over again. The way it once was, the hot need that always rose in her when he touched her, surrounded them all over again like a wall of flame that shut out the rest of the world. She only wanted to be this close to him again, always. To be part of him and make him part of her.

She had questioned, worried, wondered for so

long. Now she only wanted to be with Hayden again, to feel as only he could make her feel.

Hayden's lips slid away from hers and he pressed tiny, fleeting kisses to her cheek, the line of her jaw, that oh-so-sensitive spot just below her ear. The spot that had always made her feel so crazy when he kissed it. She shivered at the warm rush of his breath over her skin.

She laughed breathlessly and wrapped her arms around his shoulders to try to hold herself straight. She feared she would fall down and down into love with him again and be lost for good this time.

'Jane, Jane,' he whispered hoarsely, pressing his lips to her hair, 'we can't go on like this. I still need you so much.'

She rested her cheek on the curve of his neck and inhaled deeply the wonderful, familiar scent of his skin. This had always been the one true thing between them, the way their bodies knew one another, craved one another. Said things they never could in words.

And she knew in that moment she had to let go of her fears. Silently, she took his hand in hers again and led him to the old sofa in the corner. She only wanted to feel the way only Hayden could make her feel. She wanted to feel close to him again.

She laid back on the cushions and looked up at him in the shadows. His eyes glowed and his face looked taut and intent with the desire she could tell he tried to hold back. She raised her arms up to him in a silent gesture of welcome.

'Jane—are you sure?' he said roughly.

'Shh, Hayden,' she whispered. She wanted no words now. Words only shattered the spell she wanted to weave around them. To try to repair some of the damage they'd so carelessly done.

She reached up and drew the pins from her hair, letting it coil around her shoulders. He'd always liked her hair and she watched his eyes darken as he studied her every movement. Feeling bolder, she shook her hair down her back and slowly unlaced the neckline of her gown. The cool air brushed over her bared shoulders.

'Jane!' he moaned, rubbing his hand over his eyes. 'What are you thinking now?'

'Please, Hayden,' she said. She swallowed her fear and smiled up at him. 'I want you. Don't you want me?'

'Of course I do. I've always wanted you more than anything in the world. But I—'

Whatever he wanted to say was lost when he caught her up in his arms and kissed her, passionately, deeply, nothing held back any longer.

Jane felt as if her soul caught fire. She had to be closer, closer. She pushed his coat away from his shoulders and untied his cravat. For an instant, he was tangled in his clothes and they fell together back on to the sofa, laughing. But once his coat and shirt were tossed on the floor and she felt his bare skin under her hands, the laughter faded.

Her touch, light, trembling, learned his body all over again. The smooth, damp heat of his skin, the light, coarse hair dusted over his chest, the tight muscles of his stomach, his lean hips.

The hard ridge of his erection, straining against the cloth of his breeches. Oh, yes—she remembered *that* very well.

As they kissed, falling down into the humid heat of need, she felt his hands sliding over her shoulders, releasing the fastenings of her gown and drawing it away.

She kicked the skirt down and laughed as they slid together, skin to skin, the silken length of her hair twirling around them to bind them together. He pressed his open, hot breath to her neck and all thought vanished into pure sensation.

Jane closed her eyes and let herself just feel. Feel his hand on her hip, his mouth on the curve of her breast. She ran her hands over his strong shoulders, the arc of his back, and couldn't believe they were here together like this again. Her legs parted as she felt the weight of his body lower against her.

He reached between them to unfasten his breeches, then at last he pressed against her and thrust inside. It had been so long since they were together that at first it stung a bit, but that was nothing to the wonderful sensation of being joined with him again.

She arched up into him, wrapping her arms and legs around him to hold him with her.

'Jane,' he groaned, and slowly he moved inside her again. Deeper, harder, until there was only pleasure. A wondrous delight that grew and grew like a sparkling cloud, spreading all through her.

Jane cried out, overcome by the wonder of it. How had she lived all those years without that, without him?

Above her, she felt Hayden's body go tense, his head arched back. 'Jane!' he shouted out and his voice echoed inside of her, all around her.

And then she exploded, too, consumed by how he made her feel. She clung to him, feeling as if she tumbled down from the sky.

Long moments later, once she could breathe again, she slowly opened her eyes. For an instant, she was startled to find the familiar old room around her and not some new, enchanted glade. Hayden lay next to her, his arm tight around her waist. His eyes were closed, his body sprawled around hers in the way she remembered so well. Almost as if they had never been apart at all.

She closed her eyes again and fell back down into the sweet, drowning warmth of being near Hayden all over again.

Chapter Ten

It all appeared to be heading in the right direction.

Emma stood on her tiptoes to peer between a gap in the maze hedge. They weren't really talking, but every once in a while they would smile at each other, or touch hands as they passed a trowel or bucket. Emma found it most satisfactory to see those touches linger, the smiles grow longer.

There was something new, something harmonious, in the air today. Emma wasn't entirely sure what had changed, or even what had gone wrong in the first place, but it felt most satisfactory. She didn't want Hayden to go away, leaving Jane all worried-looking and lonely again.

Plus it distracted Jane so Emma could get on with her own work.

Emma ducked back into the maze. 'Come on, Murray,' she said, hurrying off along the pathway. She took the old journal from the pocket of her apron and carefully flipped the brittle pages open to the sketch she'd found. She was sure she was very close now. The treasure had to be somewhere nearby.

'Is your sister up to some mischief?'

Jane laughed at Hayden's wry question. 'Probably. She usually is.' She plunged her trowel into the rich, loamy soil of the flowerbeds and pulled up old, dead roots. Hayden tossed them into a bucket and reached out to pull up some more of the stubborn roots Jane couldn't reach.

It felt like a glorious morning. The sun was shining, the garden looked tidier and prettier under the light, and Hayden was with her. Best of all, he even seemed to be enjoying their quiet morning together.

'How old is Emma now?' he asked.

Jane sat back on her heels and swept her hair back from her damp brow. 'Sixteen. I know she can't run wild here for ever, but she seems to be so happy. After that school…'

'The school she hated?'

Hayden sounded so quiet, Jane wondered if he remembered their old quarrels about Emma when she wanted to retrieve her sister from the school and bring her to stay with them. 'Emma likes to be free,' Jane said simply. 'The school was suffocating her. I could see the light in her eyes dying, though she never talks about what happened there. I want to make it up to her. But I do sometimes wonder if I am doing her no favours by letting her run around here doing whatever she likes.'

'You want her to have a Season?'

'Eventually I suppose she will have to. But not with us being such a scandal. She would be cut before she even made her first curtsy.'

Hayden laughed wryly. 'You didn't consider that when you asked for a divorce.'

'I considered many things,' she said. 'I just couldn't see how we could go along as we have been. Married, but apart.'

'And what do you think now? How should we go on?'

Jane turned to face him. He looked so serious, so focused solely on her. If only it could have been like that years ago. If only she could have conquered her fears. If only he had listened to her then.

But he seemed to be listening to her now and that made the world of difference.

'I don't know,' she said simply. 'All these years I've thought of little else but us, the mistakes we made and how best to fix them. I could come up with no answers. After last night...'

'Things are different after last night.'

Different in a good way? Against her will, Jane felt a small touch of hope. *She* had certainly felt different after last night. She'd floated through the morning as if on a cloud, remembering every touch, every kiss. The way she woke up to find him gone, but a flower left on her pillow and a note asking if he could work with her in the garden today.

Yes, things were different. She could feel it, she knew it. But could she make it all last?

A tiny droplet of water hit her skin, then another as the skies turned a pale grey above them. She took his hand and led him in silence into the house. Once they were in her bedchamber, she turned to him and stared up at him. Her heart was bursting with hope and fear. 'Oh, Hayden, I—'

But his mouth covered hers, catching her tentative words, her senses, her balance, sending them all whirling away until there was only him.

Her passion, which had been reawakened last night, rose up inside of her again. With a moan, she wrapped her arms around him as he lowered her back to the bed. His body against hers, the weight of it, felt wondrous, perfect.

Whatever else happened between them, *this* had always been so right. In their years apart, she'd tried so hard to forget him, to push away all her feelings for him. But those feelings were stubborn things and wouldn't go away so easily. And now, as he kissed her, they burst free like the rain from the sky.

Jane pushed his coat back from his shoulders and fumbled with the knot of his cravat, desperate to touch him. He drew back from her only to tug his shirt free from his breeches and loosen the placket in the front. He lifted her skirts up around her legs and she wrapped them tight around his hips. Then his body was tight against hers, his lips seeking hers. He smelled of sunshine and clean soap, and of himself, that intoxicating scent that always drew her so close.

She ran her hands over the smooth, warm skin of his shoulders above the edge of his loosened shirt. He groaned and kissed the curve of her neck as she arched her head back and revelled in the feel of his mouth on her skin.

He pulled her up against him. She opened her eyes and stared up into his eyes as he slowly thrust forwards.

Everything vanished but their skin touching, sliding against each other. She heard his harsh, uneven breath, his moan, and she answered it with her own cry. Then the pleasure burst over her and she clung to him, sobbing out his name.

'Jane!' he shouted. 'Jane,' he whispered, thrusting harder, faster, until she felt him find his own release. 'Jane, Jane.'

Just her name, but it was enough. In that moment, it was everything.

For a long time they just lay together amid the tangled bedclothes. Jane listened to the rain patter on the windows, the soft sound of Hayden's breath, and she closed her eyes to let the moment stay for as long as it could. Soon, very soon, they would have some serious matters to consider. Would they, could they, live together again? Where, and how? Could they possibly try again to have a family? She was afraid of the answers to all those questions, but she knew they would have to be faced. The past couldn't just be erased.

But not yet. Not nearly yet.

Chapter Eleven

Whack! Whack!

The sudden thundering, pounding noise jolted Jane from sleep. The whole house seemed to be shaking, as if caught in an earthquake. She shot up in bed, the sheets tumbling around her, and for an instant she had no idea where she was or what was happening.

The noise echoed away, leaving only the patter of the rain on the window and her own harsh, uneven breath. She realised she was in her own bed-chamber. The lamp she usually left burning on the bedside table had gone out, but she could make out the shapes of the dressing table and the old *chaise*.

But what was that noise? Just a dream? Or was something wrong with Emma?

'If she let Murray run free again…' Jane muttered, remembering the last time Murray escaped Emma's room and wreaked havoc. She pushed back the blankets and swung her legs out of bed, only to freeze at the sound of a deep, rough male groan.

Hayden. Hayden was in bed with her.

Jane twisted around to see his black hair tousled on her pillow. The bedclothes were twisted around his waist, the faint light from the window playing over his bare skin. The whole evening came flooding back to her—his lips on hers, his body sliding over hers, the hot pleasure as she cried out at his touch.

He reached out and looped his arm around her waist. He tugged her closer, and she was wrapped up in the smell and heat of him. The familiar, arousing scents of bare skin and warm sheets, of the night that closed around them and made the rest of the world invisible.

'Where are you going?' he said hoarsely. His eyes didn't open, but he drew her closer against his body. She tried to resist the urge to melt into him, to nestle close to him and let everything else be damned. It felt so natural when they were together like this, so—right.

But she couldn't quite forget what woke her from her dreams in the first place.

She pushed against his shoulders as he laughed and dragged her closer. 'Didn't you hear that noise?' she said.

'What noise? I was asleep until you woke me with all your fidgeting about, woman.'

'How could you have missed it?' Jane said, then

she remembered. 'Oh, yes. You could sleep through a shipwreck.'

'Well, we're not at sea now. It was just the thunder. Come back to bed.' He bent his head to the soft curve of her shoulder and pressed a light, butterfly-dancing kiss to her skin. His lips drifted over her, soft, gentle, as his fingers lightly skimmed over her arm to grasp the edge of her shift's short sleeve.

'It's hours 'til morning,' he whispered, his breath drifting warmly over her skin.

Jane shivered and twined her hand in his tousled hair. She nearly gave in, nearly tumbled into him, until another pounding volley shattered the quiet all over again.

It was like a sudden dash of freezing water. Jane pushed Hayden away and leaped down from the bed.

'You see?' she cried. 'It's not thunder. Something is happening.'

Hayden fell back on to the bed with a groan. 'I don't suppose you could just ignore whatever it is and take that gown off.'

'Of course I can't.' Jane tugged her sleeve back into place and snatched up her dressing gown from the chaise. 'Barton Park is my home. I can't let it just be invaded by—whatever it is. Hayden, do get up!'

As she hastily tied back her loose fall of hair, Hayden reluctantly pushed himself up and put on his breeches. For an instant she was struck by the intimacy of the moment, of dressing together in the darkness. He moved so gracefully, so naturally, as if they did this every day.

There was another flurry of loud knocks, shaking her out of that stunned moment, and she spun away from the sight of Hayden pulling on his shirt. She stuffed her feet into a pair of slippers and yanked open the door.

Emma stood on the landing, peering down at the hall. Murray cowered at her feet, not much of a watchdog. Jane could hear now that the noise was someone pounding on the door.

'Who could it be?' Emma whispered, as if the invaders could possibly hear her.

'Probably just someone caught in the storm,' Jane said firmly. She couldn't let Emma see her uncertainty. No one ever accidentally wandered to Barton Park, they were too far off the better-travelled roads. 'I'll go down and see.'

'No, I'll go,' Hayden said as he stepped out of her chamber, the re-lit lamp in his hands. Emma's eyes widened, but she didn't really look terribly surprised to see him there.

'Stay here,' Jane told Emma, and she hurried down the stairs behind Hayden. He strode towards the door, looking calm and perfectly in charge despite the fact that he was in his shirtsleeves with rumpled hair. He always did manage to look as if he owned any room he was in and for once Jane was glad of that. Glad not to be alone.

He threw back the old bolt on the door and pulled

it open. The sound of the falling rain grew louder, pouring into the creaky silence of the house. Jane stood on tiptoes to peer over his shoulder.

'Hayden, my friend! We've never been happier to see anyone in our lives,' a man shouted over the thunder. 'Devil of a night, eh?'

Even though the voice was slightly slurred with drink, Jane recognised it as Hayden's friend Lord John Eastwood, who had been the best man at their wedding. She had never minded him as much as some of Hayden's wilder friends, he was a funny, quiet sort of man who carried an air of sadness since he had lost his young wife. But what the devil was he doing *here*, in the middle of the night, at her home?

'Glad you decided to rusticate, Ramsay,' another man said. 'Otherwise we'd be trapped out on that godforsaken road.'

'Carstairs, John, what happened to you both?' Hayden said with a rough laugh. 'You look like you've been dragged to hell and back.'

'So we have,' John said. 'But don't say that too loud—there are ladies present.'

'If you can call us that!' a woman cried. 'Let us in, Ramsay, it's freezing out here.'

As Jane watched in stunned disbelief, Hayden drew the door open and five people tumbled in. At first they were an indistinct, dark blur, a tangle of cloaks and great coats and water dripping in sheets on to her floor. But then she saw it was three men and two women. They laughed and cursed, dropping their wet things carelessly. She could smell the rain, wet wool, expensive perfumes and the sticky sweetness of brandy.

'I do know that,' Hayden said, his voice a strange blend of strained affability and slight irritation. 'You all remember Lady Ramsay, I'm sure.'

The cacophony suddenly ceased, like birds scattered from a tree. The gathering turned to stare at her and Jane felt her throat tighten as the lamplight fell over their faces. She knew John, of course, and the other two men were also cronies of Hayden's, fellows he often went carousing with—Sir Ethan Carstairs and Lord Browning. One of the ladies she did not know, a little apple-cheeked blonde giggling behind her hand.

The other woman was Lady Marlbury. Hayden's former mistress, or so all the gossip said. She was as tall and gloriously, vividly beautiful as ever, despite her rain-soaked red hair. She looked as if she was about to burst into delighted laughter.

Jane resisted the sudden strong, burning urge to slap her.

'Of course. Lady Ramsay. It's been far too long,' John said, the first to recover his manners. He hurried over to bow over her cold hand. 'I'm sorry to burst in on you like this. We were all on our way back to London when our carriage became mired in the mud. Luckily Carstairs remembered that Ramsay was staying here.'

Jane swallowed past her dry throat. 'It's good to

see you again, Lord John. How is your sister, Susan? She was such a good friend to me when I first arrived in London as a green country girl.'

'She is very well—just had her second child, you know. And you know Sir Ethan Carstairs and Lord Browning, of course,' John said quickly. 'And Lady Marlbury. This is Browning's friend, Mrs Smythe.'

'How lovely to see you again, Lady Ramsay,' Lady Marlbury said, still smiling. 'So kind of you to offer to provide a port in the storm.'

Jane could remember offering no such thing. In fact, every instinct told her to toss them all back out immediately. Barton Park was *her* home, *her* refuge, and they were everything she had run away from when she left London. But she knew she couldn't. Every rule of civility held her back.

She glanced at Hayden, who was studying his friends with a half-smile on his face. Was he happy to see them? Glad to have his dull country days interrupted? The warmth and contentment of the night spent in her bed, wrapped in his arms, vanished and she was so very cold. She tightened her robe around her.

'Come in, I'll fetch some brandy and get the fire started,' Hayden said, ushering them towards the sitting room.

'You'll start the fire?' Lady Marlbury said with a merry laugh. 'My goodness, Ramsay, but you *have* become domesticated out here in the wilds. What sort of upside-down place is this?'

They all followed Hayden, a laughing, jostling band who acted as if they were suddenly dropped into a seaside holiday, not stranded in a strange house—Jane's house.

Jane turned to see Emma standing halfway down the stairs, looking after them with an expression of intrigued astonishment on her pretty face.

'Emma, can you fetch Hannah?' Jane said, trying not to reveal her own stunned, uncertain feelings. 'And make cook see if she can make some sandwiches. It seems we suddenly have company.'

'Who are those people?' Emma asked, her eyes wide.

'They are friends of Hayden who were stranded in the storm,' Jane said as briefly as she could.

'Only Hayden's? You didn't know them in London?'

'Yes. I knew them.'

Emma looked as if she was aching to ask more, but she just nodded and hurried away to rouse Hannah and the cook. Murray scurried off behind her, his tail tucked down.

Jane wished with all her might that she could run off after her sister. She could already hear the loud laughter and jokes from the impromptu house party and it filled her with a sick feeling from the pit of her stomach. Her home was being invaded, just as the London house had been after they married. Already she could feel the cold tentacles of that old life, that life of fashion and lies, reaching out to grab at her again.

How could things change in only a moment like that? Jane leaned on the newel post and stared up the dimness of the staircase. When she fell asleep, she was wrapped in Hayden's arms, warmed by the most tentative and fragile of hopes. Now...

Now she just wanted to flee again. Yet if even Barton Park could be invaded, no place was safe.

Jane took a deep breath and squared her shoulders. She had her *duty*, as Hayden had often reminded her in the past. The duty of a countess and a hostess. She would see them through.

That resolve wavered a bit when she stepped through the sitting room door and saw the scene spread before her.

The cosy room where Hayden and Emma had played cards after dinner only a few hours before was transformed. The shabby sofas and chairs were pushed into a group around the fireplace. Hayden and John knelt in front of the hearth, piling up the kindling while the others shouted suggestions and jokes, and fell into fits of laughter.

Lady Marlbury rested her hand on Hayden's shoulder and leaned closer as if to examine his work. 'Really, Ramsay darling, I don't think being a chimney boy is your calling. That will never burn. You have far finer talents you should be using.'

Hayden glanced up at her with a lazy smile. 'First the fire, I think. Then...'

His hooded gaze slid past Lady Marlbury to land on Jane where she stood in the doorway. She felt utterly frozen in place, unable to turn away and unable to move forwards. She stared at Lady Marlbury's hand, resting so casually on Hayden's shoulder, and she wanted to yank out the woman's no doubt falsely red hair by the roots. She wanted…she wanted…

She wanted things to be completely different with Hayden. For Hayden and her. For a few hours, she'd even imagined they *were* different. Now they just felt horribly the same.

She closed her eyes and for an instant she was back at another house party, one where she felt like she knew no one and wasn't sure what to say or do. But Lady Marlbury knew—she was standing with Hayden, her hand on his arm, laughing up at him, making him smile at her. Making jokes with him Jane couldn't understand. That was when she had realised her life with Hayden was not going to be as she had dreamed. That he had an existence she hadn't been, couldn't be, a part of.

And when she opened her eyes she was there all over again, but it was in her own house now. The past rushing in to infect the present.

'Look, I think the fire's starting,' Lord Browning called. Everyone else turned to the hearth amid exclamations of hilarity and Hayden pushed himself to his feet.

He moved across the room towards Jane and it seemed to her as if everything had turned hazy and pale. A dream. Hayden wasn't real. Nothing was real.

But she was damned if she would let him see the deep sting of disappointment that had seized her heart. She held her head high and smiled brightly, just as she had done through all those London balls. Lady Marlbury was watching.

'Emma has gone to wake Hannah and the cook,' Jane said. 'We can get a few rooms ready very soon, if your friends don't mind sharing. We aren't really a large enough house for a proper house party.' She glanced over at the group around the growing fire. Mrs Smythe was perched on Lord Browning's knee, still giggling. 'But I am sure they won't mind sharing.'

'I'm sorry they showed up like that, Jane,' Hayden said quietly. 'I wasn't expecting them.'

'Of course not.'

'But I can't turn them out in the rain. John is my oldest friend.'

Jane saw that Lady Marlbury was watching them surreptitiously, still smiling even though her eyes were narrowed. 'Not just John, I think.'

'Jane, please. Everything was going so well. They'll be gone as soon as their carriage is repaired, and then...'

'Then what?' Jane said, and cursed herself at the sharp sound of those words. She couldn't let Hayden see, let him have the power to hurt her again. She closed her eyes for a moment, then went on, quieter.

'Don't apologise, Hayden. This is your life. I'm glad of the reminder. Now, you must see to your friends. I'll go find Emma and help put the guest rooms to rights.'

Hayden caught her hand as she turned back towards the door. 'Jane, you must listen to me. Lady Marlbury and I—'

'Not now, Hayden, please,' Jane said. She was tired, confused and her dignity was hanging on by a mere thread. 'We can talk later.'

Hayden stared down at her for a long moment. Jane dared not look at him. 'Very well,' he finally said, and let her go.

She hurried away, but as she went that laughter seemed to follow her like a dream phantom. 'Ramsay, darling, is this funny little place really where you've been hiding?' she heard Lady Marlbury say. 'You have been missing the most amusing parties while you've been buried here…'

Hayden stared after Jane as she dashed away, her shawl pulled tightly around her shoulders and her head held rigidly high. The laughing woman who had lain beside him in their warm bed was vanished and he had the sinking fear that she would never return.

In the room behind him he heard the loud laughter of his friends. Once he would have been with them in an instant, eager to pour the brandy and join in the jokes. To seize on the forgetfulness such revelry offered. Now he realised that was a mask he sought to hide behind and the mask was slipping away from him.

He had lost it in Jane's bed, when she touched his cheek with her fingertips and looked up into his eyes and they saw each other as if for the first time.

Something sharp and hot clawed at Hayden and he raked his fingers through his hair. Part of him wanted to turn to his friends, grab up the brandy bottle and dive back into his old life. Part of him was desperate to do that.

But the other part only wanted to run after Jane. To make her listen to him, stay with him. *See* him again.

'Is everything all right, Hayden?' he heard John say.

Hayden slowly turned to face him. Of all the group that had shown up on Barton's doorstep, John Eastwood was the only one Hayden would call a real friend. They had been at school together, blazed their way through society together as young bucks, drank and caroused all over town until John married—and then lost his young wife within the year. John had only just emerged out of his mourning in time to stand up for Hayden at his wedding to Jane.

They had faced a great deal together. Hayden couldn't just throw him out—even if he wished he could send everyone else in that sitting room to the devil for what they had interrupted.

'What wouldn't be all right?' Hayden said, trying to give a careless laugh.

But John's brown eyes seemed to see too much. That was the price of years of friendship. 'Lady Ramsay didn't look happy to see us.'

'I could hardly toss you back out in the storm, now could I, old man?' Hayden said. He glanced past John into the sitting room, where the others were lounging around the fire, passing the brandy bottles and snickering about London gossip.

Lady Marlbury pushed Sir Ethan's seeking hand off her leg with a throaty laugh and he merely tried again to get closer to her. She tossed back the banner of her red hair, trying to play her well-worn haughty game, and Hayden wondered what he had once seen in her. Next to Jane's laughter, Jane's fresh beauty, she was nothing.

But still there was that pull of the past. The lure of things that used to help him dull the pain. Old habits, old pleasures. It never seemed to quite let him go.

'Carstairs said he met you at some inn and you were coming here,' John said. 'I wouldn't have come if I'd known…'

'Known what?' Hayden said. He hated for anyone to know his personal business and he cursed that day he ran into Carstairs in that inn.

'That you were here trying to reconcile with your wife.'

Hayden had a flashing memory of Jane in bed with him, smiling up at him, her hair spilling across the pillows, wrapping around him. And the coldness in her eyes when she looked at his friends. 'We aren't reconciled,' he said brusquely. 'I'm merely here trying to arrange some business matters.'

John nodded thoughtfully. 'Just as you will. But I'll tell you this, Hayden, as your friend. If I could be with my Eleanor again, even for a moment, I would never waste my time with reprobates like Carstairs and Browning.'

A shriek of laughter caught Hayden's attention and he looked back to the group in the sitting room. Carstairs had given up on Lady Marlbury and was chasing Mrs Smythe around the sofa. A table overturned and laughter roared out again, even louder.

'What *are* you doing with them?' Hayden asked. 'They don't seem to be your usual crowd any more.'

John gave a humourless laugh. 'Because I *can't* be with my Eleanor. I have to take my distractions where I can. You should be beyond that now, too, Hayden.' He turned back to the sitting room. 'We'll be gone as soon as we can, I promise.'

Hannah hurried towards the door from the servants' staircase, a tray in her hands. The usually shy and scurrying maid, who he'd thought he had won over with his surprise dinner for Jane, gave him a withering glance.

'Lady Ramsay took Miss Emma upstairs, my lord,' she said. 'Before she could see any of—this. But the guest rooms are nearly ready if anyone wishes to retire.'

By Jove—Emma. Hayden had nearly forgotten his sister-in-law, so curious and alert. So young and innocent. Just one more reason for Jane to rue the day she had let him back into their home, back into their lives.

'Of course, Hannah. Thank you,' he said.

Hannah sniffed. 'Lady Ramsay also said she would stay in Miss Emma's room tonight.' She dropped a quick curtsy and scurried away.

Hayden shook his head with a wry laugh. It seemed as if, with that one sniff, the doors of Barton Park, which had just barely opened before him, slammed shut.

Chapter Twelve

It was more like studying zoology than botany, Emma thought as she watched Hayden's friends cavort around the sitting room. Plants always sat obligingly still and let one take notes, while animals would insist on wriggling about and being most unpredictable. Still, it was worth the observation.

Jane had told her last night, as they huddled in Emma's bed and listened to the unexpected interlopers stumble down the hall, that they would soon be gone and in the meantime she had to stay well out of their way. Her sister sounded again like the Jane who first brought her to Barton a year ago, so strained and worried, her eyes full of unfathomable worries.

Emma had never wanted to see that Jane again, and since Hayden came to Barton there was no sign of her. Jane had started to laugh again, to be the sister who used to play with her and tease her when they were children. Hayden, too, was losing those haunted shadows around his eyes. They all had fun together and Emma began to hope maybe, just maybe, they could all live here at Barton and find a way to build a new family.

Hope was a pernicious thing. It came and went so easily, and was so very fragile. A pounding at the door could shatter it.

So Emma resolved to watch those people and see why Jane behaved so strangely at the sight of them. Emma had promised she would stay out of their way, but Jane didn't know about this little hidey-hole in the sitting-room corner, behind a screen their mother had once painted with scenes of fat cherubs and shepherds.

Emma slipped in there when everyone was at breakfast and sat perched on a stool with her note-book open on her lap. Murray lay curled up at her feet, quiet for once. Even he seemed cowed by the sudden raucous invasion of their home.

Emma had decided to make notes as she would in any other study, but she sometimes forgot to write just from watching.

In her school, there had been girls like the daughter of a duke, the nieces of an earl and, scandalously, the illegitimate daughter of a famous theatre owner. Those girls had been wildly sophisticated and had to show off their gossipy knowledge even to an odd bluestocking like Emma. From them she heard tales of aristocratic parties, royal marriages gone horribly sour and *affaires d'amour*.

The girls' parents would have been appalled at

what they really knew behind their demure, proper façades. So would Jane, if she knew what Emma had heard from them—including gossip about Jane and Hayden's own marriage. Jane's letters had always been sunny and loving. Emma would have known nothing at all about the marriage without that late-night school gossip.

So she had heard of people like this, even though, thanks to Jane's caution, she seldom encountered them. She had to watch them now, while she had the chance.

Lord John Eastwood she had met before. He was Hayden's friend and had been at Jane's wedding. Emma rather liked him. He sat apart from the others, laughing as he watched them. Despite that laughter, she could see a deep melancholy lurking in his eyes. She remembered he had lost his wife not so long ago.

Lord Browning and Mrs Smythe had no such depths. They frolicked around like a pair of puppies. *Amorous* puppies, Emma thought with a giggle as she watched Browning snatch Mrs Smythe around the waist and haul her across his lap. She kicked out with her slippered foot and knocked over a row of empty brandy bottles with a loud clatter. Despite the fact that it wasn't even noon yet, there seemed to be a great many of those bottles.

Lady Marlbury lounged on the sofa, a luxuriously embroidered shawl wrapped around herself. She was very beautiful, in a way Emma quite envied. So tall, so exotic, with that long, waving banner of red hair. She looked like an empress, a goddess, whereas Emma herself often felt like a milkmaid. But there was such a distance with that beauty, such a veil between her and everyone else.

And Emma didn't like the way the woman looked at Hayden, the casual way she touched him. It almost made Emma wish she could yank out Lady Marlbury's hair by the roots and toss her out in the still-pouring rain, since she was sure Jane never would.

Emma craned her neck around the edge of the screen to see the rest of the room. It seemed only those four were around at the moment. Jane and Hayden were nowhere to be seen, though Emma feared they weren't together. The last time she had seen Jane, her sister was hiding in the kitchen. And that other man, the handsome one named Carstairs, wasn't there, either.

She was rather disappointed about that. She had only caught a quick glimpse of him when everyone arrived last night, but it was most intriguing. He was very handsome, always with a mysterious smile on his face, always watching. Was he one of those rakes the girls always gossiped about? Very interesting. She just hoped he wasn't like Mr Milne.

She wondered who he was and what he was doing here. Unlike with Lady Marlbury and Lord John, she hadn't been able to observe him at all.

Emma bent her head over her notebook and scribbled another line. Murray cracked open one eye and peered up at her. It was clear he only wanted these interlopers gone and his house to himself again. He was accustomed to being the only one knocking things over and being noisy.

'Perhaps I should abandon botany and take up writing for the stage,' she whispered to him. 'This would make a fascinating play.'

Murray just sighed and closed his eyes again. Emma scribbled another line and was soon lost in her observations. People really *were* fascinating; one never knew what they would do next.

Except for dull people like David Marton. One surely always knew what he would do next.

'Well, well. Who do we have hiding here?'

Emma jumped off her stool, so startled her heart pounded. Her notebook clattered to the floor, making Murray bark, and she spun around to find Ethan Carstairs smiling at her.

He leaned lazily on the edge of the screen, watching her with a wide, amused smile on his face. She'd thought when she first saw him arrive at Barton that he was handsome and in the light of day he was even more so. He could almost be a poet, with bright curls swept across his brow. He twirled a small golden coin between his fingers.

Despite all the gossip at her school, Emma hadn't really spent much time with young men, hadn't talked to them or flirted with them. With men like David Marton, she could simply lecture them about books and studies because it hardly mattered what they thought. But with a handsome young man like

Ethan Carstairs, a friend of her brother-in-law whom she trusted…

Emma was utterly tongue-tied.

'You're Lady Ramsay's sister, are you not?' he asked. His words were a drawl as lazy as his pose, slow and careless. She remembered the rows of empty brandy bottles and realised he really should be as lazy as the others today. But his shimmering eyes, though slightly red-rimmed, watched her with lively interest.

'Yes,' she managed to say as she scooped her notebook off the floor. 'I'm Emma Bancroft.'

'Well, Miss Bancroft, I'm Sir Ethan Carstairs. Most pleased to make your acquaintance.'

'I know who you are,' she blurted out.

One of his brows quirked and he laughed. 'Do you indeed? That's more than I can say about you, Miss Bancroft. It's too bad of Ramsay to keep you hidden away here. You'd be a sensation in London.'

Emma very much doubted that. Everything she had heard from the girls at school told her she was exactly the sort who would not fare well in London. But the frank admiration in his eyes and his smile made her feel strongly warm and giggly, deep down inside.

'I'm too young for a Season yet,' she said. 'Besides, I like it here at Barton.'

'I can see why,' he said, all friendly ease. 'It's a most interesting house.'

'Do you think so?' Emma said, startled. She loved

Barton very much and it was indeed interesting, hiding so many intriguing secrets in its corridors. But it surely wasn't grand or stylish, as she was sure Hayden's friends required in a house. 'It's very old, with no modern comforts to speak of.'

'That's why it's so interesting,' he said. 'Old houses like this have the best stories. Ghosts, pirates and elopements, all sorts of dastardly doings lurking in their dark pasts.'

He looked so boyishly delighted in the idea of 'dastardly doings' that Emma had to laugh. He laughed with her and she immediately felt more at ease.

'Oh, yes,' she said. 'There are indeed many fascinating tales here at Barton.'

'And you must know all of them.'

'I try to write them down,' she said and held up her notebook.

'Will you write them into horrid novels one day?'

'I have thought about that,' Emma exclaimed. 'It might be rather fun to be an authoress.'

'I'm sure you would be very good at it, Miss Bancroft,' he said, still smiling. 'I think I may have once heard a tale of Barton Park myself.'

'Really? What sort of tale?'

'Oh, the best sort. One of lost treasure.'

Emma was shocked. She didn't think anyone outside her family knew of the treasure. 'The stolen Stuart-era treasure?'

'Yes. Do you know about it, then?'

'Emma!' Jane suddenly called from beyond the screen. 'Are you in here?'

'Yes, I'm here,' Emma answered automatically. She scooped up Murray beneath her arm, trying to hush his growls as he eyed Ethan Carstairs standing there. She longed to stay and ask Ethan more about what he knew of the treasure, but Jane sounded so strained and harried that Emma knew she had to go.

She slipped past him, but before she left the cover of the screen he leaned down and whispered, 'I hope we may talk more later, Miss Bancroft. I am most intrigued.'

So was Emma. Intrigued—and flustered. She nodded and hurried past him into the sitting room. The others had left while she was preoccupied, and only Jane was there, standing in the doorway.

'Emma, dear,' Jane said softly, stopping her in her path.

'Yes?' Emma said.

'I think it would be best if you stayed in your room most of the time while the guests are here.' Jane's voice was quiet, but implacable. She didn't put her foot down very often, but Emma knew very well that when she did she meant it.

But how could she observe Carstairs if she was trapped in her room?

'Of course, Jane,' she said, and crossed her fingers behind her back. Surely what Jane didn't know couldn't matter? And there were lots of little hiding places at Barton that were perfect for quietly watching…

* * *

What a pretty girl, Ethan Carstairs thought as he watched Emma Bancroft walk away with Lady Ramsay. How much easier that would make his job here at this godforsaken house.

Emma glanced back at him just before she slipped out the door and Ethan gave her his most charming, boyish grin. The one that always made his London conquests giggle and blush. Emma Bancroft was no different, despite her unpolished, country-maid looks and unfashionable clothes. She smiled and waved, as Lady Ramsay tugged her away with a frown.

Lady Ramsay had always seemed a pale, humourless thing to Ethan. He never understood why all the fashion papers were so interested in her, how she got an earl to marry her. But she certainly had a lovely little sister, one ripe for a few compliments.

He hadn't been expecting that when he came to Barton with half-formed plans of treasure hunting. He only knew his allowance was soon to be cut off and he needed a lot of money however he could get it. But the fact that pretty Miss Emma already knew about the legend of the treasure, and was willing to tell him about it in the bargain, was a rare plum. No sneaking about to dig in dusty attics needed, which was good. He'd hate to muss his coat. He still owed the tailor for it.

Now if he could just entice the delectable Miss Emma into the garden for a little treasure hunting, all would be set. Two birds with one stone, so to speak.

'Why are you smiling like that, Sir Ethan?' he heard someone say.

He turned to find Lady Marlbury watching him. She was a rare beauty; even golden little Miss Emma paled next to her. But she had pushed him away over and over again.

What would she think of all her rejections once he was rich as Croesus? Would she rue them, pine for him? The thought made him smile even more and her eyes narrowed.

'I'm having a good time, that's all,' he said. 'Aren't you?'

'In a ramshackle house in the middle of nowhere, with endless rain and nothing to do?' she said. 'I don't know why you suggested we come here.'

'Because it was the nearest house, of course,' Ethan said, thankful once again for that rare stroke of luck. Luck—and a light hammer to the carriage wheel. 'I would have thought you'd enjoy the time to be with Ramsay again. Weren't you two something of an item?'

A dull red flush touched her sharp cheekbones. 'With his wife looking on? Don't be silly, Carstairs. Besides, Ramsay and I broke apart long ago.'

Ethan remembered Lady Ramsay's frown, the unhappy way she had studied them all since their arrival. 'Perhaps you'll have another chance with him soon enough,' he said dismissively, starting to turn away. He had treasure to seek.

'You should leave that girl alone,' Lady Marlbury called after him.

Ethan paused, his interest piqued. Lady Marlbury had noticed his talk with Miss Bancroft? 'Who do you mean?'

'That pretty little Miss Bancroft, of course. She is far out of your league, Carstairs.'

'Is she now?' Ethan shot a grin back over his shoulder at her. 'Who should I turn my attention to, then? Someone like you, perchance?'

She laughed, a sound that said all too clearly 'don't be ridiculous'. It made that anger surge up in him all over again.

'I'm only offering a bit of advice,' she said. 'If you mess about with that girl, you'll have Ramsay to contend with. And you know very well you are no match for him.'

Her words echoed in his head and, as he looked at her little smile, his anger grew and expanded like one of the storm clouds outside. How often had he heard those words? No match for his father, no match for his perfect older brother, for his so-called friends. Ethan had had quite enough of it.

He'd watched Ramsay do whatever he liked with whomever he liked in society, seen him carried along by his looks and his position and his easy fortune, for too long. Those days were over. And

Ethan would use Emma Bancroft to help him end them. His own time was coming, very soon.

'We'll see about that,' he said to Lady Marlbury, and spun around to stalk away. Her laughter followed him, but he knew that soon she wouldn't dare laugh at him any more.

Chapter Thirteen

Hayden leaned his head on the back of the dining room chair and stared up at the ceiling as his friends laughed and shouted around him. The dinner table was littered with empty wine bottles, many of which he'd helped consume. He felt the familiar sensation of heat and blurriness, of the devil-may-care-ness that alcohol used to bring him, and yet he felt strangely removed from the whole scene. As if he was someplace else entirely.

Or perhaps he only wished he was someplace else.

He squinted up at the ceiling and saw to his surprise there was a fresco painted there. A scene of a god's dinner party, surrounded by laughing cupids and pretty girls in filmy classical draperies, darkened with smoke, peeling at the edges, but still very pretty.

Hayden felt a faint stirring of interest as he thought how much Jane would like it if he had it restored. One more piece of their home brought back to life.

Their home, *Blast it all*, he thought in a sudden burst of energy. Barton Park wasn't his home; it couldn't be. It didn't matter how he'd felt since he came there, didn't matter how the rare peace of the place had crept over him and how every minute with Jane he wanted to be with her more. This wasn't his place because he hadn't earned it and didn't deserve it. Not after how he treated Jane in London, how he refused to listen to her and tried to go back to his old ways.

He'd wanted to change when he saw her again, but he could tell she didn't believe him. That she saw his London life and thought it still had a draw on him. Now that life had come back to them, into Jane's own house. He had a few drinks, a few laughs, and he felt himself slipping back to his old ways like he was tumbling over an icy cliff. It felt just as perilous, just as unavoidable.

He sat up straight and looked out at his friends, everything slightly fuzzy at the edges from the wine. They were falling and tumbling from their chairs, shrieking with laughter over a story Browning was telling about an actress and some elderly *roué* trying to recapture his naughty youth. All except Lady Marlbury, who was only smiling distantly and occasionally giving Hayden a worried glance.

Surely he was really in trouble if even his former mistress looked at him in concern.

Once he had relished such a life. The drinking, the fighting, the laughter had made him forget everything else. Taken him out of himself. When these people showed up on the doorstep and he decided to let them in and give them the last of Jane's father's wine cellar, he'd thought maybe he could recapture some of that. That perhaps his new need for Jane could be rooted out.

Instead he only felt like he was in danger of becoming the old fool in Browning's story. He found he wanted Jane more than he'd ever wanted the forgetfulness of dissipation. And that revelation hit him like a thunderbolt.

Suddenly, the dining room door banged open and Jane stood there. Her eyes blazed and her lips tightened as she swept a glance over the party. Hayden half-rose to go to her, to tell her what he'd realised, but he fell back to the chair, words lost. It seemed he'd consumed more wine than he realised.

And the burning look she turned on him told him clearer than any words that she didn't want any apologies or excuses from him now. His wife was quite, quite angry. And she had a right to be.

Nothing had changed at all.

Jane stood on the staircase landing, staring down at the flickering night-shadows in the hall as she listened to the sounds flowing up from the dining room. Shrieks of laughter, shouted curses, the ebb and flow of talk, the clink of glasses. The sound of a bottle shattering. It had only been a day since Hayden's friends had arrived at Barton, but it felt as if her house had never been her own at all.

The three years she had spent here, searching inside herself to find out what she wanted and how she should best move forwards, faded and she felt like Lady Ramsay of London again. Smiling, outwardly so serene, while she watched her husband break all her hopes. She'd run away from all that, willing to be alone, to be lonely, rather than let Hayden pull her down with him.

But then she let him back in, let him touch her heart again. She had let herself hope he could be what she once thought he was, that she once hoped they could be. Had she been a terrible fool?

Jane leaned on the railing and closed her eyes as she thought about those precious days here at Barton. Hayden working with her in the garden, lying in bed with her at night, talking so easily, as if nothing had come between them. Hayden laughing with Emma, bringing in the workmen to fix the roof.

Hayden holding her as they made love, more tenderly, more passionately, than they ever had before.

Jane curled her fists hard on the banister, holding on fiercely. No, she had not been imagining it all. These days had not been some mere fanciful dream. Hayden told her things he never had before, things about his family, his past. He had let her see him, as she had let him see her. She couldn't just let that go, couldn't let her pain and her anger drive her to run away as she once had.

This was her house, damn it all. And Hayden was her husband, whether he liked it or not.

But that didn't mean she couldn't be furious about what was happening down there in the dining room. Especially when she heard the sound of breaking glass again and a trill of musical laughter that could only be Lady Marlbury's.

Jane tightened her shawl over her shoulders and marched down the stairs. Hayden was behaving wretchedly and it had to stop now. She wouldn't let him vanish into his wild ways again. And she would not let her house be destroyed when it was just beginning to be repaired.

The dining-room door was ajar and she pushed it open to find a scene of chaos. Dinner was hours ago. She knew because she had turned down Hayden's invitation to eat with their guests and dined with Emma in her room instead, lecturing her sister about avoiding the wrong men.

Emma had begged to be allowed to go downstairs, just for a little while, just to 'observe'. The strangely eager look in Emma's eyes when she asked to go was yet another reason for Jane to want to take back her house. She didn't want her sweet, naïve sister talking to these people, especially not to Ethan Carstairs. Emma had been much too quiet and day-dreamy ever since Jane caught her behind that screen with Carstairs.

A loud clap of thunder rumbled overhead, shaking the house. Everyone in the dining room laughed even harder and raised their glasses as if to toast the storm.

The table was covered with the remains of a hastily concocted dinner that had no doubt cleaned out the cook's pantry, a tangle of platters and empty bottles. Lord John Eastwood was not there. He had always been the most sensible of Hayden's friends. Mrs Smythe perched on Lord Browning's knee, as she so often seemed to do, and Carstairs was pouring out a glass of wine. Some of it spilled out on the table. His hair was rumpled and his cravat loosened, but he didn't look quite as dishevelled as usual.

Unlike her husband. Hayden was slumped in his chair at the head of the table, his forearms braced on the table with a brandy bottle between them. His cravat dangled loose and his waistcoat was unfastened. She couldn't see his face; his black hair was tangled over his brow. He idly twirled the bottle between his palms as if fascinated by the movement.

Lady Marlbury leaned close to him to say something quiet in his ear. An instinctive flare of jealousy rose up in Jane, but even through that haze she saw that Lady Marlbury didn't look flirtatious or triumphant. She looked—concerned.

Jane shoved the door open harder, letting it bounce off the wall with a loud bang that caught everyone's attention. Browning and Carstairs scrambled to their feet, Browning's sudden movement nearly knocking Mrs Smythe over. Lady Marlbury's hand slid away from Hayden's arm and Hayden himself looked up slowly. His blue eyes were slightly reddened, his movements careful as if not to jar an aching head.

Jane's stomach clenched as she remembered her last night in London. Hayden falling asleep on the stairs after a long night out, not listening to her when she was so desperate. So shattered.

She had to be stronger than that now.

She strode into the room, ignoring everyone but her husband. As she came closer, he braced his palms on the table and pushed himself to his feet.

'Jane,' he said roughly. 'So kind of you to join us. Have a brandy?'

Jane took a deep breath, forcing herself to stay calm. She wanted no scenes, not here. Not in front of these people. 'It's very late, Hayden. Shouldn't everyone retire?'

'Late? The evening has just begun,' Hayden said, waving his arm in a wide circle. He stumbled and would have fallen over the table if Lady Marlbury hadn't caught his arm.

'Lady Ramsay is quite right,' Lady Marlbury said. 'It is late and we have trespassed on your hospitality too long.'

She was the last person Jane would have expected to come to her defence, to be the voice of quiet reason. But as their eyes met behind Hayden's back, she could see her own weary concern reflected in

Lady Marlbury's eyes. 'Come with me, Hayden,' Jane said firmly, far more firmly than she felt. But she couldn't cry now.

'We have guests, Jane,' he answered.

'I'm sure they will understand that it's time to retire,' Jane said. 'Dinner has been finished for a long while, has it not?'

'Damn it all…' Hayden said loudly, and fell against her shoulder. She stumbled back, wrapping her arm around his waist to keep them both from falling, but Jane felt herself slipping towards the floor.

Lady Marlbury caught his other arm and held them all steady. 'I'll help you get him upstairs,' she said quietly. 'Lord John retired long ago and the others won't be any help, I fear.'

The last thing Jane wanted was to accept help from Lady Marlbury, the woman who had made her feel so small, so insignificant, from the moment she married Hayden. But Lady Marlbury was right. No one else was in any condition to help and she couldn't get Hayden upstairs by herself. She couldn't even hold him upright.

'Thank you,' she murmured, and between them she and Lady Marlbury half-carried Hayden out of the dining room. He had gone quiet again, almost as if he had fallen asleep.

They led him up the stairs and down the dimly lit corridor to Jane's room. She hoped Emma really had gone to bed and wasn't hiding to spy on everyone that night.

She and Lady Marlbury dropped Hayden on to the bed. He rolled on to his back with a groan, and immediately his eyes closed and he seemed to tumble down into sleep. Jane had that feeling of being back in London all over again, watching Hayden after a long night out with his friends.

'Can you get his boots off?' she asked Lady Marlbury as she wrestled his arm out of his coat sleeve.

The redhead nodded and set about pulling off his boots. 'I truly am sorry we intruded on you like this, Lady Ramsay,' she said quietly. 'If I had known…'

'Known what?' Jane asked curiously. Lady Marlbury didn't sound at all like her usual bold, sophisticated London self. She brushed her loosened hair off her brow as she turned to look at the woman.

'Known that Hayden was here with *you*, of course,' Lady Marlbury said. She lined the boots up carefully next to the bed. 'He just disappeared from town and no one knew what he was doing.'

'I'm sure he would have returned soon enough,' Jane said. He had only come because of her extreme step of asking for a divorce, but she wouldn't tell Lady Marlbury that. Nor would she tell anyone about the foolish hopes she'd harboured in the last few days. 'He would grow bored here and go back to the parties.'

'Do you think so?' Lady Marlbury sounded so wistful that Jane was startled.

'Of course. Look what happened tonight.'

They both looked down at Hayden, sprawled across the bed, his glossy hair tumbled, his cheeks shadowed with an unshaved beard.

'No,' Lady Marlbury said. 'What he has grown bored with is the *ton* life.'

Was she right? Jane felt a tiny touch of hope, but she pushed it back down. She couldn't let hope worm its way back in again, making her hope things that couldn't be. 'Why would you say that? We have been apart for a long time. He could have left London and come here at any time. He lives his life there.'

'Perhaps once he did. Or perhaps he was only pretending. Hayden is a great actor, you know. He can hide from anyone, anywhere.'

Jane suddenly felt so very tired. She sat down on the edge of the bed and covered her eyes with her shaking hands. It was surely only her weariness that made her sit there in the darkness next to Hayden's sleeping body, talking to the woman rumoured to have been his mistress.

'I wish I had known that before I married him,' she said frankly. 'I believed so many foolish things then. I actually thought I could make him happy. I believed we *were* happy for a while, when what he really wanted all along was someone like…'

'Someone like me?' Lady Marlbury said, laughter lurking in her quiet, sad voice.

'Yes,' Jane answered. 'Someone sophisticated and elegant.'

'Oh, Lady Ramsay. He hasn't wanted someone like me in a very long time. Our association was very brief and over before he met you. Though I confess I wouldn't have minded if it had gone on longer.' Lady Marlbury sighed. 'I was what he thought he *should* want. You were what he really wanted. Everyone could see that when you married him.'

'Then everyone, including me, was clearly wrong,' Jane said, that weariness growing and growing until it covered her like the thick, dark clouds outside.

'Were we? I do wonder. He has been like a madman ever since you left, running so wildly from one party to another, never staying in one place long,' Lady Marlbury said. 'But I have learned one thing in my life, Lady Ramsay, and that is we can't ever run far enough or fast enough to get away from ourselves. I fear Hayden is learning that, too.'

She opened the bedroom door and paused there to add, 'I will leave tomorrow whether it's raining or not, Lady Ramsay. It's clear you and Hayden have matters that must be settled and I can't interfere. But if I may offer one bit of advice…'

Jane was completely bewildered by this whole conversation, one she would never have imagined having with this particular woman before. 'Yes, of course.'

'Keep your pretty sister away from Ethan Carstairs,' Lady Marlbury said. 'Unlike Hayden, who only pretends to be a careless rake out only for himself, Carstairs is the real thing. And there are rumours floating around town that he will soon be disinherited by his uncle into the bargain.'

'Yes, I know,' Jane said, surprised Lady Marlbury would even have noticed Emma, let alone Carstairs's questionable attentions to her. 'He will be gone as soon as I can manage it.'

'Good.' Lady Marlbury left, closing the door softly behind her.

As Jane rose from the side of the bed, she saw Hayden's rumpled cravat hanging loose around his neck and had a sudden idea. She wanted him to tell her why he did this, why he slid back to his old ways when everything at Barton was going so well. Why he had to make her so angry, so confused.

She slid the cravat from around his neck and went to dig out another one from his valise. He mumbled in his sleep and Jane straddled him on the bed, holding his arms down with her legs. She took one hand, then the other, and bound them as tightly as she could to the bedposts as he twisted restlessly.

The effort made her tired. Even drunk and asleep he was strong. She laid down beside her husband's bound body and closed her eyes, listening to his breath turn even and deep. Slowly, darkness drifted over her and she fell down into sleep. As consciousness slipped away, she smiled and thought that if only he was awake they might have had some fun, as they once did in their marriage bed…

* * *

'Jane. Untie me. Now.'

'What…?' Jane pulled herself up out of sleep at the sound of Hayden's voice. She'd been dreaming about him, vague, silvery images of him holding her in his arms, whispering to her. Now she rolled on to her side to find that he was awake and still with her, his eyes open and bright blue, free of the vagueness of drink. But his hands were still tied.

She smiled and sat up slowly to swing one of her legs over his hips so she straddled him again. She couldn't help it; suddenly she was feeling mischievous. 'I'm so sorry, Hayden, but I had to tie you. You were drunk and thrashing around too much with your nightmares.'

'I'm awake now,' he argued, watching her with narrowed eyes.

'Are you? I'm not quite sure…' Jane slowly leaned over to kiss the side of his neck. She parted her lips and savoured the sweet-salty taste of him, the way his breath turned harsh at her touch.

His body grew tense under hers. 'Untie me,' he demanded. 'Now.'

She laughed and reached up to loosen the cords around his wrists. 'Are you sure you want me to let you go just yet? There's so much else we could do. Don't you remember, when we were first married…?'

Before she could say anything else, he rose to meet her and his mouth swooped down over hers.

Open, hot, hungry, as if he wanted to devour her, just as it had once been between them. The thought flickered through her mind that he must be still dreaming, but as always when she was with him, it awakened something deep inside of her, that flame of longing and pure need. When he kissed her, he swept her away on a river of fire, swept her away to her true self, and she moaned.

Jane opened her lips to his and drew her tongue over his. His taste filled her, brandy and darkness, and she moaned.

As they kissed, deeper, hungrier, their tongues entwining, she laid her hands flat on his hard shoulders and felt the damp heat of his skin. He groaned deep in his throat, and his passion made her feel bold. She slid her caress lower, so slowly, savouring the delicious way his nearly naked body felt against hers. So strong, so hard, so hot. *This* was what she craved, what she needed. It made her feel alive again at last. Alive as she had only ever been with him.

She traced her fingertips over his flat nipples and felt them pebble under her touch. She scraped the edge of her thumbnail over one and he growled low in his throat. She pressed slightly harder, hard enough to give just the slightest edge of pain. His body shuddered, but he went on kissing her as if he was starved for the taste of her.

Jane slid her touch even lower, feeling every inch of his taut, damp chest, his bare skin. He felt like hot satin stretched over iron muscles and the light whorls of hair tickled her palms. She dipped the tip of her smallest finger into his navel before she moved even lower to the band of his trousers.

And suddenly she felt her newfound boldness, the temptress inside her, flee as his rock-hard erection brushed against her hand. She drew away.

'Jane, Jane—don't stop now,' he whispered darkly.

Jane smiled. Whatever else was between them, they still desired each other. Surely that was something. 'Do you like this?' She moved her hand lower and lower, a slow slide until she covered the hard ridge behind the wool fabric. She slid her fingers down in a soft caress until he groaned.

'Jane,' he whispered darkly. Suddenly he freed himself from the cords around his wrists and pulled her chemise over her head, tearing her hand away from him. She knelt on the bed in front him, her body naked for a man as it hadn't been in so long. Not since the last time they were together, before she lost the babies. A wave of sudden cold shyness swept over her as she remembered how she looked different now, thinner, paler.

When he just looked at her with those beautiful blue eyes, silent, she tried to turn away and reach for her discarded chemise. But his hands were already on her again and he spun her back into his arms.

'So beautiful, Jane,' he said roughly as his head lowered to her breast. 'You were always so damnably beautiful.'

Jane smiled. Yes—when he looked at her and

touched her like this, that strange shyness fled, and she felt beautiful again, in a way she hadn't in so long. Desirable. Wanted, and not in that way she had felt her beauty used in gaming rooms, as a commodity, a distraction. Truly beautiful. As his mouth closed hard on her nipple, drawing her in deep, her head fell back and her eyes closed. She felt the braid of her hair fall down her back and the heat of his lips on her aching breast. She bit her lip to keep from crying out. Her whole body, which had felt so frozen and numb, roared back to burning life again.

He covered her breast with his palm, his fingers spread wide to caress her. One fingertip brushed over her engorged nipple and a cry burst from her lips. She felt him smile against her, just before his teeth bit down lightly.

She reached desperately between their bodies to unfasten his trousers and push them down over his lean hips. His hard cock sprang free against her abdomen and as she held it naked in her hand at last he groaned. His teeth tightened on her nipple before he arched his head back to stare up at her.

Jane looked down into his eyes and saw that they were burning and dark, the blue almost swallowed in black lust. She bent to kiss the side of his neck, to bite at him as he had with her. He tasted salty and sweet, intoxicating.

As she kissed him, she ran her open palm up his penis to its swollen tip. Hayden's hands suddenly tightened on her backside, his fingers digging into the soft skin as he dragged her even closer. Her hand dropped away from him and he slowly pressed the tip of his manhood against the soft nest of damp curls between her thighs. He moved up and down, lightly teasing her.

'Hayden,' she whispered against his neck.

'So sweet,' he answered, in a voice so deep she didn't recognise it. He pulled her flush against his hips and then suddenly they tumbled back together to the bed. He came down on top of her, his hips between her spread legs, his lips taking hers in another wild, desperate kiss.

Jane wrapped her legs around his waist and arched up into him. He was so large, so strong and completely overwhelming. She felt surrounded completely by his heat and power. She couldn't breathe, couldn't think. She tore her lips from his kiss and tilted her head back to try to gulp in a breath, to try to find a particle of sanity. Her hands dug into his shoulders as if she would push him away—or cling to him.

Hayden seemed to sense something was wrong. His hands slid around her waist, and in one swift movement he lay on his back with her on top of him. She straddled him, her legs tight to either side of his lean hips. He stared up at her with an almost feral gleam in those extraordinary eyes, as if he was so hungry he would devour her. Yet he made no move; his body was taut and still with perfect restraint.

Jane braced her hands on his chest, letting him

support her. She slid them down, a slow, hard glide over his warm skin. He felt so tense under her caress, as if he was waiting for what she wanted to do. It made her want him even more when she saw he would give her control like that.

She reached up and released the tie on the end of her braid to shake her hair free as she smiled down at him. A muscle tightened in his jaw, but his stare never wavered from her face. She took his hands and moved them from her waist to hold them to the mattress. She leaned down and laid her open mouth on his naked chest. His hands jerked, but he didn't push her away.

She tasted him with the tip of her tongue, swirling it lightly over his flat, brown nipple. It hardened under her kiss and she felt him draw in a sharp breath of air. She nipped her teeth over him.

Surely she would always remember this, no matter what came tomorrow. It was like a dream, a lustful fantasy before she had to go back to her real life. His taste, his smell, the way his body felt as it slid against hers—she would remember it all. This had always been so right between them.

She licked at the indentation along his hip, that enticing masculine line of muscle that dipped towards his erection. She breathed softly over the base of his penis, touched him once with her tongue and sat upright atop him again.

'Jane,' he groaned. 'How do you do this to me?'

'What do I do to you?' Jane closed her eyes

and laid her hand lightly between her bare breasts. Slowly, very slowly, she traced her touch down her own body, over her abdomen, until her fingers lay over the place that was so wet for him she ached with it. She slid one fingertip downwards and then his perfect stillness shattered.

'Blast it, Jane!' he shouted. Her eyes flew open as his hands closed hard around her hips. He pulled her body up along his until his mouth closed over her womanhood just where her hand had been. She knelt over his face as his tongue plunged deep into her.

Jane cried out and grabbed on to the scarred wood of the bed as his mouth claimed every intimate part of her. His fingers dug into her buttocks as he kissed her, licked her, tasted her so skilfully. She was no longer the one in control, but she didn't even care. She only wanted his mouth on her, his touch.

His tongue flicked at that tiny spot high inside of her and she moaned. One of his hands let go of her and he drove one long finger into her as he kept licking. He moved it slowly in and out, pressing, sliding, until she cried out his name over and over.

'Oh, Hayden,' she moaned. 'How do you do this to me?'

'Just let go,' he whispered against her. 'Let go for me…'

Another finger slid into her and she felt the pressure building up low in her abdomen. He had done this to her in that warm, dusty hut, too—it didn't seem to matter where they were, who they were, only that they were a man and a woman drawn together by a deep need. That heat built and built, expanding inside her like a fire out of control. Her whole body seemed to soar upwards. Hayden's tongue pressed harder as his fingers curled inside her and she shattered completely. She screamed out loud and clutched at the bed to keep from falling.

But he wasn't done. He lifted her off of him and pushed himself up to sit against the bedpost. He drew her body down until she straddled his hips again and was spread open over him.

'Ride me, Jane,' he commanded.

She could hardly focus through her pleasure-dazed mind. She stared down at him as she held on to his sweat-slick shoulders. His eyes were still dark with lust. It made her want him, need him, all over again.

She raised herself slightly until she felt his tip nudge at her opening, then she held on to him tightly as she slid down. Lower, lower, until he was completely inside of her. His head fell back as his hands closed hard on her waist.

'Jane,' he groaned. 'You're so perfect. I can't...'

She raised up again and sank back down, over and over, faster, until she found her rhythm. His hips arched up to meet hers and they moved together, harder, faster. Until she felt her climax building all over again.

She leaned back and braced her hands on his thighs as he thrust up into her. She closed her eyes and saw whirling, fiery stars in the darkness, exploding around her in showers of green and white as she cried out his name. He shouted out a flood of incoherent curses as his whole body went rigid. She felt him go still deep inside her as he let go and soared free with her.

Jane sobbed and let herself fall to the bed. Her legs were too weak to hold her up any longer. She trembled as she let the bone-deep exhaustion claim her. The ceiling above her spun around and around as she tried to catch her breath, to make sense of what madness had just happened.

Beside her, Hayden had collapsed on the pillows. They didn't touch, but she could feel the heat of his body close to hers. His breath sounded rough and uneven, and suddenly she remembered the injuries that had brought him to her door in the first place. She sat up to frantically examine him, worry replacing the languor of sexual pleasure. Had she hurt him? What craziness had come over them to do something like that?

But he looked well enough. His leg was still bandaged in clean white linen and the cloth wasn't spotted with blood. His eyes were closed, his hair falling in damp waves over his brow. She gently brushed it back and he caught her hand in his to kiss her palm. Jane felt a sudden wave of unwanted tenderness wash over her. Tenderness—for her husband of all people! After he got drunk with his friends again! Her head was spinning, as if the reality of what had happened could hardly sink in. She had never felt quite that way before. The heat of sex and need was all tangled up with the past and she didn't know what would happen next.

She didn't even know what she *wanted* to happen next. She laid her hand gently against the side of Hayden's cheek. There was so very much she didn't know about him any more.

Jane traced the hard line of his roughened jaw and over the softness of his sensual lips. Her touch drifted over his closed eyelids and she felt his breath drift softly over her skin. His arm wrapped around her waist and he drew her down to the bed beside him.

'Jane,' he whispered hoarsely, his voice distant as if he was drifting into sleep. 'What is it that you do to me? I only feel this way with you.'

She shook her head. What did they do to each other? He made her crazy, made her forget everything else when she was with him. She couldn't let him do that to her any more.

Hayden watched Jane as she slept, half-afraid she would disappear if he turned away. A tiny smile lingered on her lips as if she was having good dreams, the worried look she wore before she fell asleep vanished. He hoped she did have sweet dreams. He hoped she dreamed of him and that for once he made her smile.

Her dark hair fell in a shining curtain over her

shoulders and the pillows, just as it had in his memories for so long. He ran a gentle fingertip along one soft strand and marvelled that after so much time they were here. Together.

Careful not to wake Jane, he lay back against the pillows and gently drew her into his arms. She sighed and nestled against him, and he felt a surge of something like triumph that she would trust him enough to stay close to him.

Could he trust himself? Once, long ago, he thought he could, when he first found Jane. But then he fell back to his old ways and came to heartily regret it. Jane had been his chance and he had foolishly thrown it away. Until he saw her again, saw how life could be here at Barton Park, he hadn't even realised just how foolish he really was.

But maybe now they could start again.

'What are you thinking about?' Jane suddenly asked softly.

Hayden glanced down to see that she was awake, watching him with her wide, calm hazel eyes, though she hadn't moved at all.

'About you and life here at Barton,' he answered truthfully.

'Good thoughts, I hope,' she said.

He smiled down at her and drew her even closer. 'The best, I think.'

Jane laughed, a wonderful, light, bright sound. 'That is good.'

And then she kissed him, and he couldn't think anything at all.

* * *

'The Earl and Countess of Ramsay.'

Jane heard the words ring out before her as she waited to step into the noisy ballroom. Ramsay. It was her title now, yet it sounded foreign. Would it ever seem as if it belonged to her, as if it fit as closely as the new kid gloves on her arms?

The countess business was so very new. She still felt as she had when she jumped into the lake at Ramsay House with Hayden and the cold water closed over her head. She just had to do as she had then and fight her way to the surface.

Hayden held his arm out to her and gave her a puzzled glance. She suddenly realised that, yes, Ramsay was her name and thus she was expected to step into the ballroom now. She gave him a shaky smile and took his arm.

'You look lovely,' he said.

'It is the new gown,' Jane answered. She shook out her blue silk, lace-frothed skirts—'The very latest from Paris, madame,' the modiste had said. 'It's far grander than anything else I've worn. Except my court gown and that was borrowed.'

'No, it's you. I shall be the envy of every man here.'

They swept into the ballroom, which was already crowded with people, the cream of the ton. Thousands of candles cast golden light over sparkling jewels, gleaming satins and masses of red-and-white hothouse flowers. Every eye in the room seemed

*to watch her, speculative, amused, wondering. The
burst of confidence Hayden's words had given her
faded, but she forced herself to keep smiling.*

*'Ramsay! How wonderful you could attend my
little soirée. I wasn't sure you were back in town
yet.' Their hostess, Lady Marlbury, hurried towards
them on a cloud of expensive perfume. Tall and elegant, with dark red hair swept up into a jewelled
bandeau and emerald-green silk swirling around
her, she was what Jane would have once imagined
a countess would be like.*

*'We wouldn't miss it for anything. Who could be
anywhere but London when your annual ball is happening?' Hayden said. He let go of Jane's arm to
kiss Lady Marlbury's hand.*

*'You are such a flatterer,' Lady Marlbury said
with a flirtatious laugh. She tapped him lightly on
the arm with her folded fan. 'But I don't mind. And
this must be your new wife. I have heard so much
about her, though I fear my wedding invitation must
have gone missing.'*

*After the pleasantries were exchanged, Lady
Marlbury begged to 'steal away' Hayden for a
dance, leaving Jane to linger alone for a moment.*

*But she was not alone for long. Susan Eastwood,
her friend from their Drawing Room débutante days,
hurried to her side, holding out a glass of wine.*

*'My dear Lady Ramsay,' she said. 'You look as
if you could use this.'*

'Thank you,' Jane said with a relieved laugh. She took a long sip and sighed. 'It is quite delicious.'

'Only the best at Lady Marlbury's ball, you know.' Susan winked at her over the edge of her own glass. 'I'm surprised you're so calm about letting Lord Ramsay dance with her.'

'I don't let him do anything,' Jane protested. 'She's our hostess, is she not? It's only polite.'

'Polite? Perhaps it is now. But my brother John, who as you know is great friends with your husband, said last year Ramsay and Lady Marlbury were quite an item. Not that it could go anywhere, of course. Ramsay has his title to consider.'

'Were they?' Jane whispered, suddenly feeling cold. Her gaze scanned the dance floor until she found Hayden and Lady Marlbury, their arms linked as they twirled around, laughing into each other's eyes.

Of course she knew Hayden had had amours before they met. He had to, a young, handsome, healthy earl. Yet to see it now, right before her, with such a very beautiful woman...

'How interesting,' she murmured and gulped down the rest of her wine.

'It's just silly gossip, of course,' Susan said. 'He has you now.'

Jane had to laugh, so she would not cry. 'Yes. Now he has me.'

Chapter Fourteen

Emma twisted the book in her hands upside down and studied the map again. It was a crude old drawing, out of scale and rough, and most of the landmarks in the garden had changed since the 1660s. But she was sure, after studying it for long hours, that she had finally deciphered it.

Unfortunately, if her new calculations were correct, the treasure was possibly buried under the summerhouse there at the centre of the maze, right across from the marble bench where she now sat.

She took her notebook out of her bag and jotted down a note next to her own sketches. It would certainly make her task a lot more difficult if that was indeed where the treasure lay. The weather wasn't making things any easier.

Emma glanced up at the sky, frowning. The rain had paused that morning, long enough for Lord John Eastwood and Lady Marlbury to depart on horseback, but the sky was still thick and grey. The ground was so muddy and churned-up she wasn't sure where to start digging, or even if she should. Maybe the treasure was better left a legend.

Or so she had thought when it looked like Jane would reconcile with Hayden. With the Ramsay money, and a true family, Barton wouldn't need the treasure. But today that all looked like a faint, foolish hope. Emma wasn't sure exactly why, but everything had changed in an instant when Hayden's friends had arrived. The bright, light days vanished and the clouds closed in around the house again.

Emma hated it. But she didn't know how to change it, so she had done what she could. She came to the garden to treasure hunt again.

A sudden rustling noise from beyond the walls of the maze made her jump to her feet. It had been so quiet, so still, since she got there that the sound made her whole body go tense. Her heart pounded and Murray sat up straight with his ears at attention. Emma slammed her notebook shut and clutched it between her hands, as if it could be a weapon.

A head peered around the edge of the wall and Emma's breath escaped in a 'whoosh'. It was Ethan Carstairs, and only when he smiled at her did she realise she had half-hoped, half-feared to see him alone again. She'd been thinking about him too much since their brief conversation behind the screen.

'I hope I didn't startle you, Miss Bancroft,' he said, stepping into the clearing. 'I thought I heard someone in here. I was just exploring a bit.'

'I— No, not at all,' Emma managed to stammer. 'It's just that no one ever comes to the maze, so I usually expect to be alone here.'

'Am I intruding, then?'

'Not at all. I'm glad of the company.' Emma slowly lowered herself back down to the bench, watching as he came closer. He really was so handsome, just what a London man-about-town should be, in her imagination. But here, outdoors in the daylight, she could see that his skin was pale, his eyes red-rimmed with the late hours she had heard everyone having last night. 'I thought everyone was leaving today.'

'I'll be on my way later, as soon as I can arrange transportation,' he said. He sat down next to her, his legs stretched before him lazily. She could smell his cologne, something sandalwoody and exotic, with the underlying tang of brandy. 'I don't think your sister likes me very much.'

'Oh, no,' Emma cried, compelled to jump to Jane's defence. There was something about his tone she didn't care for, some kind of careless laughter overlaid by a touch of bitterness. 'She is simply used to having Barton Park to herself.'

'Are you used to being alone as well, Miss Bancroft? Do you resent the intrusion of guests?'

Did she? Emma suddenly wasn't sure. She did like the quiet days at Barton where she was free to do as she liked. Especially after the torture of school. But at first having something different in the house had been exciting and interesting. New people, new gossip, new things to think about.

Then she saw how it changed Jane and Hayden, changed the way the house felt, and she wasn't sure the excitement was worth it.

She studied Carstairs closely and he watched her back with glittering eyes.

'I don't mind guests,' she said carefully. 'Especially since I couldn't have come outside much for the last few days, anyway. I liked the distraction.'

He laughed. 'So we're a distraction, are we? And now you can come outside again you no longer need us.'

'Not exactly,' Emma said cautiously. She had been interested in Ethan Carstairs before, maybe even attracted. All she knew of attraction was from books and from that disaster with Mr Milne, and there were the daydreams, the nervousness, the breathlessness she expected. Now something was making her uneasy, something slowly creeping into the edges of her consciousness. She wasn't sure what that feeling was, but it made her ease away from him on the bench. 'I'm just glad to get back to my work.'

'Your work, Miss Bancroft? And what is that? Something in that book you always have with you?'

Emma's grasp tightened on her notebook. 'It's just something silly. About what we talked of before—old houses and legends.'

His smile tightened. 'Treasure, is it?'

Something told her not to reveal too much to him,

not so soon. 'Not necessarily. I just like investigating old tales.'

'I don't think I believe you, Miss Bancroft,' he said jokingly. 'I think you are treasure hunting. Have you found anything?'

'Of course not,' Emma said, trying to laugh. She slid to the very edge of the bench, but he followed her.

'Let me see your book,' he insisted. The veneer of joviality was still there; he still smiled down at her. But now Emma could see the tight desperation at its edges and it made her chest feel painful, as if she couldn't catch her breath.

She'd thought Jane was so silly to tell her to stay away from Carstairs, from all their unexpected guests. He had seemed so fun, so flirtatious, so— admiring. She didn't know what was happening now, but she didn't like the way it made her feel at all.

'It's just silly scribblings,' she insisted.

'I doubt anything done by a smart girl like you could be silly, Miss Bancroft,' he said. 'You deserve so much more than to be buried here where no one can see you. You should be in London, where you can be admired and appreciated. I could do that for you, if you helped me in return.'

Helped him? She didn't even want to know what that meant. 'I'm happy here,' Emma gasped as she leaped off the bench. Her notebook tumbled to the ground and Murray jumped up with a loud volley of barking.

'Let me help you, Emma, please,' he said sharply, lunging to suddenly catch her arm. He dragged her back towards him, his fingers curled tightly, painfully, around her. He dragged her up against him and cold panic flooded through her.

'No!' she cried, twisting to try to break free. How had the situation spiralled beyond her so quickly? The whole maze seemed to close in around her and Murray's furious barks sounded so far away.

His other arm closed hard around her waist and pulled her closer. His lips touched the side of her neck, wet and soft, and Emma tried to kick out at him. Her skirts twisted around her leg, making her fall backwards.

As she fell, her arm wrenched free of his grasp and she managed to roll away and leap to her feet. She ran as fast as she could to the maze entrance. Just as she was fleeing the scene, Carstairs gave a ringing, furious shout.

She glanced over her shoulder and saw Murray sink his sharp little teeth into the man's leg. He kicked out and Murray flew away with a yelp.

'Murray, no! Come with me now,' she screamed and the dog came dashing towards her, limping on his back leg. She caught him up under her arm and flat-out ran.

'You little witch,' Carstairs shouted after her. 'You'll be ruined, just like your stupid sister! I offered you everything.'

Sobbing, Emma kept running until she reached

the house. She didn't know where to go, what she should do. She only knew she couldn't let Jane see her like this, couldn't let anyone see what a fool she was. Again. It was just like Mr Milne. And Jane had enough to worry about.

Emma heard Hannah singing and the rattle of china from the dining room, so she ducked down the servants' stairs to the kitchen. Cook was hunched over the stove, her back to the door, giving Emma enough time to slip into a small pantry and close the door behind her.

There in the cool darkness, she knelt on the flagstone floor and clutched Murray's soft warmth against her as she sobbed.

Only then did she realise she'd left her notebook behind in the garden.

Jane carefully folded a stack of linen to take down to the kitchen, trying not to look at the bed. But every once in a while she would glance at it from the corner of her eye, then bit her lip to keep from giggling at the sight of the rumpled bedclothes and the discarded cravats she had used to tie Hayden to the bedposts.

Every time she saw them the whole night came flooding back to her, in vivid, lightning-flash de-tail. And she could feel the heat flood her cheeks. She couldn't quite believe she'd done that. The Jane she was before she met Hayden, even the Jane who was his wife in London, would never have done such a thing.

But when she saw Hayden lying there foxed last night, and thought about all they could have that he seemed determined to throw away, she just felt so *furious*. So tired of it all. And having him there, seemingly at her mercy, though she knew very well he could easily escape at any time and tie *her* up instead, restored some of her balance. Made her see clearly again.

The fact that he let her do that, let her feel powerful for once in her life and not just buffeted about by the whims of everyone else, made some of her anger fade. She did still love Hayden, but if he preferred a life with his friends, a life of drink and carelessness, instead of what they could have together, she could do nothing about it in the end.

But, by Jove, she could show him what he was missing. She could make him sorry he chose so poorly.

If she ever saw him again.

Jane sighed as she folded the last piece of linen and stacked them in a basket. When she woke that morning, early enough to see Lord John Eastwood and Lady Marlbury ride off in the mist-shrouded dawn, Hayden was gone. His clothes had been picked up from the floor. She almost would have thought the whole crazy night was a dream, if not for the creased sheets on his side of the bed, the black strand of his hair on the pillow.

His horse was still in the stable when she checked, but she hadn't seen him. She was half-afraid to go searching, afraid that in the cold light of day whatever had happened between them last night, all that wild, frantic heat, would dissipate. And she would see there truly was no hope for them.

Hope was all she had to cling to now. She only had a shred of it, but still she held on to it. She remembered what Lady Marlbury had said—Hayden had changed when he married her. It was over with Lady Marlbury before they even met. It could all be lies, of course, and Jane feared she would soon feel even more foolish, but she had to hope. Just for a little while longer.

Unless Hayden didn't show up again.

Jane gathered up the basket and carried it out into the corridor. Lord Browning and Mrs Smythe's luggage was left in the hall, waiting for their repaired carriage to arrive, but their doors were still closed, as was Ethan Carstairs's. No doubt they were still sleeping off last night's revelries. She couldn't see any of Hayden's belongings among them, so maybe he didn't plan on returning to town with them.

As Jane hurried down the stairs, she realised she hadn't seen Emma that morning, either. Hannah said Emma had grabbed a piece of bread and an apple from the kitchen before dashing off to the garden with Murray. Emma did that so often it was hardly something Jane would worry about, but with Carstairs still around…

Jane frowned when she remembered the way he had looked at Emma when she found them talking behind the screen. He looked so—speculative. And Emma looked so dazzled, just as Jane herself had when she first went to London and met the men there. Jane knew she would have to be much stricter about Emma's education from now on.

In the kitchen, the cook was slumped over asleep in her chair in the corner and Hannah was standing over the hearth, boiling a cauldron for the laundry. Even though the low-ceilinged room was too warm, and there were piles of dirty dishes and rumpled laundry to be cleaned, Hannah was humming as she worked.

'I'm afraid there will be a bit more work once all the guests are gone, Hannah,' Jane said as she put down the basket and went to make sure the drying racks were set up.

'Just as long as they go, my lady,' Hannah said. 'It will be good to have the house to ourselves again.'

'Indeed it will.' Jane just hoped Hayden wouldn't decide to leave with them. 'Have you seen Emma again this morning?'

'Not since she went out to the garden, my lady.'

'Well, when she returns be sure to let me know at once. And if you see Lord Ramsay—'

'Oh, he's in the library, my lady.'

So he *was* still there. Jane smiled in relief. But Hayden was not exactly a bookish sort. 'The library?'

'Yes. I saw him go in there as I was carrying up the breakfast tray for Lady Marlbury.' Hannah giggled. 'He looked as if someone had dragged him through the hedgerows and back, my lady, if you'll pardon my saying so. I left a pot of good, strong tea outside the door for him.'

'No doubt he'll need it,' Jane murmured. After all that brandy, and the long hours in bed—he was surely in need of some strong tea. Which surely meant this was *not* the best time to talk to him.

Jane gathered up some jars of marmalade and pots of butter from the table and hurried off to store them back in the pantry. When she first opened the door, the light from the kitchen didn't reach its furthest corners and she blinked against the sudden dimness.

Then she heard a strange rustling sound, a sniffle and a growl. Her shoulders stiffened, as it seemed she was still on full alert after the invasion of her house.

'Who is there?' she called, hastily stashing the jars on a shelf. 'What are you doing in here?'

'It—it's only me, Jane,' Emma said, her voice small.

'Emma?' Jane cried. 'Whatever are you doing hiding in here?'

She knelt down on the cold stone floor and heard Emma slide out from under the shelves. Murray whined and a beam of light from the doorway fell over them as they huddled together on the floor.

Jane's stomach clenched painfully when she saw Emma's tearstained face and tangled hair. She looked ten years old rather than sixteen, lost and bewildered. One arm was wrapped around her dog and Jane saw bruises darkening her skin.

Jane had never felt such raw, fiery fury before in her life as she looked at her sister. She would kill whoever had done this with her bare hands. She had to force herself to speak quietly, gently, and not scare Emma further.

'What happened, Emma dearest?' she said. 'Who did this?'

'Oh, Jane, I am so, so sorry!' Emma sobbed. 'I know you told me not to speak to him and I tried not to, truly. I was in the maze and he surprised me…'

'Carstairs?' *Of course.* Jane had known the man would be trouble, had felt it in her very depths when she saw how he looked at Emma. She felt horribly guilty for not tossing him out in the rain, then and there. But he was one of Hayden's friends.

Hayden's friends—who had come here to do such things.

'Yes. He asked me about my book and I knew I shouldn't be alone with him there. When I tried to leave, he grabbed me. Murray bit him and I ran.'

'What a good dog Murray is,' Jane murmured, vowing to forgive the puppy for chewing slippers and ruining rugs. He'd protected her sister when she wasn't there.

'I'm so sorry, Jane,' Emma cried. 'I should have listened to you. I was so silly.'

Jane drew Emma into her arms and held on to her tightly as Emma's back trembled with sobs. She smoothed her sister's hair and whispered soft, gentle words.

'It's not your fault, Emma,' she said. 'You did not seek him out. You were merely minding your own business in your own house. He is a wicked man. Thank goodness you got away from him so quickly.'

After a few moments, Emma's sobs faded to sniffles. 'I won't ever be alone with a man again. Ever. I promise.'

Jane had to smile at Emma's fierce tone, despite the anger that was growing like a ball of fire inside her. 'One day there will be a man you can be alone with, dearest. A much more worthy man than someone like Ethan Carstairs. He is only a scoundrel.'

'But he was so handsome, and he—he seemed to like me. I feel ridiculous.'

'Appearances aren't everything. You know that.' And so did Jane. Hayden was *never* what he appeared to be and he always seemed to change on her in an instant.

'I won't forget it again.'

After a few more minutes, Emma sat up straight and smoothed her tangled hair. Jane handed her a handkerchief and Murray looked on worriedly as Emma wiped at her eyes.

Jane knew what she had to do. She couldn't deal

with Carstairs alone as he deserved. Hayden had brought these people into Barton Park. He had to help her now.

'Better?' she asked.

Emma nodded. 'You aren't angry with me, Jane? For being so foolish?'

'Oh, Emma. If being foolish was a great offence, I would have to be furious with myself. We will both be more careful in the future.'

'What do *you* have to be careful about? You've always been perfect.'

Jane laughed. 'Come along,' she said, helping Emma up off the floor, careful not to touch her bruises. 'You could use some tea, I think.'

Once she had Emma settled next to the kitchen fire with Hannah, Murray sitting watchfully at her feet, Jane climbed resolutely up the stairs. She marched to the library and unceremoniously pushed open the door.

Hayden sat behind her father's old desk, slumped back in his chair with his eyes closed. Her account ledgers were open in front of him, as if he had been trying to work on them, and Hannah's tea tray was pushed to one side. He didn't look as rumpled as last night; his hair was brushed and his coat was draped over the chair. But he still looked tired, as tired as she felt with everything rushing at her at once.

His eyes opened at the slam of the door and he sat up straight.

'Jane,' he said, smiling tentatively. 'The carriage is coming around to the front for the remaining guests in a moment. I was just looking at the numbers here...'

'Carstairs attacked Emma,' she blurted out. She hadn't meant to say it quite like that. She'd meant to calmly tell him what had happened and what she wanted him to do about it, but her calm was dissolving around her as she thought of Emma sobbing in the pantry.

Hayden's smile vanished and his whole face hardened. He pushed himself to his feet. 'What did you say?'

'I found Emma in the pantry, crying. She—she has bruises on her arm and she told me Carstairs grabbed her. He came across her in the garden and...'

Hayden reached for his coat on the back of the chair and shrugged into it. Everything about him seemed to have gone very cold and still in only an instant. 'Is that all that happened?'

'I think so. She said Murray bit him and she was able to run away. But...' Jane shook her head, and found that she was shaking. 'Men like that should never have been in my house, around my sister! She is only sixteen and so sheltered.'

'Where is he now?'

'I don't know. Emma said he found her in the garden maze.'

'I will find him. He can't hide from me.' Hayden paused beside her in the doorway. He reached out to touch her arm, but when she stiffened his hand fell away. His face grew even harder, as if it was carved from granite. 'This is my fault, you are right. I'll take care of it.'

'What are you going to do?' Jane called after him as he strode down the corridor.

He didn't answer, and she hurried behind him as he went out the door into the garden. She'd never seen Hayden quite like this, so silent, so still and stony. She didn't know what had happened between last night and this morning, what he'd wanted to talk to her about when she burst into the library, but this new Hayden had her most concerned.

'Hayden, wait!' she cried, but he was too far away to hear her. His long legs had carried him across the garden paths and he disappeared into the maze.

Jane ran to catch up, chasing him down the twisting walkways. As she slid into the clearing at the maze's centre, she saw Hayden was already there. And so was Carstairs.

At first the man didn't see them. He knelt in the mud near the summerhouse, digging frantically. His coat was flecked with dirt, his hair streaked with sweat and he was so engrossed in his labour he didn't notice them.

Jane's throat felt so tight and dry that she couldn't cry out. She pressed her hand hard against her stomach as she tried to catch her breath and watched helplessly as Hayden moved as quickly and silently as a large, lethal jungle cat.

He grabbed Carstairs by the back of his coat and

pulled the man to his feet. Carstairs shouted out in surprise, spinning around just as Hayden shoved him away. But Hayden wasn't done with him. He followed as the man tried to run and planted a solid facer to his nose. As blood spurted and Carstairs screamed, Hayden just grabbed him up again by the coat collar and half-marched, half-dragged him out of the maze and up to the front of the house where the carriage was waiting, with Lord Browning and Mrs Smythe already inside.

Hayden shoved Carstairs inside, watching impassively as the man fell to his knees on the carriage floor. 'Don't expect to enter the club when you return to London,' Hayden said. 'Or anywhere else for that matter. And if you ever, ever come near my family again, that broken nose will be the very least of your troubles.'

Then he slammed the door and with a slap of his palm on the carriage door sent it rolling away. Carstairs never had time to say a single coherent word.

Jane stared at Hayden, shaking with the force of all the emotions rolling through her. His shirt was torn and a bruise darkened his cheekbone. She just wanted to take him in her arms, hold him as she cried about all the things she had seen.

But there was also a part of her, a small but insistent part, that wouldn't let her forget *he* was the one who had brought these people into her house in the first place. He was the one who drank with them, who let them break the peace of Barton Park.

It wasn't completely fair, she knew that. He couldn't really have tossed them out in the storm, any more than she could have done to Hayden when he arrived in the midst of the rain. But so very much had happened—her house invaded, the strange talk with Lady Marlbury, the intense lovemaking with Hayden, Emma being attacked and the violence of Hayden's fight. She simply couldn't make her thoughts stop spinning.

She wanted to be alone to cry, to try to think.

'I have to find Emma,' she said, spinning around to run up the stairs.

'Jane…' Hayden said and she felt him reach towards her. She didn't want him to touch her, not now. She didn't want to shatter.

She slid away, not looking back. 'We can talk later, Hayden. I have to see to my sister.'

'Of course,' he said tonelessly.

She nodded and hurried into the house. Only when the door was closed between them and she was alone did she let herself cry.

She was so damnably tired of tears, she realised as she dashed them away. They never solved anything, not in London and not here. She still loved Hayden. And they still wanted such different things from life.

She wouldn't cry any more.

Hayden's blood was up. He knew he shouldn't go back to the house when he felt like that, as if he would lash out at anyone in his path. Especially when Jane looked at him like that, as if what had happened to Emma was his fault. Her beautiful hazel eyes so full of anger and sadness.

Or maybe that was his imagination. Maybe he was sending his own shattered thoughts on to her. She *should* blame him. He let Carstairs and the rest of them into Barton, let them send him spiralling back into the past. Jane had given him another chance when he didn't deserve it and he pounded her kindness into the ground. Again.

His sweet, darling Jane. His wife.

Hayden paced the muddy lane, his fists curled tightly around his bruised knuckles. He wanted to hit something again, wanted to be face-to-face with Carstairs again to beat the villain down. But Carstairs was gone—Hayden had seen to it himself, had tossed the blighter into a carriage and followed it into the lane to be sure it was headed towards London.

And he could never beat down what he was most angry at—himself.

Chapter Fifteen

⁓⁓⁓

The sitting-room door opened, and Jane sat up eagerly, the book she was pretending to read falling from her hands, only to sink back down to her chair when she saw it was Hannah standing there and not Hayden.

The clock was ticking inexorably towards dinner time, the sky outside the window darkening, and still Hayden hadn't come back. Her anger was tinged with the sharpness of worry. Where could he have gone? Was he in trouble somewhere?

She hadn't liked the wild light in his eyes when he tossed Carstairs out of the house. She'd seen that look too often and she didn't want yet more trouble.

But it was, oh, so hard to sit there and wait! To not go running out into the gathering night to find him.

Hannah put the lamp she carried down on the table and only then did Jane notice how dark it had become in the room.

'You have a caller, my lady,' Hannah said.

'A caller?' Jane said, surprised. For just an instant she was sure it was Hayden, but then she felt silly. He wasn't a 'caller', he lived there—or so she had begun to imagine. 'At this time of day?'

'It's Sir David Marton, my lady. Shall I tell him you're not at home?'

Jane shook her head wearily. That disappointment that Hayden hadn't returned lingered, but she hadn't seen Sir David in several days, not since their walk to the village. Perhaps he could be a welcome distraction. 'No, show him in. Is Miss Emma still in her chamber?'

'Yes, my lady. I just left her some tea.' Hannah paused, shuffling her feet. 'And I haven't seen Lord Ramsay come back yet.'

'Thank you, Hannah.' As the maid left, Jane went to the looking glass and tried to tidy her hair, to erase the marks of the long, strange day. She gave up after a moment, seeing it was a lost cause.

'Lady Ramsay,' Sir David greeted her as he entered the room. He gave her a bow. 'I hope you're doing well. Louisa has been complaining she hasn't seen you in ages. She says you must come to tea next week.'

'It has been rather busy here, I'm sorry to say, but hopefully very soon all will return to normal here at Barton,' Jane answered. 'It's good to see you again, Sir David.'

And it was good to see him. He seemed like a spot of calm, a sign of the orderly life she had once fashioned for herself and Emma here at Barton that had been so disturbed lately. She invited him to sit by her on the sofa and tell her of all the local doings she had missed. Soon he had her laughing at a tale of the vicar's cow getting loose from the vicarage yard and running amok around the church and she almost forgot Carstairs and the others. Even the usually solemn Sir David laughed as he told her about it.

They were still laughing when Hayden strode into the room. 'Sir David,' he greeted abruptly, his glance flickering between Jane and their guest as he frowned.

Really, that is too unfair, Jane thought, considering the trouble his friends had caused of late. Her friends were nothing compared to that. She wiped the tears of laughter from her eyes and said, 'Sir David has brought greetings from his sister and an invitation to tea next week.'

'I had no idea tea invitations were so mirthful,' Hayden said.

'Oh, no, we were only laughing at a story about the vicar's cow,' she said. 'That is nothing to London repartee, of course, but rather amusing to us locals. Perhaps you'd care to hear it, Hayden?'

As Sir David obligingly told the story again, Jane went to pull the bell to send for some tea. Suddenly, something outside the window caught her attention, some sudden flare of light in the gathering darkness.

'How strange,' she murmured, and as she hurried

to investigate Hayden and Sir David broke off their tense conversation to follow her.

'What is it?' Hayden asked, peering over her shoulder.

'I'm not sure. I thought I saw something.' The garden looked peaceful again, quiet and sleeping. She started to turn away, but a sudden burst of orange-red light shot up above the walls of the maze.

'Fire!' she screamed, spinning towards the door in a rush of fear.

Hayden and Sir David were already running out of the room. Jane dashed after them. Surely the earth was damp enough to contain any flames, but the horrible image of the gardens and house blackened and crumbling loomed in her mind.

As the men rushed into the garden, Jane hurried downstairs and grabbed the basket of linen waiting to be washed. Maybe she could use it to smother some of the flames.

'Fetch help from the village!' she called to Hannah and ran back into the hall.

When she got into the garden, the air was tinged with the sharp, metallic smell of smoke. As she ran down the pathway, the terrible visions faded and she could only hear the roar of her heartbeat in her ears, the rush of frantic activity all around her.

The fire was flaring higher and higher at the centre of the maze. Smoke rolled towards her like a silver-grey wall, stinging her eyes and burning her lungs. She could barely see the figures of Hayden and David Marton ahead of her.

Jane quickly dug out a handkerchief from her apron pocket and tied it over her nose, then she ran into the very centre of the maze. The flames were spreading from the overgrown flowerbeds, licking at the wooden walls of the old summerhouse. If they didn't get it under control, she knew they would spread to the hedge walls and out to the rest of the garden.

She dived towards the outermost edges of the flames and beat at them with one of the sheets. The heat prickled on her skin, tiny pinpricks of searing steel, and her eyes watered until she could hardly see, but still she fought on. She had to. This was her home.

She managed to put out one fire and spun around to beat at another. The figures of the men, ghostly and faint, mere blurry outlines, slid in and out of view through the smoke. She was vaguely aware of shouts, of more people running into the clearing, but all she could do was keep fighting. Keep fighting even though her arms ached as if they would wrench away from her shoulders, even though she couldn't breathe.

She fought until suddenly her knees collapsed beneath her. Coughing and choking, she fell to the ground, too weak to move. She tried to push herself to her feet, to get away from the horrible, searing heat, and she sobbed in frustration.

Suddenly, strong hands caught her by the shoulders and lifted her up. Jane blinked away the smoke tears to see David Marton standing above her.

'You need to get away from here,' he shouted above the chaos.

She shook her head, but he wouldn't let go of her. He drew her away from the charred ruins of the summerhouse, collapsing in on itself, and made her sit down in a quieter, cooler spot near the hedge. Only then did she see that most of the flames were out. Hayden was beating at the last of them, his white shirt grey and his usually immaculate hair dotted with ash. Hannah and some of the villagers who had no doubt been out in the fields nearby and saw the flames were putting out the smaller fires.

The ground was scorched and seared, the summerhouse in ruins, but it finally looked as if the rest of the garden was safe.

Suddenly it was as if every ounce of frantic fight drained out of Jane and left her shaking. She choked back a sob.

'It's all right now, Lady Ramsay,' David said. He knelt down beside her and she was glad he was there. He was so quiet and steady, just as she'd once thought. 'The fires are out.'

'But how did they start?' she said. She hated how shaky she sounded. Despite the heat of the flames, she couldn't stop shivering. 'The ground is still so damp…'

David took off his coat and gently draped it over

her shoulders. It smelled of smoke, but she was glad of its comforting warmth.

'I fear it may have been started deliberately,' he said, still so very calm. 'There was broken glass and some old rags near the building. I think it spread from there.'

Jane was shocked. Someone had done this thing deliberately? Here at Barton, which had always been her safe haven? 'Who would do that? That is monstrous! No one could possibly hate us like that…'

Suddenly an image of Ethan Carstairs flashed in her mind. His face twisted in fury as Hayden threw him out of Barton Park. *He* would hate them. And surely he had the evil nature that could do something like this.

'Oh, no,' she whispered. 'How could this have happened? All I wanted here was peace and quiet.' She couldn't hold the tears back any longer. They stung her eyes and she swiped them away.

David silently took a handkerchief from his pocket and carefully dabbed at her cheeks. His simple, kind gesture steadied her and she gave him a wobbly smile.

'You really are very kind, Sir David,' she said. 'You only came here to pay a simple call and instead you have to fight fires and comfort weeping women. How tedious for you.'

He gave her one of his rare smiles and Jane was astonished to see that it took him from a quietly good-looking man to a dazzlingly handsome one.

But still he was not as handsome as Hayden. No man was.

And she feared now she would always think that. She would always compare everyone else unfavourably to her husband. Damn him.

'Perhaps I should change my name to Sir Galahad,' he said with a wry laugh.

Jane laughed with him and when he squeezed her hand comfortingly she let him. It *was* comforting. Not confusing and enflaming and wonderful, like when Hayden touched her.

'I think we have a great deal of work to do here,' she said. 'Finding an arsonist, clearing up this mess.'

'You have plenty of friends to help you, I presume, Lady Ramsay,' he said. 'And when we catch the villain who did this, he will be very sorry indeed.'

Jane swiped away the last of her tears as she studied the scene before her, the smoky, damp pall cast over everything, the huge cleaning-up task before her.

And she found Hayden watching her from across the clearing. He stood there very stiff and still, his eyes narrowed on her. Only then did she realise David Marton's hand was still on her arm. She slid away from him, but it was too late. Hayden had already turned and vanished into the wisps of smoke.

He was touching her.

The man was actually touching Jane. He stared

across the blackened clearing at them, sitting so close together, their heads near each other as they whispered together, and at first he couldn't quite believe what he was seeing. Then pure fury roared through him, stoked by the fight in his blood from the fire.

Jane was his wife, damn it all! Maybe their marriage wasn't all it should be, maybe he hadn't beaten it into shape as he half-planned to when he rushed so impetuously to Barton. But still—she was his.

He dropped the bucket in his hand and took an angry stride towards them. He would beat that blasted David Marton, the man who was always so infuriatingly calm and cool, to a bloody stain. Then he would pick Jane up in his arms, carry her into the house and make her see once and for all that she truly belonged to him. That she had to finally give up this nonsense and come back with him to London, come back to their lives there.

But something made him freeze in his tracks and that hot anger froze, too. Marton handed Jane a handkerchief and, as she wiped at her eyes, he spoke quietly in her ear. She gave a little smile and nodded.

Hayden realised with a sword-sharp suddenness that he should *not* go to Jane now. He couldn't give her what Marton could in that moment, what she needed after seeing her garden burning—steady, quiet understanding. All the terrible things that had happened to Jane today were because he had let that

London life intrude on what she'd worked so hard to build here at Barton.

She'd run away from what they had together and rightly so. He hadn't seen what she needed, and even if he had he couldn't have given it to her. He could only see his life as it had always been, as his parents' lives had been, and that wasn't enough for Jane.

Maybe she should marry someone like Marton. But it was too late for that. Too late for them to change.

As he watched Jane smile up at Marton, something inside of him seemed to crack wide open, something he had kept locked away his whole life. He wanted to fall to his knees and howl with the pain of it.

But he just watched as Marton helped Jane to her feet and they left the chaos of the maze together. One long moment ticked past, then another, and the sharp pain faded to a dull, throbbing ache. It could almost be just another part of him now.

Hayden curled his hands into fists. He knew he couldn't fight Marton, couldn't fight the past. Yet as he battled to save Barton Park, one true thing had flashed over him. He didn't just fight to save the house for Jane, he was desperate to save it for himself. Desperate to save all Barton had come to mean to him, because without him even looking, it had become something amazing.

In those few days here with Jane and Emma, Barton had become a home. And that was something worth fighting for as he'd never fought before in his life.

'My lord,' a man called and Hayden turned to face him.

It was one of the men who had come running from the fields around the village to fight the fire. All the flames were out now, but grey, ghostly drifts of smoke still drifted from the charred grass. The ruined walls of the old summerhouse swayed in the wind and the air smelled acrid and foul.

'I'm sorry we couldn't save the building, my lord,' the man said.

Hayden shook his head. 'It doesn't matter. The summerhouse can be rebuilt. Everyone was absolutely splendid. The important thing, the only thing, was to keep the fire from spreading.' And losing Barton would have utterly broken Jane's heart—and Hayden's, too, if he still had a heart to lose.

'This was found over there, my lord, near that pile of broken glass.' The man held out a tiny, flashing gold object. 'Looks valuable. Someone might be searching for it. One of your guests, mayhap?'

So everyone knew about his scandalous guests now? Hayden gave a wry laugh as he reached for the lost object. Of course they knew. Life in the environs of Barton were quiet. People like his erstwhile friends would be a rich mine of speculative gossip. One more thing for him to repair.

As he turned the gold object on his palm, he recognised it at once. An old Spanish coin that Ethan

Carstairs considered lucky for some unfathomable reason. Hayden had often seen the man take it out and twirl it between his fingers at the card tables.

And it was lost here in the maze. Near where the fire looked to have begun.

'Thank you,' Hayden said tightly. 'I will make very sure it's returned to its owner.'

Chapter Sixteen

❦

It was raining again, the needle-sharp droplets pattering at the window glass as lightning split the night sky and thunder cracked overhead.

Emma felt like she was the only one awake to feel the old house shake with it. Jane took dinner in her room; Emma hadn't seen her since the fire had died down and everyone from the village drifted home. Hayden, too, had vanished, so Emma ate alone in the dining room and then retreated to the library to try to read. She'd neglected her botanical studies too long in the fruitless search for treasure.

But she couldn't quite focus like she once did. The smell of smoke still hung heavy in the air, though the fresh rain would surely banish any lingering sparks. But no storm could banish the terrible images in her mind, of looking out the window and seeing the garden on fire. Of her sister's tear-streaked face as Sir David Marton helped her into the house, both of them stained and reeking from the smoke. Marton had been so solicitous, so comforting in those moments of chaos.

Emma almost felt bad about thinking him just a dry old stick.

She buried her face in her hands and listened to the howl of the thunder. Murray laid his paw on her foot, whining, but she had no comfort to give him. Barton Park, which had been her family's refuge for so long, felt like it was under siege. Ethan Carstairs, the fire, Jane's sad eyes—Emma just wanted to banish it all, but she couldn't.

Jane had seemed so happy for a few days and so had Hayden. The angry look in his eyes when he first came to Barton had faded, only to come back in force when his friends showed up. Everything Emma had thought so sure, so hopeful, had vanished like that smoke outside. She didn't like it at all.

She thought about the treasure she'd been so sure was in the maze. The treasure that would save them, almost as if it was some sort of magical talisman. Maybe the fire would uncover something. But even if the old treasure was found it wouldn't fix anything. Jane and Hayden would still be apart. Emma still would be full of that restless knowledge that she couldn't fix anything.

Emma tossed her pencil down on the open book in front of her and pushed herself back from the desk. Once she'd felt so sure of so many things. Now she knew nothing.

She moved out of the circle of candlelight and into

the darkness by the window. Rain poured down in earnest now, battering the abused garden. A quick flash of purplish lightning illuminated the overgrown flowerbeds, the haze of smoke that hung in the dark air.

Suddenly she saw something, a flash of movement in the blackness. It could almost have been a shadow thrown off by one of the old statues, but then it slid away, along the path towards the house. Emma shielded the glare of the window glass with her hands and peered closer, hardly daring to breathe. After everything that had happened today, she feared it could be anything at all.

One more bolt of lightning illuminated a man's face as he ran and she saw it was Ethan Carstairs returned to Barton Park.

'That bloody bastard,' she cried, in a fit of profanity that would have horrified Jane. But she couldn't think of any other way to describe that horrible man. He had attacked her, probably started the fire—and now he was back to cause even more trouble.

Well, Emma wasn't going to allow it.

Without stopping to think, she snatched up a sharp silver letter-opener. She ran out of the library, Murray at her heels, and took a cloak from the hook in the hall. After she tugged its folds around her, she pulled open the front door.

The cold force of the rain drove her back, only for a second, but it was long enough to shake her into seeing what she was doing. Being so impetuous had got her into trouble before. She needed to get help now.

But before she could slam the door and go back, a hand shot out of the darkness and grabbed her by the arm. Hard fingers dug into her skin like sharp steel hooks and yanked her out into the storm.

Terrified, Emma opened her mouth to scream, but another hand clamped hard over her mouth, suffocating her.

'So kind of you to meet me halfway, Miss Bancroft,' she heard Ethan Carstairs say, just before stars exploded behind her eyes and she sank down into blackness.

'No!' Jane sat straight up in bed, disoriented and dizzy. What woke her? Was it the rain and wind lashing at the window? Or something inside her chamber?

Inside her own mind?

Her eyes still itched and stung from the smoke, and she rubbed at them as she took a deep breath. It must have only been a dream, a bad, strange dream brought on by the long day. Her body ached and her mind was still heavy with the sleep that clung around her. She couldn't remember her dream, but surely it involved fire and people she loved hovering on the brink of terrible danger where she couldn't reach them.

Finally her pounding heartbeat slowed and she opened her eyes to see that her bedchamber was just as it was before she fell asleep. Her shawl was tossed over the *chaise* and her half-eaten supper still lay on its tray on the table. The bathtub was still in front of the fireplace, the water grey with soot. The curtains were flung open to reveal the storm beyond her window.

Jane rubbed at her arms through her thin muslin sleeves. She'd fallen asleep in her dress. The wind rushing around the house sounded like screams and it made her shiver.

Just a dream, she told herself sternly. Yet there was something deep inside, some whisper of disquiet, that wouldn't go away.

She had a sudden strong urge to look in on Emma. It had been such a long, horrible day, for Emma more than anyone else. She'd been so quiet after the fire, retreating into her room with Murray.

Jane climbed out of bed and wrapped the shawl tightly around her shoulders before she lit a candle and tiptoed down the corridor. Hayden had retired to the room Lady Marlbury had used and the door was tightly closed. Everything was silent there.

But she couldn't think about Hayden, not now. He had looked so strangely tense and distracted after the fire, they hadn't spoken more than a few words and she almost feared to ask him how he felt. She hurried on to Emma's room. She raised her hand to knock on the door, but it swung open at her touch to reveal an empty space beyond. The bed was turned down, but not slept in.

Jane crept slowly into the room. The air smelled of Emma's light, lemony perfume, but was also cold and deserted. Even Murray wasn't there, his cushion by the window empty. The hair at the back of Jane's neck prickled and her hands went cold.

Don't be silly, she told herself. Emma could be anywhere in the house. She probably just couldn't sleep, after all that had happened, and she was still in the library. But that icy feeling wouldn't go away.

Jane hurried downstairs to the library. A lamp burned on the desk and books and notebooks lay open on its surface, but Emma wasn't there. The rainy night seemed to creep in closer and closer.

She spun around and dashed into the hall, her throat tight with a rush of panic. The door was swinging open, rain leaving the tile floor slick and glossy. Something small and shiny gleamed on the wood of the door.

Filled with the creeping stickiness of dread, Jane moved closer. The rain touched her skin, tiny wet pinpricks, but she didn't even notice that. She saw it was the letter-opener from the library, stabbed into the wood to hold a scrap of paper.

Jane snatched it down and quickly scanned the scrawled words.

The treasure for your foolish sister. Unless you want your garden to burn again. Send Ramsay to the ruined farmhouse outside the village. Carstairs.

'Oh, not again,' Jane whispered. She had thought, hoped, the man was gone for good. Hadn't he done enough to them? Hadn't they been through enough at his hands?

She read quickly over the note again, sure she must have misread it, was imagining things. The treasure? What did he mean? The old legend of the Barton treasure? That seemed so silly, so ridiculous. Yet if he'd taken Emma, it was so deadly serious.

How could she give him what she didn't have? What didn't even exist, except in her father's imagination?

'Jane? What are you doing down here?'

Jane spun around, startled at the sound of a voice, and slipped in the puddles on the tiles. She leaned against the wall and watched Hayden as he hurried down the stairs. He was in his shirtsleeves, his coat over his arm, his hair rumpled and his face hard with worry.

And suddenly she didn't feel so alone in the world, so adrift in a stormy sea of panic. Hayden had been there to help fight the fire. He was there now.

She held out the note. 'Carstairs took Emma,' she said simply.

She half-expected doubts, questions, statements that the smoke must have addled her brain. She should have known better from Hayden. The Hayden who'd so coldly beaten Carstairs up and thrown him out of Barton for touching Emma. Who'd fought the fire with her to save her home.

The Hayden she suddenly knew she could rely on, no matter what came.

'Blast!' he cursed, that one word a low, swift explosion. He took the note from her hand and read it quickly.

'The ruined farmhouse?' he said, his voice taut, as if he held himself tightly, carefully together, just as she did.

Jane watched as he put on the boots he had left discarded on the floor after the fire and shrugged into his coat. 'It's on the road just before you reach the village, behind the old tollgate. We saw it on our walk that day.'

Hayden nodded and turned to go into the library. Jane followed just as he opened a small trunk of his things that had been left there when he arrived at Barton. He drew an inlaid box from the bottom of the case and Jane recognised it right away. His duelling pistols, kept on a high shelf in the library of the London house. She'd never actually seen him use them, but she had no doubt he could.

He removed one of the pistols and secured it, along with a small bag of shot, inside his coat.

Jane didn't say a word. This Hayden was one she knew could keep her—and Emma—safe.

'Wake up Hannah, so you can start to form a search party,' Hayden said. 'They can ride out after me, while you stay here and keep watch.'

'No!' Jane cried, remembering how frightened Emma was the first time Carstairs attacked her. Once they found her, Emma would need her sister. 'I can't wait here. I'm coming with you.'

Hayden looked up at her with a frown. 'Jane, it's still storming out there. And you've already seen how desperate Carstairs is, what he is capable of.'

'I *am* going. I know the area better than you, Hayden. And Emma is my sister. She—she's going to need me.' Jane held her chin up high, swallowing her tears, swallowing everything but the knowledge that Emma needed her now and she had to be strong. 'If you make me stay behind, I will just follow on my own.'

Hayden gave her a quick flash of a smile. He came to her and took her cold hand tightly in his. He raised it to his lips for a quick kiss, and that warm touch steadied her.

'I know better than to argue with you, Jane,' he said. 'Fine, we will go together. Just stay close to me.'

Jane nodded. Of course she would stay close to him. There was no telling what they would find out there in the storm.

Chapter Seventeen

It was a hellish night.

Hayden couldn't see five feet in front of him in the impenetrable curtain of rain, which drove like relentless tiny needles into his skin. They'd managed to ride Hayden's horse for a while, until the muddy ground forced them to go forwards on foot. Now they walked, the saturated ground sucking at their boots, the wind howling around them, tearing at their clothes.

The lamp Hayden held in one hand did them no good, barely lighting their own faces. His other hand held on to Jane's, her fingers stiff and cold in his. Her pale face, framed by the sodden folds of her hood and beaded with raindrops like tiny diamonds, stared ahead with fierce determination. She was like a furious mother lion whose cub was threatened and, if Hayden didn't hate Carstairs for what the villain had done, he would almost feel sorry for the man.

Jane was indomitable when it came to fighting for what she loved.

Once she'd tried to fight for them and he had only driven her away. Given up what could have been theirs. They began with such hope on their wedding day and he just threw it away. Threw away the best thing that had ever happened to him.

But he would find her sister now. He would save the person Jane loved and make sure her life was happy from now on. Even if he couldn't be in it himself.

It was the very least he could do for her.

'Whatever you are trying to do, it won't work,' Emma said. She tried to sound brisk and cool, as Jane did when she was directing something. She couldn't show that she was scared. She *wouldn't*, not to the wild-eyed madman who paced the dirt floor in front of her.

She drew her knees up under her chin and tried not to shiver. The old roof of the ruined farmhouse was mostly gone, but she had managed to find a semi-dry spot under the eaves, where she could huddle out of the rain. Her head hurt where she had hit it on the doorstep when Carstairs grabbed her and she had to fight off waves of dizziness.

She needed all her wits about her now if she was to escape.

'Be quiet, witch,' Carstairs shouted, pacing back

and forth, shaking his head madly as if he could cast away this whole ugly night. As if he couldn't quite believe what evil he had done. Emma couldn't believe it, either. Barton was her haven, she could never have imagined such a thing could ever happen there. But it had. She had to stay calm and find a way to get out of there.

How could she ever have thought this man was handsome? How could she have listened to his flattery for even a moment?

She wrapped her arms tighter around herself, as if that could be her armour. On her sash she felt the press of something small and hard, cold through her chemise. It was the pearl circle pin that had once been her mother's, that Jane had given her to comfort her.

Before she could think about it too long, Emma tore it free and leaped to her feet. When Carstairs turned towards her again, she lunged forwards and stabbed him as hard as she could in the temple.

'Bitch!' he roared and reached out for her wildly. His hand struck her on the side of the head and she reeled backwards, but she forced herself to stay upright. She shoved him away and rushed out of the meagre shelter of the old house and into the rain.

Emma ran blindly through the pouring downfall, not knowing for certain where she was going. She heard Carstairs give a roar of fury behind her and it drove her on through the rain.

The mud soaked her thin slippers and she was sobbing with fear, but still she kept running. He was still after her, she knew he was.

She stumbled and fell, landing hard in the cold mud. She held her breath and listened carefully. Her heart thundered in her ears, along with the waters of the river rushing below the slope. Somewhere she could hear Murray barking, faint above the rush of the water. And thunder—and Carstairs shouting her name.

She pushed herself to her feet and ran towards the river.

The old ruined farmhouse was deserted.

Jane stood inside the gaping doorway and stared around the empty space in cold disbelief. She'd been so sure Emma would be there, that this would all end soon. But if her sister had once been here, she was gone. Hayden held up his lamp, his pistol held ready in his other hand, but there was nothing to see.

'Where could she be?' he muttered, his voice thick with an anger and anxiety that matched her own.

She kicked out at the damp dirt floor. A lightning strike caught a sparkle on the floor and Jane knelt to snatch it up. It was Emma's small pearl brooch, the one that had once belonged to their mother.

'They *were* here,' she said.

And then a scream split the night around them.

* * *

Emma balanced carefully on the slippery river-bank, the wind tugging at her wet skirts. Her feet were numb, holding her rooted in place. She could still hear the ring of Murray's frantic barks, but she couldn't see him.

She glanced frantically over her shoulder, sure Carstairs must be just behind her. He appeared at the top of the slope, his face white and twisted in the lightning-light.

'You stupid little whore!' he shouted. 'Come back here right now. You've caused me enough trouble and you'll be very sorry for that.'

'No!' she screamed, trying to spin away from him as he reached for her.

'Emma,' she heard Hayden call out of the storm.

She half-turned and glimpsed her brother-in-law through the rain, not far behind Carstairs on the riverbank. She tumbled off balance as Carstairs snatched at her sleeve and she fell backwards in a tumbling blur of confusion and fear. The water caught at her and Carstair's hard hands tried to push her even harder.

Through the haze, she saw Hayden catch Carstairs and ram his fist into the man's jaw, once, twice, driving him back. With a wild shout, Carstairs went tumbling into the rushing river.

Just before Emma plunged into the icy waters after him, Hayden snatched her by the arm and jerked her up and free. He fell to his knees with her, the waves lapping at her skirts, but not close enough to get her.

She wrapped her arms around his neck and clung to him, sobbing. She could feel Hayden trying to rise to his feet, but she was too scared to let go of him. So he knelt there in the mud, holding her.

'It's all right now, Emma,' he said in her ear, the words strong and calm in the midst of the storm. 'He's gone. He can't hurt you now. We're here.'

'H-how do you know?' Emma wailed. She'd been so scared of Carstairs and the crazy, wild light in his eyes. How could he be gone, just like that?

'I saw him swept down the river,' Hayden said. 'I had to pull you out instead.'

Emma nodded against his shoulder. She was still so numb, she could hardly comprehend what had happened. But somewhere in the distance, she heard the echo of a bark and it shook her out of her panic.

'Come on, we must find your sister,' Hayden said. 'She's terrified for you.'

Emma let him help her to her feet. She swayed dizzily, but his arm around her shoulders held her steady.

'Jane is lucky to have you, Hayden,' she said. 'We're both lucky you came here.'

'I doubt Jane would agree with you,' he answered. 'But I'd appreciate it if you could put in a good word for me with her.'

And together they climbed up the steep, slippery riverbank into the light.

Some wild creature was howling like it was wounded, a horrible, mournful sound. Jane clapped her hands over her ears to blot it out, only to realise that the howling was *her*. It was inside her head.

She stood balanced at the top of the riverbank, struggling to see what was happening through the darkness and rain. All she could make out was flashes of sudden, pale movement. Screams and shouts, a dog barking frantically somewhere in the distance. But she couldn't see what was happening to whom, if her husband and sister were still there somewhere.

Suddenly she saw a tall figure go reeling back into the rushing river. He instantly vanished into the water.

'Hayden!' Jane screamed. She took one lurching step forwards, only to trip and fall to her knees. Pain shot up her legs when she landed hard in the rutted mud, but she barely felt it through her fear.

There was a rush of sound, and a small, wet, warm object hit her in the chest. Murray, caked in mud, his ribs heaving, as panicked as she was. She clutched him against her, trying frantically to see what was happening down at the river. For a second she closed her eyes tightly and whispered a desperate prayer.

Let them be safe...

When she opened them, it was to a wondrous sight. Hayden and Emma were stumbling up the steep bank. Her sister's head rested on her husband's shoulder, her golden hair trailing around them in tendrils like serpents.

Jane had never seen anything more beautiful than the two of them, soaked through and covered with mud, but alive. The people she loved. Her family.

She scrambled to her feet and raced to throw her arms around them, Murray at her heels. 'You're alive, you're alive,' she sobbed, over and over.

'I'm sorry, Jane,' Emma cried. 'I never...'

'Hush,' Jane whispered. She kissed Emma's cheek, then Hayden's, just letting herself look at them, letting herself know they were all there. 'You're alive. We're together. That's all that matters now.'

And in that moment, fear still humming in her veins, cold rain pouring down on their heads, she knew that was true. It was the *only* truth. They were together. That was all that ever mattered.

'Jane...'

'Hush, don't say anything, Hayden,' Jane said as she hurried to open the bedroom door and help her husband to the bed. She tried to be brisk, nurse-like, to not show him her fear that he was bleeding. He was hurt, hurt trying to save her sister, and she had to be strong for him. Even though inside she was terrified.

Terrified she would lose him now, when she had only just found him again.

She urged him to lie back on the pillows. 'Sir David has gone to fetch the doctor, he will be here very soon. You must rest until then.'

'Emma?' he asked hoarsely.

'She is safe now. The doctor will see to her, too.'

Hannah hurried in with a tray in her hands, a basin of steaming water and pile of clean cloths. Jane wrung one out and carefully dabbed at the worst of the bleeding cuts on Hayden's face.

He suddenly reached up and grabbed her hand, holding her tightly. 'Don't leave me,' he said.

'Oh, Hayden,' she said, her throat tight. She felt tears prickle at her eyes and she couldn't do anything but let them fall. 'Don't you know by now? I could never leave you again. I was so silly and foolish when we first met, I didn't know what marriage was.'

'I was the foolish one. I couldn't see then what you really offered.'

What had she offered him, compared to what he could give her? She had loved him, or thought she did anyway, but it had never amounted to all she had hoped for. 'What did I give you? I had nothing then, just my own fanciful dreams.'

He pressed a quick, fervent kiss to her hand. 'You had everything. Love, a family, a home. All things I never had and never realised I *could* have. I saw your gentle spirit when we first met and I wanted it for myself. But just as you said, I didn't know what that meant. I was selfish.'

Jane's tears were falling now in earnest, splashing over their joined hands. She had once dreamed he would say this to her, would mean it, and now it was really happening. She thought her heart would burst. 'What went wrong for us, Hayden?'

'We just weren't ready for each other, my love. But I swear I will be a true husband to you now. I will spend every day making sure you are happy. If you will only let me.'

She wanted that so very much it hurt. It seemed she had been waiting so, so long to know he meant his words and for her to be ready to fully return them. She loved Hayden. She had loved him since the moment they met, but since he came to Barton that love had deepened, ripened.

Yet still a hard, cold kernel of fear lingered.

'What about the babies?' she choked out, and that was all she could say. The pain and fear of their lost children lingered like ice in those words.

And Hayden seemed to hear it all and understand it. He bowed his head over her hand. 'We can try again, make it work. Or if you can't, if the doctor says you should not, we'll let my blasted cousin have the title. I don't care, Jane. I only want you. *Only* you. Please…'

Suddenly he groaned. His hands fell from hers and he collapsed to the bed, unconscious.

Fear pierced through Jane, sharper than any

sword. 'Hayden!' she cried. 'No, no. Come back to me, please. I love you, too. Please, please…'

But all she heard were her own pleading words, echoing back to her. Hayden was silent.

Chapter Eighteen

Jane paced the length of the corridor, and sat down in the chair at the end, and then jumped up to pace all over again. She couldn't be still, couldn't stop and think. Whenever she stopped moving, the whole nightmare reeled through her mind again. The lightning, the rushing rain, the screams. Hayden stumbling up the slippery riverbank with Emma in his arms.

The men from the village said Carstairs's body had been pulled from the river, with roughly sketched, sodden maps of the Barton garden in his pocket. It was something of a relief to know the man would never trouble them again, but still her mind would not be calm.

Jane looked for the hundredth time towards Hayden's closed chamber door. How long had the doctor been in there? It seemed like hours. Hayden hadn't wanted to let the doctor tend him when the man came to look in on Emma, but Jane had insisted. Hayden was limping on the leg he injured when he first came to Barton and there was a deep cut on his forehead. Now they'd been in there for too long.

What if there was some terrible injury, some bleeding inside where it couldn't be seen? What if—what if she lost him again? This time for good?

Just the thought of it all, of Hayden being somewhere she could never say she was sorry, she was wrong, was utterly unbearable.

She sat down hard on the chair and closed her eyes against the pain in her head. She tried to force the fear away and imagine good things again. Hayden laughing with Emma in the garden. Hayden across the dinner table from her, smiling at her in the candlelight. Hayden in her bed, touching her, kissing her.

The peace they had found here for such brief days. The peace, the family, she had wanted all along, and lost in misunderstandings and anger. Surely it couldn't be gone for ever?

'Jane?' she heard Emma say softly. She opened her eyes to find her sister standing at the end of the corridor, Murray cradled in her arms. She still looked pale and startled, bruises standing out in stark purple relief against her white skin.

Jane pushed herself to her feet. 'Are you all right, Emma? You're supposed to be resting.'

'I can't possibly sleep.' Emma glanced at Hayden's door. 'Is the doctor still there?'

'Yes. I haven't heard anything yet.'

Emma nodded. 'I— Will Hayden leave again, do you think?'

'I don't know,' Jane answered truthfully. She didn't know what was in Hayden's mind after all that had happened. He seemed happy here at Barton. But maybe now he missed his old London life, the one his friends brought to their doorstep. The one a woman like Lady Marlbury could give him.

'I don't want him to go,' Emma said, her voice thick, as if she held back tears. Murray whined up at her. 'He isn't at all what I once thought he was.'

'No, he isn't.' Jane's husband was at once more complex and far simpler than she ever could have imagined.

'I thought I could help us by finding the Barton treasure,' Emma said. 'But I see now I didn't need it. Our treasure is right here, isn't it? It's us.'

'Yes,' Jane murmured, smoothing her hand over her sister's hair. 'Yes, our treasure is in us.'

The bedchamber door suddenly opened, and the doctor emerged with his valise in hand. Jane leaped up and Emma grabbed her hand.

'How is he?' Jane asked tightly.

The doctor shook his head. 'Lord Ramsay certainly gets battered around a bit, doesn't he, my lady? He has some cuts and bruises, and I certainly recommend rest for several days at least, but there should be no permanent damage.'

Jane let out the breath she was holding as relief

rushed through her. *No permanent damage.* Hayden was still alive; he *would* live. There was still hope. 'Thank you, Doctor.'

The doctor gave them a stern glance before he turned towards the stairs. 'I think a seaside holiday would be in order for all of you, Lady Ramsay. A month or two at Brighton would do you some good. Or even better—Italy.'

'Italy.' Emma sighed. 'Wouldn't it be wonderful if Hayden took us to Italy, Jane? I could find so many new plant specimens there.'

Jane had to laugh. Yes, it *would* be splendid. A long, sunny holiday, just the three of them, away from all that had happened. A fresh start.

If only Hayden wanted it, too.

'I should go look in on him,' Jane said, reaching for the door handle. 'You should rest, Emma.'

'Yes, of course,' Emma said, already distracted now. 'Just as soon as I find some books on Italy in the library...'

As Emma dashed down the stairs, Jane stepped into the darkened bedchamber. The curtains were drawn across the windows, blocking out the greyish daylight, and two lamps burned on the dressing table. A tray with a pitcher of water and discarded bandages was on the bedside table, and the sick-sweet smell of medicine and woodsmoke hung in the air.

Hayden lay in the centre of the bed, blankets and pillows piled around him in copious heaps. Hannah had been very solicitous towards him since he got home. His black hair was stark against the white linens, his eyes closed.

They opened when Jane clicked the door shut behind her and he watched her from across the room as she tiptoed closer.

'How do you feel?' she asked.

A faint smile touched his lips. 'As if I did ten rounds at the boxing saloon—and lost.'

That smile made Jane want to cry. She'd been so afraid she might never see it again, might never have the chance to be with him and tell him…

'I'm so sorry, Hayden,' she whispered.

His smile drifted into a frown. 'What do you mean? Jane, this was all my fault. I let Carstairs into the house, even though I never liked him. *You* have nothing to be sorry about.'

Jane hurried across the room and carefully sat down on the edge of the bed. She could feel Hayden watching her intently, but she stared down at her clasped hands in her lap and tried to decide how to tell him what she had to say. The confusion that had plagued her for days had suddenly cleared and she could see everything she should have known all along.

Everything she wanted—if it was still there for her. If it wasn't lost for ever.

'I loved you so much when we married, Hayden,' she said quietly. 'I'd never known anyone, anything, like you. So full of life, like a whirlwind. I was dazzled by you, by what I thought you were.'

'Are you saying you were deceived then, that you thought you loved me but you no longer do?'

Jane heard the confusion and pain in his voice, even though he tried to conceal them. She remembered what he told her about his family, about how he could never be good enough for them to love him, and her heart ached.

'No!' she protested. She turned to him and stared into his eyes, those beautiful blue eyes that seemed to contain the whole world. 'I am saying—back then I was young and foolish. I thought marriage would be perfect, easy, and when it wasn't I didn't know what to do. I was frightened. I loved a dream that could never be true. But now I love the reality, Hayden. I love *you*.'

And when she said those words she saw how very simple it all was after all. She loved Hayden. She loved what he'd fought against inside himself and won, loved how he had come for her, loved the life she saw now they could have here at Barton. When he had risked his life for her and for Emma, she'd known her first instincts when she met him and fell for him had been right after all.

She loved him, She didn't want to lose him again. But what if he didn't feel the same?

'I love you,' she said again, throwing herself off the cliff. 'I want us to be married again, to make a true life together. Here at Barton, in London—it doesn't matter. I just want to be your wife again.'

For a long, tense moment, he was silent. He stared at her, his eyes unreadable. Just as Jane started to turn away, sure that it was too late, his arms came close around her and he drew her against him.

'Damn it all, Jane, if I'm asleep and dreaming don't let anyone wake me up,' he said. 'I never thought I would hear you say those words again. I thought you were gone for ever. The mistakes I made, the stupid mistakes...'

Jane laughed and cried all at once, holding on tightly to Hayden as he kissed her over and over. 'We have both made mistakes, both been in pain. But we can make a new start now, if that is what you want, too.'

Hayden drew back, holding her face tenderly between his hands as he stared down at her. 'It's all I want. I love you, Jane. I want to show you how much, show you that I've changed. I can be the husband you deserve now. Let me prove that.'

'You don't have to prove anything to me. We just have to be together now,' Jane said. 'Together always.'

'Always,' he said, and there was the ring of deepest, truest promise in that one word. As if he was making his vows to her all over again. As if their marriage now was truly begun.

Always. This time, Jane knew that word was the whole world. She was Hayden's now, and he was hers. Always.

Epilogue

⥊⥈⥊

Lake Como—one year later

'Jane, look!'

Jane glanced up from the book she had balanced on the marble balustrade of the terrace and shielded her eyes from the sunlight to wave at Emma. Her sister dashed along the lakeshore, the hem of her white muslin dress wet as she threw sticks into the water for Murray. The dog, who'd grown prodigiously large on the good Italian food, joyfully dived into the waves as Emma clapped.

Jane waved and laughed, feeling more contented than she ever would have thought possible as she saw Emma having so much fun. After her kidnapping, Emma had grown so quiet and withdrawn, wandering around the gardens alone, waking at night from bad dreams, until Jane feared for her health. That was when Hayden suggested they follow the doctor's advice and take an Italian holiday.

There, under the azure skies and brilliant sun, the flowers and the good food, Emma began to blossom again. She laughed and chatted, just as she had before all the bad things happened. And, if possible, she'd even grown more beautiful. The young English bucks on their Continental tours followed her about every time she went to tour a museum or a ruin, sending flowers and letters, asking Hayden for her hand in marriage.

But Emma just dismissed them with a laugh and went on about her studies. There would be time to worry about her marriage later. Right now Jane was just glad she was happy and healthy.

And Emma wasn't the only one growing and blooming under the Italian sun. Jane rested her hand gently on her own belly, now large and rounded, and felt the baby stir under her touch. It liked to move about, kicking and turning restlessly as if her little son or daughter couldn't wait to be out in the world.

Jane smiled as she felt a tiny foot press into her palm. At first, she had lain awake worrying this child would be lost before it even had a chance to see the sun, just as her other babies had. When she'd lost that last baby, so much hope had slipped away with it, and she and Hayden were pushed even further apart.

But this child had grown and thrived, and in a few weeks she would hold it in her arms. Even if something terrible happened, she knew now she needn't fear—Hayden was with her. They were truly together now and nothing could push them apart. This last year had shown her that every day. Their love for each other grew every day, content and peaceful. They had married too young, expected too much of each other, but now they were ready for their life together. Truly ready.

'What is Emma up to now?' she heard Hayden say. She glanced back to see him coming out the open terrace doors, a platter of fruit in his hand. He had turned golden in the sun, his dark hair slightly lighter, and his smile gleamed.

It made Jane smile, too. 'She's running in the water like a hoyden, of course.'

Hayden laughed and sat down on the *chaise* next to her. He popped a glistening strawberry between her lips. Its sweetness burst on her tongue, as perfect as the day.

'I had another suitor beg me for permission to marry her this morning,' he said. 'It seems there's a line out the door every day.'

'I know.' Jane sighed. 'Yet she cares for none of them.'

'There is time for her to find the right one. None of these gadabouts are good enough.'

'I hope so. I want her to be as happy as we are one day.'

'No one could possibly be as happy as we are.' Hayden smiled and leaned over to kiss her, his lips sweeter than the strawberries, the sunlight. Sweeter than anything in the world.

It had been a long, rocky road to get here, full of storms and wrong turns. But it had led them here, to this perfect moment. To a future together, as a family.

Jane gently touched Hayden's cheek and smiled up at him. 'You're absolutely right. No one is as happy as we are.'

* * * * *

RUNNING FROM
SCANDAL

Prologue

England—1814

Emma Bancroft was very good at holding up walls. She grew more adept at it every time she went to a party, which was not very often. She was getting a great deal of practice at it tonight.

She pressed her back against the wall of the village assembly room and sipped at a glass of watery punch as she surveyed the gathering. It was a surprisingly large one considering the chilly, damp night outside. Emma would have thought most people would want to stay sensibly at home by their fires, not get dressed in their muslin and silk finery and go traipsing about in search of dance partners. Yet the long and narrow room was crowded with laughing, chattering groups dressed up in their finery.

Emma rather wished *she* were home by the fire. Not that she entirely minded a social evening. People were always so very fascinating. She loved nothing better than to find a superb vantage point by a convenient wall and settle down to listen to conversations. It was such fun to devise her own stories about what those conversations were really about, what secret lives everyone might be living behind their smiles and mundane chatter. It was like a good book.

But tonight she had left behind an actual good book at home in the library of Barton Park, along with her new puppy, Murray. Recently she had discovered the fascinations of botany, which had quite replaced her previous passions for Elizabethan architecture and the cultivation of tea in India. Emma often found new topics of education that fascinated her, and plants were a new one. Her father's dusty old library, mostly unexplored since his death so long ago, was full of wonders waiting to be discovered.

And tonight, with a cold rain blowing against the windows, seemed a perfect one for curling up with a pot of tea and her studies, Murray at her feet. But her sister Jane, usually all too ready for a quiet, solitary evening at home, had insisted they come to the assembly. Jane even brought out some of her fine London gowns for them to wear.

'I am a terrible sister for letting you live here like a hermit, Emma,' Emma remembered Jane saying as she held up a pale-blue silk gown. 'You are only sixteen and so pretty. You need to be dancing, and flirting and—well, doing what young, pretty ladies enjoy doing.'

'I enjoy staying here and reading,' Emma had protested, even as she had to admit the dress was very nice. Definitely prettier than her usual faded muslins, aprons and sturdy boots, though it would never do for digging up botanical specimens. Jane even let her wear their mother's pearl pendant tonight. But she could still be reading at home.

Or hunting for the lost, legendary Barton Park treasure, as their father had spent his life doing. But Jane didn't have to know about that. Her sister had too many other worries.

'I know you enjoy it, and that is the problem,' Jane had said, as she searched for a needle and thread to take the dress in. 'But you are growing up. We can't go on as we have here at Barton Park for ever.'

'Why not?' Emma argued. 'I love it here, just the two of us in our family home. We can do as we please here, and not worry about…'

About horrid schools, where stuck-up girls laughed and gossiped, and the dance master grabbed at Emma in the corridor. Where she had felt so, so alone. She was sent there when their mother died and Jane married the Earl of Ramsay, Hayden. Emma had never wanted her sweet sister to know what happened there. She never wanted anyone to know. Especially not about her foolish feelings for the handsome dance teacher, that vile man who had taken advantage of her girlish feelings to kiss her in the dark—and tried so much more before Emma could get away. He had quite put her off men for ever.

Emma saw the flash of worry in Jane's hazel eyes before she bent her head over the needle and Emma took her other hand with a quick smile.

'Of course we must have a night out, Jane, you are quite right,' she'd said, making herself laugh. 'You must be so bored here with just me and my books after your grand London life. We shall go to the assembly and have fun.'

Jane laughed, too, but Emma heard the sadness in it. The sadness had lingered ever since Jane brought Emma back to Barton Park almost three years before, when Jane's husband, the earl, hadn't appeared in many months. Emma didn't know what had happened between them in London and she didn't want to pry, but nor did she want to add to her sister's worry.

'My London life was not all that grand,' Jane said, 'and I am not sorry it's behind me. But soon it will be your time to go out in the world, Emma. The village doesn't have a wide society, true, but it's a start.'

And that was what Emma feared—that soon it would be her turn to step out into the world and she would make horrid mistakes. She was too impulsive by half, and even though she knew it she had no idea how to stop it.

So she stood by the wall, watching, sipping her punch, trying not to tear Jane's pretty dress. For an instant before they left Barton and Emma glimpsed herself in the mirror, she hadn't believed it was really her. Jane had put her blonde, curling hair up in a twisted bandeau of ribbons and, teamed with her mother's pearl necklace, even Emma had to admit the effect was much prettier than her everyday braid and apron.

The local young men seemed to agree as well. She noticed a group of them over by the windows: bluff, hearty, red-faced country lads dressed in their finest town evening coats and cravats, watching her and whispering. Which was exactly what she did not want. Not after Mr Milne, the passionate school music master. She turned away and pretended to be studiously observing something edifying across the room.

She saw Jane standing next to the refreshment table with a tall gentleman in a sombre dark-blue coat who had his back to Emma. Even though Emma was not having the very best of evenings, the smile on her sister's face made her glad they had ventured out after all.

Jane so seldom mentioned her estranged husband or their life in London, though Emma had always followed Jane's social activities in the newspapers while she was at school and knew it must have been very glamorous. Barton Park was not in the least glamorous, and even though Jane insisted she was most content, Emma wondered and worried.

Tonight, Jane was smiling, even laughing, her dark hair glossy in the candlelight and her lilac muslin-and-lace gown soft and pretty. She shook her head at something the tall gentleman said and gestured toward Emma with a smile. Emma stood up straighter as they both turned to look at her.

'Blast it all,' she whispered, and quickly smiled when an elderly lady nearby gave her a disapproving glance. But she couldn't help cursing just a little. For it was Sir David Marton who was talking to her sister.

Sir David had been visiting at Barton more often of late than Emma could like. He always came with his sister, Miss Louisa Marton, very proper and everything since his estate at Rose Hill was their nearest neighbour. But still. Jane *was* married, even though Lord Ramsay never came to Barton. And Sir David was too

handsome by half. Handsome, and far too serious. She
doubted he ever laughed at all.

She studied him across the room, trying not to frown.
He nodded at whatever Jane was saying, watching
Emma solemnly from behind his spectacles. She was
glad he wasn't near enough for her to see his eyes. They
were a strange, piercing pale-grey colour, and whenever he looked at her so steadily with them he seemed
to see far too much.

Emma unconsciously smoothed her skirt, feeling
young and fidgety and silly. Which was the very last
way she ever wanted to appear in front of Sir David.

He nodded again at Jane and gave her a gentle smile.
He always spoke so gently, so respectfully to Jane, with
a unique spark of humour in those extraordinary eyes.
He never had that gentle humour when he looked at
Emma. Then he was solemn and watchful.

Emma had never felt jealous of Jane before. How
could she be, when Jane was the best of sisters, and had
such unhappiness hidden in her heart? But when Sir
David Marton was around, Emma almost—*almost*—
did feel jealous.

And she could not fathom why. Sir David was not at
all the sort of man she was sure she could admire. He
was too quiet, too serious. Too—conventional. Emma
couldn't read him at all.

And now—oh, blast it all again! Now they were coming across the room toward her.

Emma nearly wished she had spoken with one of
the country squires after all. She never knew what to

say to Sir David that wouldn't make her feel young and foolish around him. That might make him smile at her.

'Emma dear, I was just talking to Sir David about your new interest in botany,' Jane said as they reached Emma's side.

Emma glanced up at Sir David, who was watching her with that inscrutable, solemn look. The smile he had given Jane was quite gone. It made her feel so very tongue-tied, as if words flew into her head only to fly right back out again. She hadn't felt so very nervous, so unsure, since she left school, and she did not like that feeling at all.

'Were you indeed?' Emma said softly, looking away from him.

'My sister mentioned that she drove past you on the lane a few days ago,' Sir David said, his tone as calm and serious as he looked. 'She said when she offered you a ride home you declared you had to finish your work. As it was rather a muddy day, Louisa found that a bit—interesting.'

Against her will, Emma's feelings pricked just a bit. She had never wanted to care what anyone thought of her, not after Mr Milne. Miss Louisa Marton was a silly gossip, and there was no knowing what exactly she had told her brother or what he thought of Emma now. Did he think her ridiculous for her studies? For her unladylike interests such as grubbing around in the dirt?

'I am quite the beginner in my studies,' Emma said. 'Finding plant specimens to study is an important part of it all. When the ground is damp can be the best time to collect some of them. But it was very kind of your sister to stop for me.'

'I fear Emma has little scope for her interests since she left school to come live here with me,' Jane said. 'I am no teacher myself.'

'Oh, no, Jane!' Emma cried, her shyness disappearing at her sister's sad, rueful tone. 'I love living at Barton. Mr Lorne at the bookshop here in the village keeps me well supplied. I have learned much more here than I ever did at that silly school. But perhaps Sir David finds my efforts dull.'

'Not at all, Miss Bancroft,' he said, and to her surprise she heard a smile in his voice. She glanced up at him to find that there was indeed a hint of a curve to his lips. There was even a flash of a ridiculously attractive dimple in his cheeks.

And she also realised she should *not* have looked at him. Up close he really was absurdly handsome, with a face as lean and carefully chiselled as a classical statue. His gleaming mahogany hair, which he usually ruthlessly combed down, betrayed a thick, soft wave in the damp air, tempting a touch. She wondered whimsically if he wore those spectacles in a vain attempt to keep ladies from fainting at his feet.

'You do not find them dull, Sir David?' Emma said, feeling foolish that she could find nothing even slightly cleverer to say.

'Not at all. Everyone, male or female, needs interests in life to keep their minds sharp,' he said. 'I was fortunate enough to grow up living near an uncle who boasts a library of over five thousand volumes. Perhaps you have heard of him? Mr Charles Sansom at Sansom House.'

'Five thousand books!' Emma cried, much louder than she intended. 'That must be a truly amazing sight. Has he any special interests?'

'Greek and Roman antiquities are a favourite of his, but he has a selection on nearly every topic. Including, I would imagine, botany,' he said, his smile growing. Emma had never seen him look so young and open before and she unconsciously swayed closer to him. 'He always let us read whatever we liked when we visited him, though I fear my sister seldom took him up on the offer.'

Emma glanced across the room toward Miss Louisa Marton, who was easy to spot in her elaborately feathered turban. She was talking with her bosom bow, Miss Maude Cole, the beauty of the neighbourhood with her red-gold curls, sky-blue eyes and fine gowns. They in turn were looking back at Emma and whispering behind their fans.

Just like all those silly girls at school had done.

'I would imagine not,' Emma murmured. She had never heard Miss Marton or Miss Cole talk of anything but hats or the weather. 'Does your uncle still live nearby, Sir David? I should so love to meet him one day.'

'He does, Miss Bancroft, though I fear he has become quite reclusive in his advancing age. He still sometimes purchases volumes at Mr Lorne's shop, though, so perhaps you will encounter him there one day. He would find you most interesting.'

Before Emma could answer, the orchestra, a local group of musicians more noted for their enthusiasm than their talent, launched into the opening strains of a mazurka.

'Oh, I do love such a lively dance,' Jane said. Emma saw that her sister looked towards the forming set with a wistful look on her face. 'A mazurka was the first dance I—'

Suddenly Jane broke off with a strange little laugh and Emma wondered if she had often danced a mazurka with her husband in London. Surely even though she never mentioned her husband she had to think of him often.

'Jane…' Emma began.

Sir David turned to Jane with one of his gentle smiles. 'Perhaps you would care to dance, Lady Ramsay? My skills at the mazurka are quite rusty, but I would be honoured if you would be my partner.'

For a second, Jane seemed to hesitate, a flash of what looked like temptation in her eyes, and Emma felt an unwelcome pang of jealousy. Jealousy—of Jane! Loathing herself for that feeling, she pushed it away and made herself smile.

'Oh, no, I fear my dancing days are quite behind me,' Jane said. 'But books are not the only thing Emma studied at school. They also had a fine dancing master.'

A horrid dancing master. Emma didn't like him intruding on every moment of her life like this. Would she ever forget him?

'Then perhaps Miss Bancroft would do me the honour,' Sir David said politely. He turned to Emma and half-held out his hand.

And she suddenly longed so much to know what it felt like to have his hand on hers. To be close to him as he led her in the turns and whirls of the dance. Surely he would be strong and steady, never letting her fall, so warm and safe. Maybe he would even smile at her again and those beautiful grey eyes would gleam with admiration as he looked at her. She wanted all those things so very much.

She hadn't felt such romantic yearnings since—since Mr Milne first arrived at her school. And look at what disasters that led to. No, she couldn't trust her feelings, her impulsive emotions, ever again.

Emma fell back a step, shaking her head, and Sir David's hand dropped back to his side. His smile faded and he looked solemn and inscrutable again.

'I—I don't care to dance tonight,' Emma stammered, confused by old memories and new emotions she didn't understand. She had made a mistake with Mr Milne, a mistake in trusting him and her feelings. She needed to learn how to be cautious and calm, like Jane. Like Sir David.

'Of course not, Miss Bancroft,' Sir David said quietly. 'I quite understand.'

'David, dear,' Miss Louisa Marton said. Emma spun around to find that Miss Marton and Miss Cole had suddenly appeared beside them from the midst of the crowd. She'd been so distracted she hadn't even noticed them approach. Miss Cole watched them with a coolly amused smile on her beautiful face, making Emma feel even more flustered.

'David, dear,' Louisa said again. 'Do you not remember that Miss Cole promised you the mazurka? You were quite adamant that she save it for you and I know how much both of you have looked forward to it.'

Sir David gave Emma one more quizzical glance before he turned away to offer his hand to Miss Cole instead. 'Of course. Most delighted, Miss Cole.'

Emma watched him walk away, Miss Cole laughing and sparkling up at him with an easy flirtatiousness Emma knew she herself could never match. She felt suddenly cold in the crowded, overheated room and rubbed at her bare arms.

'I know you think Sir David is rather dull, Emma,' Jane said quietly, 'but truly he is quite nice. You should have danced with him.'

'I am a terrible dancer,' Emma said, trying to sound light and uncaring. 'No doubt I would have trod on his toes and he would have felt the need to lecture me on decorum.'

Jane shook her head, but Emma knew she couldn't really put into words her true feelings, her fears of what might happen if she got too close to the handsome, intriguing Sir David Marton. She didn't even know herself what those true feelings were. She only knew David Marton wasn't the sort of man for her.

Emma Bancroft was a most unusual young lady.

David tried to catch a glimpse of her over the heads of the other dancers gathered around him, but the bright glow of her golden hair had vanished. He almost laughed at himself for the sharp pang of disappointment at her disappearance. He was too old, too responsible, to think about a flighty, pretty girl like Miss Bancroft. A girl who obviously didn't much like him.

Yet the disappointment was there, unmistakably. When she was near, she always intrigued him. What was she thinking when she studied the world around her so closely? Her sister said she studied botany, among other interests, and David found himself most curious to know what those interests were. He wanted to know far too much about her and that couldn't be.

He had no place for someone like Emma Bancroft in his life now and she had no room for him. She seemed to be in search of far more excitement than he could ever give her. After watching his seemingly quiet father's secret temper tantrums when he was a boy, he had vowed to keep control over his life at all times. It had almost been a disaster for David's family and their home when he did briefly lose control. Once, he had spent too much time in London, running with a wild crowd, gambling and drinking too much, being attracted to the wrong sort of female, thinking he could forget his life in such pursuits. Until he saw how his actions hurt other people and he knew he had to change.

As David listened to the opening bars of the dance music and waited for his turn to lead his partner down the line, he caught a glimpse of his sister watching him with an avid gleam in her eyes. Ever since their parents died and he became fully responsible for their family estate at Rose Hill and for Louisa herself, she had been determined to find him a wife. 'A proper wife,' she often declared, by which she meant one of her own friends. A young lady from a family they knew well, one Louisa liked spending time with and who would make few changes to their household.

Not a girl like Miss Bancroft, who Louisa had expressed disapproval of more than once. 'I cannot fathom her,' Louisa had mused after encountering Miss Bancroft on the road. 'She is always running about the countryside, her hems all muddy, with that horrid dog. No propriety at all. And her sister! Where is Lady Ramsay's husband, I should like to know? How can the earl just let the two of them ramble about at Barton Park like that? The house is hardly fit to be lived in. Though we must be nice to them, I suppose. They *are* our neighbours.'

David suddenly glimpsed Lady Ramsay as she moved around the edge of the dance floor, seeming to look for someone. Her sister, perhaps? Miss Bancroft was nowhere to be seen. David had to agree that the Bancroft sisters' situation was an odd one and not one his own highly respectable parents would have understood. The two women lived alone in that ramshackle old house, seldom going out into neighbourhood society, and Lord Ramsay was never seen. Lady Ramsay often seemed sad and distant and Miss Bancroft very protective of her, which was most admirable.

David thought they also seemed brave and obviously devoted to each other. Another thing about Miss Bancroft that was unusual—and intriguing.

Suddenly he felt a nudging touch to his hand and glanced down in surprise to find he still stood on the crowded dance floor. And what was more, it was his turn in the figures as the music ran on around him.

Miss Cole smiled up at him, a quick, dazzling smile of flirtatious encouragement, and he led her down the line of dancers in the quick, leaping steps of the dance. She spun under his arm, light and quick, the jewels in her twists of red-gold hair flashing.

'Very well done, Sir David,' she whispered.

Miss Cole, unlike Miss Bancroft, was exactly the sort of young lady his sister wanted to see him marry. The daughter of a local, eminently respectable squire, and friends with Louisa for a long time: pretty and accomplished, sparkling in local society, well dowered. The kind of wife who would surely run her house well and fit seamlessly into his carefully built life. And she seemed to like him.

Miss Bancroft was assuredly not for him. She was too young, too eccentric, for them to ever suit. His whole life had been so carefully planned by his family and by himself. He almost threw it all away once. He couldn't let that happen again now. Not for some strange fascination.

Miss Cole, or a lady like her, would make him a fine wife. Why could he not stop searching the room for a glimpse of Emma Bancroft?

From the diary of Arabella Bancroft—1663

> *I have at last arrived at Barton Park. It was not a long journey, but it feels as if I have ventured to a different world. Aunt Mary's house in London,*

*the endless hours of sewing while she bemoaned
all that was lost to her in the wars between the
king and Parliament, the filth in the streets—here
where everything is green and fresh and new, all
that is almost forgotten.*

*I know I must be grateful to be brought here
to my cousin's beautiful new manor, this gift to
him from the new king. I am a poor orphan of
seventeen and must live as I can. Yet I cannot
understand why I am here. My cousin's wife has
enough maids. I have nothing yet to do but settle
into my new chamber—my very own, not shared!
Heaven!—and explore the lovely gardens.*

*But my chambermaid has told me the most in-
triguing tale—it seems that during the wars one
of King Charles's men hid a great treasure near
here. And it has never been found.*

I do love a puzzle.

Chapter One

Six years later

*B*arton Park. Emma could hardly believe she was there again, after so much time. It felt as if she had been swept up in a whirlwind from one world and dropped into another, it was all so strange.

She stood at the rise of a hill, staring down along the grey ribbon of road to the gates of Barton. They stood slightly open, as if waiting to welcome her home, but Barton no longer felt like home. There was no longer anywhere that felt like home now. She was just a little piece of gossamer flotsam, blown back to these gates.

She gathered her black skirts in one hand to keep them from tossing around her in the wind. The carriage waited for her patiently on the road below, halted on its uneventful journey from London to here when she insisted on getting out to look around. Her brother-in-law's driver and footmen waited quietly, no doubt fully informed by downstairs gossip about the unpredictable ways of Lady Ramsay's prodigal sister.

Emma knew she should hurry inside. The wind was brisk and the pale-grey clouds overhead threatened rain. Her old dog, Murray, whined a bit and nudged with his cold nose at her gloved hand, but he wouldn't leave her side. Murray, at least, had never changed.

Yet she couldn't quite bring herself to go to the house just yet.

She'd left Barton five years ago as Miss Emma Bancroft, full of hopes and fears for her first London Season. She came back now as Mrs Carrington, young widow, penniless, shadowed by gossip and scandal. The fears still lingered, but the hope was quite, quite gone.

She held up her hand to shield her eyes from the glare of the light and studied the red-brick chimneys of Barton rising through the swaying banks of trees. Spring was on the way, she could see it in the fresh, pale green buds on the branches, could smell the damp-flower scent of it on the wind. Once she had loved spring at Barton. A time of new beginnings, new dreams.

Emma wanted to feel that way again, she wanted it so desperately. Once she had been so eager to run out and discover everything life had to offer. But that led only to disaster, over and over. It ended in a life with Henry Carrington.

Emma closed her eyes against a sudden spasm of pain that rippled through her. Henry. So handsome, so charming, so dazzling to her entire senses. He was like a whirlwind, too, and he swept her along with him, giddy and full of raw, romantic joy.

Until that giddiness turned to madness and led them on a downward spiral through Continental spa towns where there was plenty of gambling to be had. Henry was always so sure their fortunes would turn around soon, on the turn of the next card, at the bottom of the next bottle. It only led them to shabbier and shabbier lodgings on shadier streets with uncertain friends.

It led Henry to death at the wrong end of a duelling pistol, wielded by the husband of a woman he claimed to have fallen in love with at Vichy. And it took Emma back here to Barton, when she found the scandal had blocked her escape anywhere else.

'Let me help you,' Henry's cousin Philip had said, grasping her hand tightly in his when he gave her the news of the fatal duel. 'Henry would have wanted it that way. And you know how very much I have always admired you. Dearest Emma.'

Philip had indeed always been Henry's friend, a friend who caroused with him, but also loaned him money, made sure he made it home, visited Emma when she was alone and frightened in strange rooms with no knowledge of when Henry might return. She appreciated Philip's kindness, even in moments when his attentions seemed to ease over a line of propriety.

In that moment, with Henry so newly dead and the shock so cold around her, she was almost tempted to let Philip 'take care of her'. To give in to the loneliness and fear. But then she looked into his eyes and saw something there that frightened her even more. A gleam of possessive passion she saw once in Mr Milne, the dancing master, and in that villain who had once kidnapped her in the rainstorm at Barton.

The same look they had just before they violently attacked her.

So she sent Philip away, swallowed her pride, and wrote to her sister. Jane had warned her against Henry when Emma wanted to marry him, had even threatened to make Emma wait a year before she would even agree to an engagement, which led to Emma eloping and causing the first of many great scandals. And then Henry had found out that Jane and her husband had tied Emma's dowry and small inheritance from her mother up so tightly he could never touch them and some of his passion died.

While Emma wandered the Continent in Henry's wake, Jane wrote sometimes, and they even saw each other once when the Ramsays were touring Italy. They were not completely estranged, but Jane would never give in when it came to the money. 'It is yours, Emma, when you need it,' she insisted and so Henry cut Emma off from the Ramsays.

But when Emma wrote after Henry's death, Jane immediately sent money and servants to fetch her home, since Jane herself was too pregnant to travel. Jane would never abandon her, Emma knew that. Only her own embarrassment and shame had kept her away from Barton until now, had kept her from leaving Henry and seeking the shelter of her childhood home. She wondered what she would find beyond those gates.

Murray whined louder and leaned against her. Emma laughed and patted his head with her black-gloved hand.

'I'm sorry, old friend,' she said. 'I know it's cold out here. We'll go inside now.'

He trotted behind her down the hill and climbed back into the carriage at her side. For some months, Murray had seemed to be getting older, with rheumatic joints and a greying muzzle, but he wagged his plumy tail eagerly as they bounced past the gates. He seemed to realise they were almost home.

The drive to Barton was a long, picturesquely winding one, meandering gently between groves of trees, old statues and teasing glimpses of chimneys and walls. In the distance, Emma could see the old maze, the white, peaked rooftops of the rebuilt summerhouse at its centre peeking up above the hedges. In the other direction were the fields and meadows of Rose Hill, the Marton estate, and its picturesque ruins of the old medieval castle, which she had long wanted to explore.

Then the carriage came to a V in the drive. One way led to a cluster of old cottages, once used for retired estate retainers, and old orchards. The other way led to the house itself.

Emma leaned out of the window next to Murray and watched as Barton itself came into view. Built soon after the return of Charles II for one of his Royalist supporters, Emma's ancestor, its red-brick walls, trimmed with white stonework and softened by skeins of climbing ivy, were warm and welcoming.

When Emma and Jane had lived there before Jane reconciled with Hayden, the walls had been slowly crumbling and the gardens overgrown. Now everything was fresh and pretty, the flowerbeds just turning green, the low hedge borders neatly trimmed, new statues brought from Italy gleaming white. Emma glimpsed gardeners on the pathways at the side of the house, busy with their trowels and shears.

So much had changed. So much was the same.

As the carriage rolled to a halt, the front door to the house flew open just as a footman hurried to help Emma alight. Jane came hurrying out, as quickly as she could with her pregnant belly impeding her usual graceful speed. Her hazel eyes sparkled and she was laughing as she clapped her hands.

'Emma, my darling! Here you are at last,' Jane cried. As soon as Emma's half-boots touched the gravelled drive, Jane swept her into her arms and kissed her cheek. 'Welcome home.'

Home. As Emma hugged her sister back, felt her warmth and breathed in the soft, flowery scent of her lilac perfume, she could almost feel at home again. In sanctuary. Safe.

But wandering anchorless around Europe, seeing the dark depths all sorts of people were capable of, had taught her there was really no place safe. And even as she wanted to hold tight to Jane now, the guilty memory of how she had hurt her sister by eloping, of Jane's disappointment, still stung.

Emma stepped back and forced a bright smile as Jane examined her closely. Emma had learned the art of hiding her true feelings with Henry, but still it was difficult to do. 'Barton is looking splendid. And so are you, Jane. Positively blooming.'

Jane laughed ruefully as she gently smoothed her hand over her belly. 'I'm as big as a barouche now, I fear, and twice as lumbering. But I've felt much better this time than I did with the twins, hardly any morning sickness at all. I'll feel all the better now with you here, Emma. I've missed you so much.'

'And I've missed you.' More even than Emma had realised all those lonely months. 'And Barton.'

Jane took her arm and led her into the hall. Emma saw the changes to Barton were not just on the outside. The old, scarred parquet floor was replaced with fashionable black-and-white marble tiles. A newly re-gilded balustrade curved up along the staircase, which was laid with a thick blue-and-gold carpet runner. A marble-topped table held a large arrangement of hot-house roses and blue satin chairs lined up along the silk-striped walls.

But Emma didn't have much time to examine the refurbishments.

'Is that our Aunt Emma?' a tiny, fluting voice called out, echoing down the stairs. Emma glanced up to find two little faces, with two matching sets of hazel eyes and mops of blond curls, peering down at her from the landing.

'I am your Aunt Emma,' she said, her heart feeling as if it would burst at this sight of the twins, who she hadn't seen in so very long. 'You must be William and Eleanor. You are much bigger than when I last saw you. Back then you were about as large as a loaf of bread.'

The two of them giggled and quickly came dashing and tumbling down the stairs to land at her feet. They peered up at her with curiosity shining from their eyes, eyes that were so much like their mother's.

'You're much younger than we imagined,' William said.

'And thinner,' Eleanor added. 'You should eat some cream cakes.'

'Children!' Jane admonished. 'Manners, please.'

They curtsied and bowed with murmured 'How do you do's' before Jane sent them off to find tea in the drawing room.

'I am so sorry, Emma,' Jane said as they turned to follow the children. 'Hayden and I, and their nannies, work so hard to teach them how to be a viscount and a lady, but they are at such an outspoken age.'

Emma laughed. 'Rather like we were back then? Though I fear I have not quite outgrown it, whereas *you* are the perfect countess.' Suddenly she glimpsed a pile of travel trunks near the drawing-room doors. 'Are you going somewhere?'

'We were planning to go to London for my confinement,' Jane said. 'Hayden thinks I should be near the doctors there. But now that you are here…'

'You must still go,' Emma said firmly, a bit relieved she might have a few days to find her feet without Jane worrying over her as well as the new baby. 'Your health comes first. You can't worry about me now.'

'But you can't rattle around Barton all alone! You could come with us to London.'

London was the last place Emma wanted to be. All those watching eyes and gossiping tongues, all too ready to stir up the old scandal-broth of her elopement and disastrous marriage. 'Actually, I was thinking I could use one of the old cottages. They are so small and cosy, a perfect place for me to decide what I should do next.'

'Live in one of the cottages,' Jane exclaimed. 'Oh, Emma dear, no. This is your house.'

'But you said yourself, it is too big for one person. And I can't go to London now. Not yet. You wrote that Hayden was seeing about releasing my small inheritance from Mama to me soon—I can make do on that in the cottage.'

'But...' Jane looked all set for an argument, but she was, luckily, distracted by the twins calling for her. 'We will talk about this later, Emma,' she said as they hurried into the drawing room.

Emma was sure there would be a long talk later, yet she was set. A small cottage, where she could be alone and think, would be perfect for her now. She would be out of Jane's way, and she could decipher how not to make such foolish mistakes again.

The twins were already settling in next to a lavishly appointed tea table near the windows that looked out on the gardens. Light gleamed on their grandmother's silver tea service and platters of sandwiches and cakes, all cut into pretty shapes and arranged in artistic pyramids.

The children eyed the display avidly, but sat quietly with hands innocently folded in their laps.

'All this for me?' Emma said with a laugh.

'Hannah missed you, too,' Jane said, mentioning the woman who had been their maid for many years. In poorer times she was their *only* maid, but now she was housekeeper of Barton.

'Here, Aunt Emma, you must have *this* cake,' Eleanor said, passing her a pink-frosted confection.

'Thank you very much, Eleanor dear,' Emma said, sure her niece was most serious now about fattening her up. As they sipped at their tea, she studied the gardens outside. The terraces of flowerbeds sloped gently down to the maze and she was sure when summer came it would be a glorious riot of colour. 'What has been happening in the village of late? Anything interesting?'

'Oh, yes, a great deal,' Jane said enthusiastically. 'There is a new vicar, an excellent gentleman by the name of Mr Crawford. He is Lady Wheelington's son from her first marriage. I am sure you must remember my friend Lady Wheelington? She is newly home from abroad herself. Mr Crawford is sadly yet unmarried, but I am sure that will soon be remedied. His mother has hinted of a young lady from Brighton. And old Lady Firth finally won the flower show last year! It was long past time. And Sir David Marton has come back to Rose Hill at last.'

'Sir David Marton?' Emma said, startled by the name. She feared the words came out much sharper than she intended and quickly turned away to nibble at her cake. 'I hadn't realised he ever left. He didn't seem the adventurous sort.'

'So you do remember Sir David?' Jane said.

Of course Emma remembered him. How very handsome he was. The way he seemed to admire Jane's sweet ways so much. The way he would look at Emma, so carefully, so close and calm, until she feared he could see her every secret.

How would he look at her now, after everything that had happened? Would he even speak to her at all?

Somehow the thought of Sir David's disapproval made her heart sink just a bit.

'I do remember him,' she said.

'Yes. He was quite kind to us when things looked rather bleak, wasn't he? And he was such a help that night of the fire.'

He had been kind to Jane, always. 'Yet you say he left the village?'

'Yes. He married Miss Maude Cole. Do you remember her as well?'

Miss Cole, who Sir David had danced with at that long-ago assembly. Pretty, vivacious Miss Cole. The perfect wife for a man like him. 'Of course. She was quite lovely and good friends with his sister, as I recall, so such a match makes sense.'

Jane arched her brow. 'So everyone thought.'

'Was it not a good match after all?'

'No one knows for sure. Lady Marton preferred town life, so soon after the wedding they went off to London and rarely came back here. Hayden and I have mostly been at Ramsay House or here at Barton, but we heard she was quite the toast.'

'Was?'

'Sadly, Lady Marton died last year, and Sir David has come back to Rose Hill with his little daughter. We haven't seen them very much, but the poor child does seem very quiet.'

'She must miss her mother,' Emma said quietly. Surely Sir David also missed his pretty wife. She was sure he would never have allowed his marital life to grow messy and discordant as hers had. The poor little girl, how she must feel the terrible loss.

'Miss Louisa Marton, who is now Mrs Smythe, is said to be most earnestly searching for a new sister-in-law,' Jane said.

'She must surely be disappointed at the lack of scope for matchmaking around here,' Emma said, making her tone light. She didn't want to talk or think about Sir David any longer. It only reminded her of how very different things were now from when she last met with him. 'Tell me, William and Eleanor, do you like to play blindman's buff? It was your mama's favourite game when we were children, though you may not believe me now. Perhaps we could play a round later...'

From the diary of Arabella Bancroft

I think I have discovered one of the reasons I was summoned to Barton. In return for the gift of the estate, the king expects my cousin to host many parties for his court. My cousin's wife's health does not allow her to play hostess to such a raucous crowd, thus my place here. I know little of planning grand balls, but I confess I do love the new clothes—so much silk and lace, so many feathered hats and furred capes!

And the people who come here are most intriguing. I have seldom had the chance for such conversation before, and once I am an improved card player I shall surely fit in better.

I have been asking about the lost treasure, but beyond ever more fantastical tales I can find out nothing...

Chapter Two

The silence in the carriage was absolutely deafening.

David looked down at his daughter, Beatrice, who perched beside him on the seat of the curricle. Most of her face was hidden by the brim of her straw bonnet, but he could see the tip of her upturned nose and the corner of her mouth, unsmiling as she watched the lane go by. Her red-gold curls, tied neatly at the nape of her neck with a pink bow, laid in a glossy stream down the back of her blue-velvet spencer.

Bea always looked like the perfect little lady, a pretty porcelain doll in her fashionable clothes, with a real doll usually tucked under her arm as her constant companion. All the ladies they ever met exclaimed and cooed over her. 'A perfect angel, David,' his sister always crowed. 'Why, she never cries or fusses at all! And after all she's been through…'

Louisa was right. Bea *was* an angel, always playing quietly with her dolls or attending to lessons with her nanny. But was she *too* quiet? Too self-contained for a five-year-old?

Even now, on a lovely, warm, early spring day, when children were dashing along the lane with their hoops and skipping ropes, shouting and laughing, she just watched them with no expression on her little face.

'After I conclude my business in the village, perhaps we could go to the toy shop and get you one of those hoops,' David said as he guided the horses around a corner. 'What do you think, Bea?'

She turned to look up at him for the first time since they left Rose Hill. Her grey eyes were unblinking. 'No, thank you, Papa.'

'It shouldn't be hard to learn how to use it. I could teach you in the garden.'

Bea shook her head. 'Aunt Louisa says you have a lot of business to attend to since we came back to Rose Hill and I shouldn't get in your way.'

Of course Louisa would say that. It was his way of avoiding her gatherings, which seemed designed to introduce him to as many eligible young ladies as possible. But his heart ached that Bea took that to mean he had no time for *her*. Bea had been the light of his life ever since she first appeared and everything he did was for her. 'No matter how much business I have, I'll always have time for you, Bea. I hope you know that.'

'I don't need a hoop, Papa.' She turned her attention to the scenery, to the scattered cottages that marked the edge of the village and the square, stone bell tower of the church.

It hadn't always been like that, David thought with a feeling surging through him that felt near desperation. Once Bea had run through the house as lively and laughing as any of the village children. She had thrown herself into his arms, giggling as he twirled her around. She'd served him tea at her tiny table in her tiny porcelain cups, chattering all the time.

Until her mother died. No—he had to say it honestly, at least to himself. Until her mother left them, ran off with her lover, only to be killed with him when their carriage overturned on a rocky Scottish road. Bea knew nothing of that sordid tale. David had only told her Maude had become very ill and gone to take the waters, where she passed away. But ever since then Bea had withdrawn deep into herself, quiet as one of her precious dolls.

David hoped that leaving London permanently and coming home to Rose Hill, near his sister and her family, would bring her out of her shell again. Surely children thrived in fresh air and clear skies? Yet it only seemed to make Bea even quieter.

David liked to be in control of his world; he needed that. He was good at business, at running his estate, improving crop yields, taking care of his tenants and his family. When their parents died, he took care of his sister until she married. He had been a good son, a good brother, and he prided himself on that. He had even been a good husband, had given up his brief wild period of gambling and other women, and devoted himself to his wife. He had seen where such a rakish life led and he hadn't wanted it for himself in the end.

Why, then, had he failed so badly as a husband, and now as a father?

As he looked at his daughter now, her little back

so straight as she perched next to him on the seat, his heart ached with how much he loved her. How much he wanted to help her and could not.

The anger he had long felt towards Maude, which he had tried to shove away and forget, still came out when he saw how Bea had become. Maude—so pretty, so charming. So frivolous. In the beginning, she looked suitable to be his wife, until he found her charm masked desperate emotionalism, a heedless romanticism that made her utterly abandon her family and duties. Just as he had once come so close to doing.

'You should marry again,' his sister told him over and over. 'If Beatrice had a new mother, and Rose Hill had a proper mistress, all would be well. What about Lady Penelope Hader? Or Miss King?'

He had taken Louisa's advice the first time and married her good friend Miss Cole. He should not look twice at any of her candidates again. But she was right about one thing—some day he would have to marry again. But this time he would find a lady of good, solid sense and impeccable reputation and family. A lady who would join him in his duties and be content with a quiet, solid country life.

He was absolutely determined on that. He, and more importantly Beatrice, needed no more romantic adventurers in their lives.

The village was busy on such a fine day. The narrow walkways were crowded with people hurrying on their errands, and the doors and windows to the shops were flung open to let in the fresh breeze. There seemed to be a new energy in the air that always came with the first signs of green, growing things—an invigorated purpose.

David wished he could feel it too. That new, fresh, clean hope. Yet still there was only a strange numbness at his core.

Work was the answer. The forgetfulness of purposeful work. He left the curricle at the livery stables and took Bea's lace-gloved hand in his to lead her out into the lane. She went with him without a murmur, her doll tucked under her other arm.

'I won't be long at the lawyer's office, Bea,' he said. 'If you don't want to visit the toy shop, perhaps we could get a sweet afterwards? You haven't had one of those lemon drops you like in a while.'

'Thank you, Papa,' she murmured.

Their progress down the street was slow, as several people stopped David to offer him greetings or ask questions about his plans for Rose Hill. He hadn't been home long enough for curiosity to fade about his London scandal, and he could almost feel the burn of curiosity in people's eyes as they talked to him. He could hear the careful tones of their voices, from people he had known since he was a child.

Even here the upheaval of his life couldn't quite be forgotten.

As they walked past the assembly rooms, he heard his sister's voice call out to him.

'David, dearest! I didn't know you were coming to the village today. You should have sent me word and I would have made you dine with us before you go back to Rose Hill,' Louisa cried.

David turned to see his sister hurrying toward him, her two little sons tumbling after her and her pregnant belly before her. The boys were shoving and tripping each other, as they so often did, and David felt Bea stiffen next to him.

'I didn't want you to go to any trouble, Louisa,' he said as he kissed her offered cheek under the flowered edge of her bonnet.

'No trouble at all. We see you too seldom,' Louisa answered. She carefully bent down and embraced Bea, who still held her little body very still. 'And how lovely you look today, Beatrice! My, but I do hope *this* one will be a girl. Boys, stop that fighting right now! Bow to your uncle.'

As the boys quickly bowed and muttered before shoving each other again, Louisa whispered in David's ear, 'Beatrice is looking awfully pale, isn't she? You should leave her with me while you conclude your business, she can play with her cousins. I'm sure she is too much alone at Rose Hill.'

Beatrice seemed to hear her and gave David an alarmed glance. 'Thank you for the kind offer, Louisa, but we must return home very soon today. Another time, I promise.'

Louisa sniffed. 'As you like, of course. But you know what Rose Hill and Beatrice need is more children running about the halls there! New little siblings, as you and I were. Have you met Miss Harding yet? She has come to stay with her uncle, Admiral Harding, and I quite admire her already. So pretty, so steady. Just what you need.'

Bea didn't say anything, or even move, but David felt her hand tighten on his. 'No, I have not yet met Miss Harding.'

'Then you must come to the assembly next week. She is sure to be there and I have sung your praises to her already.'

'I still have so much work to do at Rose Hill…'

'Don't say you must work all night as well as all day! You must get out in the world again, David. It would do you so much good. And you will never find a wife if you stay alone at Rose Hill all the time. Will he, Beatrice darling?'

'No, Aunt Louisa,' Bea said dutifully.

'Of course not. Now, David, let me tell you about Miss Harding…'

Louisa went on talking, but David's attention was suddenly captured by a figure hurrying along the walkway on the other side of the street.

She wasn't very tall, but was very straight and slender, with an elegant bearing and purpose to her step that seemed somehow familiar. Yet he was sure she couldn't be someone he knew, for she wore a black gown and pelisse and a plain black bonnet, and there were no recent widows in the village. Still, something about her compelled him to keep watching. Something vital and almost magnetic, something—alive.

David suddenly realised he hadn't felt *alive* in a very long time. Hadn't felt captured by something as he was by the glimpses of the lady in black.

Others, too, watched her as she passed them, turned

to stare at her, stopped in their tracks. But only a few actually offered her a greeting.

She stopped at the window of Mr Lorne's bookshop and, as she turned to examine the haphazard display of dusty volumes behind the cloudy glass, David caught a glimpse of her pale profile against the black ruching of her bonnet, as pure and perfect as a Grecian coin.

'Emma Bancroft,' he whispered, shocked by the sight of her. Now that he saw her again, he was surprised at how completely he recalled a girl he hadn't glimpsed in years. But where he felt a hundred years older than the man he had been at that long-ago assembly, Emma Bancroft looked exactly the same. Golden, sunny curls, a straight little nose dusted with pale amber freckles, rosebud lips curved in a smile as she studied the books. She looked just as young, just as eager to run out and grab life.

Yet she, too, must have faced a great deal since they last met, swathed in black as she was. She pushed open the door to the shop and vanished inside, and David's strangely silent, suspended moment crashed around him. The noisy bustle of the crowd. Bea's hand in his. The ceasing of his sister's stream of chatter.

'Oh, yes,' Louisa said with another sniff. 'Emma Bancroft. I did hear she had returned to Barton Park, though I'm surprised her sister would have her back after everything that happened. Hardly befitting the sister-in-law of an earl.'

David gave her a curious glance and Louisa smiled smugly. She always liked having gossip other people did not and David had lived buried in his own business since he came home. 'You will remember, I am sure, David. Or perhaps you won't, you are always so very busy. Do you not recall her infamous elopement with Mr Henry Carrington?'

David did remember vague whispers about it all. Emma Bancroft eloped with a known rake in her first Season, against her sister's advice. Word of it had floated all the way from London back to Rose Hill, everyone saying how sad it was, but really not very surprising. Miss Bancroft, after all, had always been such an odd girl with strange fancies. Other scandals soon eclipsed it, and by the time David went to London with Maude and their new baby there were only a few titters about Lady Ramsay's wayward sister. He assumed the rake and Miss Bancroft had settled into a reasonable marriage, away from England.

And Maude's own scandal soon quite overtook everything else. But David felt strangely disappointed when he remembered Miss Bancroft's—Mrs Carrington's—true nature. For an instant there, he was actually happy to glimpse her coming down the street, felt a rush of hope. Now the sunny, lively vibrancy he had imagined seemed more hoydenish and dangerously unpredictable.

He couldn't afford any more scandal in his life. Either his own or that of others.

'They say Mr Carrington died in a duel somewhere in France,' Louisa said. 'Now I suppose Lady Ramsay has no choice but to shelter her sister.'

As David had always had no choice in his own family? Faintly irritated, he said, 'Perhaps you think she should have left her sister in a Parisian workhouse.'

'David! You are quite shocking today. Of course Lady Ramsay had to take Mrs Carrington in, though it would have been more politic of Mrs Carrington to stay away after the stir she caused. But family is family, I suppose. I just hope she will stay quietly at Barton Park and not embarrass anyone.'

'I must attend to my business, Louisa,' he said, feeling the urge to defend Emma Bancroft, even from something indefensible. 'The lawyer is expecting me so we can go over my purchase of the lands adjacent to Rose Hill.'

'Oh, yes, of course. I know you are so terribly busy, David dear. Just don't forget about Miss Harding! We shall all be expecting you at the assembly next week.'

Murmuring some non-committal reply, David led Bea off down the street. She went with him quietly, leaving him to brood on that glimpse of Emma Bancroft's face. And wanting even more of what he knew he couldn't have.

Her papa did *not* need another wife. At least not one her Aunt Louisa chose for him.

Bea swung her feet from the tall chair she sat perched on as she waited for her papa to conclude his business. He and the grey-haired, saggy-faced lawyer, Mr Wall, talked on and on with words she didn't understand and the warm close air of the office smelled of old cigars and dust, but Bea didn't care. The more they talked, and the more they ignored her as she sat quietly in the corner, the more she could watch and think.

It was a strategy that had worked very well for her since her mother went away. Things had been so very confusing for a while, the doors of the London house slamming and people coming and going at all hours. Her Grandfather Cole shouting and red-faced. Her papa, who usually played with her and laughed with her, so quiet and serious all the time.

And every time he looked at her he seemed very sad. There were no more tea parties or quiet hours for reading books together. He would send her to the park with her nanny and lock himself in the library.

And no one ever told her anything at all. Tears and shouted questions got her nothing but pitying looks and new dolls. While the dolls *were* nice, she still wanted to know where her mother had really gone and when her real papa was coming back to her.

That was when she learned to be quiet and watch. When she tucked herself away in corners, people forgot she was there and talked about things in quiet, calm ways with no baby-speak. Bea *hated* baby-speak. Her father had never spoken to her that way and most grown-ups had long ago given it up with her, until her mother left. Then no one talked to her any other way.

Especially Aunt Louisa. Bea sighed as she smoothed her doll's silk skirt and thought of Aunt Louisa. She was a very good sort of aunt, always kind and generous with the lemon drops, but her insistence that Bea play with her horrid sons was a nuisance. Those boys had no interesting conversation at all, and they always tried to steal her dolls. Once they even cut the curls off one, making Bea cry and Aunt Louisa scream.

Days at Aunt Louisa's house were not much fun. Even waiting here in this dull office was better.

But what made time with Aunt Louisa even worse was that she always told Papa he should marry again as fast as possible. She even insisted Bea needed a new mother.

Bea did not want a new mother. She'd hardly ever seen the one she once had, except for glimpses out the window when her mother was climbing into a carriage to go off to a party. She'd been as beautiful as an angel, all sparkling and laughing in her lovely gowns, but not much use. Nor would a mother like Aunt Louisa be much fun, always calling for her vinaigrette when she wasn't telling everyone what to do.

Not that Bea *completely* objected to the idea of a mother. Mothers in books always looked like lovely things, always tying their daughters' hair ribbons and reading them stories. And Papa did need someone to help him smile more.

Aunt Louisa's Miss Harding, niece of Admiral Harding, didn't quite sound like what Bea had in mind. Anyone Aunt Louisa chose would surely be entirely wrong for Rose Hill. Bea knew she was only a little girl, but she also knew what she wanted, and what Papa needed.

She just didn't know where to find it.

'…in short, Sir David, the sale of the lands should go through at that price with no problems whatsoever,' the old lawyer said. 'Your estate at Rose Hill will be considerably enlarged, if you are sure more responsibility is what you truly desire right now.'

'Have you heard complaints about my lack of responsibility, Mr Wall?' Papa said, with what Bea suspected was amusement in his voice, though she didn't understand the joke. She hoped he might even smile, but he didn't.

'Not at all, of course. You have a great reputation in the area as a good, and most progressive, landlord with a great interest in agriculture. Once you get those lands organised, you'll have no trouble whatsoever leasing the farms. But there can be such a things as working *too* hard, or so Mrs Wall sometimes informs me.'

'Is there?' Papa said quietly. 'I have not found it so.'

'A wife, Sir David, can be a great help. The right sort of wife, of course, an excellent housekeeper, a hostess, a companion. But I fear we are boring pretty Miss Marton here! Would you care for a sweet, my dear? Sugared almonds—my grandsons love them, so I always keep them about.'

'Thank you, Mr Wall,' Bea answered politely. As she popped the almond into her mouth, she thought over what Mr Wall said. A hostess for Rose Hill—another thing to put on her list of requirements for a new mother.

As they took their leave of Mr Wall and stepped back out into the lane, Bea shivered at the cool breeze after the stuffy offices.

'We should get you home, Bea, before you catch a chill,' Papa said as he took her hand.

But Bea didn't quite want to go back to the quiet nursery at Rose Hill just yet. Neither did she want to go

visit Aunt Louisa. 'Could we go to the bookshop first?'
she asked. 'Maybe Mr Lorne has some new picture
books from London. I've read everything in the nursery at least twice now.' And Aunt Louisa and her sons
never went in the bookshop. It was always quite safe.

Her papa seemed to hesitate, which was most odd,
for he was usually most agreeable to visiting Mr Lorne's
shop. He glanced towards the building across the street,
his eyes narrowed behind his spectacles as if he tried to
peer past the dusty windows. But finally he nodded and
led her across the street to the waiting shop.

Chapter Three

Emma smiled at the familiar sound of rusted bells clanking as she pushed open the door to Mr Lorne's bookshop. It had been so long since she heard them, but once they had been one of the sweetest sounds in the world to her. They had meant escape.

Could she ever find the same sanctuary in books again? The same forgetfulness in learning? Or did she know too much about what lay outside the pages now?

As she closed the door behind her, she thought about the way people watched her as she walked down the street, silent and wide-eyed. She hadn't left the grounds of Barton much since her arrival, wanting only the healing quiet of home. Days wandering around the rooms and gardens, reminiscing with Jane and playing games with the children, had been wonderful indeed. She'd almost begun to remember herself again and forget what she had seen in her life with Henry.

But now Jane and Hayden had gone off to London, and without them and the boisterous twins the estate was much too silent. Emma needed to purchase some things for her refurbishment of her cottage and she needed reading materials for the quiet evenings at her small fireside. That meant a trip into the village.

She hadn't been expecting a parade to greet her, of course. She had been gone for such a long time and in such an irregular way. Yet neither had she expected such complete silence. They had looked at her as if she were a ghost.

Emma was tired of being a ghost. She wanted to be alive again, feel alive in a way she hadn't since her marriage to Henry fell apart so spectacularly in its very infancy. She just wasn't sure how to do that.

Mr Lorne's shop seemed like a good place to start. Emma smiled as she looked around at the familiar space. It appeared not to have changed at all in the years she had been gone. The rows of shelves were still jammed full of haphazardly organised volumes, wedged in wherever there was an inch. More books were stacked on the floors and on the ladders.

The windows, which had never been spotless, were even more streaked with dust than ever, and only a few faint rays of daylight slanted through them. Colza lamps lit the dark corners and gave off a faint flowery smell that cut through the dryness of paper, glue and old leather. Once Emma's eyes adjusted to the gloom, she saw Mr Lorne's bushy grey head peeking over a tottering tower of books on his desk.

'Good heavens,' he said. 'Is it really you, Miss Bancroft?'

Emma laughed, relieved that she really wasn't a ghost after all. *Someone* could acknowledge her. She hurried over to shake Mr Lorne's hand, now worryingly thin and wrinkled.

'Indeed it is me, Mr Lorne,' she said. 'Though I am Mrs Carrington now.'

'Ah, yes,' he said vaguely. 'I do remember you had gone away. No one pestered me for new volumes on plants any more.'

'You were always ready to indulge my passion for whatever topic I fancied,' Emma said, remembering her passion for botany and nature back then. Maybe she should try to find that again?

'You were one of my best customers. So what do you fancy now?'

'I'm not quite sure.' Emma hesitated, studying the old shop as she peeled off her gloves. The black kid was already streaked with dust. 'I'm refurbishing one of the old cottages on the Barton estate, but I'm not sure what I'll do after that. I don't suppose you ever did come across any old writings about the early days of Barton?' Before she left home, Emma had been passionately involved in researching her family's home, especially searching for the legendary Barton treasure. But nothing had ever come of it.

'I don't think so.'

'Then maybe some novels? Something amusing for a long evening?'

'There I *can* help you, Mrs Carrington.' Mr Lorne carefully climbed down from his stool and picked up a walking stick before leading her to a shelf against the far wall. Just like always, she saw he had an organisational system understood only by himself. 'These are some of the latest from London. But I fear I can't help you decide what to do next any more than I can help myself.'

Emma glanced at the old man, surprised by the sad, defeated tone on his voice. The Mr Lorne she remembered had always been most vigorous and cheerful, in love with his work and eager to share the books on his shelf. 'Whatever do you mean, Mr Lorne?'

'I fear I must close this place before too long.'

'Close it?' Emma cried, appalled. 'But you are the only bookshop in the area.'

'Aye, it's a great pity. I've loved this shop like my own child. But my daughter insists I go and live with her in Brighton. I can hardly see now and it's hard for me to get around.'

Emma nodded sympathetically. She could assuredly see that a shop where stock required unpacking and shelving, and accounts required keeping, might be too much for Mr Lorne now. But she couldn't bear to lose her sanctuary again so soon after refinding it.

'That is a very great pity indeed, Mr Lorne,' she said. 'I'm very sorry to hear it.'

'Ah, well, there should be plenty of books for me in Brighton, even if I have to get my grandchildren to read them to me,' Mr Lorne said. 'And maybe someone will want to buy this place from me and restock it with all the latest volumes.'

'I do hope so. Though it would never be quite the same without you.'

Mr Lorne chuckled. 'Now you're just flirting with an old man, Mrs Carrington.'

Emma laughed in reply. 'And what if I am? I have never met another man who could talk about books with me as you do.'

'Then you must find a few of those novels and we'll talk about them when you've read them. I'm not tottering away just yet.'

As Mr Lorne made his way back to his desk, Emma scanned the rows of titles. *Mysterious Warnings. Orphan of the Rhine.* They sounded deliciously improbable. Just what she needed right now. Something a bit silly and romantic, preferably with a few haunted castles and stormy seas thrown in.

She climbed up one of the rickety ladders to look for more on the top shelves, soon losing herself in the prospect of new stories. She opened the most intriguing one, *The Privateer,* and propped it on the top rung to read a few pages. She was soon deep into the story, until the bells jangled on the opening door, startling her out of her daydream world. She spun around on one foot on the ladder and her skirts wrapped around her legs, making her lose her balance.

For an instant, she felt the terrible, cold panic of falling. She braced herself for the pain of landing on the hard floor—only to be caught instead in a pair of strong, muscled arms.

The shock of it quite knocked the breath from her and the room went hazy and blurry as the veil of her bonnet blinded her. Willing herself not to faint, Emma blinked away her confusion and pushed back the dratted veil.

'Thank you, sir,' she gasped. 'You are very quick-thinking.'

'I'm just happy I happened to be here,' her rescuer answered and his voice was shockingly familiar. A smooth, deep, rich sound, like a glass of sweet mulled wine on a cold night, comforting and deliciously disturbing at the same time.

It was a voice she hadn't heard in a long time and yet she remembered it very well.

Startled, Emma tilted her head back and looked up into the face of Sir David Marton. Her rescuer.

He looked back at her, unsmiling, his face as expressionless as if it was carved from marble. He appeared no older than when they last met, his features as sharply chiselled and handsome as ever, his eyes the same pale, piercing grey behind his spectacles. His skin seemed a bit bronzed, as if he spent a great deal of time outdoors, which gave him the appearance of vigorous good health quite different from the night-dwelling pallor of Henry and his friends.

David Marton looked—good. No, better than good. Dangerously handsome.

Yet there *was* something different about him now. Something harder, colder, even more distant, in a man who had always seemed cautious and watchful.

But Jane had said he too had had his trials these last few years. A lost wife. Surely they were all older and harder than they once were?

His face was expressionless as he looked down at her, as if he caught falling damsels every day and barely recognised her. How could this man make her feel so unsure, yet still want to be near him? Made her want

to know more about what went on behind his infuriatingly inscrutable expression?

Suddenly Emma realised he still held her in his arms,
as easily and lightly as if she was no more than a feather.
And her arms were wrapped around his shoulders as
they stared at each other in heavy, tight silence.

He seemed to realise it at the same moment, for he
slowly lowered her to her feet. She swayed dizzily and
his hand on her arm kept her steady.

'I'm so sorry,' Emma said, trying to laugh as if the
whole thing was just a joke. That was the only way she
had ever found to deal with Henry and his friends, by
never letting them see her real feelings. 'That was terribly clumsy of me.'

'Not at all,' he answered. He still watched her and
Emma wished with all her might she could read his
thoughts even as she hid hers. With Henry's friends,
who had tried to flirt with her or drunkenly lure her
to their beds, she had always known what they were
thinking and could easily brush them off. They were
like primers for children once she learned their ways.

David Marton, on the other hand, was a sonnet in
Latin, complicated and inscrutable and maddening.

'I fear I startled you,' he said, 'and these ladders are
much too precarious for you to be scurrying along.'

Emma laughed, for real this time. So Sir David
hadn't entirely changed; she remembered this protective quality within his watchfulness before. Like a medieval knight. 'Oh, I've been in much more precarious
spots before.'

A smile finally touched his lips, just a hint at the

very corners, but Emma was ridiculously glad to see it. She wondered whimsically what it would take to get a *real* smile from him.

'I'm sure you have,' he said.

'But I haven't been lucky enough to have anyone there to catch me until today.'

And finally there it was, a smile. It was quickly gone, but was assuredly real. To Emma's fascinated astonishment, she glimpsed a dimple set low in his sculpted cheek.

No man should really be allowed to be so good looking. Especially one as cool and distant as Sir David Marton.

'It's good to see you at home again, Miss Bancroft,' he said.

'Ah, but she is Mrs Carrington now, Sir David,' Mr Lorne said, sharply reminding Emma that she wasn't actually alone with David Marton.

She quickly stepped back from his steadying hand. The warmth of his touch lingered on her arm through her sleeve and she rubbed her hand over it.

'Indeed she is,' Sir David said, his smile vanishing behind his usual polite mask. 'Forgive me, Mrs Carrington. And please accept my condolences on your loss.'

Emma nodded. She was so disappointed to lose that rare glimpse of another David and be right back to distant, commonplace words. Or maybe she had only imagined that glimpse in the first place. Maybe *this* really was the true David Marton.

'And I am sorry for your loss as well, Sir David,' she

said. 'My sister told me about your wife. I remember Lady Marton, she was very beautiful.'

'You knew my mother?' a little voice suddenly said.

Startled, Emma turned to see a tiny girl standing beside Mr Lorne's desk. She was possibly the prettiest child Emma had ever seen, with a porcelain-pale face and red-gold waves of hair peeking from beneath a very stylish straw bonnet. She was very still, very proper, and if her demeanour hadn't convinced Emma this was Sir David's daughter her grey eyes would have.

Emma walked toward her slowly. She was never entirely sure how to behave toward small children. The only ones she really knew were William and Eleanor, and the rambunctious twins seemed as different from this girl as it was possible to be. Once, when she first married Henry, she'd longed for a child of her own. But later, when she saw his true nature, she knew it was a blessing she had never had a baby.

Yet this girl drew Emma to her by her very stillness. 'Yes, I knew her, though not very well, I'm afraid. I saw her at dances and parties, and she was always the prettiest lady there. Just as I suspect you will be one day.'

The little girl bit her lip. 'I'm not sure I would want to be.'

Sir David hurried over to lay his hand protectively on the girl's shoulder. 'Mrs Carrington, may I present my daughter, Miss Beatrice Marton? Bea, this is Mrs Carrington. She's Lady Ramsay's sister from Barton Park.'

Miss Beatrice dropped a perfect little curtsy. 'How do you do, Mrs Carrington? I'm very sorry we haven't seen you at Barton Park before. I like it when we visit there.'

Emma gave her a smile. There was something about the child, something so sad and still, that made her want to give her a hug. But she was sure the preternaturally polite Miss Beatrice Marton would be appalled by such a move.

Much like her father.

'I've been living abroad and have only just returned to Barton,' Emma said. 'I fear my sister and her family have gone to London for a while, but you may call on me any time you like, Miss Marton. I am quite lonely there by myself.'

'So what brings you to my shop today, Sir David?' Mr Lorne interrupted. 'Has your uncle, Mr Sansom, finally decided to sell me his library?'

'I've just come to find Beatrice a new book. She's already read the last ones you sent to Rose Hill,' David said. 'As for my uncle, you would have to ask him yourself. I fear he never leaves his estate now, though you are certainly quite right—his library is exceedingly fine.'

'Such a pity.' Mr Lorne sighed. 'I am quite sure I would find buyers for his volumes right away. Books should have loving homes.'

As Mr Lorne and Sir David talked about the library, Emma watched Beatrice sort through stacks of volumes on the floor. She came back not with children's picture books, but with titles like *The Environs of Venice* and *A Voyage Through the Lands of India*.

'Do you wish to travel yourself, Miss Marton?' Emma asked, quite sure such volumes should be too weighty for such a little girl.

Beatrice shook her head, hiding shyly behind the

brim of her bonnet. 'I like to stay at home the best. But I like looking at the pictures of other places and when Papa reads me the stories. It's like getting to be somewhere else without actually having to leave.'

'Yes, that's exactly what books are,' Emma said. 'Like trying on a different life.'

'Have you been to these places, Mrs Carrington?'

'A few of them.'

Beatrice hesitated for a moment, then said quickly, 'Perhaps you would tell me about them one day?'

Emma's heart ached at the girl's shy words. She heard so much in them that she tried to hide in herself: that uncertainty, that need for life, but the fear of it at the same time. 'I would enjoy that very much, Miss Marton.'

'Beatrice, we should be going soon,' Sir David said. 'Have you found something you like?'

Once everyone's purchases were paid for, Emma left the shop with Sir David and his daughter. As it was nearing teatime, the street was not as crowded and there was no one to stare at her. But she did notice Mrs Browning, the old widow who lived in the cottage across the street, peering at her through the lace curtains at her windows. Mrs Browning had always known everything that happened in the village.

'Did you bring your carriage from Barton, Mrs Carrington?' Sir David asked.

'No, I walked. The exercise was quite nice after the last few rainy days.'

'But it looks as if it might rain again,' he said. 'Let us drive you back.'

Against her will, Emma was very tempted. Her old intrigue with Sir David Marton, formed when she was no more than a naïve young girl, was still there, stronger than ever. When she looked into his beautiful, inscrutable grey eyes, there was so much she wanted to know. If she did sit beside him on a narrow carriage seat, all the way back to Barton, surely he could not always maintain his maddening mystery?

Yet she was no longer that girl. She had seen far more of the world than her old, curious self could ever have wanted. And she knew that men like Sir David—respectable, attractive—could not be for her. No matter how tempted she might be.

She saw the curtains twitch at the house across the street again and could almost feel the burn of avid eyes. In the cosmopolitan, sophisticated environs of Continental spa towns, where everyone was escaping from something and no one was what they appeared, she had forgotten what it was like to live in a place where everyone knew everyone else's business. Where they knew one's family—and one's past.

Emma had vowed to atone, both for the sake of herself and especially for Jane and her family. She couldn't let her sister come home to Barton to find fresh gossip, which was surely what would happen if she drove off now with the eligible David Marton. Nor did she want Sir David and his lovely little daughter to face that, only because he was being polite.

And she knew politeness could surely be all it was for him.

The curtain twitched again.

'You are so kind, Sir David,' she said. 'But I do enjoy the walk.'

'Just as you like, Mrs Carrington,' he said, still so polite. He put on his hat and the shadow of its brim hid him from her even more than he had been before. 'I hope we shall see you more often, since you have returned home.'

'Perhaps so,' Emma answered carefully. 'It was good to see you again, Sir David, and know that you are well. And very good to meet you, Miss Marton. I always love meeting other great readers.'

Little Miss Beatrice gave another of her perfect curtsies before she took her father's hand and the two of them made their way down the lane. Once they were gone from sight, the curtain fell back into place and Emma was alone on the path.

She looked up and down the street, suddenly feeling lost and rather lonely. She'd grown rather used to such a feeling with Henry. After all, he usually left her in their lodgings while he went off to find a card game. But even there she could usually find a few people to talk to, or a task to set herself. Here, she wasn't sure what she should do.

And being with David Marton made her feel all the more alone, now that he was gone.

She glanced back at the window of the bookshop behind her, at its dusty glass and empty display shelves. Like her, it seemed to be waiting for something to fill it. Suddenly a thought struck her, as improbable as it was exciting.

Maybe, just maybe, there was a way she could find

her path back into the life of this place once more. A way she could redeem herself.

She spun around and pushed open the door, moving resolutely inside. Mr Lorne, who was bent over an open volume, looked up with wide, startled eyes under his bushy grey brows.

'Mr Lorne,' Emma blurted before she could change her mind. 'How much might you ask as the purchase price for your shop?'

'Mrs Carrington is very pretty.'

David glanced down at Bea, startled by the sudden sound of her little voice. She'd said nothing at all since they left the village, the empty road and thick hedgerows rolling past peacefully on the way back to Rose Hill.

In truth, he himself had not been in a talking mood. Not since his last glimpse of Emma Bancroft—no, Emma Carrington—standing alone outside the bookshop. David had always lived his life in a rational way— he had to, if his estate and his family, especially his daughter, were to be safely looked after. But when he held Emma Carrington in his arms, felt her body against his, he hadn't felt in the least bit rational.

He felt like a sizzling, burning bolt of white-hot lightning had shot through him, sudden and shocking and just as unwelcome.

He remembered what a pretty young lady she had been before she left Barton Park and he married Maude. Her green eyes had been as bright and full of life as a spring day and she had always seemed just on the cusp of dashing off and leaping into whatever caught her attention. Her life since then more than fulfilled that promise of reckless trouble.

And now she was back, startlingly beautiful. Her pretty girl's face had matured into its high cheekbones and large eyes, and her black clothes only set off her golden hair and glowing skin. The high collar and dull silk couldn't even begin to hide the slender grace of her body.

The body he had held so close—and hadn't wanted to let go.

David's gloved hands tightened on the reins, causing the horses to go faster. He shook his head to clear it of thoughts he shouldn't even be having and brought himself back to where he should be. In the present moment, in the full knowledge of who he was and the responsibility he had.

'Don't you think so, Papa?' Bea said.

David smiled down at her. She looked up at him from beneath the beribboned edge of her bonnet, and for the first time in a long while there was a spark of real interest in her eyes.

But it was an interest she should not have. David would never let a woman hurt his daughter as his wife had when she eloped. If he did marry again, which he knew one day he would have to, it would be to a lady as fully aware of her duty as he was, someone steady and quiet. *That* was the sort of woman Bea should like and want to emulate.

Unfortunately, it seemed to be the spirited Emma

Carrington who sparked Bea's interest. And his own, blast it all.

'Isn't Mrs Carrington pretty?' Bea said again. She held up her doll and added, 'Her hair is just the same colour as my doll's.'

'Yes.' David had to agree, for really there was no denying it. Mrs Carrington *was* pretty. Too pretty. 'But there are things more important than looks, you know, Bea.'

Beatrice frowned doubtfully. 'That's what Nanny says too. She says the goodness of my soul and the kindness of my manners are what I should mind.'

'Nanny is very right.'

'Then are you saying Mrs Carrington doesn't have a good soul?'

David laughed. 'You are too clever by half, my dear. And, no, that's not what I'm saying. I have no idea what Mrs Carrington's soul is like.'

'But she is Lady Ramsay's sister and Lady Ramsay is kind.'

'Indeed she is.'

'And Aunt Louisa says you should marry again.'

This was more than Bea had spoken at one time in many weeks, and for a moment David couldn't decipher the quick, apparent changes in topic.

Then he realised, much to his alarm, that maybe they were all of *one* topic.

'Perhaps one day I will marry again,' he said carefully. 'You should have a new mother and Rose Hill a mistress. But I am sure we have not met her yet.'

'Aunt Louisa said Mrs Carrington's husband died, just like Mama did.'

'Yes. But Mrs Carrington isn't ready to marry again. And neither am I. We're happy on our own for now, aren't we, Bea?' David felt a bolt of worry over his daughter's sudden worry over his marital status. He had thought she was happy at Rose Hill, that once her mother's death had receded into the past she wouldn't be so quiet. He had thought his love and attention would see her through it all. What if he had been wrong?

'Yes, Papa,' Bea said quietly. She settled back on the seat and was silent for the rest of the drive home.

David could only hope she accepted his words and was truly content. Emma Carrington wasn't the sort of lady who could ever fit into his vision of their future and he surely wasn't the sort of person who could attract her. Not if her first marriage was her standard. He knew himself and he knew all of that very well.

Why, then, couldn't he get the memory of her sparkling eyes out of his mind?

From the diary of Arabella Bancroft

I have met the most fascinating gentleman at the dinner tonight. His name is Sir William and he appears to have no estate yet, but the king favours him. I can see why. He is so very charming, and knows much about music and theatre and books. And most astonishing, he spent much time talking to me, despite my insignificance in such company. Indeed, he did not leave my side all evening and I did not wish him to.

He has asked to walk with me in the garden tomorrow...

at the top of page, faint mirrored text visible

Chapter Four

Miss Melanie Harding was quite, quite bored.

She sighed and propped her elbows on the window-sill as she stared down at the street below. It had surely been an hour since she sat down there and not more than ten people had gone by! None of them were at all interesting either. Why had her mother sent her off to this forsaken place? It was most unfair.

She glanced back over her shoulder at her uncle, who as usual sat snoring by the fire. That was all he ever seemed to do. And she had so hoped that the home of a retired admiral would at least be full of handsome officers. That was her only consolation when her mother declared she was sending Melanie off to stay with her uncle in a backwater village no one had ever heard of.

'But why?' she had wailed in despair as she watched her mother toss gowns and slippers into a trunk at their small house in Bath. 'Why must I go *there*?'

'You know very well why,' her mother had said, never pausing an instant in her odious task. 'Because no one there will ever have heard of Captain Whitney and your unfortunate behaviour. Your uncle will keep a close eye on you.'

The Captain Whitney thing *had* been unfortunate, but surely that was his fault, not hers. She had only believed him when he said his pretty words of love and devotion and sent her such darling poems. How could she have known they were copied from a dusty old book by someone named Marlowe—or that Captain Whitney's promises were just as false?

Captain Whitney, as well as looking splendid in his red coat, had a good income and respectable connections to a viscount's family. If all had gone as Melanie hoped, as he promised, her mother would have been in ecstasy. She would have congratulated Melanie on her fine catch. But she had been deceived and now she was being punished for it.

'Why can I not go to Aunt Mary in London, then, if I must be sent away?' she had sobbed to her hard-hearted mother.

'Because London is certainly no place for you,' her mother said, still packing away all of Melanie's worldly possessions. 'There is too much scope for trouble there. No, you will stay with your uncle until you learn to behave. This family has never had a scandal on its name and we won't start now.'

So here she was. In hell. Bath was a dull enough place, full of old invalids and retired parsons, but at least once in a while someone interesting came along. But here—here there was nothing at all.

Her uncle snored even louder, shifting in his chair. Melanie knew this was the way it would be until teatime, then he would expect her to read to him from some book of sermons or naval reports or a history of the Armada.

The only people besides her uncle and his servants she had even met in the village were shopkeepers, old Mrs Browning and Mrs Louisa Smythe, who at least had some interesting conversation on the few times they had met. Mrs Smythe knew lots of gossip, even from London as well as of local worthies Melanie hadn't met yet. Mrs Smythe had invited her to an assembly, which seemed like the only bright spot on Melanie's horizon.

As she stared out the window, kicking her feet under her hem, she saw a carriage rolling past. It was the first she'd seen in over an hour and she leaned forwards eagerly to see who it was.

She glimpsed a man she hadn't met before, and from what she could see beneath his hat he was rather handsome. And not old. Plus the curricle seemed to be an expensive one, if painted a rather dull dark-green colour rather than a fashionable yellow. She stood and watched until the equipage was out of sight, her spirits considerably raised.

At least there was one handsome gentleman somewhere in the vicinity! Now she just had to find out who he was. And she knew just who could tell her more about him—her new friend, Mrs Louisa Smythe.

Chapter Five

Emma turned her face up to the sky and closed her eyes as the warmth of the sun touched her skin. After the grey, rainy days, it felt like heaven.

She pulled the door of her cottage closed behind her and hurried up the narrow path of her little garden. She wasn't sure where she was going, she just knew she had to move. She tied her shawl around her shoulders and pushed up the sleeves of her old yellow muslin gown, the first thing not in black she'd worn for weeks. The warm breeze brushed against her skin, drawing her out into the world again.

She ran up the gentle slope of a small hill and spun around to look at Barton spread out all before her. Jane had just sent her a letter that morning saying the baby hadn't arrived yet, so they would be in London for a while longer. So the house was still shut up, but Emma could see the gardeners scurrying around the grounds getting them ready for summer and the new life that would soon fill them. New flowers, new trees—new babies.

Emma felt the stirrings of something new inside herself, too. Some hint of her old restlessness that stirred up what she had thought were cold, dead embers of life.

She turned in a slow circle, taking in the old maze, the outline of her own cottage, where she had left Murray snoring by the fire in his dog dreams. It was her own home, the first she had ever had, and though it was small and quiet it felt like a place where she could be herself. Where she could hide. But maybe, just maybe, she didn't want to hide any more.

Emma took out a letter she had tucked into the folds of her shawl. It had arrived most unexpectedly with that morning's post, from a man named Mr Charles Sansom at Sansom House. When she got the direction from Mr Lorne, she hadn't really expected to hear back. After all, Mr Sansom had already said he wouldn't yet sell any of his extensive library to Mr Lorne, so why should he sell it to her?

But here it was. Emma unfolded it and read it again.

To Mrs Carrington—such a delightful surprise to hear from you, and to know that such a valuable business as Mr Lorne's will go on as before. I have placed many an order with him and he found me some rare volumes in our younger days. Also, though you will not remember it, I knew your late father, who was an excellent authority on local architecture and history. I do not go out into society a great deal now, but you must come and inspect my library at any time that is convenient.

*I have a few volumes on Barton Park itself you
might find of interest.
Yours very sincerely,
Charles Sansom.*

Volumes on Barton Park. Emma found herself most
curious to see what those could be. Once, before she
married, she had found a diary belonging to a lady who
lived at Barton in the seventeenth century. It sent her
off on an ill-fated treasure hunt, yet another reminder
that she had to learn caution.

But surely whatever books Mr Sansom had could
do no harm? He had said he knew her father, who had
also been fascinated by the legend of the Barton treasure. She really did want to get a glimpse of that library.

And she had certainly not forgotten that Mr Sansom
was David Marton's uncle. Not that she thought she
could catch a glimpse of Sir David at Sansom House.
She hadn't seen him since that first day she ventured
into the village and that was all for the best.

She tucked the letter away again and twirled around
to study the long, snaking grey line of stone wall that
divided Barton from Rose Hill. All she could see of that
estate from her perch atop the hill was rolling green
fields and a few white dots of sheep, but she knew it was
there. In the distance she could see the tumbling stone
ruins of the old medieval castle. Who knew what went
on behind Rose Hill's serene pale-grey walls? It was
like a book in a language she didn't yet know.

The wind suddenly swirled around her, catching at
her skirts and hair. It tugged strands from their pins

and tossed them around. Emma laughed and twirled with it. She took off running down the hill, letting the bright day carry her.

She hadn't run in so very long. Life had been small and confined for so many months. Now, just for a moment, she felt free. Faster and faster she went down the hill, the momentum of her movement carrying her until she almost flew over the ground.

She knew there was no one to see her there, no one to judge, and she had almost forgotten how that felt. She ran all the way to the stone wall and twirled around in a little dance step. Maybe life would be well after all. Maybe she could redeem herself, find her place. Maybe...

'I fear I've quite misplaced my dancing pumps,' someone suddenly said.

Emma gave a startled shriek and spun to a sudden halt. But her skirts didn't quite stop with her. They wrapped tightly around her legs and made her stumble against the rough stone of the wall.

For an instant she thought she must have been imagining things, because she couldn't see anyone nearby but two indifferent sheep. Then she glanced up and saw David Marton perched up in a tree beyond the border of the wall, watching her as she ran and twirled and generally behaved like a hoyden.

He *did* have a great talent for catching her unawares.

She held on to the wall and wished that the ground would just swallow her up. The sense of delicious freedom she had felt just a moment before drifted away like a curl of smoke and the coldness of shame she remembered too well from her time with Henry took over.

But then she pushed the coldness away and realised something amazing. David Marton was in a *tree*.

Mystified by the strangeness of the moment, she watched as he climbed down, branch to branch, and leaped to the ground. His lean body moved with a fluid, powerful grace, much like a troupe of Russian acrobats Emma had once seen perform. They had amazed her with the deceptive power of their elegant movements and Sir David could easily have been one of them, tumbling and twirling along thin wires. Rescuing fair damsels from thorny towers.

You have been reading too many novels, Emma told herself sternly. Imagining David Marton as a rescuer of fair ladies, slayer of dragons…

Oh, dear heavens, but he wore no coat. Emma stared at him, hoping she wouldn't go slack-jawed like some country milkmaid, as he reached for a blue coat slung across a low branch. His shirt was very white in the sunshine and the breeze moulded the thin linen to his back and shoulders as he stretched for the coat.

Obviously, he did not spend all his time poring over estate ledgers in the library, or carousing and gambling as Henry and his friends had. The strong muscles she had felt as he caught her in his arms were no illusion. His broad shoulders and powerful arms tapered to narrow hips and long legs encased in tight doeskin breeches.

Emma turned sharply away before she could gawk at his tight backside.

'Out enjoying the fine day, Mrs Carrington?' he asked.

She heard the rustle of fabric as he slid into his coat and only then did she look at him again. The coat concealed his torso, but he wore no cravat and the throat of his shirt was open to reveal the tanned skin of his neck. The wind caught at his glossy dark hair, tousling it over his brow.

In such dishabille, with his hair dishevelled, he almost looked like a different person. Just as handsome as ever, but younger, freer, wilder. More at home here, under the sun and sky, on his own land, than he was in an assembly room.

Perhaps, just perhaps, she had judged Sir David too hastily? Perhaps there was more to him than the serious and responsible estate owner?

Then he slid his spectacles from the pocket of his coat and covered his beautiful grey eyes with them again. A faint frown flickered over his lips as he looked at her and her instant of wild hope was gone.

'Yes,' she said brightly, suddenly remembering that he had spoken to her. 'I was just out for a walk. I hadn't realised I was so near to the edge of your estate.'

'Shall I have you arrested for trespassing, Mrs Carrington?'

For an instant, Emma was shocked, sure he was serious. Then she saw his frown whisper into a smile and her shock grew. Had he made a *joke?*

'Only if I cross the wall,' she said. 'And I shall be very careful not to.'

He laughed and it sounded startled and a bit rusty,

as if he didn't do that very often. 'Fair enough. Then I will stay here and we can talk at a safe distance.'

Yes, that would surely be best if she stayed at a safe distance. Especially since she had seen what he looked like without his coat. 'Were you climbing trees?' she asked, unable to contain her curiosity any longer. 'I wouldn't have thought it of you, Sir David.'

He shook his head ruefully. 'It's not my usual pastime, I confess. Not since I was about Bea's age, anyway.'

'I find it hard to imagine you as a child,' Emma blurted out. Somehow Sir David seemed the sort of person who would spring into the world, Athena-like, fully grown and ready to take care of business.

'We all must come from somewhere, Mrs Carrington. I gave up the tree-climbing after I was caught as a boy by an exceptionally stern tutor, though.'

'Then what drove you back to it today?'

'All of this…' He gestured toward a wide swathe of flat-grounded meadow, from the cluster of trees near the wall to a small, open-sided shelter in the distance. 'This used to be an orchard and quite a productive one. Until my grandfather took the trees out to try and make a more picturesque vista. These few trees are all that is left and they've given us a good apple crop every year until now. My gardener suggested I take a look, but I know little of such things. I'd like to see them restored, though; I was hoping to expand the orchard again.'

Emma peered up at the tree. 'I can see little sign of disease from here. You should read James Lee's volume, it is very helpful in such matters.'

'Ah, yes. I had forgotten your interest in botany.'

'I haven't studied it in a long time, but I do remember Mr Lee. I wanted to use some of the information to make some improvements on the gardens here at Barton.' She glanced back at the house, all peaceful and shimmering in the sun. 'There wasn't much use for such things after I left and my interests turned to other matters.'

'Your sister said you have been living on the Continent,' he said, in that maddeningly neutral tone of his.

'Yes.' Emma started strolling slowly along the wall and Sir David fell in step with her on his side of the divide.

'Barton Park must seem dull to you now.'

'It's not dull at all,' Emma protested. 'I get to be close to my sister again, to be at home. I've missed it.'

'And you don't miss things like balls and routs? Meeting new people and seeing new sights? The village bears little resemblance to Paris or Rome, I fear.'

Emma laughed, remembering the crowded, smelly streets of Paris, the hordes of people jostling together between the tall, close-packed buildings and the glittering shop windows. 'No, it's not like Paris. I confess I do miss the great scope for people-watching there. But the village does have its own pleasures.'

'You enjoy people-watching?' he asked, sounding doubtful, as if such a pastime was not quite…correct.

'Of course. Doesn't everyone? People do such endlessly fascinating and strange things. I suppose that's the only thing I miss in being by myself at Barton, though I do have the characters in the books I read.'

'You should come to the assembly next week, then. The crowds won't be as fashionable as Paris, but they ought to supply you with conversation enough.'

Emma had moved a few steps ahead of Sir David, but now she stopped and turned to look at him. Had he really said she should come to the village assembly? 'I haven't been to a gathering there in a long time.' Not since the party where she watched him dance with Maude Cole, the two of them so beautiful, so perfect-looking together. As if they belonged there, in that very place with those very people, with each other.

Suddenly she felt terribly selfish for ever thinking Sir David only cold and aloof. He had lost his wife, the mother of his adorable daughter. She, too, had lost her husband, and even though Henry had proved to not be what she had hoped for in the end, she had mourned him. Mourned the possibility of what he might have been. How much worse it must be for Sir David.

She didn't know quite what to say to him and for once she held herself back from blurting out commiserations he surely did not want, not from her. Instead she just smiled at him and said, 'I remember how enjoyable events at the assembly rooms were. But I'm not sure I should go.'

His head tilted a bit to one side and he gave her a narrow-eyed, quizzical look, as if he was confused by her sudden smile. Emma resolved to be friendlier in the future, to not always leap to conclusions about people.

'Because you are still in mourning?' he said.

'Actually I should be in half-mourning now,' Emma answered. She just didn't have the money to replace her black with greys and lilacs, not until her inheritance from her mother came through. And then most of that would go to buying Mr Lorne's shop and replenishing its stock. But Sir David didn't have to know that. 'Appearing at an assembly shouldn't cause much comment, unless I become completely foxed and dance about wildly on the refreshment tables.'

David laughed again. Twice in one day. Emma was sure it had to be a milestone. 'Do you do that often?'

'Only when the mood strikes me,' Emma said breezily. 'But here at home I'm sure I would be a pattern-card of propriety. I'm just not sure many people would be happy to see me there. Not after…'

After the scandal she caused by eloping. The infamy would surely follow her always. Emma felt her cheeks turn warm and she turned away to sit down on the edge of the wall, busying herself with arranging her skirts around her.

'You have more friends here than you realise, Mrs Carrington,' David said gently. 'They would all be glad to see you again, dancing wildly or not. And if you plan to run the bookshop…'

Emma looked up at him in surprise. 'You know about that?'

'I was in the village again yesterday and Mr Lorne mentioned it.'

'You don't think that's terribly shocking—for a female to run a shop?'

David sat down next to her on the wall and was silent for a moment. She had the sense he was weighing his thoughts. He always seemed to do that. She wished she could learn how.

He braced his palms on the wall and said, 'It is not the usual thing, of course. But it's not as if you were proposing to take over the butcher shop. Many young widows find projects to fill their days. Charity, embroidery—why not books?'

Emma was startled. She would never have thought David Marton would espouse such an open-minded attitude. Maybe his years of marriage had changed him. Or maybe the years had changed her. Hadn't she just decided she should not judge people hastily? They were too ever surprising. 'Or an orchard?'

He looked down at her, his brow arched. 'An orchard?'

'Young widowers surely need to distract themselves as well,' she said. 'You are said to be the hardest-working landowner in the area.'

'I take my responsibilities at Rose Hill seriously,' he answered slowly.

'My sister says you lived much in London when Lady Marton was alive. You must be going through many—adjustments now.'

'As you are, Mrs Carrington?'

'Yes. As I am.' Emma had always felt as if she and David Marton were such different personalities they could scarcely talk together, no matter how much she enjoyed looking at his handsome face. But perhaps now they had become more alike, both suddenly adrift in a new, uncharted sea.

His compass, though, seemed more reliable than

hers. He had his purpose at Rose Hill, his secure place in the life of this village. She was still floundering.

'My wife preferred town life,' he said. 'Luckily London is within easy enough distance that I could take care of Rose Hill from there and still see to my family. But when she died I wanted Bea to know her home.'

'Miss Marton is very pretty,' Emma said. 'And she seems quite clever, if the books she chose are anything to go by.'

David smiled, and just as he had when he first jumped out of the tree he looked suddenly younger. Lighter. His grey eyes seemed to glow as he thought about his daughter. 'Bea is too clever by half. And, yes, she is very pretty, though I do say so myself as her papa. I fear it may get her into trouble one day.'

'Not with such a fond papa watching over her,' Emma said. Surely any man who cared about his child so had to be good inside? She thought of her own father, so distracted by his own projects, but so much fun when he was with her.

'She has had a difficult time since she lost her mother. I was hoping that coming back to Rose Hill would help her, yet she still seems rather lonely. There are few children here her own age for her to befriend and my sister's sons—well, Bea has little in common with them.'

Emma thought of Mrs Smythe's boys, romping through the streets of the village. 'I would imagine not.'

'I sometimes wonder if a school might not be good for her.'

'Oh, no!' Emma cried, unable to stop herself. 'Not a school, Sir David, I beg you.'

David's brow arched again. 'You don't think a school would be a good idea?'

'I—I don't mean to interfere in your own family business, of course. But I went to school for a time after my sister married, and it was not where I wanted to be. Girls who love books and dreaming, as it seems Miss Marton does…'

'Could easily get lost there,' David murmured. 'Thank you, Mrs Carrington. You have confirmed that I should indeed be selfish and keep her with me. It is hard at times for a father to know what best to do for his daughter when she has no mother. My own parents died too young and I had to look after my sister. I fear it has all made me too protective.'

Emma nodded. He did seem to understand, in a way few men would. It certainly surprised her. 'Miss Marton can always come visit me at the bookshop and read all she likes, since you say my shopkeeping has not shocked you too much,' she said, trying to tease him, to make him laugh. To put herself on more familiar ground with him, when she was shaken by the sudden surge of tender feelings.

He didn't say anything. Before he looked away, Emma saw a shadow flicker through his eyes. Even though he was obviously too correct, too reserved, to say anything, Emma felt the familiar cold touch of faint disapproval. Of course a man like him would not want his young, impressionable daughter spending much time with a woman like her. Her past mistakes were still there with her.

Emma jumped up from the wall, unable to sit so close to him any longer. She felt like a fool, wanting him to like her, wanting to know him better, but knowing he would not. The old wildness that had always plagued her, always lurked inside of her, swept over. She clambered atop the low wall and danced over it, balancing on her toes, letting the wind brush over her and tug at her hair again.

'Mrs Carrington, be careful,' Sir David called. He jumped up from the wall and held up his hand as if he would catch her.

Somehow the gesture only made her feel sadder. She twirled away and called, 'It's a beautiful day, Sir David! You should dance here with me.'

'This wall is a bit rougher than a dance floor, I fear,' he said, his hand still held out to her.

'All the better, then, because there is no one to see us.' Emma held out her arms and ran lightly over the uneven stones. He stayed close beside her, and when she spun around again she heard him make a choked sound, half between a laugh and a disapproving growl.

She glanced down at him, at his eyes shielded behind his spectacles and his windblown hair, and she wanted to touch him. To feel those locks against her fingers, the warmth of his skin on hers. She turned sharply away. 'Don't worry, Sir David. I can take care of myself— I've been doing so for a long time.'

'Sometimes in life we have to let other people take care of us, Mrs Carrington.'

Surprised by his solemn words, Emma stumbled to a halt and looked down at him again. She thought of what Jane had said, of how he took care of Rose Hill and all its tenants and servants, took care of his giggly sister and his daughter and his wife. 'Oh, Sir David. I'm not sure you are quite the right person to teach that lesson.'

He stared up at her and his handsome face hardened. It seemed like a veil dropped before his eyes and he was even more hidden from her than ever. 'Please get down from there now, Mrs Carrington.'

Feeling chastened, Emma finally reached out for his offered hand. But the toe of her half-boot caught on a crevice of the stone and she stumbled and started to fall towards the ground.

But his arms closed around her waist and swept her up again, saving her from disaster. Disaster of her own making.

Emma held on to him and closed her eyes tightly as she tried to breathe. 'Th-thank you. Again.'

'So you can always take care of yourself?' he asked, a hint of lurking amusement in his voice.

Emma's eyes flew open and she looked up into his face. That handsome face that always dazzled her and that hid so much of his true self behind it. 'Perhaps—not always. Not by choice, anyway. But sometimes we have no choice.'

'No,' he answered quietly. 'Sometimes we don't have a choice.'

'If *you* ever need someone to catch you…'

Sir David laughed and suddenly spun around with her

in his arms. Emma squealed and held on to his shoulders as the world turned blurry and giddy around her.

'Would you stand below my ladder and my wall, waiting for me to tumble down?' he shouted over the wind. 'I fear you would send us *both* crashing down!'

'I'm stronger than I look,' Emma cried, laughing.

'Now that I do believe.' David came to a sudden halt, but Emma was still dizzy. As she struggled to catch her breath, to stop laughing, he went very still.

She looked up at him and was caught, mesmerised by what she saw there. He stared down at her, his grey eyes glowing, unwavering, and she knew she couldn't have turned away from him if the world was crumbling around them. He was all she could see, all she knew. He leaned towards her; his lips parted, and she knew, knew with the most certain certainty of all her life, that he would kiss her. And that she wanted him so desperately. His mouth barely brushed hers…

'Papa!' At the sudden cry, David pulled back abruptly. A look of raw horror crossed his handsome face before it went all mask-like again and he carefully lowered her to her feet.

Emma spun away from him to press her hands to her warm cheeks. She was so bewildered, so excited and sad and confused all at the same time that she didn't know what to do. What to feel. She only knew she had to compose herself before David's daughter saw her. Before she faced him again after what they had almost done, what she had wanted so desperately for him to do.

'What are you doing today, Bea, my dearest?' she

heard David say. His tone was light, affectionate, betraying none of her turmoil.

'I'm out for my walk, of course,' Bea answered. Emma heard the sound of footsteps rustling over grass, the whisper of muslin and silk stirred by the wind. 'Is that Mrs Carrington?'

'Indeed it is,' David said. 'I met her on her own walk.'

Emma pasted a bright smile on her face. At least she had learned *that* in her life with Henry, how to put on a social face to hide her true feelings. She turned to see Miss Beatrice beside the wall, a stout older lady in a starched grey nanny's uniform hovering nearby. Watching everything, as if she planned to talk about this encounter in the servants' hall later.

Beatrice was beautifully dressed again, in a pink pelisse and ribbon-trimmed bonnet, her small hands encased in pink kid and a book tucked under her arm. But today she actually had a shy smile on her pretty, pale little face.

'How do you do, Miss Marton?' Emma said. 'I'm very glad to see you again so soon after the bookshop. Have you been enjoying your new volumes?'

'Oh, very much indeed,' Beatrice answered enthusiastically. 'I should like to tell you all about what I read about India, it's ever so interesting. Have you ever seen an elephant, Mrs Carrington?'

'As a matter of fact, I have,' Emma said. 'In a menagerie in Austria. Though I fear he was quite an elderly fellow and not decked in grand jewels as I'm sure they are with the maharajahs.'

Beatrice's eyes widened. 'Really? Oh, Mrs Carrington, you must tell me if—'

'Bea, dearest, I'm afraid Mrs Carrington was on her way home now,' David said, much more abrupt than his usual carefully polite style. 'We must not detain her.'

Beatrice bit her lip. 'No. Of course not, Mrs Carrington.'

'I am sure we will meet again very soon, Miss Marton, at least I hope we will,' Emma said quickly. She meant every word. Her heart was touched by this quiet little girl, who seemed so alone despite the love of her father. Beatrice Marton reminded her too much of her childhood self. 'I can tell you all about the elephants then, as well as the parrots and monkeys I saw.'

'I would like that,' Beatrice said quietly. 'Good day, Mrs Carrington.'

'Good day, Miss Marton—until next time.' Emma watched as Beatrice's nanny bustled forwards to take her hand and lead her away. Beatrice glanced back once and gave a little wave, which Emma returned with a smile.

David bowed politely. 'I'm glad I happened to be here to catch you, Mrs Carrington,' he said quietly.

'Again, you mean?' Emma smiled and curtsied. As she straightened to her feet, the letter from Mr Sansom fell from her shawl.

She bent to pick it up just as David reached for it. He glanced down at it as he held it out to her.

His brow arched in that way she was coming to hate. It always seemed to mean something disapproving. It made her feel so cold, so—in the wrong. 'You are writing to my uncle?' he said.

'Yes, Mr Lorne was kind enough to send me Mr Sansom's direction,' she said. 'I wanted to know more about his library. He says he knew my father.'

Sir David's jaw tightened. 'My uncle is an elderly man who just wants to be left alone with his books. He already told Mr Lorne he doesn't want to sell.'

Emma was confused. 'Yes, but I—'

'You what, Mrs Carrington?' he said, his tone too polite, too quiet.

She tucked the letter away. 'You've made it clear that you don't entirely approve of how I live my life, Sir David, but I assure you I mean no harm to your uncle. I merely wished to enquire about his library. Thank you for rescuing me—again. Good day.'

She spun around and hurried away before she could become careless yet again and say things she would regret. She had determined to make a new chapter in her life, a more respectable one, and she had to do that.

No matter how angry or unsure Sir David Marton made her feel. Or how very much she longed for him to kiss her.

By Jove. Had he actually almost kissed Emma Bancroft?

David, after an hour of trying to go over the Rose Hill accounts, finally gave up and tossed down his pen. Images of Emma's eyes, greener than a summer meadow, brighter than his mother's old emerald ring, kept getting in the way of black-and-white numbers.

Usually nothing could have distracted him from his work, but Emma did it now.

You've made it clear that you don't entirely approve of how I live my life, she had said, those eyes flashing.

And he didn't. He couldn't, not after Maude. He had too much to protect, and he had never known a freedom quite like the kind that shone all around Emma. After his father's hidden flashes of raw anger when he was a child, David had vowed to always keep tight control over himself.

For a time in his youth he had let himself loose, let himself run wild, and it hadn't ended well. Emma just brought out those old feelings.

And yet—yet he also couldn't help but grudgingly admire Emma as well. She had come back here, to a small place she hadn't seen in a long time, and was trying to rebuild something. To make herself useful. That could not be an easy task.

But that didn't mean he would let her bother his elderly uncle, who needed rest and quiet. Nor could he let her beautiful eyes disrupt *his* life. He would never make such a mistake again. When he remarried, it would be for practical, sensible purposes.

Two things Emma Bancroft could never be.

A knock sounded at the library door and he welcomed the distraction. 'Come in,' he said, carefully closing the ledger.

It was Bea's nanny who stepped into the room and made a wobbly curtsy. She was a good woman who in her younger days had been a junior nursemaid to Louisa and David, and later took care of Louisa's brood before coming to look after Bea following Maude's death. But David had begun to notice she was getting older, less sturdy, and even a quiet child like his daughter could get away from her at times.

One more thing he would have to take responsibility for very soon.

'Yes, Nanny, what is it?' he said. 'Is Miss Beatrice unwell?'

'Not at all, Sir David,' she answered. 'But she has been pestering me today for more books. I can't do anything beyond lessons on some Bible verses and such, and I fear she will become bored and troublesome. Perhaps more education is needed soon? More advanced books to keep her occupied?'

David laughed ruefully. *More educated—more books.* It sounded very much like the lady he had just been trying so hard not to think about.

But it seemed she wouldn't let herself be forgotten, even here in his own house.

Chapter Six

⚜

'I say, Phil, but you are racing off too early tonight. It's hours 'til dawn. Plenty of trouble to get into before then.'

Philip Carrington laughed as he tied the elaborate loops of his cravat. He studied Betsy's reflection in the mirror as she lolled around on the rumpled bed behind him. Her long, bright-blonde curls were tangled up with the sheets and she pouted at him.

'I never want to leave you, Betsy my beauty,' he said. 'You know that.'

'Then why go? You were gone abroad for ever so long, I just got you back.'

'I'm afraid I left some business undone on the Continent,' he muttered, reaching for his brocade waistcoat. 'So tomorrow I have to go to the countryside and finish it.'

'The country! I wouldn't think you'd like it *there,*' Betsy said. She sat up against the haphazard piles of pillows and wrapped the blue-satin blankets around her luscious nakedness.

'No, I certainly will not. But it must be done.'

His troublesome cousin Henry, rot his soul, had died owing him and Philip was not a man to forget debts owed. If Henry weren't here to do it, then Henry's widow would have to.

At the thought of Emma, Philip's fingers tightened on the carved buttons of his waistcoat. Emma—so beautiful, so sweet. Henry never knew what he had in her, always running off and leaving her alone and vulnerable.

It should have made his task easier. Seduce that idiot Henry's grateful, lovely bride and find what he needed. What Henry stole from Philip's father. But Emma had proved more loyal than Henry deserved and only professed gratitude for Philip's 'friendship'. And then she had left before Henry even knew she was gone.

But Henry was dead now. Surely Emma's time alone had made her want company? And he found himself strangely eager to see her again.

'It has to do with money, doesn't it, Phil?' Betsy said. Usually Betsy was all fun all the time, always up for a dance or a bottle of wine or a romp in the bedchamber. That was why he liked her, why out of all the lightskirts in London he kept coming back to her.

But now she sounded serious. Hard, even. Philip turned to look at her and she peered at him over the garish satin blankets with narrowed green eyes.

Green, like Emma's.

'Why would you say that, my dove?' he asked. 'Have I not taken care of you sufficiently today?'

He glanced pointedly at the bracelet on her wrist, the

one his jeweller threatened to be the last one he would get on credit.

'You've been worried ever since you got here,' she said with a little pout. 'And I know nothing would take you to the blighted country unless it was dire. Must be money.'

Philip dropped the coat he had just picked up and strode across the room to the bed instead. He couldn't bear the look of worry and scepticism in Betsy's eyes any longer. She was the only one who ever thought he could do no wrong. He didn't want her to think differently, as his family always had.

At the thought of his family and their demands, a wave of hot anger washed over him. He pushed it away and kissed Betsy instead, devouring her with his mouth, demanding she help him forget.

But Betsy held him away, staring up at him with her hard eyes. 'You should marry, Phil,' she said.

He choked out a laugh. Betsy was certainly full of surprises tonight. 'Marry?'

'That's how toffs like you get money when they need it, right? From what I hear, the streets of Mayfair are paved with heiresses just ripe for the plucking.'

'Not exactly,' he answered, bemused. Marriage had never been in his thoughts; there was too much fun to pursue in life to worry about such matters. But maybe Betsy had a point, in her own way... 'And heiresses tend to come with strict guardians.'

'I wager you could charm the guardians as well as the heiresses,' Betsy said. She lay back down beneath him and stretched her plump white arms over her head as she grinned up into his eyes. 'You have to marry some day, right? Might as well make it of good use.'

Philip laughed and kissed her again, feeling the sweet, yielding softness of her lips on his. He would fix this any way he could, no matter what he had to do. And Emma Bancroft Carrington had to be the key.

Chapter Seven

$\sim\!\!\infty\!\!\sim$

Emma drew in a deep breath as she looked up at the assembly rooms before her. During the day, the building was a rather dull, low, squat rectangle of dark brick and green-painted shutters, quiet and still. A place to hurry past on the way to the draper's or the bookshop.

Now, in the gathering blue-black twilight, with its shutters and doors thrown open, and light and music and laughter spilling out, it seemed an entirely different place. A place full of life and movement.

It had been quite some time since Emma went to dance, and even longer since she attended a gathering here at home. She swallowed past a nervous lump in her throat and stared up at the amber glow of the windows as if they were about to swallow her up.

You can go home, a tiny voice whispered in her head. Run back to the shelter she had made of her little cottage. She glanced back over her shoulder to see that Jane's coachman had already driven away. She couldn't flee without chasing him down, or walking home in her satin slippers.

Besides, Sir David was right. She had to meet people if she wanted to be part of the life of the village, if she wanted them to come to her bookshop. She had to find a way to get them to like her again.

And, if she was being honest with herself, she wanted to see David Marton again. That was really why she had taken such care with her appearance tonight.

Straightening her shoulders and holding her head high, she marched up the stone steps and through the open doors into the vestibule. Girls she didn't recognise, girls who had probably been children when she left, were gathered in front of the mirrors there, giggling together and exclaiming over each other's gowns. They made room for her with no judging glances—so far so good.

Emma glanced in the mirror. She had borrowed one of the housemaids at Barton to help her with her coiffure, a girl eager to gain lady's maid's experience, and the results weren't half-bad. Not as elaborate as the stylish young ladies around her, but surely most presentable. Her blonde waves were smoothed into curls and bound with blue-and-black ribbons. She wore one of her black gowns, her only new evening dress of taffeta and a pattern of sheer silk ribbon embroidery. She had added a bunch of blue-silk forget-me-nots at the sash and her mother's pearl pendant.

Surely she looked respectable and presentable. Maybe even a bit—pretty?

Emma sighed. It had been so long since she felt pretty. It seemed like a lot to ask now.

'Mrs Carrington? Is that really you?'

Emma turned to see a lady hurrying towards her through the crowd that had just swept between the front doors. A purple-plumed turban bobbed above grey-streaked dark curls and bright brown eyes. With a flash of delight, Emma recognised Jane's friend Lady Wheelington.

'Lady Wheelington,' she called, trying to fight her way upstream through the swirling crowd to the first familiar face she'd seen that night. 'How lovely to see you again. Jane said you had recently returned home.'

'I had to, my dear.' Lady Wheelington reached Emma at last and reached for her hands. 'My son Mr Crawford is the new vicar. What's your excuse for coming back?'

Emma laughed, suddenly more at ease. This was not entirely a foreign land; it was her home, or it once had been. She was the one who had changed, not it. 'I missed you all too much, I suppose.'

'You mean you missed our thrill-a-moment ways? Why, Mr Price's pig, who won some terribly important agricultural show just last month, escaped from his pen and ran quite amok in Mrs Smythe's flowers...'

Without faltering over a word in her tale, Lady Wheelington took Emma's arm and steered her neatly toward the doors leading into the ballroom. She couldn't escape then if she wanted to.

And she was very glad to have a friendly face beside her as she stood before the gathered crowd. It seemed as if everyone in the village, from the ninety-year-old Mrs Pratt who had once run the draper's shop, in the corner with her ear trumpet, to a little toddler in leading strings lunging for a tray of lemon tarts, was gathered there. And they all turned to look at her with shocked expressions on their faces.

Emma held her head high and made herself keep smiling. She had as much right to be there as anyone else. She was their neighbour; she had bought a ticket. And she intended to make her new life here among them.

Curiosus semper—cautious always. That was the motto of the Bancroft family and Emma meant to live up to it now.

'My dear Mrs Carrington, you remember my son Mr Crawford, do you not?' Lady Wheelington said as they came to a couple standing near the tall windows at the back of the room. 'He is finally living here. And this is his new fiancée, Miss Leigh of Brighton.'

Emma smiled at the two of them, as young and adorable and eager as pretty puppies, and luckily, they smiled back. The approval of the local clergy was always important.

'Best wishes to you both on your engagement. I did enjoy your sermon last week, Mr Crawford,' Emma said. She had slipped into the back pew of the old church, near her own father's memorial plaque, and left when the last notes of the closing hymn died away. But Mr Crawford's sermon had indeed been mercifully short and spiced with hints of humour. She would happily attend his services every week.

'Wasn't he wonderful, Mrs Carrington?' Miss Leigh said, gazing up starry-eyed at her betrothed. 'Mr Crawford writes the most eloquent sermons I have ever heard.'

As she chatted with their little group, Emma surreptitiously scanned the crowded room. The little ripple of shock caused by her entrance seemed to have faded, though everyone who passed would slow down to stare at her. She gave them smiles and nods, which sent some scurrying away, but also brought some to greet her. Soon she found herself in the midst of quite a group, Lady Wheelington leading their conversation about plans for an upcoming garden fête to benefit the church's efforts to restore some of the medieval monuments that were crumbling away.

Emma tried to picture Henry here with her, listening to such chit-chat about local affairs as the amateur musicians noisily tuned their instruments in the corner. He would have fled in a panic as soon as they stepped through the doors, running until he found a card room. Only he would have fled there as well, as Emma remembered that only penny-ante wagers were allowed there. And old Mrs Pratt always won anyway.

Emma almost laughed to imagine Henry's reaction if she had asked him to live this life with her. Then she glimpsed David Marton just coming into the ballroom and her smile faded.

He was taller than everyone around him, so for a moment she could see him quite clearly. He looked so different than when he had leaped out of that tree, in his fashionably sombre dark-blue coat and impeccably tied cravat skewered with a small pearl pin. His dark hair was combed back to reveal the austerely carved lines of his face, the metallic glint of his spectacles. Emma felt a warm rush of excitement flow over her to see him again.

For an instant he was very still, studying the gathering as if they were a scientific experiment that was not going quite as he hoped. But then he bent his head and smiled, and his face softened.

Emma saw that it was his sister, Louisa Smythe, on his arm. Mrs Smythe went up on tiptoe to whisper something frantically in his ear as she tapped his sleeve with her fan. As Emma watched, Mrs Smythe used that fan to wave someone over. It was a lady in a pretty pink-sprigged muslin gown trimmed with fluttering pink ribbons, with more pink ribbons in her fashionably tumbled pale curls.

The two ladies embraced as if they were long-lost bosom bows and then the pink lady curtsied to Sir David.

The lady half-turned as she smiled up at David and Emma saw she was as pretty and spring-fresh as her dress, with blushing cheeks and a dimpled chin. She swayed close to him as he talked to her, her eyes wide as if she could see only him. Finally he held out his arm to her and she took it with a soft laugh. He led her towards the gathering dancers, while Mrs Smythe looked after them with a cat-in-cream smile on her face.

And Emma felt foolish for feeling that warm rush of excitement on seeing his face again. It seemed as if she had been catapulted back to the last time she was there in those very rooms. Watching Sir David dance with Miss Maude Cole.

This lady, whoever she was, seemed to be the image of his late wife. The perfect pretty bride, where Emma had long ago blotted her copybook beyond any hope of being such a thing.

'That is Miss Harding,' Lady Wheelington said close to Emma's ear, pulling her back to where she was. Who she was.

'I beg your pardon, Lady Wheelington?' Emma said.

'The young lady whose gown you seemed to be admiring. Her name is Miss Harding and she is a new arrival to the village. Her uncle, Admiral Harding, retired here last year and she has come to stay with him for a time. She and Mrs Smythe are always seen together of late.'

'Are they?' Emma murmured. An admiral's niece *and* best friends with his sister. Of course Sir David would want to dance with her.

And smile at her. Emma watched as the music started and the dancers skipped down the line, David hand in hand with Miss Harding. They twirled around, perfectly in step with each other.

'I shouldn't trust it,' Lady Wheelington said. 'Look what happened last time poor Sir David listened to his sister's marital advice.'

Last time? *Poor* Sir David? Emma turned to Lady Wheelington, concerned. 'Whatever do you mean, Lady Wheelington?' she asked, but her question was lost as Lady Wheelington turned to greet Mrs Smythe as she joined their small group.

'Mrs Carrington!' she exclaimed with a little flutter of her silk-gloved hands in front of her obviously enceinte belly. 'Such a surprise to see you here tonight. I've seen you rushing around the village here and there, but I didn't think to see you out in society just yet. But then, you always did have your own way of doing things. Just a *joie de vivre*.' She gave a trilling laugh.

Emma politely smiled. She could see echoes of Sir David in Mrs Smythe's pretty face and dark hair, in the blue-grey eyes she squinted slightly as if she eschewed her brother's spectacles even though she needed them. But Mrs Smythe had none of his calm stillness, his careful observation. She was like a bird, fluttering around, always looking for the next moment.

'It was getting very lonely at Barton with my sister gone, Mrs Smythe,' Emma said. 'I wanted to see old friends again.'

'But I see *you* have been making new friends, Mrs Smythe,' Lady Wheelington said. 'Was that Admiral Harding's niece you were greeting? Such a pretty girl.'

'Oh, yes!' Mrs Smythe cried with another of her trilling laughs. 'And she is quite as sweet as she is pretty. I have quite come to admire her in the short time we've known each other. Such an asset to our little community.'

They all turned to look at where Miss Harding was dancing with Sir David, graceful and light in her little hopping steps as she turned under his arm and smiled up at him.

'I am hoping she can somehow be persuaded to stay here much longer than the planned visit with her esteemed uncle,' Mrs Smythe said. 'It is so hard for my poor brother to find dance partners who match him so well in grace. Especially after my poor darling sister-in-law.'

Mrs Smythe sniffled and Lady Wheelington gave her a sideways glance Emma couldn't quite read. She did, however, read Mrs Smythe's intentions quite well. She was set that her brother should marry the pretty Miss Harding.

Emma watched the two of them dancing, so well matched, like the picture of a perfect couple in a novel. She suddenly wished there was a wall nearby in need of being held up so she could hide there.

She didn't know why her spirits should sink at the thought of Sir David standing at the altar with Miss Harding, kissing her, holding her, taking her to Rose Hill to take her rightful place as the second perfect Lady Marton. Emma had so little in common with Sir David. She shouldn't even want to be in his company, let alone feel sad he should marry again. She had made such mistakes with her emotions before, with Henry and long ago with Mr Milne, the dance master. She could not be trusted now.

And yet—and yet there was the way she felt when he held her in his arms. So safe, so right, so full of excitement and peace all at the same time.

'Excuse me for a moment,' Emma murmured to Lady Wheelington and Mrs Smythe. 'I suddenly feel in need of some refreshment.'

'Are you quite all right, my dear?' Lady Wheelington asked with a concerned frown. 'You do look rather pale.'

Emma made herself smile to hide her confusion.

'Nothing a glass of punch can't cure. I will return directly.'

She threaded her way through the thick crowds around the edges of the dance floor. A few people even greeted her and issued tentative invitations to tea, a sign of some progress, she hoped. Yet she was always aware of David dancing with Miss Harding so nearby. It was a distraction she couldn't afford.

At last she reached the refreshment table and gratefully sipped at a glass of cool, sweet punch. She noticed Mrs Smythe's portly, usually absent husband lurking nearby, putting away a silver flask in his coat pocket. She wished he would splash some of it into the punch bowl for the rest of them.

The room suddenly felt too warm, too close-packed. The music and laughter and indistinct voices blended into a blurred roar that made her head spin. She closed her eyes and imagined her little sitting room waiting for her, a fire in the grate, a pot of tea and some toasted cheese, a pile of books and Murray snoring at her feet.

But then the contented image shifted and someone was sitting in the chair next to hers, reaching for her hand. He raised it to his lips for a warm, lingering kiss and whispered, 'Now isn't this so much better than going out on a chilly night?'

In her daydream, Emma shivered at the kiss and looked up—to find David Marton smiling at her in the firelight, his beautiful eyes full of promise.

Emma's own eyes flew open in shock. She was still in the crowded ballroom, still standing by herself. And David was finishing his dance with Miss Harding.

Emma quickly swallowed the last of her punch and scanned the room for some escape route. Tucked in a darkened corner she saw a door that she knew led out to a small garden attached to the assembly rooms. She hurried towards it, hoping no one would notice her hasty exit, and slipped outside.

The garden, a formal expanse of winding gravel paths past orderly flowerbeds and groupings of stone benches, was usually a place for resting between dances, exchanging whispered secrets—or for gentlemen to escape their wives for a few minutes. Even though Emma could tell such escapees had recently been there by the faint smell of cigar smoke in the air, the space was nearly deserted. Except for one young couple sitting close together on one of the benches, staring into each other's eyes, she was alone for a moment.

Emma made her way to a low iron railing that divided the garden from its neighbour. There was a cluster of tall old trees there where she could hide. She could hear the echo of laughter from where the coachmen waited in the narrow lane behind the building, but where she stood was blessedly quiet and dark.

No one could see her ridiculously flushed cheeks there.

Emma drifted to the far end of the garden, where a large, ancient tree offered shade to strollers by day and shelter to shy wallflowers at night. And Emma needed a place to shelter at the moment.

When she first came back to Barton, she'd expected many challenges. But she certainly hadn't expected David Marton to be one of the greatest. When he was near, she couldn't concentrate on anything else. She wanted him to notice her—but then she was scared of what he thought when he did. And he had looked so right dancing with Miss Harding…

Emma leaned back against the rough trunk of the tree, letting its strength hold her up as she examined the darkened windows of the bookshop across the lane. *That* was what she needed to think about. What she needed to do next. Not things she couldn't have.

As she studied the quiet street, she heard the assembly-room door open. There was a blast of music and laughter, quickly cut off, and the soft rustle of footsteps on the pathway.

Emma quickly straightened and pasted a bright smile on her face before she turned to face the newcomer. But her smile faltered when she saw it was David who stood there.

She was now alone with David in the moonlight.

He gave her a small, quick flash of a smile and laid his palm against the tree. 'Diagnosing the diseases using Mr Lee's treatise, Mrs Carrington?'

Emma gave a choked laugh. 'Since this is an oak, Sir David, I am sure it can have nothing to do with your orchard. I just needed a breath of fresh air.'

'Perfectly understandable. I find it hard to breathe at such things myself.'

'But you seemed to be enjoying the dance,' Emma said. She thought of how he smiled down at Miss Harding as she turned prettily under his arm. Emma shivered, wondering why the night felt so cold.

'Are you chilled, Mrs Carrington?' he said. To her

surprise, he quickly shrugged out of his coat and gently draped it over her shoulders.

She was suddenly wrapped in the warmth, the clean scent of him. And yet it made her shiver all the more.

He drew the edges of his coat closer around her, yet he didn't move away. Emma stared at the white glow of his cravat in the darkness and felt him watching her closely. She slowly reached out and rested her hands on his shoulders.

'I do like to dance sometimes, Mrs Carrington,' he said, his voice rough. 'But I like it best with the right partner.'

It had been so long since she was close to a man like this, and even back when she thought herself so in love with Henry it hadn't felt like she did now. So giddy and dizzy, like a glass of sparkling champagne! So warm and safe, like a summer's day. All of her senses whirled and all she could think about was David so close to her. The way his strong shoulders felt under her hands, so hard and warm and alive.

'We—we shouldn't be here like this...' she managed to whisper.

'Definitely not,' he said hoarsely. Yet his head bent toward hers and she instinctively went up on tiptoe to meet the kiss she so longed for.

The touch of David's lips was soft at first: warm, gentle. When Emma whimpered and wrapped her arms around his neck to hold him with her, he deepened the kiss. Their lips parted, tasted, and with that taste they slid down into urgent heat.

Something deep inside Emma, something reckless

and passionate she had tried so hard to banish, surged back to life at the taste of that need. Passionate need— from David Marton! And, oh, but he was such a *good* kisser, his lips moving over hers so skilfully, his tongue sliding over hers to draw her into him. Who could have ever guessed? He knew just how to touch her to make her want to touch him back. *Need* to touch him.

Something in her heart called out to him, a rough, wild excitement that burst inside of her until she knew she would explode from it. She moaned and pressed her body even closer to his as his arms held her tight. She forgot everything: who she was, who he was, the crowd in the building just behind them. Scandal mattered nothing to how he made her feel in that one perfect, frozen moment.

A moment too quickly shattered by a laugh from behind the tree that hid them from view. Emma's sensuous dream shattered like a fragile glass bubble and dropped her back down to the heavy earth. She tore her mouth from David's and drew in a deep breath of air. It felt like surfacing too fast after diving into a warm pool.

It was too dark for her to see his face, but she feared she wouldn't like what was written there if she could.

He stepped back from her, his shoulders heaving with the force of his breath. 'Oh, blast it all,' he said roughly, and she could swear she heard nothing but horror in his hoarse voice. 'Emma. Emma, I am so…'

'No,' she whispered. She pressed her fingertips to her tender lips and willed herself not to cry. She hadn't cried in so very long; tears never solved anything. But she wanted to cry now, from some strange, ineffable, hollow sense of loss.

Was she sad because he had kissed her so unexpectedly, awakening needs she had thought she had banished? Or because he had stopped?

'Don't say you're sorry, I beg you,' she said.

'But I am sorry. I don't know what insanity came over me. Forgive me, Mrs Carrington.'

Insanity. Of course. That was surely what he thought it had to be if he desired her. Emma shook her head, beyond words. She spun around and dashed out of the garden, careful to keep to the shadows where no one could see her. His coat tumbled from her shoulders. Somehow she found her way to the blessedly empty ladies' withdrawing room.

She barely recognised the sight that greeted her in the mirror. Her cheeks were very red, her hair dishevelled. She had lost the silk forget-me-nots at her waist and her sash was half-untied. She quickly set about tidying herself.

She had just smoothed her hair and tugged her gloves into place when the door opened to let in another blast of music and laughter from the party outside. Emma tensed, but then saw it was only Lady Wheelington.

'There you are, Mrs Carrington!' she cried, joining Emma at the mirror to adjust her turban. 'I wondered where you disappeared to.'

'I found myself a bit overwhelmed,' Emma confessed. 'I needed a breath of air.'

Lady Wheelington nodded sagely. 'I completely understand, my dear. All of us feel that way sometimes when faced with Mrs Smythe. She is quite the chatterer, I fear.'

'I often got the feeling when I lived here before that she did not like me very much,' Emma admitted.

'Of course not. You are much too smart for her.' Lady Wheelington turned sideways to study the fall of her dress in the glass. 'Their parents, rest their souls, were kind people and very dutiful, but it's always been quite clear their son inherited whatever brains were in the family tree. Sir David is a treasure to our community indeed. I hope he shan't make the mistake of taking his sister's marital advice again. What a mistake that would be.'

Against her will, Emma felt her curiosity piqued. Hadn't she just vowed to stay away from Sir David? Vowed never to let her emotions rule her again, as they had with Henry and Mr Milne? That David was bad for her peace of mind, for the future she wanted for herself. Yet here she was, eager to hear any gossip about him.

'Was it a mistake the first time?' she asked, hoping she sounded only light and neutral. She looked down to fuss with the button on her glove. 'I left Barton before Sir David's wedding to Miss Cole, but I remember what a handsome couple they were.'

Lady Wheelington gave a sound that sounded suspiciously like a snort. 'Handsome in appearance, mayhap. And certainly Miss Beatrice Marton is the prettiest of children. We must hope she inherits her father's steadiness and not her mother's sad flightiness. What a scandal it was!'

'A scandal attached to Sir David's name?' Emma said, startled. 'I can hardly warrant it.'

Lady Wheelington's eyes widened in the glass. 'My dear, never say you don't know?'

Confusion swept over Emma, a feeling she was becoming all too familiar with. 'Don't know what?'

'Oh, yes. I forgot you have been gone for a long while, and your dear sister is probably not the sort to share local gossip in her letters. Well, Mrs Carrington, what *do* you know?'

'Only that Sir David and Lady Marton lived mostly in London while they were married and that Lady Marton died there.'

Lady Wheelington pursed her lips. 'Yes, but I fear that is not all of it. Lady Marton died in a carriage accident near the Scottish border—where she had eloped with her lover, a cavalry officer. A handsome young rake, so I've heard. We all wondered why she insisted on living in town, when Sir David has always been so devoted to Rose Hill. When she died, it all became clear. She wanted to be close to her lover.'

Emma had never been so deeply shocked in her life. Sir David's wife had run away from him with a lover? Eloped and left her husband with a little daughter and a terrible scandal hanging over their heads? How awful it must have been for such a proud, reserved man to face down such a thing. And poor little Beatrice…

Then Emma sighed as another terrible thought struck her. Lady Marton was a romantic eloper, just as Emma herself was. No wonder David looked at her with such distance sometimes. No wonder she could never quite read his thoughts. Surely he looked at her and saw the shadow of his late wife.

But why, then, would he kiss her, so wonderfully and thoroughly?

Her head was spinning with it all.

'…but Mrs Smythe was delighted when he married Miss Cole, though the rest of us had our reservations that they suited as a couple,' Lady Wheelington was saying. 'I hope he won't listen to his sister's advice now about Miss Harding. She may be a perfectly lovely girl, of course, but who around here knows her?'

Emma shook her head, trying to bring herself back to the present moment and out of her own shock and confusion. 'Isn't Miss Harding an admiral's niece? That sounds most respectable.'

'Yes, but who are her other people? Why was she sent to stay with her uncle so suddenly? Sir David should be doubly cautious now. After Miss Cole, and little bits of gossip we heard about him in his youth…'

Cautious about associating with questionable ladies. Emma understood that very well. And she was sure any 'bits of gossip' about David himself had been only that. Gossip. 'So should we all, I think,' she murmured.

Lady Wheelington gave her a kind smile. 'Oh, my dear, you needn't worry about such things now. You are home again. You must come to tea soon and tell me how you are settling in.'

Emma started to reply, when the door opened and Mrs Smythe and Miss Harding appeared, arm in arm, heads bent together as they giggled over some joke.

'Oh, Lady Wheelington! And Mrs Carrington,'

Mrs Smythe cried. 'How lovely it is to see you out and about.'

'Thank you, Mrs Smythe,' Emma said politely, even though Mrs Smythe already told her that once.

'You must meet my new friend Miss Harding, who has quite brightened our little corner of the world since she arrived,' Mrs Smythe said. 'Miss Harding, you know Lady Wheelington of course, but this is Mrs Carrington, who is sister to Lady Ramsay at Barton Park. She has been gone for quite some time.'

Emma and Miss Harding made their polite curtsies and greetings, and Emma studied the other lady as Mrs Smythe went on chattering. Miss Harding's smile quirked, as if she had got the measure of Emma and found her no threat. And Emma was sure she could *not* be a threat where Sir David was concerned, not after all that had happened in her life.

But then, it was not her business who Sir David Marton married, she reminded herself. She had caused scandal just like his wife had and therefore wouldn't be suitable in his eyes or the eyes of their friends. And he did not even know everything she had seen in her life with Henry. No, Miss Harding was obviously a pretty and suitable young lady. And Emma shouldn't even be thinking about David, or anything else but repairing her life.

Why, then, did she just want to hide in a quiet corner somewhere and cry?

David scooped up his coat from the ground and paced to the end of the garden and back to the tree, a terrible restlessness seizing him. He had guarded against such passions all his life, fearing a hidden temper like his father's lurked inside of him. But with Emma he couldn't guard against anything at all.

When he looked into her wide green eyes, so full of life, he could see nothing else.

He had to be rid of these feelings. They could do nothing good, for either him or her. The more he saw her, the more he *wanted* to see her. The more he admired her boundless spirit.

But it was the kind of spirit that led only to ruin in the end.

David shook his head, trying to rid himself from memories of that kiss. Of the way Emma tasted, the warm, soft sweetness of her body against his.

A ray of moonlight caught on something at his feet and he bent to study it. It was the branch of silk forget-me-nots fallen from Emma's sash. He slowly picked it up and turned it between his fingers. They smelled faintly of Emma's perfume as he inhaled deeply.

And something drove him to slip the flowers into his coat and carry them with him back to the assembly rooms. He would have to return them to her later...

From the diary of Arabella Bancroft

My first kiss! I feel foolish indeed admitting to such a thing after my time here in such sophisticated company, but there it is. I have just had my first kiss tonight, in the garden with Sir William. And it was all I could have dreamed of. He told

*me I was beautiful, that he could see my true heart
as it is like his. I know better than to believe such
poetry, but those words were sweet to my ears.*

*For a moment I was sure I found a place where
I truly belonged.*

Chapter Eight

Melanie Harding struggled to climb up the slope of the hill, holding on to her bonnet as the wind tried to snatch it away. Nature really was terribly horrid. But going for a walk seemed like the only way she could escape her uncle's snoring for a while.

She reached the top of the hill and turned to study the village laid out before her as she tried to catch her breath. She could see all the little streets laid out in their short, straight lines, the old church, the people moving in and out of the shops like lines of ants.

Once she had thought Bath a poky little place, boring and narrow. Now she saw what 'narrow' really meant. She longed to escape, to run away, yet she knew there was no place to go. This terrible little village was where she was trapped.

She had to find an escape within her purgatory, clearly. And Melanie had learned to be resourceful if nothing else. Captain Whitney had abandoned her. Even her own mother had sent her here to rot. She could only depend on herself now.

And on the few friends she had been able to make. Melanie studied the stolid stone building where the assembly was held. Assembly—it was hardly worthy of the name, nothing like the assembly rooms in Bath where at least there was real music and a choice of dance partners. But at least she was able to wear her pink muslin again instead of letting it moulder in her trunk.

And she had also met Mrs Smythe's brother there.

Melanie made another impatient grab at her flying hat. Mrs Smythe was indeed a good friend, the only person of any interest she'd met since she arrived at her uncle's house. Mrs Smythe knew about London fashions and *on dit,* and was always ready for a laugh. Everyone else here seemed too serious to laugh, too preoccupied with nonsense like crops and fences and tenants. Mrs Smythe cared for none of that and she seemed glad to have Melanie's company, too.

Mrs Smythe also had a very handsome brother. A handsome brother with a nice estate and a good income.

Melanie turned her back on the horrid little village to look towards where she knew Rose Hill lay. She'd walked by it on one of her escaping rambles before, peeking over walls and past gates for a glimpse of the house. It was quite fine and modern. It could use some extension and renovation, of course, but that was what the mistress of a house was for.

Yes, Rose Hill definitely had potential. And gossip said the estate was prosperous enough to fund a London house as well. That was most important. It wasn't as if he was an earl or marquess, but at that point she would happily settle for being Lady Marton of Rose Hill.

The fact that Sir David was good looking and smelled nice, and was not an old, bald man with gout like her uncle's cronies, made it even better. He wasn't much fun, of course, not like Captain Whitney…

Captain Whitney. Melanie sighed as she remembered him and his flirtatious laughter. Being with him had been like being swept away on a tidal wave, giddy and fast and wonderful, but so quickly gone. How she missed him! Sir David was nothing like that. She had a feeling that days—and nights—with him would be something of a trial, no matter how handsome he was.

But maybe, with the security of money and a proper name behind her, there could be men like Captain Whitney again. With no harm done this time. If she was clever and careful, as she knew she could be. She had learned her lesson.

Yes, she was lucky in Mrs Smythe's friendship, as Mrs Smythe's brother was her best chance in a long time. She wasn't about to let it go.

Suddenly fed up with the wind catching at her skirts and the annoying birds wheeling overhead, Melanie strode back down the hill towards the road. She turned back towards the village, thinking maybe she could take tea at Mrs Smythe's before she had to go back to her uncle and his silent, stuffy house. She trudged slowly beside the hedgerow, caught up in thoughts of Rose Hill and being a wealthy married lady at last.

For several long moments all she could hear was the whine of the wind, which carried the stench of damp grass and woolly sheep to her nose. Yet another horrid country thing.

Then she heard something else, the rumble of hooves pounding on gravel behind her, coming on fast. She peered over her shoulder, holding on to her bonnet, to see a large, gleaming black horse barrelling down on her. It was suddenly so close she could see the sheen of sweat on the beast's flanks and the capes of the rider's greatcoat flapping around him like wings.

Terrified, she shrieked and dived toward the hedgerow, sure she would be trampled by the hooves. She tripped and fell into a puddle, her redingote quickly soaked.

'Blast it all,' she cursed. Tears of rage choked her. What else could go wrong with her life? It was all so terribly unfair!

Melanie pounded her fists on the ground, sending up more muddy splashes. Now she would have to go straight back to her uncle's house to bathe and change, no consoling gossip with Mrs Smythe.

'Are you quite all right, miss?' a man shouted. 'I am so terribly sorry. I thought no one was around.'

Melanie looked up to see the greatcoated man swooping down on her. He swept off his wide-brimmed hat and for an instant she was dazzled by the halo of light around him.

She blinked and saw that he really was quite angelic-looking. Dark coppery-blond hair fell in curls to his collar and his eyes were a deep, dark, chocolate brown set in a handsome face. Surely he was some sort of dashing poet, like Lord Byron!

She felt like she was caught in a beautiful dream.

'Are you injured?' he said.

'N-no,' Melanie gasped. 'I do not think so.'

'But I did at the very least cause you a fright, for which I am profoundly sorry,' he said. 'Please, let me help you to your feet.'

Melanie held out her hand to him. His gloved fingers closed around hers, strong and warm, and he supported her as he raised her up. He held on to her until she could stand on her own, the dazzling dizziness slowly righting the world around her. All the boredom she'd felt only moments before was gone when she looked at her rescuer.

'I have not seen you here before, sir,' she whispered.

'I have just arrived in the area on a business matter,' he said with another dazzling grin. 'I would have come much sooner if I had known there were such beauties to be seen. May I beg to know your name?'

Dizzy with his compliments after so long in the arid loneliness of no society, she laughed. 'I am Miss Melanie Harding, sir.'

'And I am Mr Philip Carrington, very pleased indeed to make your acquaintance,' he said. He lifted her muddied glove to his lips for a gallant kiss. 'Please, let me see you home to begin to make amends for my terrible behaviour.'

'Thank you, Mr Carrington,' she answered. The name was vaguely familiar to her, but she couldn't quite fathom why amid the delightful feelings of Philip Carrington's touch on her arm as he led her to his horse.

Not since Captain Whitney first appeared in her life had she felt that way.

He lifted her up into his saddle, his hands strong and steady on her waist. Then he swung up behind her, holding her close to him as he urged the steed into a gallop. The wind rustling past her seemed exhilarating now where before she had hated it.

Suddenly the world seemed fun again.

Philip watched as his pretty damsel in distress dashed up the narrow steps to a village house. She paused at the door and turned to give him a flirtatious little wave. Even under the dust of her fall to the road, Philip could see how lovely her pert little face and the pale curls peeking from beneath her bonnet were.

An angel lurking in the dismal depths of the countryside. Who could have imagined such a thing?

Miss Melanie Harding. Philip tipped back his head to peer up at the tall, narrow house. He had a feeling he would be hearing that name again soon. He was determined to see that fair face and slender figure once more.

Philip sighed and wheeled his horse around. In the meantime he had to find lodgings and seek out the agent of this dismal journey—Emma Carrington.

At least things looked a little more fun now…

Chapter Nine

❦

Sansom House didn't look very forbidding, Emma thought as she studied its front door. All the novels she had been reading lately led her to think the house of a recluse would look like a medieval fortress. That it would come complete with a moat and a watchtower, at the very least some crenellated walkways where the hidden occupant could lurk about and watch for intruders.

She was a bit disappointed there was nothing like that at all. Sansom House was more a large cottage than a castle, comfortable and modern with a pretty front garden and smoke curling out of the chimney. It wasn't even particularly hidden, merely tucked off the main lane behind a stand of trees.

Mr Sansom hadn't been seen about in a long time, but Emma supposed if one had to be reclusive it could be done just as well in comfort. She wondered what sort of man she would find inside. Would he be something like an older version of Sir David?

Emma rather hoped not. She'd already spent too much time thinking about Sir David since they last met at the assembly. She kept images of him away well enough during the day, as she walked Murray on the Barton grounds, worked on decorating her little house and spent time with Mr Lorne learning how to run a bookshop. When she was busy, there was no time to remember how it felt when he kissed her. How it felt to feel life stirring within her again.

But at night, when her cottage was quiet around her and she had only the company of a book and her dog, the thought of him would not be banished. That was when she dreamed of what it would have been like if his kisses had gone even further…

Emma shook her head and climbed down from the seat of the pony cart she'd borrowed from Jane's stable. She couldn't have Sir David in her life. She knew that very well, especially after hearing the sad tale of his wife's scandalous elopement. She shouldn't even have thoughts of him.

A groom hurried over from the side of the house to take the reins and she made her way along the walkway to knock at the front door. She straightened her bonnet and smoothed her new lilac-coloured spencer jacket that she had bought now she had received her inheritance. Surely Mr Sansom could not be so very fearsome, yet she still felt quite unaccountably nervous as she waited. Her reception in the village had been so varied, she didn't know what to expect here at this house.

A neatly clad maid in a white cap and apron opened the door and took Emma's card. 'Of course, Mrs Carrington,' she said, bobbing a curtsy. 'Mr Sansom is expecting you, if you'll just follow me.'

She was expected—that was surely a good sign. Emma trailed behind the maid as she was led through narrow, winding corridors and past closed doors. She could see why Mr Lorne was so eager to do business with Mr Sansom. Every inch of space was taken up with books, piles and stacks and overflowing shelves full of books. They blotted out most of the light from the windows and she was eager to stop and peruse the titles, to explore the treasures that might be hidden there.

But the maid kept up too brisk a pace for any explanation and Emma had to keep up with her. They came to the end of a dim hallway and the maid pushed open a door.

'Mrs Carrington to see you, sir,' she said.

'Send her in, send her in,' a voice, much heartier than Emma would have expected, called. 'And fetch us some tea, please.'

Emma ducked past the low doorway and into what seemed a cave of wonders. There was a crackling fire in the grate and comfortable dark-velvet chairs and sofas grouped around it, but every other inch was covered in more books. Stacked on every table, around the floor, teetering on shelves. Finally, behind the highest stack of all, Emma saw a man.

He sat in a deep armchair close to the fire, wrapped in a warm shawl with another over his legs, despite the mild day outside. Except for the spectacles perched on his nose, he didn't much resemble Sir David. He was thin and waxy-white, with sparse, untidy waves of grey hair. But his blue eyes were bright as he waved her forwards.

'Mrs Carrington, so good of you to come to my little house,' he said. 'Do forgive me not standing, my rheumatism you see…'

'Oh, not at all, Mr Sansom!' Emma cried as she hurried to greet him. 'I don't want to put you to any trouble at all. It was kind of you to answer my letter.'

Mr Sansom pushed forwards a chair for her and gave her a twinkling smile that made her like him right away. 'Not at all. I'm always happy to meet another book lover. Mr Lorne is a good friend, but we have known each other so long we have little left to say to each other. It seems all my other old friends have left the world without me.'

'Life does have a way of changing when one isn't looking, doesn't it?' Emma said.

'Quite right. But books are always the same. Books can always be relied upon. I know you must agree with me, as you are your father's daughter. Now there was a man who valued learning.'

'So he did, Mr Sansom,' Emma said. 'I was so excited to learn that you knew him.'

'We shared many interests. And I'm sure he would be most intrigued to learn you intend to take over the good Mr Lorne's shop.'

'I hope to. I need something useful to occupy myself and earn my bread, and books seem to be the only thing I know well. That is why I'm hoping you could help me.'

Mr Sansom chuckled. 'By letting you sell my books? I confess I would find it very hard to part with my old friends, though I know some day I must. I suppose seeing them go to new homes where they would be appreciated would be best, even if they must be separated.' He gestured to the portrait hung over the fireplace mantel, an image of two young, dark-haired ladies in the stiff satin gowns of the last century. 'You see them?'

'Yes,' Emma answered. 'They are very pretty.' And she couldn't help but notice the younger one had very familiar-looking bright grey eyes.

'My sisters. Anna, the elder, married a diplomat and went off to ports unknown, where she used to write the most fascinating letters to me. My health never let me travel as much as I would have liked, but through her I did. She died young with no children. Amelia, the younger, married Sir Reginald Marton of Rose Hill and lived close, but sadly she was a girl of little imagination. Her only son is a most intelligent man, but he is so busy he does not have the time to read as he should. So I have no family who would want all these dusty tomes.'

Emma thought Miss Beatrice Marton might one day want the 'dusty tomes', as well as Anna Sansom's letters from ports unknown. She was dying to ask Mr Sansom more about David. What was he like as a child? What other secrets lurked in his family's past? But fortunately the maid appeared with the tea tray before she could appear too eager to learn about his nephew.

'Perhaps you could pour, Mrs Carrington, while I find the books I have here that once belonged to your father,' Mr Sansom said. As Emma sorted out the tea, he dug about in the piles of volumes next to his chair.

'I was most excited to hear you had some of them, Mr Sansom,' Emma said.

'Yes, he sent them to me before he died, my poor

friend. Was afraid your mother might sell them off if he didn't, I dare say.'

Emma had to laugh. 'I fear she might have. Mother wasn't a great reader, nor did she share some of my father's—ideas.' Like the search for the lost Barton treasure. The idea of it consumed her father and sent her mother into fits of temper, and he never even found it in the end.

Nor had Emma.

'I like you, Mrs Carrington. You are not missish at all. I can't bear missish women.' Mr Sansom came up with a bundle of faded green leather-bound volumes. 'Ah, here they are. Handwritten, of course, and not the easiest to read, as I'm sure you will find. But rewarding, if you are interested in local history as your father was.'

'I am indeed,' Emma said. She passed Mr Sansom a plate of cake and took the books in exchange. 'I hope to settle here again and learn all I can about the area.'

'Done with wandering, are you, Mrs Carrington?'

'I hope so.'

'Then I do hope you can make a go of the bookshop. This place would be an utter desert without it. Tell me your plans for it.'

As they finished their tea, Emma told him some of her ideas for expanding Mr Lorne's business and finding new, further-flung clients interested in antiquarian works. She also told him about Jane and Hayden's work at Barton Park and listened to some of Mr Sansom's most recent studies. The time was passing so pleasantly that Emma was startled when the maid reappeared.

'Sir David Marton is here to see you, sir,' she announced.

'Well, well! Two visitors in one day. I am becoming quite popular,' Mr Sansom said cheerfully. 'Send him in. Mrs Carrington, you have met my nephew, have you not?'

'We have met a few times,' Emma murmured. She felt her cheeks turn warm at the memory of what happened the last time they met, the overwhelming kiss that exploded between them. The memory that wouldn't leave her. She turned to stare into the fire, hoping she could excuse her sudden blush on its heat.

'It is very good to see you again, Mrs Carrington,' David said quietly. 'I am sorry, Uncle. I didn't realise you had a guest or I would have called another time.'

Mr Sansom chuckled. 'Because I usually live so hermit-like? That is very true, David, but Mrs Carrington has kindly come along to remedy that. Sit, join us for some tea.'

David stood in the doorway for a long moment and Emma began to wonder if he would make his excuses and leave. If he couldn't stand to be around her and remember his uncharacteristic loss of control. But then she heard the echo of his boots on the old wooden floor and he moved some books from the chair next to hers before he sat down.

He was so close Emma could feel the warmth of his lean body brush against her skin, more enticing than any fire on a cold, lonely day. He smelled of the sun and the wind, and of the faint, clean cologne she remembered from the assembly. It made her want to bury her nose in his cravat and inhale him, to be as close to him as she could.

But she just glanced at him and gave him a tentative smile, half-fearful of his response. He smiled at her in return, a careful, polite smile, but it was a start. At least they could be in the same room together without her melting into a puddle of embarrassment.

Hadn't Mr Sansom said he admired her for not being missish? She felt terribly missish now, as if she would start giggling at any moment! That simply wouldn't do.

'Shall I ring for more tea?' she said briskly as she pushed herself to her feet. She hurried across the room to tug at the bell pull.

'Don't go to any trouble for me,' David said. 'I shouldn't stay long and interrupt your conversation.'

'We were just talking about books, weren't we, Mrs Carrington?' Mr Sansom said. 'An endlessly fascinating topic. Mrs Carrington is going to run the bookshop.'

'So I have heard.' David watched Emma as she went back to her seat next to him. The firelight glinted on his spectacles, hiding his eyes from her. 'Were you trying to beg my uncle's books, Mrs Carrington? After he declared to Mr Lorne he didn't want to sell at the moment?'

Emma felt vaguely discomfited by his question, as if she were caught doing something she shouldn't. She knew that feeling very well. She fidgeted with her skirt, trying to decide what to say.

'Don't be so ungallant, David,' Mr Sansom said with another chuckle. 'It's not at all like you. Mrs Carrington was merely offering assistance in finding good homes for my friends.'

'Forgive me, Mrs Carrington,' David said with a small bow.

'Not at all,' Emma answered, still pleating her skirt between her fingers. 'You are quite right to look after your family. Perhaps Miss Beatrice would care to take some of Mr Sansom's library? She seems to have very advanced reading tastes for her age.'

David picked up the large volume on top of the teetering stack next to him and glanced at the spine. 'Perhaps not quite ready for Tacitus. But you are right that she has advanced beyond lessons with her nanny.'

'A bluestocking in the making, is she?' said Mr Sansom, clapping his hands in delight. 'Most gratifying indeed. You must take her any of these books you think she would like.'

David picked up another book and examined it. He didn't look at Emma, but she glimpsed the quirk of an almost-smile at the corner of his lips. Was he—could he be—softening toward her?

'Perhaps Mrs Carrington should advise us what Beatrice might like to read, Uncle,' he said. 'My daughter has said more to her in the few times they've met than she has to anyone else of late.'

Emma couldn't help a warm flush of pleasure at the knowledge that Miss Beatrice liked her, for she was a most intriguing child. But did this mean that David would let her be around his daughter, after his wife's scandalous elopement? 'I would be happy to help Miss

Marton any way I can,' Emma said. 'She's a lovely child.'

'That all sounds settled, then,' Mr Sansom said. 'You must both help me sort out which books to sell and which to start little Miss Marton's library. In the meantime, David, tell me if you could use anything in those agricultural pamphlets I sent you. I could make little of them, but then I am not a farmer…'

After another half-hour of tea and pleasant chatter about books, Emma took her leave along with David. She found her pony cart waiting at the garden gate, along with David's horse, saddled and ready to go.

'Your uncle is a most interesting man,' Emma said. She concentrated on tugging on her gloves, uncomfortable to be suddenly alone with him.

'He is that indeed,' David said. 'I always enjoyed our visits to him as a boy. I have been trying to help him with his financial straits lately, as he has not been in good health.'

'Yet you don't think he should dispose of his books, Sir David?'

David shrugged. 'They are his books to do with as he sees fit. I just worry that he would find himself too lonely if they were gone, and then his health would decline even further. You heard how he calls them his friends. He shouldn't be pressed to dispose of them before he is quite ready. I'm always here to help him if he requires it.'

Of course he was. If there was one thing Emma had heard about David Marton, it was that he always did his duty. He always looked after his own. And that was a trait Emma had seen so rarely in the men in her life. She couldn't help but admire it.

Even when she longed to see another glimpse of the *other* David Marton, the one who kissed her so passionately, so freely. The one she was sure he kept locked down inside somewhere.

'It was good to see you again, Sir David,' she said as she put her foot on the rail of her cart to climb in. 'Please give my greetings to your daughter and your sister.'

He suddenly reached out and took her hand to help her up. His hand was warm and strong and steady through her glove. Like when he touched her, she felt— safe. Secure. As if he would never let her fall in any way.

But Emma knew that was only a sad illusion. Men like him weren't for women like her.

'May I see you home, Mrs Carrington?' he said. 'There is something I should like to talk to you about, if you can spare a few moments.'

Surprised by his words, Emma stared down at him from her perch on the seat. He looked back at her, the greyish light carving his face into solemn, beautiful lines.

'Of course, Sir David,' she said. 'I have no social occasions this afternoon. Perhaps you would care to follow me? I am staying at the old gatekeeper's cottage at Barton.'

'Not in Barton itself?' he said. She couldn't read his tone. Was it surprised—or disapproving?

'It's much too large for me with Jane in Town. I'm cosier in the cottage, though it can be a bit hard to find.'

'I will follow you, then. Lead on, Mrs Carrington.'

Emma nodded and gathered up her reins as David swung up into his saddle. She tried to look as calm as possible, but inside she was utterly bursting with curiosity. Whatever could he want to talk to her about?

She could hardly wait to find out.

Chapter Ten

〰〰〰

'It isn't much,' Emma said cheerfully as she pushed open the door to her cottage. 'But I call it home.'

She led David through the short hall to her sitting room and hurried around opening the curtains to let in the light. She didn't look at him as she tried to hastily tidy things up, but she was avidly aware that he stood there in her doorway, watching her.

That David Marton was in her house. She never could have fathomed it before, despite her strange and fleeting fantasies of him beside her by the fire. She couldn't help but be nervous, wondering what he thought when he looked at her little room.

She quickly swept a tangle of ribbons and thread into her workbox and glanced around to make sure there was nothing embarrassing around.

Everything seemed to be in order. The room was small but tidy, furnished with modern, bright pieces Jane had sent over from Barton, shelves full of books, and a few knickknacks from Emma's travels. The colours were light and fresh, all yellows and pale blues,

with a watercolour of Barton hanging over the fireplace
and miniature portraits of Jane and the children on the
mantel. Surely Sir David couldn't object to any of that?

Then Emma saw the book she had been reading lying
open on her favourite chair. *Lady Amelia's Scandalous
Secret.* She quickly swiped it into the workbox with the
ribbons and gave him a bright smile.

'It's charming,' he said. 'It suits you, Mrs Carrington.
But do you not get lonely here? It seems some distance
from the main house.'

'Not at all. I would be much more lonely there with
Jane gone,' Emma said. She watched as Murray roused
himself from his bed by the fireplace and trotted over to
greet their guest. David knelt down and rubbed at Murray's greying head, making the dog's plumy tail sweep
across the carpet. 'I have Murray here, as you see, and
a maid comes over to help me every day. She's probably
in the kitchen reading fashion papers now. She has a
cherished ambition to be a lady's maid. But I think she
can scramble together some tea for us.'

'You mustn't go to any trouble, Mrs Carrington,' he
said. 'I don't want to take up too much of your time.'

'Not at all. Please, do sit down, Sir David, and let
me ring for tea. Like your uncle, I'm glad of the company,' Emma said. Then she suddenly felt flustered, remembering how he hadn't seemed very happy she had
visited his uncle. She hurried over to ring the bell and
leave her hat and gloves on the table.

He sat down in the chair next to hers, looking a bit
stiff and not entirely at ease. Murray followed him, resting his head on David's knee.

'I'm so sorry,' she said. 'Let me put him back in his bed before he leaves fur all over you.'

'No, please, let him stay,' David said. 'It's been a long time since I had a dog. It's quite nice.' He smiled down at Murray, who wagged his tail even faster.

Emma watched him, astonished. Murray was never an unfriendly dog, but life with Henry had taught him to be wary of men and protective of Emma. That he would be happy to see David, so quickly, amazed her. Against her will, she felt her feelings growing tenderer towards David again. He was baffling.

'Murray does seem to like you,' she said.

'I remember when he was a puppy, when you last lived at Barton,' David said. 'Now he's getting as grey as me, poor fellow.'

Emma laughed. 'I don't see any grey in *your* hair, Sir David.'

He smiled up at her. 'That's because I have a valet who is very clever at cutting hair. He hides my decrepitude from the rest of the world.'

'Decrepit indeed,' Emma murmured. She thought of the easy, powerful way he rode his horse as they made their way to Barton, as casually elegant in the saddle as if he were a centaur. The grace of his dancing. The strength of his arms around her as he kissed her...

Fortunately, Mary the maid hurried in to interrupt such wildly distracting thoughts. Emma ordered tea and sat down in her chair, carefully arranging her skirts.

'Oh, Mrs Carrington, the post just came,' Mary said as she turned toward the door. She took a bundle of papers from her apron pocket and left them on Emma's worktable. 'There was a letter from London, as you've asked me to look out for.'

'Thank you, Mary,' Emma said happily. 'It must be from my sister, Sir David. I have been longing to hear how she's doing.'

'You must read it, then. I shall talk to Murray while you do.'

As Emma reached for the letter on top, with the direction written in Jane's neat hand, she smiled to see how content Murray seemed to be, still leaning against Sir David's leg. 'He does seem to enjoy your company.'

'Perhaps I should get Beatrice a dog. Something a bit smaller than Murray, though, I think.'

'Everyone should have a dog.' Emma broke the seal on her letter and quickly scanned the contents. It wasn't very long, as it seemed Jane was still confined to bed, but the news Emma had been aching to hear was good. 'At last!'

'Good tidings, I hope?' David said.

Emma smiled up at him. 'Very good. My sister is safely delivered of a healthy daughter, named—little Emma! They are both recovering very well. She says they hope to return to Barton by the summer.'

'That is indeed excellent news. You must send my congratulations to Lady Ramsay.'

'Of course I will.' Emma carefully refolded the letter, remembering how, years ago, she had suspected Sir David admired her sister. Nothing could have ever come of it, of course. Jane was married, even though she and Hayden were then estranged. And surely David was too much a gentleman to ever pursue such a thing. Still,

Jane *was* pretty and such a perfect lady at all times. Unlike her younger sister...

'You wanted to talk to me about something, Sir David,' she said quickly, pushing away such memories.

He blinked, as if surprised by the sudden change of topic. But he nodded and followed her lead. 'It was about Beatrice.'

'Would you like me to find a puppy for her?'

David laughed. 'Perhaps one day soon. I would only know how to procure farm dogs, not young lady's pets. But I would like to ask a rather presumptuous favour.'

'I doubt it could be very *presumptuous* if it involves Miss Marton. I quite enjoy her company and would like to help her if I can.'

'That is very kind of you. I do my best for her, but it cannot be easy for a girl of her age without a mother to help her. Her own mother...'

Had not been much of a mother. Emma remembered the tale of Lady Marton's sad elopement and wild ways. Surely something like Emma's own misjudged past. Yet here he was asking her for a favour for his daughter. Surely that was some sort of good sign, a kind of progress?

'I am going to look out for a suitable governess for her,' David said. 'Someone who can teach her a little more than French and etiquette. She is becoming too clever for her nanny and me.'

'A bluestocking in the making?' Emma said, remembering Mr Sansom's jolly words.

'I don't know where she gets it. My mother and sister

were never readers and Beatrice's mother—well, Maude knew a great deal about hats and the theatre, I suppose.'

'But not much about books concerning travels in India.'

'Quite. I know Beatrice has been very quiet since she lost her mother and we came back to Rose Hill, but she does seem to enjoy learning. And she also seems to like you.'

Was that a note of doubt in his voice? Did he marvel that Beatrice could like her at all? 'I enjoy her company as well.'

'Then would you perhaps be willing to give her a few lessons until I can find a suitable governess? She could come to you here, or at the bookshop, and I would provide any volumes you need. I think it might help to distract her.'

'I would be most happy to give Miss Beatrice lessons,' Emma said, surprised but delighted. 'It would give me distraction as well and something useful to do. I am not sure I know enough to actually teach her, but I am willing to find out. Perhaps she and I can discuss new topics together.'

'I would be most grateful to you, Mrs Carrington. In return, perhaps I could help sort through my uncle's books and see what might suit you.'

'I thought you didn't like me "bothering" your uncle, "pestering" him to let me have his books.' Emma couldn't help but tease, just a bit.

David gave her a rueful smile. 'I do tend to be quite protective of my family.'

'And quite right.' Emma felt a bit wistful as she wondered how it would feel for him to protect *her*. But at least, perhaps, they were starting to be friends. It was better than nothing and the best she could expect.

Mary came back with the tea tray and arranged it neatly on Emma's worktable. As the maid left, Emma studied the china cups and bowls of sugar and lemon, and a mischievous thought seized her.

'I think I have quite had my fill of tea for one day,' she said. 'My sister's news deserves a bit of celebration, don't you think, Sir David?'

A doubtful frown flickered over his handsome face. 'A celebration?'

'Yes,' Emma said firmly. She hurried across the room to rummage through a crate she hadn't yet unpacked. It was full of odds and ends of her peripatetic life with Henry that she hadn't yet been able to dispose of—including a bottle of fine French champagne he had won at the card tables one night. She had hidden it before he could drink it, then he had died the next week in that duel.

'I think this is fitting to toast the new baby,' she said. 'I was told it's quite a rare and expensive vintage.'

David laughed. 'What *is* that?'

'Champagne, of course. Don't tell me you have never seen such a thing before, Sir David, for I happen to know there is reported to be quite a fine cellar at Rose Hill.'

'Yes, my father was a collector. But where did you get it?'

'From my husband. Henry won it in a card game. I was utterly furious when he brought it back instead of

money for the rent.' Not as furious as she was a week
later, though, when Henry fought that fatal duel. And
his weeping, married lover landed on her doorstep to
tell her about it. Emma pushed away those terrible memories and held the bottle up to the light. 'It's terribly
dusty, but it should still be good, I think.'

'You should have sold it. It would have paid your rent
for many weeks, I think.'

'Really?'

'Yes.' David came and took the bottle from her hands
to study the label. 'It's a '96. A very fine vintage.'

'Truly?' Emma peered closer at the label, which was
so faded she could hardly make out the French words.
'Perhaps things were not so hopeless as I feared, then.'

He held it out to her. 'You should put it in a safe
place.'

Emma shook her head. 'I still think we should drink
it. To toast baby Emma's good health.' And perhaps to
celebrate her tentative new hopes for friendship with
Sir David.

'Are you quite sure?'

'Yes. Can you open it?'

He nodded and turned away to do something complicated to get the bottle open. 'I confess I am quite curious
to taste it. Since the war, bottles have been quite rare.'

'I'm glad to be of help, then.' Emma laughed and
clapped her hands as the cork popped free with a fizzy
little explosion.

David laughed too, a wonderful sound she had never
heard before. He quickly poured out some of the pale
gold liquid into the teacups and passed her one. His

bare fingers slid along hers, warm, enticing and too quickly gone.

He stepped back and held up his cup in a salute. 'To baby Emma.'

'To baby Emma,' Emma agreed. She clinked the gilded edge of her cup with his and took a long sip. It slid over her tongue in a sweet, effervescent rush, making her shiver. 'Oh, that *is* nice. Like—like liquid sunshine.'

David also took a deep drink and smiled. It was a sweet, deeply satisfied smile and Emma couldn't help but wish he would smile at *her* like that. 'Very fine indeed. Are you sorry now you didn't open it sooner?'

'Not at all. This seems like the perfect moment for just such a thing.' Emma sat back in her chair and happily sipped at her champagne until, all too soon, it was gone. David refilled their cups, and a delightful, warm, comfortable feeling spread over her.

After a few quiet moments, David suddenly said, 'Did your husband gamble quite often?'

Emma frowned, some of the warmth ebbing away. She didn't want to think of Henry, not now when she was having such fun. 'Why do you ask?'

David held up his cup. He seemed to notice then it was empty again and he refilled both his and hers. 'Because you said he brought home wine instead of rent money from the gaming tables.'

'Oh, yes. That.' Emma took another sip and Henry once again seemed very far away. A pleasantly blurry memory, which was just what he should be. 'He was very fond of a card game, as well as many other things he couldn't quite handle. I didn't quite realise that when we married.'

'Things such as what?' David asked. 'What sort of man was your husband?'

The wrong sort for any lady. 'But I don't want to think about Henry any more!' Emma cried. She jumped up out of her chair, suddenly unable to sit still any longer. Her whole body felt like the champagne itself, fizzy and warm and alive. Alive—as she had not felt in so very long!

David laughed and she spun around to look at him. She could hardly warrant this was the same man who first came into her cottage so cautiously. He leaned back in his chair, his long, lean legs stretched in front of him. His cup dangled loosely from his elegant fingers and his hair curled over his brow. He smiled up at her lazily and suddenly she couldn't breathe.

'What do you want to think about, then?' he asked.

'I want to dance,' Emma blurted out. At least she didn't say the very first thing that popped into her head—*I want to kiss you.* 'It's been too long since I danced.'

David set aside his empty cup and slowly rose to his feet, as graceful and deceptively powerful as a panther. He reached for her hand and gave a low, courtly bow as Emma watched in thunderstruck astonishment.

'And there is no finer ballroom for it,' he said. 'Mrs Carrington, may I have the honour of this waltz?'

Emma laughed and curtsied deeply before taking his hand. 'Sir David, I would be honoured.'

He took her into his arms and hummed a waltz tune

as they twirled around the room, faster and faster until they were both laughing, until she had to cling to him to keep from falling.

'I've never waltzed like this before!' she cried.

In answer he whirled her around faster and faster, until they stumbled to a stop. Their laughter faded as they stared at each other in the hazy daylight.

Emma reached up to touch his face, trailing her fingertips over his finely carved features as she marvelled at him. He was so contradictory—she couldn't decipher him at all. One moment so strict, so remote, and the next, closer to her than anyone had ever been. He made her feel so safe with his quiet strength, but at the same time he made the world crumble around her until she didn't know what was happening.

She swept a light caress over his sensual lips and he smiled against her fingers.

'Emma...' he said roughly, and then he did what she so longed for. He kissed her.

She went up on tiptoe to meet him, twining her arms around him so she wouldn't fall. So he couldn't leave her. His hands closed hard around her waist, pulling her even closer to him.

Emma marvelled that they seemed to fit so perfectly together. Their mouths, their hands, their bodies—as if made to be just like they were now. She parted her lips and felt the tip of his tongue sweep over hers. Lightly, enticingly, but it made her feel as if she had tumbled straight down into the sun itself. The kiss turned frantic, full of raw need and burning desire.

She felt him press her back against the wall, his

hands strong and hungry as they slid over her shoulders and traced the soft curve of her breasts through her muslin bodice. Emma was astonished and delighted at his boldness, at the way he seemed to know just how she needed to be touched. She moaned at the delicious sensations that shivered through her, like sunrays and snow showers all at the same time.

Oh, this is terrible, she thought. Terrible and wonderful all at the same time. She knew she shouldn't be doing this, but she couldn't stop.

Through the silvery, sparkly haze of desire, she heard him whisper her name.

'Emma, Emma,' he said, as if he was in pain. 'What do you do to me?'

What did she do to *him*? He cracked apart her whole world and reformed it, just by being near her. She didn't know why or how. All she could do was hold on to him.

She felt his fingertips trace the edge of her bodice, caressing the bare skin of the soft upper curve of her breast. She was shocked—and delighted. She drew him closer to her, desperate for him not to leave her. To have him touch her again. She'd felt so cold, so alone, for so long, and now she finally felt warm again.

Because of David.

Her head fell weakly back against the wall and her eyes drifted shut as she tried to blot out everything but the feel of his touch on her skin. His warm, slightly rough fingertips, the brush of his cool breath—it was all so wondrous. She wanted more of it, and yet more and more.

He bent his head to press a hot, open-mouthed kiss

to her neck, to the soft, sensitive spot just below her ear. She shivered as his kiss trailed over her collarbone, the curve of her shoulder over the thin muslin of her gown, like a silky ribbon of fire.

The tip of his tongue lightly traced a teasing circle on the slope of her breast, just above the ribboned trim of her gown. His touch came teasingly close to her aching nipple, just the merest brush, but it made her cry out.

Emma arched against him. Through the layers of her dress and his doeskin breeches, she felt the heavy length of his manhood, hard with a desire that echoed her own. As her body touched his, he groaned against her skin and his mouth found hers again.

Emma buried her fingers in the silky waves of his hair, almost sobbing at the intense force of connection that flowed between them.

The haze of her passion cleared a bit as she felt him draw back. His kiss slid away from her lips, leaving her chilled. His hands loosened their hold on her waist, his fingers tense on her skin, and he braced his forehead on her shoulder. Their rough breath mingled and Emma was sure he could hear the pounding of her heart in the sudden silence of the room.

She reached up to smooth a gentle caress over his rumpled hair and her hand trembled. She wanted to cry with the terrible yearning that grew inside of her, the longing for what she couldn't have. A new life, a new beginning. Her mistakes had made those impossible. But she still longed for them, here with David.

'Oh, Emma,' he whispered hoarsely. 'What is it that you do to me? What is happening here?'

Emma choked out a laugh. 'I have no idea,' she managed to answer. She pressed a lingering kiss to the top of his head, clinging to him for as long as she dared before she let him go. She feared this precious moment close to him would be the only one she might ever have.

As his touch left her, she turned away from him and adjusted her gown. She drew in a deep breath, then another and another, until she felt her trembling slowly stop. Her thoughts still swirled, but at least she could feel the ground under her feet again.

Behind her, David braced his fists against the wall, his head hanging between his shoulders. His inner struggle almost felt like a physical thing between them, a building of a wall as thick as any stone. How could they be as close as any two people possibly could be one moment, and so far the next? She longed to know what he was thinking, for him to take her in his arms again and tell her what was happening.

She glanced back at him shyly, just in time to see him stand up very straight. He seemed to draw the invisible protection of his infallible dignity around him. He straightened his coat and raked his hands through his hair.

'Emma, I...' he said, his voice rough and sad.

'No, David, please,' she answered, trying to laugh, to be light. Not to cry. 'Don't say you're sorry. I should never have opened that wine. I never had a head for it. It seems to cast such a strange spell...'

'Not just the wine,' he muttered.

No—not just the wine. Emma shook her head. She had more words, no more excuses.

'I hope that my behaviour doesn't mean you won't spend time with Beatrice in the future,' he said.

Emma was shocked. She would have thought he wouldn't *want* her to tutor his daughter, not after her wantonness. 'Of course not.'

'Thank you,' he said, his voice still tight, as if he held all his emotions on the tightest of leashes.

Emma wished she could do the same. She felt as if she was about to crack with it all and just wanted to be alone so she could cry.

'I am sorry, Mrs Carrington,' he said. 'I don't know what madness came over me.'

Madness. Of course. That was what it had to be, if he desired her. Emma swore she could hear her heart cracking apart inside of her…

'Is that someone at your door?' David said.

'Wh-what?' she gasped. The whole world seemed to be spinning madly around her and for an instant she wasn't sure where she was. She tilted back her head and stared up into David's glowing grey eyes.

He seemed almost as bewildered as she felt, a frown forming on his brow as he stared down at her. His hair was tousled, his eyes intent as he looked at her. He had never looked so attractive to her, like a flame she beat against helplessly, like a moth drawn again and again to the very thing that was worst for it.

She opened her mouth, only knowing that she had to say something, *anything,* to snap the taut, sizzling tension between them. Then she heard the loud pounding sound again and she realised it was *not* her heart.

Someone was at the door.

'I suppose I should get that,' she said, feeling very slow-witted indeed.

David nodded and slowly stepped back. Emma swayed, hoping she could walk without tumbling down on her trembling legs. She spun around and hurried toward the door, her feet moving automatically.

In the hallway, she glanced back over her shoulder just in time to see David stoop to pick up his spectacles from the floor. Murray gave a confused little whine and David absently reached out to rub at the dog's head. David stared down at the spectacles in his hand, frowning. She longed to go back to him, to feel him touch her again and beg him to tell her what he was thinking.

But she knew very well that he wouldn't tell her. He'd said it himself; he was sorry for what had just happened. Probably sorry he had lost control with a woman like her, no matter how momentarily.

When he kissed her, in that instant she felt safe, as if she belonged, as if she didn't have to be lost. But now she felt even lonelier than ever.

Another knock sounded at the door and it was very clear Mary wasn't going to answer it. Emma quickly smoothed her skirt and tucked her hair back into its confining combs. She had no idea who would come calling on her, as no one had yet made their way to her cottage sanctuary. She only knew she had to get rid of them, whoever they were. And then she had to get rid of David, so she could be alone and think, and remind herself sternly why she was done with romance.

Any hint of the blighted thing was obviously very bad for her.

She pulled open the door, a polite smile pasted on her lips—and froze.

It was Philip Carrington. Henry's cousin and best friend, his partner in carousing. And the only one who had stood as *her* friend during her misbegotten marriage.

Philip stood on her doorstep in a stylishly cut greatcoat and impeccably fitted doeskin breeches, tall-crowned hat in his hand. The breeze tossed around his honey-coloured curls and he grinned at her in a show of dazzling delight.

For an instant, all Emma could do was gape at him. Surely he was some sort of illusion? It had been months since she refused his offer of help and left him in that dingy lodging house. She'd thought she would never see him again, yet here he was. Right on her doorstep.

Emma shook her head, mingled disbelief and delight sweeping through her. Philip had been her one friend during life with Henry, even though he had often been in trouble himself.

'Philip,' she gasped. 'Whatever are you doing here?'

'I came because I couldn't bear not to see you again, Emma. The Continent is a complete wasteland without you.' His smile widened and Emma remembered how all the ladies would flutter their fans at him. Would practically chase him down through the casinos and shopping stalls.

Yes, he was just as handsome as ever. As handsome as Henry had once been. But what was he doing there? They hadn't parted on the best of terms. And she wasn't one of his swooning admirers.

Even though she could see why those ladies were enthralled. His smile *was* disorientingly sensational.

But not half as disorienting as David's rare flashes of humour.

Oh, good heavens. *David.* David was just down the corridor in her sitting room. This was not good at all.

'Philip, I—I am quite astonished,' she managed to say. 'You should have written.'

His confident grin faltered a bit. 'No time to write, Emma my dear. I could travel faster than a letter and I was most eager to see you. I can see now I should have travelled faster. You are looking lovelier than ever.'

'Philip…' Emma said, her desperation growing.

'Blast it, Emma, I missed you so much,' he said. Before she saw what he was about, his gloved hand slid out and grabbed her wrist to pull her towards him. 'You are more gloriously pretty than I remembered!'

His arms closed hard around her waist and he lifted her completely off her feet. As she curled her fists into the fine fabric of his coat, trying her hardest to push him away, he twirled her around and around.

'Didn't you miss me, too, Emma? Just a bit?' he shouted. 'Say you did or I vow you'll break my heart!'

'Philip…' she cried.

'I can see I'm quite interrupting. I'll just take my leave, Mrs Carrington, and be out of your way,' David suddenly said.

Over Philip's shoulder, she saw David standing in the corridor just beyond the open door, his hair and clothes impeccable again. As if nothing at all had happened.

What was worse—far worse—was that he watched

her seemingly cavorting with Philip with no sign of emotion on his face at all. No frown, no anger, only that calm, cool mask she had come to dread.

The man who kissed her so passionately had completely vanished.

Chapter Eleven

'Philip, put me down!' Emma cried, hating the thread of desperation in her voice. 'This instant.'

'It's been so long since I've seen you, though, Emma,' Philip protested. 'Haven't you missed me just a bit? I…' Then he looked beyond her and saw David standing in the doorway. His teasing grin slowly faded and he lowered her to the ground. 'I didn't realise you had company. I thought that horse there was yours.'

Emma staggered back, trying to pretend to at least a modicum of dignity. She really just wanted to scream, or run away, or rewind the clock to take her back an hour before this all happened. Or really, if she had such a magic cloak, she should turn it back to before she made the supreme mistake of marrying Henry Carrington.

But all of those things were quite impossible. She straightened her shoulders and said, 'Philip, this is my neighbour, Sir David Marton. Sir David, may I present my late husband's cousin, Mr Philip Carrington?'

'A neighbour, eh?' Philip said as he offered David a bow. 'You have settled back here quickly, Cousin.'

'Is that not what home is for, Mr Carrington?' David said quietly. 'A place to belong, no matter how long we have been gone from it?'

'I'm sure my late cousin would want his wife to be with family, no matter what,' Philip said.

'And yet his own family has taken so long to call on her?'

Emma felt as if a conversation in some foreign language was going on over her head as Philip glared at David. She didn't like that feeling at all. And she couldn't like the solemn, watchful way David studied Philip. It made her feel like she had done something horribly wrong, when for once she had not.

'Mr Carrington has quite taken me by surprise today,' she said. 'I thought he was travelling on the Continent.'

'You were the one who left in such a hurry,' Philip said, a thread of querulous irritation darkening his sunny demeanour.

'Then I will leave you to be reacquainted,' David said. 'Thank you for the tea, Mrs Carrington. I am sure either my uncle or I will contact you regarding the books very soon.'

He gave her another bow and hurried down her garden path toward the gate where his horse was tethered. He moved with such swift, elegant dignity, so quick to leave her.

As if their dance, their kiss, had never happened.

Emma longed to run after him to catch his arm and

tell him everything. To beg him to believe her when she said she was not expecting Philip. But she knew she couldn't do that. It would surely only make him think worse of her and he wouldn't believe her anyway. Why should he? She surely looked the veriest wanton now, just like his wife.

With David, she always felt like one baby step forwards—or one great kiss forwards—pushed her ten steps back. She wanted so much more from him, even though she knew that was foolish indeed.

'Good day, Sir David,' she called as his horse turned on to the drive that led away from Barton land.

He gave her a quick wave and urged his horse to a gallop. All too soon he disappeared from her view.

'I hope not all your neighbours are quite so dour, Emma,' Philip said.

Emma's hands curled into fists as she turned back to face him. 'Sir David is not dour. He merely has many responsibilities, which he takes seriously. Unlike the Carringtons.'

Philip held up his hands as if in surrender and gave her a rueful smile. 'Pax, Emma. I am sorry I was too impatient to see you to write first. But I *have* missed you.'

Emma sighed and rubbed her fingertips against the headache forming at her temples. It really was not Philip's fault that the timing of his arrival was so rotten. Once he had been very kind to her when she had so little kindness in her life.

It wasn't his fault that he was part of a past she wanted only to leave behind.

'Do come in, Philip,' she said. 'I can ring for some

tea and you must tell me what you have been doing since I saw you last.'

Philip's grin returned and he offered Emma his arm to lead her back into the house. 'Missing you, mostly. It really has been horribly dull without you and Henry.'

'I find it hard to believe you could find no amusement at all,' Emma said. She hastily kicked the empty bottle of wine behind a sofa and piled up the used teacups on the tray before she rang for Mary and set about straightening the chair cushions. Her emotions were still roiling inside her, confusing and bewildering, but she was suddenly glad she wasn't alone.

'You would be surprised,' Philip muttered. He examined her little room with his hands clasped behind his back, frowning a bit as he glimpsed Murray. The dog whined at him and sat up at attention. Murray had never much liked Philip, Emma remembered. 'I was astonished when the housekeeper at Barton told me you were living alone here in this old cottage. Never tell me your sister cast you out?'

'Oh, no, nothing like that. Jane is in London right now and I felt too lonely in the great house all alone.' Emma sat down and gestured Philip towards the chair next to hers, trying not to think of how David had just sat there. Of how close she had come to him—only to be pushed away again.

'It still seems a harsh place for the sister of a countess,' Philip said. He fiddled with the china ornaments on her side table, a curious look on his face.

'You know how Henry left me placed,' Emma said softly, embarrassed to even mention his cousin's bad behaviour. Philip had encouraged Henry in some of it, true, but it was not Philip's fault he could handle it and Henry could not. Philip had tried to be her friend and now he had come all this way to see her. She couldn't be unfair to him.

'Do I?' he muttered. Emma could hear that hint of some darkness again and it made her fidget in her chair. But then he smiled and it seemed as if a grey cloud scuttled away. 'Yes, I fear my cousin did not deal well with either of us in the end.'

Mary hurried in with a fresh tea tray. For a second, the maid's eyes widened in astonishment to see a different man there. But Philip turned his sunny smile on her and she giggled as she set down the tray with a clatter. Her cheeks were bright pink when she dashed away. Such was the effect of Philip's angelic looks on every female he encountered.

Emma remembered that it was last a darkly exotic Polish countess, which made her wonder again why he had come so far to dull old Barton.

'No, I suppose he did not,' Emma said. She poured out the tea, knowing she would never offer a guest wine again. It only caused trouble.

'He left you nothing at all?'

A strange intensity in the question made her glance at him sharply over the teapot. 'You know he did not. But I am finding ways to look after myself.'

'Your family, I'm sure. Or perhaps you are planning to marry your ever-so-serious neighbour?'

Emma gave a choked laugh. Marry Sir David? Surely

it would as easy for her to fly to the moon. 'I am not the sort of wife Sir David Marton would require.'

'The more fool him, then.' Philip gave her another smile as she handed him the cup, a different smile. One quieter, more intimate. 'You really are looking lovely, Emma. The countryside seems to agree with you.'

'I am quite content here,' she said. 'I wish that you could find the same. You really have been a good friend to me, Philip. You deserved better from Henry.'

'Oh, I think I am closer to finding contentment than ever before,' Philip said mysteriously. 'Now, tell me more about your new life here, Emma. I find myself quite intrigued…'

David urged his horse faster down the lane until they were galloping, the wind rushing past and the hedge-rows turning to a green blur as they soared by. Zeus was glad to have his head and tossed his glossy black mane back in joy. But the wild run didn't set David free.

Usually a fast ride released the tension built inside of him, took him out of himself, but not today. Today the recklessness and burning anger he kept tied up inside threatened to consume him.

He sent Zeus soaring over a ditch, bent low against the horse's neck as they flew. He had no right to feel jealous of anything Emma Carrington did, yet he feared that was exactly what fuelled his fury now. When he saw that man holding her in his arms, David just wanted to grab the blighter by his dandyish coat and plant a facer on him.

And then he wanted to grab Emma in his own arms

and kiss her until she never wanted to look at another man but *him*. Until she cried out his name only.

The fierceness of his primitive instincts appalled him. He didn't recognise himself—or at least not the man he had long strictly schooled himself to be. Responsible, reliable, never thoughtlessly angry. And he had now long lived by the dictates of control and decorum.

Until Emma. She brought out a recklessness he had thought conquered. Not even Maude, who he had once desired, ever made him feel that way. Her scandalous desertion had only made him more determined to exert control over every aspect of his life, to protect his daughter and his family name.

But Emma—she brought out the old wildness in him. Every time he looked at her, every time she smiled or laughed and he saw her green eyes brighten like a warm, lazy summer's day, he only wanted to be closer to her. To be a part of her light, fun spirit and see the world as she surely did.

Her husband had disappointed her, just as Maude had with him. But Emma didn't seem defeated by it. How did she do that? He wanted that for himself—he wanted *her*. Wanted her as he had never wanted anything else—wildly, passionately.

And he had to beat that down, just as he did every desire, every attempt of his darker side to defeat him. Passion had no place in his life. It only led to destruction and ruin. He needed order in his life and Emma Carrington was the very definition of chaos.

Why, then, did he keep remembering the way she felt

in his arms? The way she tasted, the smell of her perfume all around him, the sound of her sighs? When he danced with her, kissed her, he never wanted to stop. Never wanted her to go away.

And then that man—Philip Carrington—appeared. When David saw Emma in his arms, the two of them laughing as he spun her around, anger as strong as his desire threatened to overwhelm him. But he should have been grateful for Mr Carrington's timely arrival. It was a vital reminder to David that he always had to remember who he was and what his life was about. And who Emma was.

It was obvious Emma and Philip Carrington had once been close. The familiar way he touched her, the looks they exchanged, spoke of a friendship. Who knew what had gone on in Emma's life with a disappointing husband on the Continent? Perhaps Philip Carrington had been a comfort to her.

Even as a new wave of anger rushed through David at the thought of such 'comfort', his rational side knew he could hardly blame her. Henry Carrington had let her down in some way and she was alone in strange cities, far from her family. She had made mistakes, misjudged people, as everyone did. He himself had misjudged Maude and it almost ruined him and Beatrice.

He couldn't afford to misjudge again, no matter how beautiful or spirited Emma was. No matter how much her kiss awakened fires in him he thought long extinguished. He had to be very careful.

David turned Zeus down the lane towards home, drawing the horse in a bit. Zeus snorted and tossed his head, obviously not happy with being reined in and re-minded he had to be civilised.

'Believe me, old boy, I understand,' David said with a rueful laugh. Once wilder impulses were released, it was almost impossible to lock them away again. But it had to be done. He just felt that way because he had been too long without a lady's intimate company.

Yes, that was all it was. He had his natural urges and had suppressed them.

The gates of Rose Hill were just ahead and David glimpsed something most unwelcome there. His sister sat in her open carriage, waiting for the footman to open the gates. And beside her, the two of them giggling to-gether, was Miss Harding.

'Blast it all,' David cursed. This was the very last moment he wanted to see his sister and her friend, and play the genteel host.

But all his years of self-control were not for nothing. He slowed Zeus to a walk and felt a sense of icy calm and remoteness come over him as he moved closer to home.

'Louisa,' he said as he drew Zeus in beside his sis-ter's carriage. 'I didn't know you were planning to call today. And Miss Harding, a pleasure to see you again.'

'Miss Harding and I were just visiting Mr Crawford at the vicarage and I thought she might like to see Rose Hill since we were so close,' Louisa said with a giggle. 'Really, David, what have you been doing? You look quite wild! Not at all like you.'

David was sure he couldn't look half as wild as he felt. But he loathed the idea that it showed to other people. 'I have just been for a ride. Poor Zeus has been quite restless lately. If I had known you were coming—'

'Oh, Sir David, you mustn't be cross with your sister,' Miss Harding cried. 'It was entirely my fault. I have heard so much about the beauties of Rose Hill and I begged her to let me catch a glimpse for myself. Do forgive us for intruding.'

David bowed his head to Miss Harding, who smiled prettily back. She was all pink cheeks and bouncing pale ringlets in her fashionable beribboned straw bonnet and blue redingote, the very image of demure young ladyhood. The niece of an admiral, friend of his sister—exactly the sort of proper young woman he ought to be seriously thinking about at such a time in his life.

The sort who would grace Rose Hill and the area, look after Beatrice and give him more children—and never arouse his darker side with passionate desire. Yes, exactly what he needed.

But as she gave him a shyly sweet smile, all he could see was Emma staring up at him with brilliant green eyes and kiss-red lips.

'Not at all,' he said carefully. 'My sister and her friends are welcome at Rose Hill at any time. Please, do come inside.'

'I knew you would be glad to see us, David,' Louisa said. 'Dear Rose Hill is in such need of a feminine presence, isn't it?'

David led his sister's carriage up the gravelled drive to the front doors, which were opened by Hughes, the old butler who had been at Rose Hill since David's parents' time. He left Zeus with the grooms and helped Louisa down from her carriage.

As he handed down Miss Harding, she leaned gracefully on his arm and peeked up at him shyly from beneath the brim of her bonnet.

'Thank you so very much, Sir David,' she said. 'You are always so gallant.'

'You are very welcome, Miss Harding,' he answered politely. 'I hope Rose Hill doesn't disappoint you after the good reports you have heard.'

Still holding on to his arm, she tilted back her head to study the house's façade of pale-grey stone, with its twin stone staircases leading to the front doors and soaring rose-pink marble columns. The windows sparkled in the sunlight.

'Not at all,' she said. 'It is most pretty indeed.'

'You do not see any improvements you would make?'

Miss Harding's smile turned mischievous. 'Not at present. But I should have to see the inside. That is where ladies really excel, you know, in curtains and cushions and such.'

'Indeed,' David murmured, remembering how Maude had filled the London house with bolts and piles of fabrics and wallpapers and pillows the instant they arrived. Everything in the very latest style.

And then he thought of Emma's cosy sitting room, all books and family portraits and dog beds.

'Hurry up, you two,' Louisa called out merrily, pulling him out of his thoughts. Out of his impossible desire to be back in Emma's cluttered cottage, beside her. 'Stop whispering now. I am quite longing for a cup of tea.'

'Of course, Louisa.' David led Miss Harding up the steps into the cool shadows of the hall, with its black-and-white stone floor and rows of classical statues brought back by his grandfather from the Grand Tour. They hadn't moved since.

'Yes, I do see what you mean,' Miss Harding whispered. 'No colour at all.'

Before David could answer, Mrs Jennings the house-keeper, like Hughes a remnant of his parents' time, came hurrying over.

'Louisa, Miss Harding—Mrs Jennings will take you into the drawing room and send for some tea,' he said. 'If you will excuse me for a moment.'

'Oh, David dear, no need to be so formal,' Louisa said with a laugh. 'Rose Hill is still my family home, too. I can play hostess—until a new Lady Marton comes along, of course.'

Miss Harding blushed prettily and gave him a flashing smile before she hurried after his sister into the drawing room.

David went up the stairs toward the family chambers, shaking his head. He was no fool when it came to matchmaking family and friends. Almost everyone he knew had immediately begun producing their pretty young daughters, sisters and cousins as soon as Maude died. He saw their kind intentions and always knew one day he would have to marry. But being in no way prepared for the emotional demands of a marriage, and having his stunned and sad little daughter to think of, had sent him back to the quiet haven of Rose Hill. Alone.

He had foolishly not counted on his sister's tenacity on the subject of his marriage. Louisa hadn't learned much from the mistake of her friendship with Maude, it seemed. And now Miss Harding was her object.

David paused on the landing to glance back down at the drawing-room door. Laughter floated out to him, a softly feminine echo that Rose Hill hadn't heard in a very long time. He couldn't be unfair to Miss Harding. She *did* seem to be exactly the sort of lady he required as a wife—young, respectable, biddable. That she could be friends with Louisa was surely a mark in her favour; she would get along with his family.

But doubts lingered, a toxic mix of bad memories and a strong desire never to make a mess of his life again. He couldn't afford to make another wrong, scandalous marriage. Miss Harding bore some watching.

And yet—yet he couldn't get the memory of Emma out of his mind. Emma in his arms, Emma's lips under his. Emma driving him to bedlam with his need for her.

David pounded his fists on the carved railing and silently cursed, trying to drive the thought of her away. Emma was most decidedly *not* the sort of wife he needed. She was too impulsive. And he was not the man for her, not if she sought adventure as she had with her first husband. They were deeply wrong for each other.

If only his mind could convince his body.

He heard a rustling noise, a sigh, and he glanced up to see Beatrice on the landing above. She sat between two gilded posts, her legs dangling down and a doll clutched in her arms as she stared down at him with large, solemn eyes.

'Is that Aunt Louisa, Papa?' she said.

'Yes, it is. And where is Nanny? You should be in the nursery,' David said. He strode up the rest of the stairs to scoop his daughter up in his arms.

'She fell asleep by the fire. I was reading, but then I heard voices and wanted to know who was here.' She peered down at the hall far below. 'I was rather hoping it was Mrs Carrington.'

Beatrice was hoping to see Emma Carrington? David studied her closely and saw an interested light in her eyes that hadn't been there for a long time. He had thought he should not let Emma tutor Beatrice, not when he needed to learn to control himself around her, but if she could make Beatrice show an interest in something at last...

It was rather a conundrum.

'It is your Aunt Louisa and her friend Miss Harding,' he said as he turned toward the nursery wing.

Beatrice wrinkled her little nose. 'Miss Harding? Why is *she* here? She doesn't talk about anything interesting. At least she did not that time I met her at Aunt Louisa's.'

'She is here because she's friends with your aunt and you need to be polite to her.'

Beatrice looked doubtful. 'I'll be polite, of course. If I must see her.'

David tried not to laugh. He had to teach Beatrice to learn to be a proper lady, after all. 'You must, as they are visitors in our home. You said you see her at Aunt Louisa's house.'

'I must be nice because one day you might marry her?'

David stopped suddenly in his tracks, startled by her quiet question. 'Where did you hear that I am to marry Miss Harding?'

Beatrice stared back at him, wide-eyed. 'From Aunt Louisa, of course, when I went to play with my cousins yesterday. She was talking to Mr Crawford's fiancée, and she said she hoped that soon Mr Crawford would have another ceremony to perform—for you.'

'Well, it was wrong of your aunt to speculate like that,' David said, appalled to realise that surely now the whole village paired him with Miss Harding. He would have to have a word with his sister about little pitchers and big ears. 'I can't say what might happen in the future, but Miss Harding and I are not betrothed. If we were, *you* would be the first one I would tell.'

'Really?'

'Really. We are a family, you and I, and we must always be able to tell each other what we really feel.' David hugged his daughter close, an unbearable feeling of tenderness threatening to overwhelm him. She was his child and he would protect her in any way he could. And the first way he would do that was in being very careful about what new stepmother he brought into her life.

'Then Miss Harding is not to be my stepmama?'

'No one is going to be your stepmama at present. We do well enough by ourselves, don't we?'

Beatrice nodded and even gave a smile. 'For the present we do. But I must tell you honestly, Papa, that you don't smell very good right now. You should not be entertaining guests to tea.'

David laughed, relieved that her worries seemed to have passed. But if there was one thing he knew about Bea, it was that she was too good at hiding the depths of her feelings. Though she was quite right; the wine and the fast gallop outdoors probably did not make for an appealing perfume. 'What have we said about manners, Bea?'

'But you just said we should tell each other what we think.'

'I have just been riding and was just coming upstairs to clean up and make myself presentable.' David nudged open the door to the nursery sitting room. Nanny was indeed snoring by the fire and Beatrice's dolls were set up around their tiny table for a tea party. Open books lay scattered around everywhere and he remembered her need for lessons.

And her happiness at the mention of Emma's name.

Yes, it was definitely time for Beatrice's education to advance. She was becoming far too clever for the nursery. The realisation that his darling daughter was growing up, becoming a most independent spirit, gave him a pang.

He put her down on her small chair and picked up some of the scattered books to tidy them into a pile. Against his better judgement, he knew what he had to do.

'I do have some news you might like, though, Lady Impudent,' he said.

Beatrice frowned doubtfully. 'What is that, Papa?'

'I am going to look out for a governess for you, a lady who can help teach you all the things you want to know. In the meantime, so that you will be ready when she comes, you will go to the bookstore to have a few lessons with Mrs Carrington.'

'Mrs Carrington? Truly?' A smile suddenly burst across Beatrice's face, brighter and happier than any David had seen in a long while. And it was Emma who had put it there.

Emma who somehow made the world brighter and lighter just by existing. Emma—with her doubtful past and unpredictable spirit.

'Oh, thank you, Papa,' Beatrice cried. She jumped off her chair and came running to hug him around his waist, holding on tight. 'I will study so very hard with Mrs Carrington, you'll see. You are the best papa in the world.'

'Just promise me you will do your work and be very careful,' David murmured, holding Beatrice close. He hoped he was not making another terrible mistake.

Yes. This place would do very well.

Melanie studied the drawing room as she sipped at her tea and listened to Mrs Smythe chatter on. The colours were not at all stylish, of course, much too dark and heavy, but the elaborate white plasterwork of the ceiling was very pretty and the space quite large. It could accommodate some grand parties.

She thought of the rooms in Bath where she and her mother had lived for so long, the tiny little bare space they could barely even afford to heat. How very different Rose Hill was from all that! A whole different world, really. It would be so very splendid if she could bring her mother here and show it to her as their new house. If she could finally take care of her mother and not be a disappointment to her...

Melanie closed her eyes and imagined the look on her mother's face when they drew up to the portico of Rose Hill in a fine carriage. The delight, the joy—the relief that they would never have to struggle again. How wonderful that would be! To have a secure place. To be Lady Marton of Rose Hill.

And all she would have to do was marry Sir David Marton to get it.

Melanie's eyes opened and she felt as if cold water had just been flooded over her delightful dream. Marriage was surely a small price to pay for such a prize? She had been completely ready to marry Captain Whitney. And Sir David was far from unattractive. He was very handsome, indeed, and came with that lovely security.

But—but why did she feel nothing when she looked at him? When she danced with him? When Captain Whitney led her on to the dance floor at the Bath assembly rooms, it felt as if a wonderful fizz, like champagne, sang through her veins. That giddiness made her long to risk everything just to feel it again. And when it was gone—blackest despair.

She'd felt the tiniest fizz again when that gloriously

gorgeous Philip Carrington lifted her up on to his horse. He was so dashing, like a Galahad rescuing a fair damsel! It was like a dream.

But she couldn't afford dreams now. Dreams were what got her packed off to this dull village in the first place. Dreams were why they were so poor, because her mother fell in love with a poor curate who then died young. No, Melanie couldn't have dreams of great romance right now. She needed this house. Maybe some day, when she was established, she could find someone…

She just had to find a way to get all that.

The drawing-room door opened, interrupting Mrs Smythe's flow of chatter, and Melanie looked up to see Sir David come into the room. He had changed into a fresh coat and his dark hair was damp and combed back neatly from his face.

Something inside her perked to a new attention. Yes, he *was* good looking. Surely once they were married she could do something to make him more fun? More impulsive, more laughing. More like…

More like Philip Carrington.

No, Melanie told herself sternly. She wouldn't think again about Mr Carrington, no matter how beautiful or exciting he was.

'Sir David,' she said brightly. 'Your home is so lovely, I am quite, quite overwhelmed by it all.'

Then she saw the little girl who held his hand and she froze. She had met Miss Beatrice Marton before, of course, at Mrs Smythe's house. She was a pretty child, but so quiet and so strangely old for her age. It was a bit—spooky.

And Melanie had quite forgotten that Sir David and his lovely house came with a strange little fairy-child who seemed to see right through Melanie with her weird grey eyes.

'Say good day to your aunt and Miss Harding, Beatrice,' Sir David said.

Melanie made herself smile and rose to her feet to hurry toward them. 'Such a charming little girl, Sir David!' she cried. 'You must be so very proud.'

If this was to be her life—and she was grimly determined that it would be—she knew she might as well start now.

From the diary of Arabella Bancroft

I hardly know how to write this, but it seems my darling Sir William is not all that he appears. The king does invite him to court for his handsome looks and charming conversation, but his family has long been penniless. He is here to seek an heiress to marry, or failing that...

He must return to highway robbery as he did during the wars. My poor William. How desperate his life must have been, must still be.

And I am no heiress.

Chapter Twelve

'And this is *galgan*,' Emma said as she pulled the spiky little plant from the damp ground. 'It's very useful for fevers, but it looks a bit like *venich*, which has no good use and shouldn't be eaten.'

Beatrice carefully studied the plant and compared it to the drawing in the book she held. 'I don't think I can ever remember so much, Mrs Carrington.'

Emma laughed and added the new specimen to their basket. 'That's what I'm here for, Miss Marton, to help you learn.'

'May I try to find one on my own?' Beatrice asked.

'Of course. Just don't go too far.'

As Beatrice scampered away, her botany guide in hand, Emma straightened and stretched her back. She laughed as Beatrice happily dug in the dirt, the sun shining on her red-gold hair. They had only been out for an hour, and already the girl was glowing with the brisk, bright air of the outdoors.

Not bad for a first lesson, Emma thought happily.

Surely David Marton would be content that she was the proper person to teach his daughter.

Not that she cared about what David thought about her, of course. Not at all.

To distract herself, she snatched up the basket of plants she had gathered with Beatrice and turned to follow the girl. It really was a lovely day, the spring sun bright and warm in a cloudless sky, the rich smell of green growing things on the breeze. Back in nature, which she had once loved so much and had lost for so long, she could almost feel like she had come back to herself again. Her true self.

It was too bad her true self still insisted on thinking about David Marton and the way it felt when he touched her.

'Mrs Carrington! Look at this,' Beatrice called.

Emma started to follow her, when suddenly she heard the rumble of wheels coming along the lane over the hill. She turned and saw it was Sir David himself, driving his curricle. He looked as if he had been visiting tenants, for he was casually dressed in a dark-blue coat and fine doeskin breeches that clung to his strong legs. A wide-brimmed hat shadowed his face.

'How goes the lesson, Mrs Carrington?' he asked as he drew in the horse.

Emma walked slowly toward him, still caught between her daydreams of him and the reality of his sudden appearance before her. She was unsure how to react to him.

'Very well, I think,' she said. 'Botany seems a good subject to begin with.' Emma felt a blush touch her cheeks when she remembered how disapproving his sister once was of her muddied hems. 'Although I haven't had the chance to study it in a long time, I fear.'

'Papa!' Beatrice cried. 'Look at what I found.'

His smile widened, transforming his already-handsome face to something truly wondrous. He climbed down from his curricle and quickly tied up the horse before he strode towards his daughter. Emma hurried after him, holding on to her straw hat as the wind tried to snatch it away.

Beatrice's little face and pink muslin dress were streaked with dirt as she held up a clump of mud-trailing plants, and her own hat fell from her head. Emma remembered how beautifully turned-out the child always was and felt a jolt of alarm that David would upbraid her for letting Beatrice get into such a state.

But he knelt beside Beatrice and carefully examined the leaves she held out to him. He swept his hat off and let it dangle in his hand, and the wind caught at his dark hair and tousled it over his brow.

'Very nice, Bea,' he said. 'What is it?'

'It's a—a…' A frown flickered over Beatrice's little face. 'What was it called, Mrs Carrington?'

'*Galgan*,' Emma said.

'It's good for a fever,' Beatrice said earnestly.

'Fascinating,' David said. 'What else have you learned today?'

Emma couldn't help but smile as she watched them there together, the tall, strong, handsome man and the adorable child. The sunlight shimmered on their hair, dark and bright. It was such a tiny, perfect moment, so unlike anything she could ever have imagined in her life before. If she could only freeze time and keep it for ever, she thought wistfully.

'Mrs Carrington?' Beatrice said, and the moment jolted into full light-filled motion again.

Emma smiled and went to kneel down next to them. She told Beatrice more about the plants, concentrating on the little girl even as she felt David's gaze on her, studying her. She felt a flutter deep down in her stomach, a nervous self-consciousness she didn't know what to do with.

Eventually Beatrice scampered off to examine something on the slope of the hill, her hat bouncing by its ribbons on her shoulders. David held out his hand to help Emma to her feet and she smiled up at him.

'Miss Beatrice is very curious about the world,' she said as they strolled along the road behind Beatrice, side by side.

David laughed. Like his daughter, he seemed lighter outdoors, more natural. He made Emma feel more comfortable too. 'Too curious sometimes, I fear. It's kind of you to share your knowledge of botany with her.'

'I've forgotten so much of what I once learned. I've enjoyed rediscovering it today,' Emma said. 'I think—

Her words were once again interrupted by the clatter of wheels on the dusty road. Emma glanced back over her shoulder to see an extraordinary scene, a fine open carriage painted a bright, glossy red, driven by a coachman clad in red-and-gold livery. It looked like no other equipage in the area.

As she watched, astonished, the carriage lurched to a

halt and a lady's face peeked over its gilded edge. Like her vehicle, she was—different. Bright blonde hair sparkled under a copiously feathered hat and her beautiful heart-shaped face was set off by a marabou-trimmed pink spencer.

'By Jove,' she cried, her voice caught by the breeze like the toll of a silver bell. 'It *is* David Marton. My, but it's been an age, hasn't it?'

Next to Emma, David stiffened. She studied him out of the corner of her eye and saw that his earlier easygoing, smiling demeanour, the casual warmth that had drawn her closer, was quite vanished. A small frown curled his mouth downwards and his eyes were narrowed as he looked at the beautiful woman in the carriage.

'Mrs Dunstable,' he said, his quite deep voice giving nothing away. 'It has been a long time.'

She laughed again. 'It's Betsy, remember? You used to call me that, anyway.'

'You are a very long way from London,' David said. Emma felt as if she watched a theatre scene she had come to late and couldn't follow.

'I was just giving a ride to a friend who needed to come to your quaint little village,' Mrs Dunstable—Betsy—said. 'I quite forgot you had come to live in this funny little place. After your marriage, wasn't it?'

'Yes,' David said shortly, still so quiet.

'Yes,' Betsy echoed, her sparkle dimming just a bit. 'It really has been too long. It's good to see you again.'

'And you, Mrs Dunstable. You look very well, as always.'

The fine carriage went on its way and David led Emma back towards where Beatrice was digging in the dirt again. 'An old acquaintance,' he said briefly.

'Of course,' Emma murmured. Yet inside she was afire with curiosity, and a tinge of what felt ridiculously like—jealousy...

'How are you settling back at Barton, ma'am?' Mary the housemaid said as she brought the tea tray into Emma's little cottage sitting room.

'Very well, I think,' Emma answered, pulling herself away from wondering who Betsy might be. 'It's a bit strange coming back to the places I knew as a girl and trying to reacquaint myself with everyone.'

'You'll make new friends, surely, ma'am,' Mary said. The china clattered as she laid it out.

Emma thought about that one sunny moment as she watched David and Beatrice, of how perfect it all seemed. How quickly it vanished. 'I hope so. I shall have to go into the village more often, I suspect.'

'Or call on more neighbours, ma'am?'

Emma laughed. 'I don't think we have many of those, Mary.'

'There is Rose Hill, ma'am. My sister worked in the kitchen there, 'til she went off to Bath.'

'Did she?' Emma asked in interest. Servants so often knew everything that went on in a house. 'I just saw Sir David Marton and his daughter today.'

'My sister said it was a lovely place to work and Sir David is very generous to all the servants,' Mary said approvingly. 'When he was there. He used to live in London, you know, when Lady Marton was alive.'

'I had heard that. It does seem strange, considering how much he seems to care about his estate.'

'So he does, ma'am, everyone says so. But...' Mary paused and bit her lip.

Emma was intrigued. 'But?'

'Well, Mrs Carrington, I did hear that once, a long time ago, when Sir David was young, he got into some trouble in London.'

'Trouble?'

'I'm not sure what exactly. Drink, maybe, or an unsuitable woman,' Mary whispered. 'But then his father almost let the estate go to ruin while he was gone and he came back. That's all I know. Just a bit of gossip, ma'am.'

'Yes,' Emma murmured. It was clear the maid would know no more. 'Thank you, Mary.'

As the maid hurried away, Emma sipped at her tea and turned those intriguing titbits of gossip over in her mind. So, once upon a time, the responsible Sir David had had a wild streak. Perhaps that was when he knew Betsy. But Rose Hill had brought him back, just as Barton Park had for her.

Most intriguing....

Chapter Thirteen

❦

'So, is young Miss Marton to join us today?' Mr Lorne said.

Emma glanced up from her book, blinking and startled to find herself in the dusty, quiet bookshop and not in the colour and chaos of Restoration England. She had been immersed in Arabella's diary for what felt like hours now. It was a welcome distraction from thoughts of David and all that had happened between them. Of the gossip she had heard from Mary.

She smiled at Mr Lorne and said, 'I believe so. That is what Sir David's letter said.'

She'd been most surprised to get his message after their day outdoors. And, she was ashamed to think of it now, excited too, when she had seen it came from Rose Hill. She hadn't seen him since that day, and she was sure he regretted that he asked her to help Miss Beatrice. She avoided the village, afraid she might see him there and become quite tongue-tied and ridiculous when forced to make polite greetings to him and pretend nothing had happened.

But that didn't mean she ceased to think about him. Unfortunately, that was not the case at all. At night, she laid wide awake in her bed, remembering his kisses. The wondrous, soaring delight, and how she never wanted them to end.

And the way David looked when he saw her in Philip's arms. So cold, so remote—as if they hadn't just been so very close. And when Mary told her the tale of Sir David's youth, it was as if she didn't know him at all.

Emma wanted to cry when she thought about it all. Everything was so tangled up and upside down. She was mooning over David Marton like a silly schoolgirl and she hated it. Like the silly schoolgirl she herself had once been, in fact, fancying herself in love with the handsome dance master, Mr Milne. She'd been a fool then and she felt a fool now.

David was no Mr Milne, preying on a girl's fancies, she knew that very well. He was no Henry Carrington, either, living only for the moment and the desires of that one instant. David was a respectable man, as well as a devilishly attractive one. But that made him not for her and her dreams of his kisses were a hopeless waste of time.

But then again—he *had* asked if he could send Beatrice to her today. Surely that meant something? Feeling silly, Emma carefully laid aside the old diary.

'Sir David says he intends to hire a proper governess for his daughter and wishes for her to have some lessons to catch up first,' she said. 'I agreed to help if I can, but I fear Miss Marton may be too smart for me.'

Mr Lorne chuckled. 'She is a clever one, that child.

The quietest ones often are. Sir David is quite right to keep her mind occupied so she won't get into mischief. But I wouldn't worry, Mrs Carrington, you are quite equipped to teach any child. Did you not go to school yourself?'

Emma shook her head, thinking of her school. There had been little education there, among the worldly, gossipy daughters of fashionable families. And the too-handsome, deceitful dancing teachers. 'A finishing school for stylish young ladies with dancing and a little music and French. And Jane and I never had a proper governess. I learned haphazardly from my father's library. At least he never cared what we read, we had free rein among his books.'

'Books contain every answer, if we know where to look for them,' Mr Lorne said as he shelved a new shipment of poetry volumes from London. 'I understand you visited my friend Mr Sansom?'

'I did. He was most charming. He gave me these old diaries from Barton Park. I'm finding myself quite fascinated by them.'

'Did you have any luck in getting him to sell us his collection?'

Emma smiled at his use of the word 'us'. It made her feel as if maybe she was finding her place at last, even if it was behind the counter of a bookshop. 'Not yet. But I am sure he will let us have at least some of them soon. In the meantime, I feel as if I have made a new friend here.'

'Friends are a good thing to have.' Mr Lorne gave

her a sly smile over a stack of volumes. 'I hear that another one of yours has recently arrived in the village.'

Puzzled and disconcerted by his words, Emma said,
'I don't know what you mean, Mr Lorne.'

'I heard that a relation of your late husband was lodging at the Rose and Crown.'

Emma almost groaned aloud. If even Mr Lorne knew
of Philip's presence, surely that meant everyone did.
And she had come home to Barton hoping to escape
gossip! Philip had sent her notes asking for another
meeting since that day of his sudden arrival, but she
wasn't yet prepared to talk to him and find out his true
reason for coming.

She realised then she should have settled things with
him that very moment. If only her head had not been
whirling from David's kiss!

'Mr Carrington is my late husband's cousin, yes,'
she said quietly. 'He is passing through on his way to
a business appointment, I believe, and stopped to pay
his respects.'

'Mrs Smythe and her friend Miss Harding were in
to buy some of the new Minerva Press titles yesterday,'
Mr Lorne said. 'They were all a-flutter about how handsome this Mr Carrington is, and how he promised to
attend the next assembly. I'm sure they would be most
sorry to see him leave again too quickly.'

'Yes,' Emma murmured. Philip was indeed handsome. But nothing at all compared to David.

She thought of Miss Harding dancing with David,
the two of them looking so right together. And Mrs

Smythe's hopes for her brother's new match. Miss Harding would be a fool indeed to let Philip turn her head.

But no more a fool than Emma herself was for letting David turn *her* head.

She laughed at herself and turned back to the brittle pages of the old diary in front of her. Better to lose herself in the hopeless romances of people long gone than worrying any more about her own.

The bell over the door jangled and Emma looked up to see Beatrice entering the shop with her nanny. The little girl looked just as tidy and pretty as ever, like a little candy box in a pink pelisse and net bonnet, her hair tied at the nape of her neck with pink ribbon, unlike her messiness when they looked for botanic specimens. But her usual quiet, watchful air, so much like her father's, had vanished in a new smile. She hurried eagerly to the counter on her little pink kid boots.

'What are we going to learn today, Mrs Carrington?' she asked, her eyes shining.

'No, Miss Beatrice,' her nanny chided. 'Remember your manners.'

'Of course,' Beatrice said, bobbing a curtsy. 'Good day to you, Mrs Carrington. Mr Lorne. So delighted to see you again.'

Emma laughed. 'Good day, Miss Marton. I'm very happy you're so eager to continue your lessons.'

'Oh, yes, I am,' Beatrice said.

Her nanny took her leave, saying either she or Sir David would return for the child before teatime, and Emma helped Beatrice change her pastel pelisse for an apron. Mr Lorne lifted Beatrice up on to the stool next to Emma's, behind the pile of books Emma had chosen for her.

'These look marvellous,' Beatrice said. Emma wondered where the pale, quiet little girl had gone. Beatrice fairly shone with excitement.

'I wasn't sure where you wanted to start,' Emma said. 'I found some children's books on English history and some pamphlets on botany...'

Beatrice examined a copy of Aristotle that was nearby. 'When can I learn Greek, so I can read this?'

Emma laughed again, delighted at her eagerness. The little girl quite chased away her earlier silly broodiness. 'I'm afraid that Greek is quite beyond me. I can teach you French, and a little Italian and German, which I learned on my own travels. You'll need a special tutor for Greek, when you are older. In the meantime, we can start learning about another young lady who was eager to learn...' Emma pulled a biography from the bottom of the stack. 'Queen Elizabeth. I think she would be an excellent example for you and I found this lovely biography written for girls just your age.'

'Oh, yes,' Beatrice said as she opened the book to examine the engraved portrait on the endpapers. 'I saw a book from my father's library about the Spanish Armada once. I didn't realise she was once a child like me.'

The time happily passed with Beatrice reading about the young Queen Elizabeth and asking Emma questions about Tudor England as she went along. Emma continued in between with deciphering the old diary, making notes of things she found interesting.

'What are *you* reading, Mrs Carrington?' Beatrice asked.

'A very old diary your father's uncle gave me,' Emma said, showing her the faded ink writing on the crackling pages. 'It was written in the 1660s by a girl who once lived at Barton Park.'

'Did she know Queen Elizabeth, then?'

'No, the queen had been dead many years by then. But she does write about Charles the Second, who once visited Barton after he gave it to one of his friends. She mentions the family at Rose Hill, too, though I fear it's the old castle and not the one you live in now.'

Beatrice's eyes brightened and she leaned closer to examine the pages. 'Really? What else does she say? What was her name?'

Emma gave her an abbreviated account of the life of Arabella Bancroft, a poor cousin of the Bancroft who was given Barton Park by the king. Arabella witnessed parties at the new house and heard rumours of Court politics, all of which she shared in colourful detail. Arabella also had a budding romance with a handsome Cavalier, which Emma feared would not end well.

But Beatrice didn't need to know that part. Emma told her what houses like Barton and Rose Hill were like two hundred years ago and about the treasures of lost Royalist gold Arabella wrote about.

'A lost treasure?' Beatrice said. 'It sounds like a storybook.'

'It is, in a way. I've heard tales of the legend of Barton treasure since I was your age.'

'But is it true?'

'I don't know for sure. My father always thought it was true, but he could never find out where it was hidden.' And it drove him crazy in the end. Emma could never forget that.

'But he didn't have Arabella's diary, did he?'

'He gave it to Mr Sansom a long time ago.'

'Then maybe there is a clue in it your father didn't see,' Beatrice said thoughtfully.

Emma was somewhat alarmed to see the same spark for adventure and romance in Beatrice's eyes that had once been in her own father's. And her own, she feared. 'It is just a local legend. Queen Elizabeth is a much more important subject.'

Beatrice reluctantly went back to her book, until the bell over the door rang again. Emma looked up, expecting a customer—only to find it was Philip. There could be no more avoiding him now.

'Who would have guessed the loveliest ladies in all the village could be found in the bookshop?' he said cheerfully. 'And I have been searching for them for days in vain.'

'Good afternoon, Philip,' Emma said. 'As you can see, I have been working.'

'Working too hard even to see your cousin, eh?' Philip said, but he didn't seem put out by her avoidance. He smiled and strolled over to lean his elbows on the counter. 'And who is this fair maiden?'

'This is Miss Beatrice Marton,' Emma said. She felt strangely unsettled, but she couldn't quite decipher why. 'Miss Marton, this is Mr Carrington, who was cousin to my husband.'

Beatrice gave him a doubtful look. 'How do you do, Mr Carrington?' She slowly held out her hand to him.

Philip gallantly bowed over it. 'How do you do, Miss Marton? You must be the daughter of that chap I met a few days ago, Sir David Marton.'

'Yes, I am,' Beatrice agreed.

'I'm amazed he is so fortunate to have such a beautiful daughter,' Philip said teasingly. 'I hope he is very protective of you and carefully guards such a jewel.'

To Emma's surprise, Beatrice laughed. 'You sound like a character in a book.'

'The book you are reading right now?' Philip said, peeking at Beatrice's volume upside down across the counter. 'A life of Good Queen Bess, eh? Sounds quite weighty for such a petite girl.'

'I like it,' Beatrice said. 'Maybe you could have been someone at her Court, Mr Carrington. They liked to give compliments too.'

'Very wise of you, Miss Marton, to know so much about the Elizabethan age already,' Emma said, quite enjoying watching their light banter. Beatrice was actually smiling. 'Never believe flatterers, no matter what era they live in.'

Philip laid his hand over his heart and affected a wounded air that made both Emma and Beatrice laugh. 'I vow I speak only the truth! But Mrs Carrington is quite right, Miss Marton. You must read all you can and learn all about the world and the people in it. Tell me more about Queen Elizabeth.'

Beatrice showed him some of the illustrations in her book, explaining the various chambers of old palaces, the food and gowns and servants. Emma was amazed she had already absorbed so much information.

'And this is a great banquet for a foreign ambassador,' Beatrice said. 'I wish I could have seen the dances then. Were they much like the ones we have now at assemblies, Mrs Carrington?'

Before Emma could answer, Philip held out his hand to Beatrice and said, 'If you would do me the honour of partnering me, Miss Marton, I would be delighted to demonstrate a Spanish gavotte. Which my mother once made me learn to show off at a fancy dress party when I was about your age.'

Emma frowned. 'I am not sure…'

'Oh, please, Mrs Carrington!' Beatrice said eagerly. 'I do so want to try it.'

'I, too, would like to see a gavotte,' Mr Lorne said, leaning on the crate he had been unpacking.

'Oh, very well.' Emma gave in with a laugh. 'We are meant to be learning lessons, after all. Dancing should be included.'

Philip helped Beatrice off her stool and led her to a cleared space in front of the shelves. He bowed low and she gave a giggling curtsy.

'First we step like this,' Philip said. 'Then to the left. Hop. Hop, clap and spin.'

Soon they were whirling and twirling between the piles of books, Philip humming horribly out of tune as Emma and Mr Lorne clapped in time.

'Look, Mrs Carrington!' Beatrice called merrily. 'I am dancing.'

Emma laughed to see the delight on her pretty little

face. 'So you are—and very well, too. Philip, you have hidden talents!'

'If my fortunes wane, I can find work as a dancing master,' he answered.

'May I have this dance, Mrs Carrington?' Mr Lorne said with a wobbly bow.

'I would be honoured,' Emma said, and soon the four of them were twirling and spinning amid laughter and cries.

'These are the best lessons ever!' Beatrice called out, just as the door opened amid a jangle of bells.

David stepped over the threshold—and went very still at the sight of their hilarity. His solemn gaze swept over them, casting a chill over their impromptu ball.

Emma staggered to a stop and Beatrice suddenly toppled over, her hair bow askew. Philip lifted her up, until he too saw David watching them in silence.

'Papa,' Beatrice cried, 'I'm learning Elizabethan dances.'

'So you are,' David said quietly. 'It's not quite what I envisioned when I said you should have lessons…'

'Sir David…' Emma gasped, suddenly cold and dizzy after the giddiness of the dance. David was the last person she ever wanted to look foolish in front of, yet she always seemed to end up doing it anyway. 'We were reading a book about Queen Elizabeth, and Mr Carrington came in…'

'I do see,' David said, still very still and serious looking. He strode over to Beatrice and quickly retied her hair bow, drawing her away from Philip. 'It's getting rather late, I fear. We should be going home, Beatrice.'

'But, Papa…' she began.

'Now, if you please. Nanny will have your tea ready.'

Emma saw something she had never before glimpsed on Beatrice's face—the beginning of a pout. She leaned over to grab the child's hat and pelisse, and helped her put them on. She felt flustered and unsure and she didn't like that feeling at all.

'You must take the books with you, Miss Beatrice, and tell me what you've read in them next time I see you,' Emma said.

'Oh, I will, Mrs Carrington. I promise, I will read them all,' Beatrice said. 'Can I come back here very soon?'

'I'm sure Mrs Carrington must be very busy, Beatrice,' David said. He took his daughter's hand and led her toward the door. 'We cannot monopolise all her time.'

'Oh, but—' Beatrice cried.

'Say good day, Beatrice,' David said firmly.

The pout became fully formed, but Beatrice obediently made her curtsy. 'Good day, Mrs Carrington, and thank you very much.'

Then, to Emma's surprise, Beatrice ran over to hug her around the waist. Emma longed to hug her back, to hold her close, but Beatrice left as quickly as she had come. She hurried back to take her father's hand, her eyes downcast, all her giggling gone.

'Good day, Mrs Carrington. Mr Carrington, Mr Lorne,' David said. He led his daughter away and the door shut behind them, leaving stunned silence behind them.

'Well,' Philip said jokingly, 'he isn't much fun, is he?'

Emma had the strongest urge to rush to David's defence. After all, surely she herself was in the wrong for letting Beatrice's lessons get out of control? And yet—yet she was angry with David, too. They had been doing nothing wrong. She ran out the door just in time to see David helping Beatrice up into his curricle.

'Sir David,' Emma called.

He turned back to look at her, his handsome face blandly polite. She had come to hate the way that expression concealed so much from her. 'Mrs Carrington?'

'I—I hope you aren't angry at the…er…exuberance of today's lesson,' she said, a bit out of breath after her dash from the shop and desperately eager that he should not be angry with her. 'It won't be that way again. Mr Carrington came in most unexpectedly and—'

'Mrs Carrington, please don't worry,' he said politely and yet somehow impatiently. 'It is none of my business who your relations are, of course. I must only be concerned with my daughter.'

And being with her would not be good for Beatrice? 'Of course you must be. I only—'

'David, dear! What are you doing here at this time of day?' Mrs Smythe and her friend Miss Harding suddenly emerged from the draper's across the lane, waving to David and turning his attention from Emma.

Emma turned away, most unwilling to let the ladies see how flustered she was. The last thing she needed was more gossip in the village. She rushed back into the bookshop and slammed the door behind her. As she turned to pull the shades down on the window, she glimpsed Miss Harding linking her arm through David's and smiling up at him.

Emma spun around and marched back to the counter where she blindly shuffled books around. Mr Lorne had vanished behind the shelves.

Behind her, Philip peered past the edge of the shade, an expression of amusement on his face.

'If that's the level of amusing company in this place, Emma, I'm amazed you stay here,' he said. 'Especially after Italy and Germany. There's nothing like that life here, is there?'

Emma remembered all those spa towns, the casinos and ballrooms, the drunken men. 'No, and that is why I came back here. That is why I am trying to make a new life here, to fit in.' And she was obviously doing a very poor job of it.

'With such dry sticks as that Sir David Marton? He even looks bored right now, talking to that charming Miss Harding.'

Emma slammed a book down on the counter in a sudden fit of anger. She'd once thought David a 'dry stick' herself, when she was young and stupid, before life with Henry taught her what 'amusement' could do. Now she saw how very foolish she was then.

Now that it was all too late.

'Sir David is a very respectable and amiable man,' she said. 'Why are you here, Philip? I know this place cannot amuse you.'

He looked back at her over his shoulder, a grin still on his lips. 'I came here to see you, of course, Emma. We parted much too abruptly after Henry died.'

'I had to come home. There wasn't much choice.'

'But there was. I offered you my assistance, Emma. Indeed, I was most eager to give it.'

Emma closed her eyes against the spasm of pain the memory of that terrible time gave her. She had felt so alone, so lost. She'd only wanted home, peace, a place to belong.

For a few precious moments, when David kissed her, she had felt just that.

'You were very kind, Philip,' she said.

His face darkened and he let the shade drop into place. 'I wanted to be more to you, Emma, and you would not let me.'

Disconcerted, Emma glanced toward the shelves where Mr Lorne was hidden.

'Let me walk you home,' Philip said. 'I can see we have much to talk about.'

Emma didn't want to walk home with him. She didn't want to be reminded of the past any longer, to be in the company of one man when all she wanted was to be with another. Another who didn't seem to want her. But she knew she had to hear Philip out, for once he had been her only friend.

She quickly gathered her hat and the diaries, and bid Mr Lorne goodbye. When they left the shop, David's carriage was gone and Mrs Smythe and Miss Harding were nowhere to be seen. But Lady Wheelington was walking past and she stopped to greet Emma with an airy kiss on her cheek.

'Mrs Carrington, my dear, how lovely to see you!' Lady Wheelington cried. 'I must hurry on my way, for I am meeting Mrs Smythe, Miss Harding, and my future daughter-in-law at the church to plan Sunday's flowers. I think we may expect an interesting announcement there soon.'

Emma was still distracted by everything that had happened so quickly, but she did not want to be rude to Lady Wheelington at all. 'Indeed?'

'Oh, yes,' Lady Wheelington said with a laugh. 'Mrs Smythe is quite sure her brother is on the very verge of a match with Miss Harding, which would be quite the *on dit* in our little community, don't you think? A new Lady Marton for Rose Hill…'

He was so near to getting engaged? To Miss Harding? Emma swallowed hard and hoped she didn't look as stunned as she felt. 'Quite the *on dit,*' she managed to agree.

'But then, one can never quite rely on Mrs Smythe's information,' Lady Wheelington said as she headed on her way. 'I just hope my son will have plenty to occupy him in his place as vicar now. Come to tea soon, my dear, and we will have a long chat!'

In a daze, Emma turned toward the road to Barton, Philip walking silently beside her until they had left the village behind.

'So your respectable Sir David is to marry that pretty Miss Harding,' he said. 'Amazing.'

Emma glanced up to see a flash of something like anger in his eyes. He quickly covered it in a smile. 'You know Miss Harding, Philip?'

'I met her when I first arrived. She and Sir David

seem quite different from each other. But then, we all must do what we must.'

'Is that why you are here?'

'I came because I wanted to be sure you are well.'

'You could have written to me for that, rather than taking such a long journey. I know how much you enjoy life on the Continent.'

Philip was silent for a long moment, the only sound the crunch of the dirt and gravel under their feet, the chatter of the birds in the hedgerows.

'I did wish to see you again, Emma,' he said, his tone darker, angrier than she had ever heard from him. 'But also I wanted to show you this. I have had it on my conscience for some time.'

'Conscience?' Emma said, puzzled. 'Whatever do you mean?'

Philip took a much-folded, faded piece of paper from inside his coat. As they stopped near the gates to Barton, he handed it to her.

Emma quickly scanned it and found it was a promissory note signed by Henry and dated nearly a year ago, right before his death. It appeared Henry had lost a game of cards to Herr Gottfried, a man Emma remembered all too well. Herr Gottfried had then signed it over to Philip.

It was for a great deal of money.

Emma did not know what to make of it all. 'Henry still owed you this money when he died? But he assured me he had paid off all his debts before...' Before he intended to run off with his married lover. Before he was killed in that duel.

Philip leaned his fist against the stone wall that guarded Barton. 'I didn't want to burden you with it, Emma. Not when I had hopes we could be—closer.'

'Philip...'

'No, don't say anything else. I see now that my hopes were impossible, that you want a different sort of life than we could have together. I was going to forget this note, but...'

'But what, Philip? Surely we can be honest with each other now.'

Philip nodded, his face still shadowed. Distant. 'So we can. The truth, Emma, is that I had to use much of my legacy from my mother to buy this note. Herr Gottfried was not a nice man and Henry would have been in a great deal of trouble if this debt had stood. Henry vowed to pay me back, but as you see he died soon after. And I have found myself in rather dire straits since then.'

'You came here to ask me to pay back Henry's debts?' Emma said, a terrible certainty dawning over her. Her troubles with Henry were far from over.

'I came to see if you could possibly be interested in me, care for me, as I do you, Emma,' Philip said. 'But as I see now that is impossible, I must ask for something else. I need the repayment.'

Emma stared down at the creased note in her hand. It was a great deal of money, much more than she possessed, even with her legacy from her own mother, which was to go to the bookshop. She had tried so hard to pay off Henry's debts to tradesmen, forcing her to depend on Jane to get home to Barton. Philip had said nothing of it to her before, but she had no reason to doubt him. Philip *had* helped Henry out of trouble. Why bring it to her now, though?

She looked up at him over the paper and it was as if she was watching a stranger. Philip stared back at her, his face as hard as granite. Every vestige of Henry's laughing, carousing cousin, a man she herself had counted on as a lighthearted friend, was vanished.

'I am very sorry for it, indeed,' she said slowly. 'Henry was a careless man to us both. I wish you had told me of this before.'

'Perhaps I should have. But as I said—I had hopes.'

And now that he realised she couldn't love him, he thrust *this* at her? Emma's head was spinning at how quickly matters had changed between them. She didn't know what to do.

'I am afraid I can be of little help, Philip,' she said. 'You see how I am set up here. I live on the kindness of my sister right now.'

'Surely she would help you settle a debt of honour for your husband? She is married to an earl, after all.'

Yes, perhaps Jane and Hayden could help. Yet Emma could imagine the looks on their faces as she told them of another of her failures. As she asked them for help again, after she had vowed to herself she would look after her own needs from now on. They had enough to think about now with the twins and the new baby. Baby Emma. Whatever would her namesake think of her wayward aunt?

Emma just had to find a way to fix this herself.

Surely Philip's pride could not be so hurt that he had entirely forgotten their friendship?

'I cannot ask Jane,' she said.

'Really? I thought families were supposed to always be loyal to one another. That is what Henry always said. That is why I tried to help him, even when it was to my own detriment.'

Emma nodded. She remembered that very well. The nights Philip brought Henry home drunk and babbling, his money gone. The day Philip tried to stop Henry from duelling. Yet she also remembered that Philip was very often the one who led Henry into trouble in the first place. Philip, who was so much cleverer about *finding* trouble than Henry could ever have been.

'Jane has already helped me so much,' she said.

'Then perhaps they might come to know more about Herr Gottfried and his friends,' Philip said in a granite-hard voice. 'And the circumstances under which this was obtained. Surely you remember them, Emma?'

Emma shook her head, appalled to think of the night she had gone to the casino at Baden with Henry, hoping her presence there would make him behave a little better. Far from it, of course. Herr Gottfried and his loathsome friends had made her horrible propositions in German she could barely understand—until one of them grabbed her and pulled her on to his lap.

Henry had only laughed, already filled with brandy, and asked the Germans if they cared to make *her* part of the wager. She'd been forced to slap the horrible grabber in the face and kick him in his fat leg with her heeled shoe before she ran away, their coarse laugh following her.

Philip saw her home that night and every vestige of her affection for Henry vanished for ever.

She would be so ashamed if Jane knew that sordid tale, knew the sort of life Emma really lived as Henry's wife. The people who had been around her. She'd hidden the incident with Mr Milne, the school dancing master, from Jane for so long. She meant to hide as much as she could. What Jane already knew was bad enough.

And now Philip of all people was trying to *blackmail* her? She longed to slap him as she had that German bounder! To kick him and scream at him. But impulsiveness was what had got her into this mess in the first place. She had to be calm now and work out the best thing to do.

She slowly folded the nasty note. 'I will find your money. Jane doesn't need to know about this.'

Philip gave her a stiff nod. 'I am sorry it has come to this, Emma. I had sincerely hoped...'

Emma held the paper out to him. She was careful not to touch him when he took it back. 'Just leave now, Philip. Please. I will send you word when I have decided what to do.'

'Very well. Just don't take too long. I don't wish to stay at the Rose and Crown any longer than necessary.' He turned and strode away down the road, back towards the village.

Emma watched until she was sure he was gone, then she spun around and ran through the gates of Barton.

She didn't stop running until she had gained the safety of her own cottage and locked the door behind her.

She tore off her bonnet and tossed it to the floor. The books under her arm followed and she sat down heavily on the wooden planks to bury her face in her hands. Why was everything in such a mess?

She heard the click of Murray's paws on the floor and he nudged her with his cold nose and a whine.

Emma wrapped her arms around his furry neck and hugged him tightly. 'I'm such a fool, Murray,' she whispered. He answered with a lick to her cheek that made her laugh. 'But we can't sit here for ever. We have to figure out what to do now.'

Murray barked as if in agreement. Emma gathered up the books, the old diaries Mr Sansom gave her. As she dusted off the faded leather covers, she suddenly remembered the old tale she was reading in the bookshop, the one her father had loved so much.

The stolen treasure of Barton.

From the diary of Arabella Bancroft

The treasure is real! I must scribble these words in pencil as I am running away forthwith. My William has found where it must be at—among the ruins of the old medieval castle of Rose Hill. We are going there to search it out before anyone can discover us.

Please God let it be there. It would be the answer to all our troubles and we could be together at last.

Chapter Fourteen

'Papa! Papa, where are you going?'

David turned from Zeus to see Beatrice standing at the top of the stone steps, looking down at him on the drive. She wore an old brocade curtain around her shoulders for a cloak and he was sure she was pretending to be Queen Elizabeth again. She had done that a great deal since her day with Emma at the bookshop.

The day he found them dancing so freely with Philip Carrington—in a way he himself could never have been free.

'On an errand into the village,' he answered. 'Where is Nanny?'

'Asleep, of course. I was reading in the window seat and saw you down here.'

David made a mental note that it was time to talk to nanny about retiring. It was clear Beatrice was becoming far too lively for her.

And for him. Every time he turned around now, his quiet, watchful daughter was into some mischief. He suspected it was Emma's influence.

She hurried down the steps, her cloak flowing behind her. 'You aren't going to see that Miss Harding, are you?'

'I am going to see the lawyer,' he said, making another note not to let Louisa talk too freely around Beatrice about her matchmaking attempts. 'Why would you think I was going to see Miss Harding?'

'Aunt Louisa brought her here that day and told me to be nice to her. Aunt Louisa likes her. But I don't, not very much.'

David knew very well he should not encourage Beatrice's new outspokenness, but he still wanted to laugh. He'd been so worried about her since Maude died, afraid her spirit had gone into hiding for ever. Now it was back, stronger than ever.

And he had the feeling it was Emma to thank—or blame—for that. Emma, with her own imaginative delight in life. Beatrice had spoken of nothing but her since that day in the bookshop.

But he wasn't sure that was a good idea at all. She brought things out in him he had thought long suppressed.

'That isn't very kind, Beatrice,' he chided. 'Miss Harding was most polite to you.'

'I don't think she means it. I think she is only saying what she thinks she ought.'

'Sometimes that is what being polite means, I'm afraid. But why would you think that?'

'The way her eyes crinkle when she talks to me,' Beatrice said.

'Miss Harding is a most respectable young lady. She might be in the village for some time.'

'I don't mind if she stays in the village. I just don't want to try to talk to her very much. She knows nothing about anything interesting. I doubt she even knows who Queen Elizabeth was.'

David struggled not to laugh. 'Well, you don't have to talk to Miss Harding today. Go and read your Queen Elizabeth book and try to keep out of trouble until I get back.'

'I will.' Beatrice slid the toe of her slipper along the gravel of the drive. 'Papa, when can I go to the bookshop again for another lesson? I must tell Mrs Carrington I need new books to read.'

Mrs Carrington—he wanted to see her too, far too much. And he didn't think that was a good sign. She was becoming too much a bright spot in their lives. 'I'm sure Mrs Carrington is very busy. But we'll see. We can talk about it when I get back.'

He bent down for Beatrice to kiss his cheek and then swung up into Zeus's saddle. At the turn of the driveway, he glanced back and waved. Beatrice waved back from the top of the steps. With her reddish-gold curls and brocade drapery, she looked like a young queen. He realised with a pang that his daughter was indeed becoming a young lady and very soon he would have to make decisions about her future and his own.

He had to do something he never liked to do—examine his feelings.

Outside the gates of Rose Hill, he started to turn towards the road into the village. Suddenly he changed his mind. He tugged on Zeus's reins and sent the horse galloping toward Barton Park instead.

It was time for Emma Carrington and him to cease dancing cautiously around each other, to fully acknowledge the lightning of attraction and caution and need crackling between them.

It was time for him to be honest with himself and her. It was time to find a way to end things, once and for all. Before it all went too far and his passion got the better of him.

The old castle at Rose Hill. Surely that was where it had to be.

Emma looked up from the open diaries spread on the table in front of her, surprised to see the light at the window was a pale pinkish-grey sunset. She had given Mary the day off and settled down hours ago to read Arabella's diaries and finish deciphering them. Now the day was almost gone and the pot of tea she made herself long gone cold.

But surely she had the answer now, unless Arabella somehow carried the treasure off later, after her lover died. Yet the diary ended abruptly and Emma had no way of knowing what happened to Arabella Bancroft without more research. Arabella could not have gone too far, not if her diaries stayed all this time in the village. And the couple's last refuge was in the old castle.

Emma stood and stretched out her aching back, sore after so long bent over the old books. Her eyes itched from deciphering the faded ink and she was hungry, yet she also felt strangely energised. The hunt for the

Barton treasure was a futile idea, surely. It had been a legend for so long and no one had ever found it.

And yet—if she *could* find it, she could pay back Philip with no one ever hearing the whole shameful story of her life with Henry. She could refurnish the bookstore, too, make a real life here again. And surely then Philip would know for good that she could never, ever live with him.

If nothing else, Arabella's story had taken her out of herself for a while. Given her something to think about, dream about, besides David Marton.

Emma sighed at the thought of him. She hadn't seen him since he took Beatrice out of the bookshop so suddenly. Surely he would never let his daughter see her again after the chaos of her 'lessons' and Philip's presence there. Surely he had seen she was no good example for a little girl like Beatrice.

Possibly he was even engaged to the pretty Miss Harding now, as Lady Wheelington said.

Emma hurried over to kneel down by the fire and stir the embers to life. Murray roused himself from his bed to watch her and whined as if to remind her what time it was.

'I know, you haven't yet had your tea, poor old Murray,' she said, reaching out to pat his head. 'Perhaps you and I should do a bit of exploring tomorrow? We could go take a look at the old castle at Rose Hill, see what we can find.'

And if David didn't catch them there. The last thing she wanted was to look silly in front of him yet again! To be caught trespassing would be too embarrassing.

As she rubbed at the dog's soft ears, Emma thought about the treasure. If it *was* at the old castle, it wasn't terribly surprising her father had never found it. Her parents were never great friends with David's, despite how near their estates were. The Martons were too respectable and conventional for the eccentric Bancrofts. They wouldn't have let him on to their land, so he mostly dug about on Barton Park.

Murray whined again and Emma smiled down at him. 'I know. I'm just as hopeless as my father. But I must do something to make Philip go away.' Or she would lose everything here she had so carefully begun to rebuild.

Suddenly, a knock sounded at the door. Murray barked, and Emma jumped to her feet, startled.

'Don't let it be Philip,' she whispered, a cold sweep of panic touching her. He had said he would give her time. Surely it hadn't been long enough.

She heard another knock, and she knew she couldn't just hide. Hiding never solved anything. She quickly smoothed her hair and her simple muslin day dress and hurried out of the sitting room, Murray at her heels.

She pulled the door open and to her shock saw it was *not* Philip on her doorstep. It was David.

The dying sunlight cast his dark hair in a golden halo and he looked more handsome than ever. She thought her heart even skipped a beat at the sight of him, just as the silliest poets always said.

'I am sorry for calling unexpectedly, Mrs Carrington,' he said.

'Not at all,' Emma gasped, still in the grip of surprise. 'Please, do come in. I was just about to make some tea.'

'Thank you, I won't trespass on your time very long,' he answered, patting Murray's head as the dog eagerly clambered to greet him.

'I'm glad of the company,' she said, half-truthful. She *was* happy to see him. But she also worried about what he had come to say. She couldn't help but feel ridiculously hopeful.

Murray glimpsed a squirrel in the garden and dashed to chase it as Emma shut the door behind David and led him to the sitting room. She was very conscious of him close behind her with every step, and she couldn't believe he was really there, in her home. Almost as if her daydreams had conjured him.

'Please do sit down,' she said as she hastily rearranged the chairs. 'Mary has the day off, but I have learned how to warm my own tea at least.'

David slowly lowered himself into the chair where he sat the last time he was there and Emma couldn't help but remember the champagne. The dance. The kiss. Oh, good heavens, the *kiss*. Emma hastily turned toward the fire and reached for the kettle.

'Don't go to any trouble, Emma,' he said.

At least he was calling her 'Emma' again. Surely that was a good sign.

Maybe it would be a good time to ask him about the treasure and the castle. But she had to curb her impulses and be courteous.

'I was just doing a little reading,' she said. 'I have been wondering how Miss Marton was faring.'

'She is well,' he said. 'That is what I wanted to talk to you about.'

'I am sorry about the way you found us in the bookshop,' Emma said quickly. 'Philip quite surprised us, you see, and when he saw Miss Beatrice was reading about Queen Elizabeth—well, I fear he can be a bit… er…spontaneous.'

'Like his cousin, your husband?'

Yes, too much like Henry. She could feel herself turning warm at the thought that David knew that much about her erstwhile family. 'Something of the sort. But you must believe me, Sir David, I would never endanger Miss Beatrice in any way. She is a lovely, clever girl and I am very fond of her.'

She glanced back at David in time to see the austere, solemn lines of his face soften a bit. 'She is, indeed, and I know she much enjoyed her time with you. She keeps telling me facts about the Elizabethan age every time I see her. But she has no mother now and I must be very cautious for her.'

Emma swallowed hard. 'Of course you must.'

David leaned back in his chair, his fingertips tapping at the wooden armrest. 'I am sure you must have heard something of how I lost my wife.'

Maude Marton's infamous elopement. 'I have and I am very sorry.'

'Bea doesn't know the truth, of course, but I will never allow her to be hurt like that again. I won't allow scandal to touch her.'

'I do see,' Emma said slowly. She wanted to wrap her

arms around herself, to hold away the hurt she feared was coming. 'You are saying you fear I would embroil her in scandal if she spent time with me?'

A frown flickered over his face and then his jaw hardened again. Emma turned away to tend to the kettle, afraid to look at him any longer.

'Beatrice likes you very much,' he said, so careful, so controlled. Emma wished with all her might she could shake up that awful control. 'Indeed, you are the first person she has shown enthusiasm for since her mother died. I would like to find a way for you to spend time with her, if you are agreeable. But we must be—careful.'

Emma spun around to face him. She bumped into her sofa and impatiently pushed at the piece of furniture. 'Because your fiancée might see things the wrong way?'

The frown became full-fledged. 'My fiancée?'

'Miss Harding,' Emma said, feeling disappointed that the rumours could be true.

'Miss Harding? I am not engaged to Miss Harding, or anyone else. Where did you hear that?' he said, a puzzled look replacing the frown.

'Well, I...' Emma stammered, suddenly confused.

'I assure you, I am not engaged to Miss Harding. My only concern, Emma, is my daughter. I hope you do not misunderstand me.'

'I—no, of course not. I...' Emma was utterly baffled. David always had her in a whirl. Her feelings for him, the puzzle of him. 'You surely must marry *someone*. Everyone says so.'

David suddenly rose to his feet, anger and amusement warring in his expression. 'Will *you* marry again? Because everyone says you should?'

'I have had quite enough of marriage,' Emma scoffed.

'And so have I. You shouldn't listen to gossip, Emma. Surely you and I both know how very wrong it can be.'

Emma shook her head and pressed her hands over her eyes. She wished she was merely watching this scene on a stage, that she could make the actors go back and erase lines, start again in a way she could understand. 'My life has been ruled by gossip, for as long as I can remember. There is no escape. I thought if I came home, I could escape it and begin again. But all I found is that it's even worse here. At least on the Continent, no one knew me, not really, but here, with people I care about so much…'

Emma spun around, unable to face him a moment longer. She had almost given herself away. The atmosphere in her little sitting room suddenly seemed to crackle, like on a stormy night when lightning flashed against the windows.

'People you care about?' he said softly.

She felt him move closer to her in the strained silence of the room, felt the warmth of his lean body. The clean, heady scent of him. How could he not know? Surely he saw how she had foolishly come to care for him. All the reasons she had disliked him when she was a silly girl—his quiet dignity, his care for the people around him, his subtle good humour—drew her to him now. He was all she was not and she craved that so very much.

She craved *him* and the way he made her feel when he was near. The way he made her want to be better, to be worthy of a life with him. But she had no idea how to even begin to do that.

'I would never want my actions to hurt Beatrice,' she said roughly. 'I know you think I am not the sort of woman she should be around. You gave me a chance and I just ruined it—'

'You have no idea what I think, Emma,' he suddenly burst out. She felt his hand close hard on her arm, spinning her around to face him. Her eyes flew open and she stared up at him to find his face dark and hard, his eyes glowing fiercely. 'You have no idea what I feel.'

'Because you will not let me see!' she cried, afraid she would start sobbing at the taut, hot emotions of the moment. At his nearness. 'You won't let anyone see.'

'I can't let anyone see,' he said. His other hand closed around her other arm, holding her with him. She could feel the tension in his whole strong body, as taut as a drawn bowstring. 'I can never lose control, too much depends on me. But I *do* feel, Emma. By Jove, but I feel so much, especially when you are near. I've never known anyone like you. I think about you far too much. I can't be like…'

Emma's tears fell in earnest now, she couldn't hold them back. She'd held them in far too long, held back her emotions that had been growing and growing for David until she feared they would drown her.

But now he was holding her close, words exploding from him in a torrent she would never have imagined could come from him. She wanted more and more of it, wanted to know everything about him.

'Be like what?' she sobbed.

Instead of answering with words, he pulled her closer.

Chapter Fifteen

David silenced her tearful words with the simple expedient of his mouth over hers in a hard, desperate kiss.

How she had longed for this! Dreamed of it in her lonely bed at night. How *right* it felt, her emotions swinging wildly from anger to hot desire.

And David seemed to feel the same. His tongue thrust into her mouth, as if he was hungry for the taste of her, and she met him with an equally fiery need. She felt as if she had jumped into a volcano, consumed by flames. She didn't want to escape, though. Ever.

Her hand slid from his shoulder down his hard, warm chest. Her fist curled into his slippery silk waistcoat and she drew him even closer. She could feel the alluring heat of his body through her muslin gown and she knew it still wasn't close enough. Feeling suddenly bold, she tugged open the buttons of that silk waistcoat and slid her fingers between the folds of his shirt to at last touch bare, smooth, warm skin. The lean, hard strength of him.

She felt him groan against her hand. He deepened

the kiss and she went up on tiptoe to meet him eagerly. She was determined to remember this glorious moment, every taste and touch, every glorious pleasure. His mouth slanted over hers and their kiss tumbled down into frantic need.

There was no turning back, not for her. Not for him either, as his hands closed hard on her waist and held her up against him. His warm lips traced the curve of her throat as her head fell back, and he kissed the soft skin of her shoulder through the thin muslin of her gown.

She remembered rumours that once upon a time David had not been quite so proper as he was now and it seemed sometimes that old naughtiness still came out. She was wildly glad to see it.

'David, please,' she whispered, burying her fingers in his hair. It slid like silk against her skin and she suddenly felt ecstatically happy.

'Oh, Emma,' he groaned. His hand closed over the gathered edge of her sleeve and he slid it down a mere inch. 'Let me see you, please.'

'Yes,' was all she could say. She was overcome by the raw, heady pleasure of his touch.

They tumbled back to the sofa and David drew her loose bodice down to reveal her lace-trimmed chemise. His dark head dipped and his lips closed over her aching nipple through the soft cotton. His other hand grasped the hem of her gown and chemise and he dragged them up over her leg until the fabric was wrapped around her waist. She wore no stockings, and she felt the heat from the fire on her bare skin, the fine wool of his breeches a delicious friction that made her moan.

And she felt his erection, hot and hard, straining against the confines of the fabric.

He laid her back against the cushions of the sofa behind them, his body heavy over hers, his mouth warm on her breast. She wrapped her legs around his hips and held on to him.

She was spread beneath him, vulnerable, open to all his desires—and her own. She closed her eyes and let herself fall down into the whirling, sparkling darkness of need.

'Emma,' he whispered. The top of his tongue circled her nipple as his hand slid over her bare thigh, drawing her higher and harder against him. He traced an enticing pattern on her skin, and then to her delighted shock she felt his fingertip press to the seam of her damp womanhood. She cried out at the rush of sensation from that one light touch.

'Do you want me, Emma?' he whispered roughly. 'As I want you?'

Did she want him? She had never felt anything like this desperate, primitive need.

'Yes,' she moaned. 'Yes, more than anything.'

He rose up over her and his mouth covered hers with a sizzling kiss. She felt his hand reach between them to unfasten his breeches, freeing his manhood at last from its confines.

'Emma, I'm sorry, but I can't wait,' he said hoarsely. 'I need you now.'

'Yes,' was all she could say.

With a twist of his hips, he slid deep into her and they were joined at last.

Emma arched up into him, crying out at the wondrous pleasure. She pushed his shirt away from his strong shoulders and held him close. She could hear his breath, the pounding of his heartbeat in rhythm with hers.

They moved together, apart and together again, deeper and deeper, faster, as the passion overcame them.

'Hold on to me,' he said as his lips slid along her neck and his arms came around her to draw her body tight against his.

She wrapped her legs close around his hips, holding on to him as she let herself move higher against him. She felt him thrust even deeper and she cried out at the sensations.

She called out his name incoherently, pushing her hands under his loosened shirt to trace the shift and flex of his muscles as he moved even faster. Even then she did not feel quite close enough. She wanted to be part of him and make him part of her. She hadn't realised until that instant that he was exactly what she longed for, for so long. And he was here with her, as close as two people could be.

How could she ever let him go after this?

He moved faster, less controlled, more frantic. It was never like this with Henry and his hurried, drunken fumblings. She'd never felt such pleasure before.

Deep down inside, she felt a hot pressure growing, expanding, covering her whole body. Sparks seemed to dance over her skin, consuming her. Every coherent thought fled, and all she could do was feel.

'David,' she gasped. 'What...?'

'Let it happen,' he said hoarsely. 'I'm here. I'll catch you.'

He buried his face against her shoulder and his body stiffened as he groaned at his own climax. He shouted out her name and suddenly drew out as delight exploded within.

He fell back beside her on the sofa, their arms and legs entangled. Emma closed her eyes and let herself float for a moment. She could feel David's weight pressed against her side, their heat of their damp skin pressed together, the night gathering around them to enclose them in its dark privacy.

'You are so very beautiful, Emma,' he whispered hoarsely.

Emma felt her cheeks turn warm and she turned her face away from him. It seemed ridiculous to feel so shy over a compliment after what they had just done, how intimately they lay together now, but the deep sincerity in his simple words made her want to cry.

'David,' she murmured.

He ran a gentle caress over her hair. 'Surely you've head that many times and far more poetically than I could ever say it.'

Emma turned on to her side and curled up against him as he covered them with his coat. She had never felt warmer, safer, than she did in that moment with his arms around her. It made her feel content, as she never had before in her life. She wished she could smash the clock over the mantel and make that moment stay for ever.

But she knew she couldn't. She could just revel in it now and hold him close.

She twined her fingers with his where his hand rested on her waist. She knew she had to give him honesty now.

'I've been given compliments before, yes,' she said. 'And when I was young and wilful, I let my head be turned by them. I hope I have learned better now, that I have learned to tell a sincere truth from a manipulative lie.'

David gently turned her in his arms so she looked up at him. His hair was rumpled, his eyes bright as he looked frankly into hers. He traced his fingertip lightly over her lips and the curve of her jaw, looking at her as if he studied her, memorised her. As if he really *saw* her. Not the scandal, but the real her.

'Well, you can believe me when I say that you are beautiful,' he said, his voice deep and rough. 'The most beautiful woman I have ever seen.'

He pressed a gentle kiss to her brow and Emma closed her eyes against the wave of emotion that swept over her. She turned again in his arms and listened to the crackle of the fire, the sound of his breath.

'Will you tell me what happened to you, Emma?' he said. 'What hurt you so much you can't believe anyone would think you are beautiful?'

Emma shook her head, thinking of Philip and how he insisted he had to hurt her because he cared about her so much. 'The past should be gone. I *want* it to be gone. But it won't let me send it away.'

'I know what you mean,' he answered slowly. 'There are people, things, that can never be changed or erased.'

Emma remembered what she had heard of his marriage, and she wondered if that was what he spoke of. If his wife still made him so cautious. 'Your wife?'

David went very still and she feared perhaps she'd said too much. Pried too far. 'Yes. She is one of those things that can't be changed or forgotten.'

Emboldened by the quiet, steady seriousness of his voice, Emma said, 'Did you love her very, very much?'

'I am sure you must have known what happened with Maude in the end,' he said starkly.

'I know she ran away and then died. But that doesn't mean that perhaps you didn't love her at first. I thought I loved Henry, until I discovered who he truly was. And then I mourned for my dream of him when he was gone.'

'Yes. I suppose I was much like that with Maude, though I never thought of it that way.'

'Do you try not to think of her at all?'

David gave a rueful laugh. 'I fear my sister and her love of a gossipy tale would never let me do that. She is still quite convinced there was just some misunderstanding between Maude and me that would have mended if she hadn't died when she did. Louisa thinks if she could just find me another woman like Maude…'

A woman like the pretty, vivacious Miss Harding? A better Lady Marton, a more faithful one, but just as sociable and perfect as Maude Cole once seemed. Emma shivered. 'But you don't?'

'Maude and I were mismatched from the beginning, though I was far too busy and too selfish to see it,' he answered. 'It was time for me to marry and she seemed very suitable. We got along well enough. I thought once she settled into being Lady Marton she would be happy. But I could never have made her happy. She wanted things I simply don't have to give.'

'I can't imagine that could be true,' Emma said. David was handsome, kind, perceptive, intelligent— and a wonderful lover, too. What else could the silly woman have wanted? He was all Emma could desire— if she hadn't been a foolish girl and ruined her future in one impulsive act. Now all she could have with him was this night.

'She wanted adventure. I have Rose Hill and my family and tenants to think of,' David said. 'She put all I care about most at risk. But she did give me Beatrice, so I can never hate her. My daughter was a great gift.'

'Yes,' Emma said quietly. 'Beatrice is a lovely child indeed.' And it was obvious David loved her with all his heart. She was another thing he would fiercely protect.

'Did you love your husband, Emma?' he asked.

Emma swallowed hard past the knot of emotion in her throat. 'I—I once thought I did. I thought I loved him so much that such a love would be worth defying even my sister's advice, that if we were only together all would be right in the end.'

'It didn't end up that way?'

'No,' Emma said. And then she told him something she had never admitted to anyone, not even herself. 'I was only a challenge to Henry. Once he had me, he wasn't quite sure what to do with me. And I was no great heiress who could support his lifestyle.'

She took a deep breath and went on. 'Before Henry, when I was at school, there was a dance teacher named Mr Milne. He flirted with me a bit and I must admit I was flattered. I was lonely at school, you see, away from family for the first time, and I wanted him to like me. I fear he took it for encouragement and tried to kiss me one night in a dark classroom.'

'Emma....' David said, his tone very dark. His arms went still around her.

She laughed. 'When I slapped him, he said I had lured him on with my beauty. That I could not blame a man for being so tempted when I wouldn't behave like a lady. That is why it is hard for me to believe it when someone says I am beautiful, that they don't want anything from me in return.'

In silence, David turned her again in his arms and softly kissed her lips. Looking into her eyes, he said, 'Emma Bancroft. You are truly beautiful.'

Emma was sure she would start crying at the stark simplicity of his words. With David, she believed them.

'Just sleep now,' he said, drawing his coat closer around her. 'I'll make up the fire and let Murray in. Don't worry about anything.'

Suddenly very weary, Emma nodded and closed her eyes. She let herself sink deeper into his arms and let the warm darkness of sleep close around her. It blocked out everything she worried about—Philip, money, the future, the past. All she knew was David next to her, holding her.

She knew it wouldn't always be this way. But she would hold on to it as long as she dared.

* * *

From the diary of Arabella Bancroft

We are discovered.

My cousin found out we had run here, and he cannot bear for anyone else to have the Barton treasure he is sure must be his. We hid in the old cellar, holding on to each other, but William was snatched from my arms. Now I am locked in my chamber and I fear my William is gone for ever.

Chapter Sixteen

David lay very still next to Emma, watching her as she slept. The flickering red-coral firelight gleamed on the tumbled spill of her golden hair and the smooth perfection of her skin. Her lips curved in a small smile, as if she was lost in a pleasant dream.

He would give anything to have been the one to make her smile like that. To give her that sort of happiness. But he feared he could never be that person.

David gently slid away from the enticing warmth of Emma's body and quickly righted his clothes before letting her dog in from the garden. Murray gave him a suspicious glance, but quietly settled into his bed by the fire. David found a blanket tossed over one of the chairs and tucked it around Emma so she wouldn't be chilled.

She sighed and stirred in her sleep, but she didn't wake. David sat down in the chair beside her and stared into the dancing flames.

He'd come to Emma's house, after pacing in front of her gates for a long time trying to decide what best to say, to tell her they should try to be as distant as possible. That it couldn't be good for them to try to be friends—not when he longed to kiss her every time he saw her. Not with that tugging rope of attraction always between them.

He remembered what she said about how their world was ruled by gossip. It was all too true. He had always tried to shield his family, his daughter, from it as much as possible. Especially since Maude's recklessness almost destroyed them. Beatrice didn't need to know such sordid things about her mother.

Emma couldn't help but attract gossip, with her beauty, her spirit, the impulsive affection of her nature. She was precisely the sort of person he had vowed to stay away from in his life.

And yet it was exactly those qualities—her glowing, vibrant, joyful life—that drew him close to her over and over. That made him crave to be in her presence.

Emma had an unquenchable glow within her that refused to be extinguished, and it warmed the coldness that had always seemed lodged like a paralysing shard of ice in his heart. Her passion for life, for sensation and fun and learning, made him want them too.

Ever since he saw her dancing in the old orchard, her arms outflung, her hair glowing in the sun, he had wanted her and all she was more than he had ever wanted anything. He fought against it, fought to stay frozen in his old, safe ways, but he couldn't stay away.

Emma murmured in her sleep and David reached over to gently tuck the blanket closer around her. He smoothed a gentle caress over her hair, letting the warm, soft length of it trail over his arm as a bolt of sheer, burning longing washed over him.

She was so fragile, so soft under his touch. The thought that anyone could dare hurt her, as her villain of a husband had, made him utterly furious. If the man wasn't already dead, David would find him and strangle him right then.

Emma's trusting, impulsive nature had led her into so much trouble. Once he had been sure she was something like his wife, willing to cause scandal for her own self-ish ends. Emma was so very different from her quieter sister. But he saw now that Emma had none of Maude's cold heart. Emma would never willingly hurt a child as Maude had Beatrice. The fact that Bea, who was usually so very cautious, had clung to Emma so fast, and that Emma returned her affection and even understood what Bea needed in a way he couldn't, showed him that.

Emma's own stark pain over her past, the hope for the future in spite of it all, her love for her sister and willingness to work hard at the bookshop, showed him so clearly that he had been wrong about her.

And yet, the past was still there and always would be. Emma's impulsive nature was still there. And so were his own cautious ways. He couldn't afford to abandon them, not even if he had come to care too much for Emma. To want her, crave her.

Yes, he wanted to watch over her, to make sure she was never hurt again. He wanted that more than he had ever wanted anything. And that realisation scared him.

David pushed himself up from the chair, suddenly

restless to take action. He had to know the truth, the *whole* truth. Then he would know what to do.

He quickly put on his coat and bent down to kiss Emma's cheek one last time. Her skin was soft and warm under his lips, and desire surged through him. He wanted to crawl under the blanket with her, to claim her mouth with his and feel her body move against his again. But he steeled himself against the burning lust. He had work to do now and no time to lose.

Her eyes fluttered open, and she gave a sweet, sleepy smile. 'Is it morning? I thought maybe it was all a dream…'

A dream indeed. One David was reluctant to wake from, but he knew he had to. 'Not a dream, I promise. It's not morning yet, but I need to leave before it is.'

She blinked and the sleepy sweetness vanished. She looked worried before she turned on to her side, her face half-hidden from him. 'David…'

'I won't apologise, Emma, I promise,' he said fiercely. He couldn't bear to hurt her, as so many people had, to make her feel ashamed. But neither could he yet make her fully his. Not until he could be sure. And maybe that would never be possible. 'I will see you again very soon.'

'Of course,' she said, 'soon.'

David kissed her one more time, then hurried out of the cottage before he could give in to the strong temptation to stay. He had work to do now and he couldn't afford to let his heart lead the way. Not with so much at stake.

But he still couldn't help but pluck a small blossom from the first of the rosebushes over her door and tuck it into his pocket to remind him of Emma. Half-hidden beneath the bush, he glimpsed a folded letter, no doubt lost in the mail delivery. He slid it back under her door and turned for home, with his keepsake rose safe with him.

If only he could hold Emma just as safe.

Chapter Seventeen

'David! You cannot let Beatrice visit that woman again.'

'Good day to you, too, Louisa,' David said as he looked up from the estate ledgers open on his library desk just in time to see his sister sweeping into the book-lined room. The tall plumes on her bonnet waved madly, along with her lace-gloved hands. She was obviously in a state over something, as usual, but he was damned if he knew what it could be.

He could barely even see the numbers in front of him. All he could think about was Emma. Emma, as he had last seen her, sleepy and sweet, her skin bare to him.

'What seems to be amiss?' he said, pushing away those lascivious memories as his sister continued to flutter around the room.

Louisa plumped herself down in the armchair across from the desk. 'Is it true that you let Beatrice see Mrs Carrington? At the bookshop?'

Ah, so *that* was what this unannounced visit was about. He didn't like the pinched, disapproving look on Louisa's face when she said Emma's name. He sat back in his chair and studied her calmly over his steepled fingers.

'Indeed she did,' he said. 'Bea has proved to be quite fond of learning, and has been reading with Mrs Carrington while I look for a suitable governess. Is there some sort of problem, Louisa?'

Louisa threw up her hands. 'Brother, what can you be thinking! You are usually so very sensible; we all rely on you. But you must see that Mrs Carrington is not suitable to be a companion to a young girl like Beatrice. Children can be so impressionable. One can never be too careful.'

David almost laughed at his sister's temerity in lecturing him about parenthood, when everyone in the village saw how wild her sons were. But he could not laugh at her disparagement of Emma. Certainly not after what happened last night.

'Mrs Carrington is from a family whose estate has long neighboured our own,' he said carefully. 'Her sister is a countess and she herself is known to be a most intelligent lady. Bea likes her.'

'And I see that you do, too!' Louisa cried. 'Oh, David, how could you? And Miss Harding so very fond of you. I was so hoping you would escort her to the assembly rooms next week for the concert. I know she hoped so as well.'

David could see he needed to nip all this in the bud right at that moment. 'I never encouraged Miss Harding in any way, Louisa, you know that very well. And just because I allow Beatrice to spend time with Mrs Carrington does not mean I am contemplating anything improper with her.'

No, he was not contemplating it—he had already done it. And he wanted more than anything to do it again. The question now was, where did he and Emma go next? Would she have him? Or would they only be making a terrible mistake together, re-enacting the mistakes of the past?

Either way, it was not the business of Louisa or anyone else. He wouldn't let Emma be exposed to any more gossip.

'I think we have said enough on this topic, Louisa,' he said firmly. 'When I have made matrimonial decisions in the future I shall inform you of them. But no more matchmaking, I beg you.'

'Well,' Louisa huffed. 'I only ever try to help, Brother. And I am quite shocked at your lack of judgement when it comes to Mrs Carrington. Why, only just this morning I heard Lady Firth say that her butler, who had gone to run an errand a few towns over, saw her going into the shop of Mr Levinson the jeweller. And you know what *that* means.'

David froze. 'It probably means she was buying a gift for her sister's new baby.'

'Certainly not!' Louisa cried. 'Everyone knows Mrs Carrington is in no position to give expensive gifts to anyone, not after her shockingly bad marriage. Everyone also knows that Mr Levinson gives a very good price for jewels when ladies find themselves in shocking debt.'

David frowned as he tapped his fingertips on the

ledger page. He had always had the suspicion that he didn't know everything about Emma, not even after their night together. What had she been doing at Mr Levinson's shop this very day? It was true what Louisa said. Everyone knew that often ladies who found themselves in embarrassed circumstances went there to sell jewels. But Emma shouldn't be in such trouble now that she was home, now that she had Lord and Lady Ramsay to protect her.

But the Ramsays weren't home and Emma was alone. David had the sense that Philip Carrington must have something to do with it all, something Emma was hiding. Especially if he was like his rakish cousin.

The man's appearance in the area, his hanging around everywhere like the bookshop, was annoying to say the least. Louisa giggled about how handsome he was, how charming, but David didn't like the possessive way the man looked at Emma. He had to find out who the blighter really was, what he had in his past. That could require a trip to London, but now David did not want to leave Emma unprotected.

Whatever trouble Emma had got herself into, he had to find out what it was. Now.

David pushed himself back from the desk and strode to the library door. 'I'm sorry, Louisa, but I must go out on an urgent errand.'

'Right now?' his sister said. She scurried after him into the hall just in time to hear him send the footman for his horse. 'David, what is the meaning of this?'

'I will explain later, Louisa,' he answered, though his thoughts were far away, with Emma.

'You must come home with me at once,' Louisa said. 'I am meeting Miss Harding this afternoon and I am sure all can be mended with her now you know the truth about that unfortunate Mrs Carrington.'

The truth about Emma? David feared he had only just begun to discover the many enticing, surprising layers that made up Emma Bancroft Carrington. And now he was afraid for her.

If she was in trouble...

David hurried out the front door and grasped Zeus's reins to swing himself up into the saddle. He had to find out what was happening to Emma. Now.

Beatrice stared down past the gilded railings to the hall below, watching as her aunt burst into tears. Past the open front doors she could see her father galloping down the drive, not even wearing a hat. The footmen, usually so perfectly postured and expressionless, gave each other bewildered glances.

It felt as if Rose Hill had been turned upside down and shaken hard. She hardly knew what to think.

Even in London, when her mother would breeze in and out of the house so unpredictably and there were often parties of odd people laughing in the drawing and dining rooms, her papa was a quiet, calm constant. Today there were tears and angry words, and her aunt having hysterics.

Beatrice almost stamped her foot in consternation that she hadn't been able to hear the whole conversation between her father and aunt. All she knew was that Aunt Louisa said they should have nothing to do with

Mrs Carrington any more and that Papa should marry that silly Miss Harding.

Well, Beatrice was having none of that. Mrs Carrington was wonderful and Bea would *not* give her up. Ever.

If she was still a baby, she would have laid down on the floor and wailed out her woes. But grown-up ladies could do no such thing. Grown-up ladies had to find other ways to get what they wanted. Reading about Queen Elizabeth had taught her that. When Elizabeth was a young, powerless princess, she had to be very clever and very sneaky to stay out of trouble and achieve her ends.

Only when she was queen could she pitch fits.

Beatrice would just have to find a way to show her papa what was really good for them: Mrs Carrington. But how?

Aunt Louisa swung around to storm back toward the library. Beatrice ducked down so her aunt wouldn't see her. Only once the library door slammed shut did she tiptoe back up to the nursery.

Nanny was snoring by the fire, as usual. The Queen Elizabeth book lay open on the window seat and Beatrice went to fetch it. Yet she couldn't quite lose herself in its pages as she usually could. She stared out the window at the sunny day, trying to figure out what she should do.

Then she glimpsed the tumbling stones of the old castle in the distance and remembered Mrs Carrington's tale of the lost treasure and the parties they used to have at Barton Park and Rose Hill, when Charles the Second was king.

It was a nice day. Maybe she needed a bit of exercise. That was what nanny always told her—to run along and play, and not be bothersome. Usually Beatrice just wanted to sit and read her books, but today a bit of exploration sounded fun.

And just maybe she could slip over to Barton for a bit, too…

'I heard he has even been letting his daughter visit her. He must like her a great deal, though I must say I am surprised at Sir David.'

'Quite. A careful, respectable man like him—and Mrs Carrington? Most unaccountable.'

'But she is a countess's sister, so she would be a fair match for him, I suppose. If only…'

Melanie Harding had not stayed any longer in the doorway of the draper's shop to listen to old Lady Firth and her equally elderly friend gossip. She'd heard all she needed to hear.

He was never going to marry her. Rose Hill was never going to be hers. She hadn't imagined the look of polite indifference on his face when she called with Mrs Smythe. He preferred an old widow like that Mrs Carrington. The fool.

Melanie hurried down the street, not seeing anyone she passed or any of the enticing window displays. All she could think of was what she had lost, before it was even really hers.

Suddenly she caught a glimpse of Philip Carrington

striding toward the Rose and Crown, and some spark of reckless hope took flame inside of her. The sunlight gleamed on his poetically tumbled golden curls, and his shoulders looked so broad and strong in his dashing greatcoat. Surely he was far more handsome, far more interesting than David Marton could ever be.

And Melanie was quite, quite desperate. She did not want to go back to her uncle's dismal house.

'Mr Carrington!' she called as she hurried across the street toward him. 'What a delightful coincidence to see you here today. Do you perchance have time for tea?'

Chapter Eighteen

~~~~~~

Emma paced the length of the forest clearing and back again. The coins in her reticule felt heavy, the fruits of selling her wedding ring and her mother's pearl pendant to a jeweller in a town several miles away. It hadn't been as much as she hoped, but maybe it would be enough for now. She desperately hoped it would be enough.

If she ever hoped to be good enough for David, she had to make Philip go away. His presence in the village was always a reminder of her past. She had to be done with all that now.

She turned and paced back again. The only sound she could hear was the harshness of her own breath, the brush of her boots through the leaves, the whistle of the wind in the leaves. Pale, watery sunlight filtered through the trees on to patches on the ground. She had never felt quite so alone.

Surely Philip would come? That was what his note said, to meet him here at this hour. Even despite his blackmail, she had to believe he would keep his word.

He couldn't be all bad. Her old friend must still be in there somewhere.

At last she heard the pounding of horse's hooves along the pathway and she spun around to see Philip come into the clearing. His hat hid his face and she couldn't see his expression.

'I thought perhaps you weren't coming,' Emma said.

A whisper of Philip's old grin flashed over his face, only to be quickly gone. 'I asked you to meet me, did I not? A bargain is a bargain, Emma. You have something for me, then?'

Emma held out the purse and he came down from the horse to walk towards her. Her chest felt tight and she wondered if this had perhaps not been the wisest place to meet him. They were alone, so far from everyone else.

Yet that was why it seemed like a good place. She couldn't let anyone see her with Philip. And she felt the weight of the small dagger tucked into her sash under her spencer.

He took the purse and opened it to peer inside. 'This isn't the amount we agreed,' he said angrily.

Emma took a deep breath, forcing herself to stay calm. 'I know. I will find the rest later. This is all I have now, but it is more than enough for you to leave here and establish yourself somewhere else.'

'It's not good enough, Emma,' he said.

'I know, but I want to help you, Philip. I do,' Emma said desperately. 'We were both ill treated by Henry and we deserve a new start. Don't we? I am willing to help you make yours, if you will help me make mine.'

Philip was silent for a long, heavy moment. He stared down into the purse. 'It's because of that David Marton, isn't it? He is the reason you are so very eager to be rid of me.'

'Why do you say that?' Emma said, trying to sound casual, to not give anything away.

Philip snapped the purse shut. 'I've seen the way you look at him. He's the reason you're so anxious to forget about your old life, your old friends.'

'Sir David has nothing to do with this,' Emma said, suddenly angry. 'My family...'

'Your family has nothing to do with this!' Philip shouted, frightening her. 'He isn't worthy of you, Emma. He is too dull, too...'

'No,' Emma cried, shaking her head fiercely. 'I won't hear you speak against him. He is the best of men. If anything, I am not worthy of him, or you would have nothing with which to blackmail me now.'

'Blackmail? Such an ugly word to use, Emma.'

'What else could it be?'

'I wanted to have you as my own,' Philip said roughly. 'When you wouldn't listen to reason, what else could I do?'

'So you claim to love me, yet seek to hurt me?' Emma shook her head, bewildered. But she saw one thing so clearly now, thanks to David. 'Once I mistook pain and drama for love, too. But no more. Love is not cruel, Philip. Love is—is...'

Philip suddenly lunged forwards and grabbed her in his arms. Panic and fear rushed over her, blinding, just like with Mr Milne and Herr Gottfried. She struggled to twist away, but he held her too tightly and she couldn't breathe. His lips came down on hers, suffocating her.

Philip was a skilled lover and he put all his expertise into that kiss, Emma could feel it through her fear. Yet his kiss was nothing like David's and she longed only to be free of it.

She managed to slip her fingers into her sash and grasp the hilt of the dagger. It was a ridiculous thing, an antique that once hung on the wall in her father's library along with his other curiosities, but now she was desperately glad she brought it with her. She yanked it free and pressed the tip to Philip's side.

He froze and his lips finally slid away from hers. 'Emma…' he said hoarsely.

'Just let me go,' she whispered. 'Let me go and leave this place. I can't love you, Philip. And you never really loved me.'

He slowly backed away from her and Emma held up the knife until she was several feet away. Even as he reached for his horse's reins, she held it firmly in her fist.

'Very well, Emma, I am going,' he said. 'But this strange spell Sir David Marton has you under will fade. You have too much life for him, too much spirit. I will be waiting for you.'

'Don't do that, please,' was all Emma could say. 'This is where I want to be, where I have always wanted to be.'

Philip pulled himself up on to his horse and wheeled away. To her deepest relief, he spurred the horse into motion. 'This isn't over, Emma,' he shouted. 'I promise.'

Only once the hoofbeats had faded did Emma let

herself drop the dagger. She collapsed to her knees on the ground and struggled not to cry. Not to give in to despair.

'Let him be gone,' she whispered. Let a new life truly be possible. Even if David didn't want her, even if she had to find a way forwards alone, their night together had truly changed her and she knew she couldn't go back.

She slowly made her way to her feet. She left the clearing and found the path back to the road. Philip was gone and there was no one else to be seen. She had to go home now. Back to her cottage, to Murray and poor Arabella's diary, and try to find that way forwards.

Yet she found her steps taking her not toward Barton, but in the direction of Rose Hill. At the top of a rise in the road, she could see the crumbling stone ramparts of the old castle. Arabella's last refuge with her lover.

Somehow Emma found herself drawn there now and she left the road to climb over a low rock wall and head toward its romantic allure.

Chapter Nineteen

⊱⟞⟠⟞⊰

The old castle looked stark and empty against the pale-blue sky as Emma slowly made her way toward it. The blank windows set in the crumbling, ivy-coated walls seemed to stare down at her, watching her warily as she approached.

How much those walls must have seen over the centuries, she thought. Wars, elopements, broken hearts, deaths and births, and still it looked on in silence. Suddenly she was glad she came there so impulsively. The old walls felt like a refuge, a place she could hide for a while and where she would not be judged. Her sins were surely only small ones compared to all the walls had seen.

Emma made her way carefully around the edge of the outer wall, studying the faint lines in the overgrown grass where chambers once stood. She wondered where Arabella and her swain had sheltered from their pursuers, what they felt as they held on to each other against the rest of the world. Were they frightened, or exhilarated by their passion?

She almost wished *she* could run away, too. Could just run and run until she collapsed some place just like this, hidden and ancient, protected by the old lingering spirits. Yet even here she knew there was no hiding. The past was always there, waiting. And running never solved anything at all.

Emma sat down on a low wall and studied the column of what must have once been a chimney in front of her. Perhaps Arabella had even stashed the treasure in a fireplace just like that one, before they were caught? How could it have been for her, knowing in that moment that all she hoped for was gone? That love could be real, but could be lost so suddenly.

'Help!' someone cried, a tiny, far-off sound.

Emma jumped up from her seat, her heart pounding. Had her melancholy thoughts of Arabella conjured the girl's ghost? Was a spectre about to float into view?

'Don't be silly,' she told herself sternly. No matter what the novels said, there was no such thing as ghosts. It was only the wind, whistling past the old stones.

'Help,' someone cried again, and she heard it very clearly that time. A real voice, not a ghost.

'Where are you?' she called back, spinning around in a circle to scan the castle grounds. She couldn't see anything but a few sheep grazing nearby, a wisp of smoke from the chimneys of Rose Hill. 'Can you hear me?'

'Mrs Carrington! Is that you? Help me, please.'

Beatrice. Emma's heart pounded even harder as a rush of panic seized her. 'Bea! Where are you?'

'Down here. Oh, help me, please.'

Emma followed the sound of the child's frightened

voice, but she still saw nothing. 'Keep talking, Bea, so I can find you. I'm here, I won't leave you, I promise.'

Beatrice started singing, a wobbly little nursery song, and Emma followed the sound until she found an old caved-in section of what must once have been a cellar. Beatrice's voice echoed up from its dark depths.

'Beatrice, darling, what are you doing down there?' Emma called, forcing down her own fear so she could help the girl. 'I can't see you.'

'It's so dark,' Beatrice said and Emma could hear the panic in her voice.

'Just move toward my voice, dearest. Are you hurt?'

'I—I don't think so. I was just looking around the old castle, I didn't see the hole in the ground and I fell into it. I can't find my way out.'

'You were here by yourself?' Emma said. She could hear a rustling sound as Beatrice moved around. 'Where is your father? Your nurse?'

'Nanny fell asleep, of course, and Papa dashed off on some errand. Aunt Louisa was there and I didn't want to talk to her. So I came exploring.'

'But why here? It's very dangerous, Beatrice darling.'

'I loved the stories in the old diary you showed me. But I will never, ever go off alone again, I promise!'

Emma knelt down at the edge of the opening and at last she glimpsed a pale flash in the shadows. Beatrice's little face peered up at her. She blinked in the ray of light and her cheeks were streaked with dirt.

'Oh, Mrs Carrington,' she sobbed. 'I'm so sorry. I am not as brave as Queen Elizabeth.'

'It's quite all right, darling, I'm here now.' Emma

sighed. 'I know what it's like to be tempted by adventure. We must get you out of there, though.'

'There's a stone here, I think. Maybe there were steps once?'

'Can you stand on it and reach for my hand?'

Beatrice clambered up and reached out her small fingers. But Emma couldn't quite reach her. She quickly studied her surroundings and came up with a desperate plan.

'I will lower myself down there and help you up,' Emma said. 'Then I will pull myself up again. Can you move back a bit?'

Once Beatrice went back into the shadows, Emma grasped the edge of the pit and eased herself down carefully until her feet touched the rough, broken stone. Once she was down in the old cellar, Beatrice suddenly hugged her hard around the waist, her face buried in Emma's skirt.

Emma hugged her in return, deeply thankful to have a safe, healthy child in her arms.

'I'm so, so glad you're here, Mrs Carrington,' Beatrice sobbed.

'You are very, very lucky I happened by today, Bea,' Emma said as she kissed the top of Beatrice's rumpled head. 'You might have been lost for days. Your father will be frantic. So we must get back to Rose Hill right now.'

'I'll be so good from now on, Mrs Carrington, I promise.'

'I know you will be. Now, let me lift you up.' Emma hoisted Beatrice in her arms and balanced carefully on the stone. Using all her strength, she lifted Beatrice up and over, practically tossing her over the edge and into the light.

But as Beatrice launched herself away, Emma felt her foot slip out from under her in a rush of panic. She toppled to the hard-packed ground and her ankle twisted painfully beneath her.

'Mrs Carrington,' Beatrice cried. 'What happened? Are you hurt? Say something!'

Emma could hardly breathe with the pain, but she didn't want to frighten the child any more than she already was. 'I—think I have injured my foot,' she managed to say. The pain swept over her in drowning, nauseous waves. When she tried to stand, she feared she would faint.

Beatrice let out a wordless wail and Emma feared the child would go into hysterics.

'Beatrice,' she shouted sharply. 'None of that now. You must—you must run home at once and fetch your father, or someone else who can help. You must be very strong and brave now, just like Queen Elizabeth at Tilbury.'

'I will be back in only a moment, Mrs Carrington, I swear it.'

As Emma heard Beatrice's running footsteps fade, she let the dizziness and pain overwhelm her. Darkness closed over her just as she glimpsed some toppled old shelves in the corner by the dirt wall.

'Hurry, David,' she whispered. Then everything faded.

Chapter Twenty

'**P**apa, Papa!' David heard Beatrice's cries just as he handed Zeus's reins to the waiting groom. He'd never heard such panic in her voice before and he spun around in alarm to see her running towards him across the lawn.

His usually quiet, composed, ladylike daughter was streaked with dirt, her hair tangled and sleeve torn. David raced toward her, frantic to know what had happened.

'What is wrong, Bea?' he said. He knelt down as Beatrice threw herself into his arms. He felt her little wrists and ankles, and nothing seemed broken, but she was shaking like a leaf in the winter wind.

'You must come with me right now, Papa,' she gasped.

'No, we need to get you inside and send for the doctor,' David said. 'You can tell me what happened in the house.'

'Yes, yes, we will need the doctor, but not for me.'

Tears were pouring down Beatrice's cheeks, choking her.

'What do you mean, Bea? What on earth has happened?' he demanded. 'I go into town for a couple of hours and look what happens!'

Indeed, the weight of the package he had had just redeemed from Mr Levinson's shop was still heavy in his pocket. The pearl pendant he had seen Emma wear twice at the assembly rooms—and which she had for some reason sold to the jeweller. He had brooded over it, over her, all the way back to Rose Hill, but that was lost in Beatrice's panic.

'Tell me what happened,' he said firmly.

Beatrice gulped in a deep breath. 'It's Mrs Carrington who needs the doctor. She fell down into the cellar at the old castle and hurt her leg. Now she can't move and she can't get out.'

It was *Emma* who had got into trouble with Beatrice? Emma was hurt? David felt his confusion and anger freeze in fear and the need to move immediately to save her. 'The old castle? She took you there?'

'No, Papa!' Beatrice frantically shook her head. 'I went there on my own, to look around. It seemed better than talking to Aunt Louisa. I fell down into the cellar first and she found me. She hurt herself helping me.'

'Come along, Bea, quickly, and show me where,' David said. 'There is no time for the whole tale now, but you will tell me later.'

'Yes, Papa,' Beatrice whispered.

David hastily retrieved Zeus from the groom and sent the boy to fetch more servants to help at the old castle with ropes and blankets, and then into the village for the doctor. As David swung himself back into the saddle with Beatrice front of him, he forced his concern for Emma down. She needed him now; there was no time for his own fear.

And who knew what they would find at the old castle.

Emma felt as if she were sinking down into the dark warmth of an ocean, drifting down and down as something dragged at her limbs and wouldn't let go. She fought against its hold, the suffocating heat, even though part of her just wanted to fall back into it. She knew she had to wake up.

But when she forced her eyes open, she realised why she just wanted to drown. Stabbing pain shot up her leg and she cried out.

Then she remembered where she was, what had happened. She lay alone on a dirt floor, the only light a small yellow circle high above her head. She could smell the damp, green smell of the dirt and rotting wood, it pressed in all around her.

How long had she been unconscious? Would Beatrice return soon?

Please, please, Emma thought. Let Beatrice be back soon with help, before she became mad with panic.

Emma took a deep, steadying breath and forced herself to sit up. She ground her teeth against the pain and dizziness, and was able to slide back until she could lean against the wall. As she waited for the wave of nausea to pass, she examined her surroundings. They were not promising.

Surely, this had once been a cellar beneath the old kitchens, but most of it was caved in now. A few old rotten shelves, surrounded by broken shards of crockery, lay haphazardly on the floor. The stone she had stood on to lift Beatrice out was indeed an old, broken step.

Emma shivered in the cold damp and closed her eyes. She thought of Arabella and her lost lover, sheltering in just such a place. And she thought of David, holding her in his arms, keeping her so warm…

'Emma! Emma, are you there?' she heard someone shout, pulling her out of her half-dazed dream.

She sat straight up. 'Yes, I'm here!'

David's face appeared above her, peering down into her prison. He was surely the most beautiful thing she had ever seen.

'Are you hurt?' he asked.

'Yes, I twisted my ankle. I can barely move, I fear.'

'Don't worry, I'll have you out in only a moment.' He disappeared again and a rope fell down through the opening. As Emma watched in astonishment, David nimbly climbed down the rope until he dropped lightly to the dirt floor. He wore no coat and the white linen of his shirt gleamed in the darkness. He seemed like an angel of rescue to her.

He hurried over to kneel beside her and Emma bit back a sob as he took her gently into his arms. She clung to him, knowing she was safe at last.

'Where are you hurt?' he asked roughly.

'My—my ankle. That's all, I think,' Emma answered.

He carefully eased up the hem of her skirt and slid her boot from her swollen foot. Her stocking was torn and spotted with blood, and she gasped as his strong fingers slid over it carefully.

'Not broken, I think, but badly sprained. The doctor should be waiting at Rose Hill, he can examine you there.' David yanked his cravat from around his neck and wrapped it tightly around her ankle. 'Bea said you fell helping her out of here.'

'Yes,' Emma said. She wiggled her toes; the pain was eased a bit by the tight bandage. 'I'm glad I happened by. I promise I don't usually trespass on Rose Hill property. Something just told me to come here today, I think.'

David shook his head, his face drawn in stark, serious lines. 'Come, we have to get you out of here. I will try not to jostle you too much.'

Emma nodded and braced herself as he lifted her high in his arms. The pain washed over her again, but she knew she could bear it in his embrace. He pushed her up and out of the opening, much as she had with Beatrice, and footmen waited there to catch her. The sunlight blinded her for a moment after the dank darkness of the cellar, but she heard Beatrice cry out her name.

'Mrs Carrington, I am so, so sorry,' Beatrice sobbed and Emma felt her little arms slide tight around her neck. 'I will never be naughty again.'

'Adventures are quite all right sometimes, Beatrice,'

Emma said, laughing despite the pain. 'Just not alone, promise me.'

'Never again, Mrs Carrington. I will only go on adventures with you.'

'I think Mrs Carrington is done with your adventures, Bea,' David said. 'Come, we must go back to Rose Hill. The doctor will be waiting.'

David lifted her gently into his arms and helped her into a blanket litter the footmen had fashioned. She closed her eyes, safe but scared. Was he angry with her for what happened? What could ever happen next?

'You are very lucky, Mrs Carrington, to be in no worse shape after such a tumble.' The doctor snapped his bag shut and gave Emma a stern glance. 'Only a sprained ankle, I would say. Nothing broken. But you must be very careful for a few days. No dancing.'

Emma grimaced as she sat up against the cushions of the *chaise* in one of the guest chambers at Rose Hill. The mild sedative she had been given was starting to take hold of her senses, but the ankle still throbbed. 'I think I can safely promise you I won't be dancing, doctor. I will stay safely by my own fireside for a long time.'

'I am most glad to hear it.'

'How is Miss Beatrice?'

'Only scared and a bit muddied. Not hurt, thankfully. I will stop by Barton on my way back to the village and leave word for your servants there.'

Emma nodded, most relieved. As the doctor left, she could hear him talking with David in the corridor, quiet mutters she couldn't quite understand. She propped her freshly bandaged ankle on a pillow and studied the room around her, with its comfortable chintz draperies and overstuffed chairs scattered around the flowered carpet. It was a pretty, comfortable, inviting room, one where she wished she could stay for days and days, wrapped in the warmth of Rose Hill. But she feared she would be gone from there all too quickly.

She had to be gone. Obviously her impulsive ways hurt the people she cared about most and she wouldn't hurt them any more. She had to leave them for their own good.

'I owe you a great deal of thanks, Emma,' David said as he entered the chamber. He softly closed the door behind him.

Emma laughed, the warmth of the room and the medicine, and David's presence, wrapped around her. She would enjoy them while she could, for those fleeting moments were precious. 'You were the one who climbed down a rope to rescue me, David.'

'You injured yourself rescuing my daughter.' He sat down next to her on the *chaise* and gently put his arm around her.

Emma rested her head on his shoulder with a sigh and suddenly the pain and fear vanished into a sweet, soft weariness. She remembered how it felt after they made love and he held her against him in the firelight. How all the turmoil and worry of life quieted in his arms. If only it could always be like that.

She ran a gentle touch over his shoulder, tracing a streak of dirt on his coat and smoothing the silk lapel.

'I am just glad I happened to be there to find her. Poor Beatrice.'

'Yes,' he said quietly, his heartbeat steady under her hand. 'Why *were* you there, Emma?'

She froze, her hand in mid-stroke over his coat. Oh, yes—why she had been wandering around the bleak ruins all alone. She had almost forgotten, in the drama of her rescue and the doctor's sedative, and now it all came rushing back to her. Philip and his crude black-mail scheme, and her fear and loneliness.

'I cannot tell you,' she whispered. 'It is all too em-barrassing. And anyway, it doesn't matter now.' Or she hoped it did not matter, that Philip had left and she had time to get her life organised again.

'Emma, have you learned nothing about me? Your secrets are safe with me, as I hope mine are with you. I am no gossip like my sister. If you are in trouble…'

Emma shook her head. 'No more than usual.'

David's arm tightened around her and she felt him press a kiss to the tip of her head. She squeezed her eyes shut, afraid she would start to cry at his tender-ness. Tenderness she did not deserve.

'Who has hurt you, Emma?' he said quietly. 'Is it some trouble to do with your late husband? Is it that cousin of his?'

Somehow David's very quietness, his still, gentle strength, broke something in her. She buried her face in his shoulder and held on to him as all the fear and pain of the past poured out of her. She trembled with the force of her emotion and wished she could wail with it all, as Beatrice had in the old cellar.

'Shh,' David whispered. He softly caressed her hair, holding her against him. 'Don't be afraid, Emma. I'm here. I'm your friend.'

Her friend. Somehow that word was so precious, yet so insignificant compared to what she felt for him.

But his closeness, his touch, the pain and the medicine the doctor had given her, all conspired against her. She found herself holding on to him and telling him about Philip. She explained that Philip had threatened to tell details about her life with Henry, that she had tried to pay him because she couldn't hurt Jane any more.

She didn't tell him about Herr Gottfried, or any of the other horrid people Henry knew, but she was sure what she *had* said was quite enough for David to refuse to have anything more to do with her. Her heart felt as if it cracked in two and crumbled away with the knowledge that David and Beatrice would be gone from her.

Yet she knew, deep in her soul, that it was right for him to know. After all they had done, all he had meant to her, at last she could give him her honesty. David had changed her life, made her believe that real goodness, real loyalty, was actually possible once more. That it could touch her life, however briefly, and leave it transformed for the better.

He had given her that. And surely now that he knew how great her past mistakes were, he would leave her. Yet she would always remember how his arms felt around her right now.

'I am so sorry, David,' she whispered brokenly. 'So, so sorry. You have been kind to me and I have been...'

'Shh,' he said again. He gently urged her to lie back

on the *chaise* and carefully tucked a fur-trimmed throw around her. 'You honour me with your honesty, Emma. I will never betray it.'

'You deserve so much more from me,' Emma murmured. Her head felt cloudy, dizzy, and she closed her eyes against it.

'Trust me to know what I deserve. What we both deserve,' he said softly, in a neutral tone she couldn't read. She wished now more than ever she could read his thoughts, but they were carefully hidden from her. 'Just sleep now. I will send for the carriage and take you back to Barton when you have rested for a while.'

Emma nodded, the darkness of exhausted sleep closing around her. Yet it was so different from the hot, painful blackness of the cellar. 'I wish I didn't have to leave Rose Hill.'

'You don't yet. Just sleep.'

She felt his hand cover hers, warm and strong, like a lifeline holding her above the drowning waves. She held on to it and let herself sleep.

The bastard.

David braced his clenched fists on the desk, fighting down the urge to break the wood under his bare hands. It wasn't the innocent desk's fault that his temper was up. It was that blighter Philip Carrington's.

How dare he threaten Emma? How dare he even come near her?

The force of his fury surprised David, since it had been so long since he felt anything even near to it. He kept his emotions so carefully at bay all the time; it was the only way for him to always see to his duties, the only way he could survive. But Emma had changed all that and he suddenly realised how very much. His feelings for her had changed everything. Only when he was afraid he would lose her, lose the vibrant light of her irrepressible spirit, had he known how much he needed Emma.

David pushed himself back from his desk and snatched up his riding gloves. Carrington had to know Emma was not alone now. There would be no more taking advantage of her gentle heart, her generous spirit. No more threatening her over the past. Philip Carrington was going to leave and he was going to do it now, even if David had to bodily toss him into the street in front of the whole village.

Even if he had to cause a scandal. After Maude, he had vowed never to cause talk about his family again. But now, when he thought of Emma's tear-streaked face, he knew so clearly that some things were worth facing scandal.

Some things were worth any sacrifice at all.

He strode out of the library, calling for the butler. 'Hughes,' he shouted. 'Have Zeus brought around at once. I have an urgent errand in the village.'

Hughes looked shocked as he emerged from the drawing room. 'Right now, sir?'

'Yes,' David said firmly. If he was going to start being shocking, he might as well start at home. 'Right now.'

'But—but someone is here to see you, sir. I was just coming to announce him—'

'No need,' a brusque voice said and a man emerged from the drawing room behind the butler.

It was Lord Ramsay, Emma's brother-in-law.

'Ramsay,' David said slowly, pushing down his martial urges to face the one man Emma wouldn't want to find her here. 'I didn't realise you had returned from London.'

Lord Ramsay slowly slapped his leather gloves against his palm. 'Jane and I just arrived back at Barton to find a curious message you had sent to the housekeeper there. My sister-in-law is *here?* With you?'

'She is here, yes, but she is resting,' David said as he made his way toward the stone-faced man. He considered the Ramsays to be friends, but he knew he had to tread very carefully with them now. 'She had a very trying experience today.'

Ramsay's eyes narrowed. 'I think you had best explain, Sir David, and quickly. My wife was frantic for word of her sister and it was all I could do to persuade her to stay at home while I fetched Emma back to Barton. Jane is tired after the journey and should not be wearied further.'

David led him back into the drawing room and shut the door. He quickly told Ramsay the whole sorry tale, as briefly and simply as possible. About how Emma rescued Beatrice and was injured herself. He said nothing of how Emma had come to be wandering around the old castle in the first place, of the growing…whatever it was between them. He couldn't even find the words for it yet himself, though he knew that he was coming to rely on Emma's presence in his life far too much.

Ramsay was quiet for a long moment; the only sound in the tense air between them the slow, thoughtful slap of the gloves.

'You and Emma have become friends of late,' Ramsay said.

'I have tried to be a friend to her, yes,' David replied carefully. 'When she will let me.'

Ramsay laughed. 'Yes, she can be a stubborn one, no denying that. Jane worried about her all the time we were in London, but I told her Emma was better off at Barton right now. I hope I was not wrong. Is she much injured?'

'She needs rest.'

'I have brought the carriage to take her home. I see that you are on your way to some errand, so we shan't intrude on your hospitality any longer.'

His hospitality? Such a tepid word for what David was coming to fear he wanted to offer Emma. But for now Ramsay was right—Barton was the right place for Emma while he took care of business. She would be safe there. 'I hope I may call on Mrs Carrington at Barton very soon. And Lady Ramsay, of course.'

Ramsay stared at David for a long moment before he finally nodded and David knew there was a silent understanding between them.

He would do right by Emma, the strangest, kindest, most spirited woman he had ever known. He just didn't know yet what right might be. Every instinct told him to grab her in his arms and never let her go again, never let his life be the arid, lonely desert it was without her.

But he had to make sure she was safe first. That he could make her happy.

Because when David held her there in the dank darkness of the cellar and felt the warm, vivid life of her against him, he knew with a terrible certainty that making her happy was the only thing he wanted to do.

He was leaving her?

Emma leaned against the window frame and watched as David rode away down the drive. He never even looked back. And she had never felt more desolately alone. She had no idea why that should be: he had rescued her from the cellar; he owed her nothing, especially not explanations for why he would leave her. But the pain was still there.

She closed her eyes tightly against it. She should have expected nothing else. She and David were truly nothing to each other beyond a couple of wild moments desperately seeking comfort in each other's arms.

But he had given her more. He gave her hope. And now she felt foolishly, unaccountably bereft.

There was a knock at the chamber door and Emma hastily swiped at her damp eyes. She turned away from the window, from the sight of the empty lawn, and limped back to the *chaise*.

'Come in,' she called.

A maid peeked in with a quick curtsy. 'Begging your pardon, ma'am, but Lord Ramsay is here to fetch you. He's waiting in the drawing room and wishes to know if you require assistance.'

Emma gave a rueful laugh. So that was why David

left—he had handed responsibility for her troublesome self over to her brother-in-law.

Surely she would no longer see him next to the fire in her cottage. Whatever was between them seemed ended, as suddenly and strangely as it had begun. And she had never felt quite so lost before.

She remembered her earlier resolve, to leave David and Beatrice behind for their own good, before her propensity for trouble affected them too. She knew now that was the only right thing. She sat down at the small desk in the corner and reached for a sheaf of paper to do what she had to do.

From the diary of Arabella Bancroft

> *I would not have thought such grief was possible. Such pain. Surely I will fall into pieces if I must breathe for another moment. William is dead, the treasure is still lost, and I am being sent back to London.*
>
> *I hope those stinking streets will soon hold my doom.*

Chapter Twenty-One

David took the rickety wooden steps at the back of the Rose and Crown two at a time. The inn was quiet at that time of day, the tavern room empty and no new guests arriving. But the proprietor said that villain Carrington was in his rooms, that he had come in hours before and locked himself away. And that Carrington also owed him money for the stay.

It was the perfect time for David to confront the blighter and tell him in no uncertain terms that Emma was no longer unprotected. She no longer had to fend for herself against predators like the Carrington cousins. She was at home now, where they took care of their own.

He was there to take care of her. She had done an admirable job of it on her own for far too long, but he would see to it she didn't have to again.

As David stepped on to the second landing, he could hear Carrington moving behind his door. David pounded on the stout wood.

'Who it is?' Carrington called out, muffled, impatient.

'It is David Marton,' David answered, equally impatient.

There was silence, thick and heavy. 'What do you want?'

'Open the door and I will tell you.'

'I have nothing to say to you.'

'That's too bad, because I have a great deal to say to you. Open the door, Carrington, or I will be forced to break it down. And I don't think you would want such a scene. It would just add to the amount you owe the innkeeper.'

Once, a 'scene' would have been the last thing David wanted as well. His respectability, his name, his daughter—they were everything. But now taking care of Emma was equally as important. She deserved that—and so much more.

So, yes, he *would* break down the door if he had to.

Finally there was a creaking sound and the door swung open. Carrington stood there, his cravat hanging loose, his eyes bloodshot.

David pushed him back in to the room and stepped after him, slamming the door behind him. 'I should have you up before the magistrate for blackmail. It's a hanging offence, you know.'

A smile twisted Carrington's cracked lips. 'So she told you, did she? I am shocked. Emma was always one to bear her burdens alone.'

'So you thought she would be an easy mark for your villainy?' David said, his fury growing. 'She is not alone any longer, and if you value your skin at all you will return her money to her and crawl back to hell.'

'The white knight, are you?' Carrington sneered. 'I tried to be that for her once. But I wasn't good enough for her. No title, I suppose. The little whore.'

David's temper snapped at that vile word. He reached out and grabbed Carrington by his stained shirtfront, the fierce urge to bash the smirk off his unshaved face burning through him. His fist pulled back…

'You leave him alone!' a scream rang out.

David spun around, his fist still twisted in Carrington's linen shirt, to see Miss Harding standing in the doorway between the small sitting room and the bedroom. She wore only a chemise and her hair fell in a tangled skein over her shoulders.

A different kind of shock overtook David's anger. Had Carrington been victimising *all* the women in the area? 'Miss Harding…' he began. With another banshee-like scream, she launched herself at him and pounded at him with her little fists.

Not exactly a victim, then. David had to let go of Carrington and try to hold her back. She was shockingly strong.

'Well, well,' he said, once she backed away, panting. Carrington took her in his arms and quieted her. 'This is most unexpected. I think we might negotiate after all, Carrington…'

'Emma!' David called as he ran up the stairs at Rose Hill. He found himself ridiculously eager to share the tale of Carrington and Miss Harding with her, to see her reaction and maybe hear her laugh at the awful absurdity of it all.

It was the strangest sensation, wanting to share something after being alone for so long. But he wanted to tell Emma everything. Share everything with her.

He pushed open the bedchamber door, only to find the space completely empty. The blankets on the *chaise* where she had laid were neatly folded. In his excitement, he had forgotten that her family had already taken her away.

Then he saw the note, neatly folded atop the desk, labelled with his name. A cold finger of disquiet touched his earlier excitement and the house suddenly seemed so cold.

He slowly took it up and unfolded it to read the words looped across the paper. It was short and all he could see was her last message.

I've seen now how I can only be a misfortune in your life, David. I cannot stop my hoydenish ways and I have led you and Beatrice into danger. I have been careless too long and I can't do it any longer, not to people I care about as I do you. So I must go...

David crumpled the paper into his fist and tossed it away in a sudden rush of anger, and—and of fear. He hadn't realised until Emma was hurt how much he needed her in his life, and in Beatrice's too. He would even face scandal for her.

If she thought she could run away now, she was much mistaken.

Chapter Twenty-Two

'Are you sure you feel quite well, Emma dear?' Jane said as their carriage rolled closer to the village. 'I fear you still haven't quite recovered from your fall. If you want to return home...'

Emma turned from staring out at the gathering darkness beyond the carriage window and gave her sister a reassuring smile. 'Of course not. I've been looking forward to this concert and feel perfectly capable of sitting and listening to music for an hour or two. You need an outing, as well. You've seen almost no one since you returned to Barton.'

'I've seen my family and that's all that matters,' Jane said firmly. 'Though I fear the twins have not exactly been helpful in expediting your recovery.'

Emma laughed. She had insisted on staying in her cottage to recover, but Jane and the children were there every day anyway. Jane came bearing picnic baskets of healing jellies and soups, the nurse carrying the gurgling, pink-cheeked baby Emma behind her and the twins running ahead of her. It was quite true that they chased Murray and knocked over piles of books in their wild games.

But they were the only things that kept her from brooding over David, remembering every moment with him. When he held her in his arms, kissed her so tenderly, she had dared begun to hope…

But she knew she was right to have left him that note. Perhaps David *did* care for her, in some way. In fact, she was sure he did. He was no cad like the Carrington men, no consummate actor who could feign affection for a lady until he got what he wanted and then left. He deserved better in his life. And she knew it was best if they parted now, before she created some terrible scandal in his life. She had to be sensible, practical, and do what was best for David and Beatrice. Even if 'best' was not her.

Why, then, did being so sensible make her feel as if she was being cracked in two?

'I love their company,' Emma said. 'And yours. I can't tell you how happy I am you're home, Jane! But I think it will do us good to get out of the house for a while.'

Even though her first instinct when Hayden suggested they attend the concert at the assembly rooms had been to hide in her cottage and lock the door behind her for ever. What if she saw David there and had to be polite? What if she ran into Philip and he made his vile threats again? But even in her fears she knew Hayden was right and she should go. This place was her home now. The sooner she faced down her fears and got on with her life, the better.

Jane sighed and tapped her folded fan on the edge of the carriage seat. 'I confess, as much as I adore my children, I am happy to have an outing. I'm terribly behind on the local gossip and you are of no help there since you spent all your time buried in the bookshop while I was gone.'

Emma was saved from having to admit she had not spent *all* her time in the bookshop when the carriage lurched to a halt outside the assembly rooms. They were a bit late, so there was no line of vehicles waiting to disgorge their passengers. The windows glowed with flickering light and laughter spilled out of the open doors. Emma took up the cane Mr Sansom had sent her when he heard of her injuries and followed Jane into the building.

'My dears!' Lady Wheelington called out as soon as they stepped into the hall. They had barely handed their wraps to the attendant when she took their arms and led them toward the ladies' withdrawing room, the only place for a quick gossip. 'Have you heard the very latest news?'

Jane laughed. 'Of course not. I have only just returned from the wilds of town. But do tell. The design in coming here tonight was to hear everything.'

Emma nodded, though she was not quite so sure. What if the news was that David was to marry Miss Harding? Or had gone back to London? How could she maintain her façade of polite interest then?

'Well, my dears,' Lady Wheelington said, 'it seems that deliciously handsome Philip Carrington, who appeared in our midst only a few weeks ago, has already vanished again. His rooms at the Rose and Crown are utterly cleaned out. And you will never guess who vanished with him!'

Jane was wide-eyed with interest, but Emma feared where this tale might be going, even as relief swept through her that Philip was really gone. But she knew she couldn't trust whatever trouble he left behind.

'I can't even imagine,' Jane said with a sidelong glance at Emma. 'You must tell me at once.'

'The admiral's niece Miss Harding!' Lady Wheelington cried. 'We all thought Mr Carrington was here for you, Miss Emma. And that Miss Harding was all set to marry Sir David Marton. That's what Mrs Smythe was sure of, anyway. And now they have eloped together. People are ever surprising, are they not?'

Emma was actually rather shocked by the ending of this tale. And—and relieved. Miss Harding was not to marry Sir David? David was free?

But even if he was free, that could mean nothing to her.

'Is it quite sure they have gone together?' Jane said. Emma could feel her sister's gaze on her and she feared the truth of what Jane would read there. Her sister knew her all too well.

'The impertinent girl left a note for her uncle saying as much,' Lady Wheelington answered. 'The admiral actually managed to rouse himself enough to send searchers after them, but no trace can be found.'

'How shocking,' Jane murmured. Emma hoped her sister was not remembering Emma's own 'shocking' elopement. All of that seemed to have happened to an entirely different person, a foolish girl who let her heart rule her head, when it was obvious her heart had no idea what it was about.

Yet how different was she now, really? She had certainly let her heart rule when it came to David.

'That poor girl,' Emma said.

'Ah, well. Perhaps Mrs Smythe will be careful of her matchmaking in the future,' Lady Wheelington said. 'Shall we go in? The music should be most entertaining tonight...'

As they followed Lady Wheelington into the ballroom, Jane linked her arm with Emma's and whispered, 'I thought you said your husband's cousin did not stay long in the village?'

'He didn't, obviously,' Emma whispered back, still bemused by all they just heard. 'He just stopped to pay his regards. I had no idea he was involved in a secret romance.' With Miss Harding—who everyone expected David to marry.

'If you want to call it a romance,' Jane said. 'Lady Wheelington is right—people are ever surprising.'

Emma studied the crowd as they found seats at the side of the room, near the doors to the garden. She didn't see David there, or even his sister. Which was most surprising, since Mrs Smythe was never one to miss a social occasion.

Emma was relieved not to face him again quite yet, but also felt the pangs of sharp disappointment. She managed to smile and chat with the people who stopped to greet Jane, but all the time she wondered where he was. Where he had gone.

The musicians on their dais in front of the rows of chairs finished tuning their instruments and launched into their first selection, saving Emma from having to make further polite conversation. It was a lively, slightly out-of-control rendition of a local folk song and under its noise she could lose herself in her wistful thoughts.

Suddenly she felt a warm prickle at the back of her neck, as if someone had just trailed a caress over her skin. She rubbed at the spot with her gloved fingertips and glanced over her shoulder. Yet she was already quite sure of what she would find there. No one else's presence could ever give her that sudden lightning-shock of awareness.

David stood just inside the doorway, a lean, austere figure in black-and-white evening clothes, his hair swept neatly back from his face, his spectacles gleaming. He looked so different from the dusty, dishevelled man who had rescued her from the cellar. He looked like the Sir David she had once thought so cold and remote.

But now she knew the truth of what was hidden in him. She knew the real fire of his passion and it had warmed her for her whole life.

And despite all her resolve to let him go, to forget him, she realised that was the last thing she could ever do. David was emblazoned on her heart. She couldn't forget him.

She tried to turn away from him, to hide what she was feeling, but his gaze found hers across the room and she couldn't let go. An expression flickered across his face, a flash of pleasure that was so swiftly gone she feared she had imagined it.

He gave her a small nod, and as she watched he slipped out the door into the garden.

'Excuse me for a moment, Jane,' Emma whispered.

'Are you unwell?' Jane asked, a concerned look on her face. 'Shall I come with you?'

Emma shook her head. 'I won't be long.'

Once she was sure Jane's attention was on the music again, Emma quickly slipped out the door behind him. As the darkness of the evening closed around her, her heart pounded in her chest so hard she could barely breathe. Barely think.

She scanned the pathways, but she couldn't see him and for an instant she feared he had already left. Or worse, was hiding, appalled she had followed him.

Then a ray of stray moonlight fell on a dark silhouette, half-hidden at the far end of the garden. He waited under the tree where they once kissed, so still he could almost have been a stone Roman statue. Yet the warmth of his living body drew her to him.

'How have you been, Emma?' he asked quietly when she drew close to him, moving carefully with her walking stick.

'Very well,' she answered carefully. 'My sister has been an excellent nurse. How is Miss Beatrice?'

'She is quite well and asks after you daily. Her behaviour has been exemplary since her little—adventure. A new, younger nanny helps as well.'

Emma had to smile to think of Beatrice. 'I am glad.'

A silence fell between them, and in the moonlight she could feel David studying her quietly, carefully. 'I am very sorry I haven't written,' he said at last. 'There were a few matters I had to take care of before I could see you again and once I was sure you were safe with your sister and brother-in-law.'

'Matters?' Emma asked curiously. 'What can…?'

As she looked up at David in the moonlight, she glimpsed a flash of sudden laughter in his eyes, and a suspicion struck her. 'David, did you have something to do with this shocking news of Philip and Miss Harding?'

A muscle flexed in his jaw, almost as if he tried not to smile. 'I have no idea what you are speaking of, Emma. But I do assure you, Philip Carrington will not be causing you trouble in the future.'

'I must admit that I am not sorry to see the last of him,' Emma said slowly, still reeling from the knowledge that David had got rid of him somehow. 'But poor Miss Harding…'

'I believe you mean the poor new Mrs Carrington.'

'They married?' Emma cried, even more shocked than before.

'They did, for better or worse. You are done with him, Emma, I promise.'

'But what did you…?'

'Never mind that now,' David said. He reached inside his coat and took out two small items he held out to her. 'I believe these are yours.'

Emma stared down at his hand to see the pearl pendant she had sold to pay Philip, and the tiny bunch of silk forget-me-nots she lost from her sash the night of her first assembly back here.

Amazed, she murmured, 'Where did you…?'

'I obtained the necklace from Mr Levinson's shop, where it had sadly been misplaced,' David said. 'The flowers I confess I have been keeping far too long.'

He had kept her flowers? Emma swallowed hard at the knowledge that he had done such a thing. 'How did you know I went to Mr Levinson's? I was desperate and I heard Lady Wheelington say once that ladies sometimes went there.'

'It doesn't matter how I found out,' David said with a laugh. Emma stared up at him, astonished to see him laughing—and confused.

She had no idea what was happening. She'd been in despair, sure she could never see David again. Now here he was, smiling at her, giving her back her necklace—with the whole village merely feet away, where anyone could come across them.

'The only important thing is that I did find it,' he said. 'And that I can say this now—no one else will ever hurt you again, not while I'm here. And I won't let even you stand in our way, Emma. My dear, noble-hearted Emma.'

Emma shook her head, afraid to hope. She had hoped for so many things so many times before and been so cruelly disappointed. Did she dare endanger her heart one more time, for the thing she hoped for above all else?

'David, what do you mean?' she whispered. 'What are you saying?'

'I am saying I have never been happier in my whole life than when I am with you, Emma,' David said. 'I am saying that you have shown me the joy of what being alive can mean. I didn't realise before you that I was only living a half-life. Don't make me go back to that. When I read your note, I was so angry, so unhappy to think I would never see you again. I never want to feel like that.'

Emma was so confused. It seemed like the world had turned upside down. 'But—I haven't seen you since I came back to Barton. I thought you were angry with me for leading Beatrice into trouble. That you...' She choked on her words, unable to go on.

'I am so sorry, Emma dearest. I went to town for a few days because—well, because I didn't feel I could declare myself to you without this.' David reached into his coat again and withdrew a tiny box.

As Emma watched, her heart pounding, he opened it to reveal an emerald ring surrounded by smaller diamonds that sparkled in the moonlight.

'It was my mother's, and her mother's before her,' he said. 'It never seemed to belong to Maude; I could never bring myself to give it to her. But I think it is rightfully yours. It's the colour of your eyes. The colour of summer, which is how it feels whenever you're near.'

Emma was sure he must have deep feelings for her, if it made him so poetic. As she watched, David slowly knelt before her and held out the ring.

'It is yours, Emma, if you will have me with it and Beatrice, too. She adores you, as I do,' he said solemnly. 'I know I am not exciting or adventurous. Life at Rose Hill will have no casinos or court balls. But I promise to always love you, to always work as hard as I can to make you happy.'

Tears pouring down her cheeks, flowing freely as she let her emotions fly out at last, Emma knelt next to David and covered his hand with hers. 'You already make me happier than I ever thought possible. There at Rose Hill, with you and Beatrice—that's where I felt I at last belonged. I didn't think you wanted me.'

David laughed, a glorious, musical sound she had heard too rarely. But maybe now she would hear it every day for the rest of her life, if she dared hope for that. 'I want you more than anything. I don't think I realised quite how very much until you were hurt and I feared to lose you. Please, Emma, say you will marry me. Or do I have to run into that concert and declare that I have ruined you in front of everyone to make you say yes?'

Emma had to laugh at the image of David, her calm, cool David, making such a dramatic scene. 'Such scandal! Just like me, I fear.'

'I'm not afraid of any scandal, as long as we face it together. All of the things I have guarded against all my life—none of them matter next to you.'

And nothing in her life mattered next to him, either. He was truly the best man she had ever met. The only man she wanted. 'Then, yes. Yes, Sir David Marton, I will marry you.'

David took her hand and slipped the ring on to her finger. It *did* look like summer, she thought as she looked down at it. Like warmth and light, and the promise of a happy life where she belonged. The promise of a life with David, the man she truly loved.

She threw her arms around him as he drew her close

for a long, sweet, fiery kiss that said everything she ever needed to know.

As his lips trailed to her cheek, she smiled as happiness greater than any she could have ever imagined broke over her. 'Oh, David,' she whispered. 'I suppose you are not such a dull old stick after all...'

From the diary of Arabella Bancroft

It has been a year since I last wrote in this book, and I am sure this will be my last entry. I have not been able to find words, find light, for so long, but today the sun has come out again. Today is my wedding day.

I shall never forget the glorious love I found with my sweet William. But George Marton is a good man who I have come to care for. And with him I can leave London—and seek the treasure once more...

Epilogue

⌒⌒~⌒⌒

One year later

'Oh, Lady Marton, it looks lovely. Just perfect.'

Emma stepped back to survey the new window display of books freshly arrived from London. Mrs Anston, the young widow she had hired to manage the shop after Mr Lorne retired, clapped her hands as she looked at the array of volumes.

'Yes, Mrs Anston,' Emma agreed as she slid one book just a shade to the right. 'I think you are quite right. We should be ready for our re-opening party next week.'

Wiping her hands on her apron, she turned to scan the space. There were just as many books as ever, but now they were neatly shelved in categories, with displays laid out on tables from the attics at Rose Hill and Barton Park. A few comfortable chairs and sofas were also scattered about for easy perusing of volumes and pretty yellow curtains hung at the newly scrubbed windows.

It was a lovely sight indeed, her idea of the perfect bookshop. And it was all her own.

Emma had feared that once she was married, she would have to give up the shop and Mr Lorne would close it. But David had insisted she keep it, and even found Mrs Anston, the widow of a kinsman of his, to run it for her. Part of Mr Sansom's library had already found buyers, the beginning of Emma's antiquarian clients, and new book-buying ventures to London were all the 'adventures' she ever needed again.

Well—that and what happened in the grand, curtained bed at Rose Hill every night. *That* was proving to be quite adventurous indeed.

Emma felt herself blushing fiercely to think of it and she quickly turned away to readjust a display. Yes, life as Lady Marton was continually proving to be all she had ever dreamed. And more.

Beyond the window, she heard the church bell toll and she glanced up, startled. 'Is that the time already? I must go…'

'Don't worry, Lady Marton, I will unpack the last of the new books,' Mrs Anston said. 'You can't be late today.'

'No, indeed, or my sister would be furious.' Emma quickly changed her apron for a satin pelisse and tied on her bonnet. Her pearl pendant gleamed at her throat. She glanced in the mirror to see that her cheeks were still pink, but hopefully everyone would just think it was the spring day, the happiness of the occasion. Not that she had been daydreaming about what her husband did to her in their bedchamber.

She gently smoothed a caress over the still-small bump under her pelisse. It was still a secret to all but her sister, but in a few months Bea would have the new brother or sister she persisted in begging for.

Emma smiled to think of it. Her family. Her husband and children. Their home. All things she had once thought could never be hers.

With a quick goodbye to Mrs Anston, Emma hurried out of the shop and towards the church. Lady Wheelington's carriage was already there, outside the churchyard gates, and Mrs Smythe and her rambunctious brood were making their way up the path.

Jane and Hayden waited with the vicar at the church door, the twins helping little Emma toddle around on her leading strings. Beatrice tumbled around with them, laughing, until she saw Emma walking toward them.

'Mama!' she called, and dashed towards Emma to hug her. 'I got to hold the baby. He is very small, but I was so careful.'

'Of course you were,' Emma said with a laugh. Bea was always careful, always polite, always with a book in her hands. But she was learning to play too, which Emma was happy to see.

'And he's named Edward, just like Queen Elizabeth's brother,' Beatrice said. 'Come and see.'

'Yes, Emma, come and see your godson,' Jane said, holding up the lace-swathed baby in her arms. Hayden beamed down at them, every inch the proud papa. 'You were almost late for his christening.'

'I never would have missed this for anything,' Emma said. She took baby Edward carefully from her sister, marvelling at his tiny nose and silky lashes, the sweet scent of him. She couldn't believe that very soon she would have one of her own.

She felt a gentle touch on her shoulder and glanced up to find her husband smiling down at her. Even after a year of being married, just the sight of him made her heart swell and the day turn golden-bright.

He bent to kiss her and Emma knew that finally she was right where she belonged. For ever.

* * * * *

LET'S TALK
Romance

For exclusive extracts, competitions
and special offers, find us online:

Get in touch on 01413 063232